HOME, AWAY

HOME, AWAY

a novel by

JEFF GILLENKIRK

———

SUMMER 2010
CHIN MUSIC PRESS
SEATTLE

Copyright © 2010
by Jeff Gillenkirk

チン・ミュージック・ベースボール

PUBLISHER:
Chin Music Press
2621 24th Ave W
Seattle, WA 98199
USA

www.chinmusicpress.com

All Rights Reserved

COVER PAINTING: John Musgrove

Printed by Imprimerie Gauvin, CANADA

Library of Congress Cataloging-in-publication data is available.

EDITOR'S NOTE: *Go Tribe!*

DISCLAIMER: This is a work of fiction. Any resemblance to
individuals either living or dead (except for Craig Counsell) is totally
coincidental.

ANOTHER EDITOR'S NOTE: We in no way mean to imply that Mr.
Gillenkirk condones the message in our previous note. But if he did,
he'd be a better man for it.

To Marv and Lucas

HOME, AWAY

Preface: Father, Son

FATHER, SON

H E CRUSHED THE WHATABURGER bag and gripped it tightly in his right hand. Ridges of calluses ran the length of his index finger, connecting through the web around the inside of his palm to a gnarled thumb covered with a blackened, concave nail. He squinted at his son through the smoke from his cigarette.

"Your mom tells me you're quite the ball player."

"I almost made the All-Star team," the boy smiled.

"Almost! What the hell good is almost?"

The boy's smile fell as quickly as sand through the cracks of the building's old wooden steps. 'Almost' was pretty good for a kid who had spent the past five years in Alaska, but he knew better than to bring that up. The fact was, there weren't a lot of baseball diamonds in Point Barrow. Sometimes guys used to clear off the snow from the parking lot behind the piping depot and shoot baskets, but for eight months out of the year baseball wasn't an option. The kids in Texas got to play year around.

"I'm not as good as some of these guys —"

"Horseshit," his father said. "The only reason you're not as good as those guys is you're lazy."

They were sitting on the back steps of the apartment his mom had rented after they returned from Point Barrow. It was an old building with two dilapidated railroad flats — one up, one down — covered with chipped asbestos shingles streaked with rust from the clothesline reels. The concrete yard dead-ended at a plank fence facing a massive K-Mart parking lot across the alley. The flats didn't look long for the world, which is probably why they were were so cheap. Whether they would fall of their own accord or be scraped by bulldozers to clear the way for more Texas sprawl was an open question. The boy had heard his parents arguing about why she'd rented such a godawful place. He had worked his ass off for five years at forty below, his father shouted, and deserved a little luxury. Luxury, she laughed — what the hell did he know about luxury! But this time, their arguments didn't end with curses and door slamming and his father disappearing for days. One night he had heard his father talking about "The Program," and his desire to take the money he'd made in Alaska and invest it in a liquor store and buy a house.

"There's always money in liquor," he said. But he had one more job to do. Royal Dutch Shell had hand-picked a team of veterans to run some state-of-the-art platforms off the coast of Norway. When Mom complained, his dad shouted what the hell was he supposed to do — "I've got to go where the oil is and it ain't in Texas any more." It was the last big field. There wouldn't be any more like this one, he said, and then he'd be home forever.

The heavy bruise of an impending Gulf storm settled over K-Mart. His father arced the Whataburger bag across the yard, where it disappeared into the battered trash can with a soft thud. "Let's play some catch." Jason leaped up and grabbed his glove and a hardball from the shelf on the porch just inside the door. "You don't have a glove," he said. Jack Thibodeaux smiled and held up his right hand, as tough and discolored as a slab of leather.

They slipped through a hole in the back fence and set up ninety feet apart in the nearly deserted K-Mart lot. Jason lobbed the ball softly at first, but the throws came back hard and unforgiving. They played without speaking, which was fine for the boy. When his father spoke to him it was usually a complaint or a command: You need a haircut. Pick up your clothes. Get ready for school. They rarely did anything together except eat or ride in cars across godforsaken landscapes — oil fields or expanses of tundra or prairies or swamps about to become oil fields. When his father worked, he worked. When he didn't work, he slept or drank. But this was something different. There were no complaints, no instructions, no judgments — just the ball rocketing back and forth, and glimmers of surprised contentment passing between them when they caught each other's eye.

The sound of the ball in the boy's glove made a sharp retort — against his father's hand a slap, like a rolled up newspaper. He couldn't believe his father was playing without a glove; he had been a superb ball player in his day but decided to chase the certainty of Louisiana oil ... Texas oil ... Alaskan oil rather than the dream of playing professional ball. "Doesn't it hurt?" His father shook his head. "Throw harder!" he shouted. But the harder Jason threw, the harder it came back. They were

8

at a level he had never played before, back and forth, back and forth in a charged relentless rhythm that Jason could have kept up forever. And then it began to rain. And as it did in Galveston during summer, it began as a deluge and quickly worked its way to a torrent. Wind-driven sheets of water swept across the parking lot, accompanied by fusillades of thunder.

But the ball kept coming. Jason couldn't believe it, he could barely see, water streamed over his eyes, his glove was soaked, his father was nothing but a slim shade ninety feet away in the downpour. He grinned, filled with a giddy and profound sense of connection with his father.

Then, "Jack! Jason!" his mom cried from the back porch, breaking the reverie. A jagged streak of lightning scarred the sky. The air crackled with a sound like sheet metal ripping apart.

"Lightning!" he shouted to his father. "We should go in!"

"Why, you got a metal plate in your head?"

His dad fired the ball through the rain and Jason speared it, laughing. He couldn't remember feeling happier, playing his favorite sport and defying the gods back-to-back with his old man. It was like a dream, a promise fulfilled, some kind of payback for the fifteen years of wandering in the desert of his father's life. Nothing had prepared him for this, just as nothing prepared him for what was to come.

Jack Thibodeaux walked a few steps closer to his son. "I'm going away tomorrow," he shouted. This was another monumental change. Every other time, he just left. Jason was always the last to know where or why or for how long, just that he was gone. But now it was different. His father cared about him. He was going to do one last job and come home and do it right.

"Mom said you're going to Norway!" he shouted back.

His father whizzed a fastball to him, low and away. It hit the pavement and skittered past, all the way to the base of the building. Jason chased it down and when he turned to throw it back, his father was gone.

STRIKE ONE

Grass, horizons of shimmering green grass, its loamy perfume sweet in his nostrils. Lunge, snatch, throw ... lunge, snatch, throw ... the crack of Vuco's fungo bat beats methodically as he fields grounder after grounder on the tightly clipped turf of Sunken Diamond. A sheen of sweat spreads across his back, then Vuco shouts, 'You wanna throw?' He steps on the mound and tosses a fastball to Barf Connolly and the radar gun shows Double Zero. He throws another pitch even harder but the gun shows Double Zero again. 'Vuco!' he calls but his coach just stands there. 'That must have been a hundred!' Then he looks behind the backstop where Rafe was playing with his Big Truck and he's gone. He tries to run but his spikes snag the turf. 'Barf, for Christsakes where is he?' Sweat pours from his face, he can't breathe, a hole opens in his stomach, he has no idea where his son is.

He runs behind the concession stand, then down the asphalt path towards the stadium. A jumble of trees and tangled underbrush lines the path, places where Rafe could be lost. Then somehow he's a mile down Campus Drive, running across the lawn toward their apartment though Rafe could never have gotten this far, he wasn't even two years old. He stares up at the apartment's balcony then down the boulevard, trying to retrace every step, every clue, but his thoughts float out of reach.

'Rafe!' he shouts. 'Rafe, where are you?'

JASON SHOT STRAIGHT UP FROM the sofa bed, scattering books, papers, pencils onto the floor. "Rafe!" he called, crossing the room with two giant strides into the nursery fashioned from the Murphy Bed closet. There he was, surrounded by Pooh and Noodles and Doggie and Fuff in the sky-blue crib Jason had painted with rising suns and phases of the moon, spread out on his back beneath the posters of Sandra Day O'Connor and Randy Johnson, his breath sliding in and out in the sweet reassuring sleep of innocence.

"Jesus Christ!" Jason exhaled. He leaned over and hoisted Rafe into his strong arms. At two years old he was no heavier than a full bag of groceries. He carried Rafe into the kitchen and poured two glasses of milk — one in a regular glass, the other in a sippy cup festooned with transparent butterflies. Rafe continued sleeping against his neck but began to stir at the smell of the pear Jason was slicing.

"Time to face the music, Buddy," Jason said, switching the radio on to KSJO — *All Rock, All the Time.* "You gotta wake up or you'll never get to sleep tonight. And tonight," he said joyfully, waltzing with his son across the small kitchen, "your mommy's finished with law school." Rafe stared blankly as Jason strapped him into the old wooden high chair. "Dude," Jason cooed. "Can you say *freedom?*"

The backpack, the stroller, the pale blue plastic baby bag — Vicki could deal with these now. Tomorrow he was going back to baseball. Tomorrow ended the unprecedented — and some said unwise — leave of absence from Stanford's baseball program to be a full-time dad. He would rejoin his quest for what he and everyone who knew him assumed would inevitably be his — a professional baseball career. And Rafe would go back to being just his kid, rather than a full-time job.

Rafe stared at the pear slices on his tray, then picked one up in his chubby hand and flung it to the center of the floor. "Whoa, you gotta hit your cut-off man!" Jason cried. He knew Rafe was never hungry after waking, but he was anxious to accelerate the program. Vicki's eighteen hour days, the endless cycle of studying and tests and papers — it was over *today.* He didn't know what came next, but it couldn't be any worse. Right from the start it had been 'Vicki Vicki Vicki, Rafe Rafe Rafe.' Finally, it was his turn.

He hurried into the living room and found the foam rubber baseball under the sofabed. Rafe's eyes rose with a smile when he saw the ball in his father's hand.

"Catch!" Rafe shouted.

Jason laughed and softly tossed the ball. Rafe's hands came together several beats after the ball bounced off his chest. Jason threw it again and again until Rafe managed to squeeze it against the high-chair tray. "Good! Now throw it to Daddy." Happily, with a jerky flap of his arm, Rafe tossed the ball into his father's waiting hands.

"Yay!" Jason cried. "You're gonna be a ballplayer, my little man."

After a dinner of ravioli and green beans, he sat Rafe on the living room floor with a pile of wooden blocks and his favorite stuffed animals. "Let's build a zoo," Jason said. He quickly formed a square enclosure and placed Pooh Bear in the center. Rafe recognized the game and began forming new enclosures for his stuffed animals. Jason popped open a metal cookie can holding thirty-forty small plastic cars and arranged them into a parking lot, then grabbed a copy of *Sports Illustrated* and read two articles before Rafe began impatiently mixing the blocks and cars together. Not that it made any difference. The living room was a mess, the morning newspaper still tangled with the sheets on the pull-out couch that transformed their living room into a bedroom. A plate of half-eaten raviolis, sneakers, socks, a kitchen towel, issues of *Baseball Digest* littered the floor.

At nine o'clock Jason rolled over and squeezed Rafe's belly. "Two minute warning, Buddy. Night-night time." Rafe carefully set the animals on their sides. "Night night," he sang. Jason carried Rafe into the bedroom, where he changed Rafe's diaper and dressed him in his orange fire-retardant footsies.

"What should we read tonight?"

"The birdie book!"

"All right!" It could have been a plumber's manual, Jason wouldn't care. It was over. He could feel the rock rolling away, freedom blowing into his life. The trips to the pediatrician, to Gymboree for clothes, the afternoons cramming on park benches while Rafe scampered up and down play structures, the meals prepared, baths drawn, diapers changed, loads of laundry washed … it was all over, today. *Finis. Terminado.* Done. That was Vicki's job now. His job was to play baseball.

He sat in the living room chair with Rafe warm and clean-smelling in his lap, leafing through the *Encyclopedia of North American Birds* for the umpteenth time. Ten minutes into it Jason saw the tell-tale wavering of Rafe's eyelids, the softening of his mouth. He carried him to the balcony where they faced eastwards and began their nightly litany: "Good night Gramma," they recited together. "Good night

Grampa … good night Mommy." And tonight, because it was there, "Good night moon."

Rafe had brought a carrot stick and pointed it to the sky. "Do stars eat carrots?"

Jason smiled. "I don't know, hold it up and see." Rafe thrust the carrot towards the sky and waited, his dark eyes shining with anticipation. After a moment, he turned to his father with a wondering look.

"Maybe they're not hungry," Jason offered. "They probably already ate." Rafe studied his face, then pushed the carrot against Jason's mouth. He grasped it with his teeth and began chewing. "Mmmm, daddies love carrots. That's why daddies are *strong*."

He lay Rafe down in his crib and pulled the yellow cotton blanket up to his neck. "Good night, sweet boy. Have a great sleep."

Rafe stared at him placidly in the half light of the room.

"Good night, Daddy," he said, and closed his eyes.

Rafe's breathing was soft and steady by the time Jason reached the door. He left it open the width of his fist and hurried into the kitchen. The clock on the stove said 9:27. Vicki should have been home by nine, but what else was new? He looked at the cluttered table and realized that he should have bought some champagne or something to celebrate the end of law school, whatever good that would do. Their relationship sucked, there wasn't anything they'd ever found to make it better, so why pretend?

He cleared a space at the table and began reading from *Analysis of Sociological Data* for his midterm. At 10:30 he slammed his fist down. He'd never make it to work on time. It was his last night at the physical plant where he scrubbed, cleaned, painted, patched and monitored the machinery that cooled and heated half of Stanford's sprawling campus, from eleven PM to seven AM — payment for extending his baseball scholarship another year. Gutfried Oderbach — Field Marshall Oderbach, they called him — would be all over him for being late, even if it was his last night.

He pulled on a pair of frayed khakis and the sweatshirt he'd worn the past two nights. He was in the bathroom brushing his teeth when the front door opened.

"Glad you could make it!" he called sarcastically. Vicki ignored him and tip-toed into Rafe's room. She leaned over the railing and kissed him lightly on the lips. She smiled as Rafe's eyes fluttered and the corners of his mouth lifted sweetly.

Then Jason loomed over her shoulder. "You said you'd be home by *nine*."

She gazed tenderly on Rafe, his soft corn silk hair pressed against his temple. "I'm sorry," she said, pulling the blanket away from his chin. "Something came up." She turned and hurried from the room. Jason reached over and yanked the blanket back up to Rafe's chin, then followed Vicki into the kitchen.

"What do you mean something came up? It's over, right? This is the last day."

She took a blueberry yogurt from the refrigerator and sat tiredly at the kitchen table. She ran her hand through her long, shimmering hair. "I really wish we could talk once without you yelling."

"I'm not yelling! I'm frustrated. I've been waiting for two hours ... two *years!*"

Vicki breathed deeply and closed her eyes. "It hasn't been *two years*." When she opened them he was leaning over the table, his head thrust towards her.

"What is it now?"

"I was trying to change my Bar Boards schedule. They put me in the afternoon class by mistake."

"Bar Boards? What are *Bar Boards*?

"I told you — I've got two weeks of prep classes for the Boards. These last three years are down the drain if I don't pass."

"No, you didn't tell me." He glared at her. "I've got practice tomorrow. You said you'd take Rafe."

"It's just for tomorrow."

"Naw, Vicki, naw — this is your time now. You promised."

She shrugged. "It's the best I could do."

The red numerals of the digital clock burned into his eyeballs — 10:49. "No, that's not your best," he said. "You gave your best to constitutional law. You gave your best to Professor Hairpiece. You give your best to everyone but me. I get crap."

"That's because all you know is crap. You dish it out all the time."

The argument wasn't new, only the circumstances. They both had waited for this moment since Rafe's birth — the end of law school, the pursuit of some kind of normalcy in a marriage that had never really had any. It was that promise, that distant hope that had held them together for the past two years. Now, it was suddenly clear that that point could just as easily be an end as a beginning.

He snatched her tub of yogurt and threw it as hard as he could. It exploded high above the stove, showering rays of pale blue cream across the wall and down the side of the refrigerator. "I've fuckin' had it!" he shouted. "This marriage is over!"

Vicki scrambled from her seat and backpedaled towards the door. "Then get out! Get out — nobody wants you here!"

He stepped towards her. Their altercations had never been physical; the sound, the spray, the audacity of the exploding yogurt shocked them both.

"Stay away from me!" Vicki cried.

"I wouldn't touch you if you paid me!"

Vicki's foot hit a pool of yogurt and she slid hard against the wall, banging her shoulder. "You asshole!" she screamed. Jason stood over her, uncertain what to do.

"Get away from me!" Vicki screamed louder. "You hear me? GET AWAY FROM ME!"

Rafe was crying now. The day Jason had dreamed about for more than a year somehow had turned into a nightmare. He grabbed his Stanford jacket from the living room chair and fled down the front stairs two at a time, striking out on a run across the dark lawn towards East Campus Drive. The sound of Rafe's crying chased him like a siren.

THE STANFORD DAILY
CARDINAL FATE HINGES ON DAD'S RETURN
STANFORD ACE HITS 1,000 (DIAPERS) IN OFF-SEASON

When "JT" Thibodeaux takes the field today in the opening practice of the Cardinal's baseball season, for the first time in a year he won't be playing with a Nerf ball. A two-time high school All-American recruited out of Henry Beaumont High in Galveston, Texas (where he was known as "Heat"), JT elected to take a leave of absence to raise his one-year-old son while his wife completed Stanford Law.

"I'm ready to play," Thibodeaux told the *Daily* on the West Campus playground, where we caught up with him on the swings with his fledgling Cardinal, Raphael. "I wouldn't trade this year with my boy for anything," JT said, though he is looking forward to trading in his diaper bag for a duffel bag.

Thibodeaux was an overpowering 16-1 as a junior in the Cardinal's near-trip to the College World Series two seasons ago. With the birth of his son to second year Stanford Law student Victoria Repetto, Thibodeaux red-shirted his final year of eligibility in order to take primary responsibility for raising him.

"I can always pitch," the hard-throwing 6'4" left-hander said. "But I won't ever have the opportunity again to raise my son. It's just something I decided to do. I think it worked out great for both of us."

A Sociology major in the School of the Humanities, Thibodeaux managed to earn three credits towards his degree on his year off. Working with department staff, he turned his fathering experience into a year-long sociology tutorial, recording his son's developmental progress. Thibodeaux estimates that he read nearly forty books on child-rearing — in addition to "changing a thousand diapers."

Thibodeaux's coaches and teammates are happy to see their ace return. "JT has always done things his way," one teammate said. "I don't care what he does off the field. I just want to go to the World Series."

—

THE MORNING session was hell. The new conditioning coach, Brad Sievert, started them with a half hour of calisthenics, then running drills and wind sprints from line to line before shagging flies. Pitchers and catchers took fielding drills with the equipment manager, Donnie Burt — or "Toast," so named because two seasons ago one of the dryers caught fire and burned the team's uniform pants — rolling simulated bunts onto the infield grass. At eleven o'clock the pitchers practiced covering the bag on balls hit to first.

Jason worked as hard as he'd ever worked in his life. His legs ached. His t-shirt was soaked. His thighs screamed from sprinting from the mound to first base. He loved it. Men being, trying to be, pretending to be the fastest, the most powerful, the most prolific players in a game that Americans had played for as long as most Americans could remember. He was embarrassed for ever giving it up. But that was the past. He could forget the year he had taken off. He could forget his blow-up with Vicki, the sound of Rafe crying, the yogurt sprayed across the wall and floor of the kitchen. Here, inside the sanctuary of Stanford's legendary stadium, it was all baseball, only baseball, a wholly self-contained and self-referential world.

Lunch was catered, with mounded platters of pasta, risotto, baked chicken breasts, buttered green beans and biscuits with honey, all passed up and down the table. Jason sat with the other seniors — Jeremy Asher, his battery mate since freshman year; Barf Connolly, the baby-faced infielder from San Diego with the social mores of John Belushi; Damon Lister, the stuck-up world government major from Perth, Australia, who played center field like a roadrunner; John Corliss, scion of Corliss Software; Artemio "Artie" Garza, the son of a real Texas Ranger from San Antonio and premier base stealer on the team; wide-body first baseman Brent Seligman. Jason had searched his teammates' faces for any sign of disapproval and found none. But neither did he discern any interest in what he had done the past year. The chatter was generic. It was an emotion-free zone.

"Hey Selly, you eating clean up or hitting it?"

"What this needs is a good white wine."

"Whine, whine, whine … Pass the honey, will you?"

Jason slid the jar to Garza. "You know if a kid under two eats honey, he can have a seizure and die?" Nobody said a word. "Scarlet fever, bee stings, choking on a peanut — there's a million things can kill a kid."

"Nobody ever does that, do they?" Corliss said skeptically. "The honey thing."

"Naw, naw, people know," Jason replied. He beat the table with his open palms. "It gets passed down from generation to generation, like drumbeats."

The sound of forks scraping, large mandibles chewing, chairs squeaking. "So how's marriage?" Seligman asked with a sardonic drawl.

Jason nodded as if he'd never heard the question in his life. He hated to acknowledge defeat. It was an awful marriage, but he was hardly willing to admit that. "Having a kid is awesome," he replied enthusiastically. "They're kinda like Mini-me's: they do whatever you do, but they do their own shit too." A large plate of green beans made its way around the table. Jason heaped some onto his plate, then began filling the plate beside his. "But one thing Rafe loves to do, I don't know where he gets it — he loves to sing in his bed in the mornings. He wakes up and just starts singing whatever comes into his head —"

A strong hand seized his forearm. "I don't like green beans," Lister said in his imperious Australian accent.

"Sorry, mate," Jason smiled. "Rafe loves them. He calls 'em 'bean beans.'"

Lister swept the beans off his plate with a fork. "I'm not your fuckin kid." Corliss laughed with a single, sharp bark. Jason blushed and passed the platter along. Rafe's image came to him, running toward him in his comical, top-heavy toddle. He saw his sparkling eyes, his tiny mouth calling out "Da-Da!" He was surprised by how much he missed him — and how little his teammates cared.

AFTER LUNCH came more running, more calisthenics, more stretches, loosening muscles that had tightened during the break. Jason lay on his back, his legs twisted to the right, his left shoulder straining to reach the ground when Vucovich's shadow crossed his face. He looked up and saw his own reflection in Vuco's Robocop shades. Bill Vucovich was a ramrod straight, square-jawed, thirty-three-year-old former second baseman for the Anaheim Angels who had torn an anterior cruciate ligament at twenty-seven and never returned to play. As a former Stanford Cardinal, coaching at his alma mater was the closest he could get to recreating his dreams of stardom. The will to play still burned in his taut body. It was a will that made him impatient with players who didn't give 100% or more.

"You been throwing?" Vuco asked.

"Yeah."

"Let's see what you got."

Jason stood on the mound with the new ball in his hand, the leather as familiar as his own skin. He looked over and saw head coach Milt Baptiste talking with an assistant, his hands thrust in the back pockets of his uniform, shoulders rounded, abdomen thrust forward looking as if he had been born in a baseball uniform. A hundred fans lounged in the stadium seats, die-hards of the senior set or parents of prospects there to give their offspring some moral support.

Jeremy Asher squatted behind the plate and offered his mitt as a target. "Show 'em how it's done, JT."

Jason rocked into motion, his right knee rising against his belt, his long left arm sweeping from three-quarters above his shoulder toward the plate. The echo came milliseconds after the ball slammed into the pocket of Asher's mitt, like a sonic boom. Heads turned — Lister, Seligman, Connolly, the new guys who only had heard stories about the flame thrower from Texas who gave it up to raise a kid. Jason nodded to himself. The thrill of being able to do something that only a van full of guys could do was deeply satisfying. This was his world. This was his ticket to the Show.

The coaches lined up along the first baseline and watched their big lefthander throw fifteen, eighteen, twenty pitches. They never used the radar gun this early in the season, but it was clear he was throwing heat. Jason felt good — for himself, for the team, for Vuco. Vuco had gone out on a limb to keep him in the program. He never knew what he had said exactly, but Baptiste had finally agreed to red-shirt him rather than release him. Red-shirting was something teams did all the time — but at the team's instigation, not the player's. Guys were held back for injuries, for academic reasons, because they had another player at your position who they wanted to play ahead of you. But raising babies? No one had ever seen that before, at least on the men's side of Stanford sports. It was a first that Baptiste hadn't wanted to earn for his esteemed program, but he had to. He could hardly teach personal responsibility while forcing a young man to abandon his child for baseball — or vice versa. And then, there was the 98-miles-per-hour fastball.

Jason started his motion but stopped when he saw Vuco walking towards the mound. "I thought the kid was covered."

"What do you mean?"

Vuco gestured towards the dugout. There was Rafe with his babysitter, Carmen, dressed in the tiny Stanford uniform Vicki's father had bought for him, the number 1½ stitched below little letters spelling out "Thibodeaux." He could see Rafe's wide brown eyes, his fair hair fringed at the bottom of his cap.

"It's just for today," Jason tried to explain. "Vicki had a conflict."

Vucovich rubbed his eyes beneath his shades, then reached for the ball. Jason handed it over and trudged past Baptiste without looking. Rafe's eyes danced happily as his father drew near. "Da-Da!" Carmen looked at him apologetically. "Vicki can't come until 4 o'clock," she explained. "I have to go to my other job."

Jason shoveled Rafe with his Rugrats backpack into his arms, snatched the stroller from Carmen and hauled them down the right field line towards the clubhouse. He could feel forty pairs of eyes burning into his back as Rafe played with the bill of his hat. Goddamn Vicki, he steamed. Fifteen months caring for Rafe and she still wouldn't pull her weight. This was his *career*, not some Sunday pick-up game.

He set Rafe down and looked at the clock on the clubhouse wall — 2:40. Twenty minutes to nap time. If he could get him down he could get back to the workout before Vicki showed. Rafe, however, ran straight for the free weights laying on the floor. Jason grabbed his right arm and snatched him back.

"Nap time, Buddy."

Rafe tried to squirm away. "*Jugo! Jugo!*" he shouted, using the Spanish word for juice that Carmen taught him. He was excited, the clubhouse was something new.

"Come on, Rafey — it's time to take your nap!"

Rafe's small face collapsed. "I-want-some-*jugo*," he cried, tears streaming down his now-reddened cheeks.

"Oh for Christsakes." He pulled Rafe into the clubhouse and opened the huge refrigerator stocked with juice and soda. Rafe grabbed a Pepsi from the bottom shelf but Jason yanked it away. Before Rafe could even think of crying again, Jason opened a bottle of Orangina and filled Rafe's sippy cup and shoved it into his hand. He carried him to the big leather couch where they could see through the open glass doors as Eric Freeholder spanked grounders to the infielders and Baptiste skied fly balls to the outfielders and Vucovich huddled with the pitchers and catchers down the left field line. As Jason watched, Rafe pulled a pile of magazines off the slate coffee table. Jason heard them hit the hardwood floor with a thud, and turned to see Rafe spraying the magazines with orange soda from his sippy cup.

He caught Rafe's arm and shook him. "That's a NO-NO!" he shouted. "NO-NO!" The toddler's face contorted and a pitiful wail escaped his mouth. A wave of guilt swept over Jason, then utter frustration. He should have lined up another babysitter, but he never thought Vicki would actually leave him in the lurch. What the hell was he supposed to do now?

He pulled a tissue from the bag and wiped the streams running from Rafe's nostrils. "I'm sorry, Buddy," he said. But Rafe was inconsolable. The blare of his crying burrowed into Jason's brain like a dentist's drill. He jumped up and slid the clubhouse door shut. He wanted heads turning at the thud of his fastballs, not his son's tantrums.

He took a deep breath and looked closely at his agitated boy. Of course — he'd forgotten to ask Carmen when he'd been changed last, when he'd eaten, when he'd slept. He pulled Rafe to him and peeked inside his pull-ups — dry as a bone. He found a box of Saltines in the cupboard and pulled out a stack, set Rafe on his lap, wiped off his tears and held out a cracker. "No!" Rafe pouted, but Jason could see his

23

face soften. Soon Rafe was chewing the cracker, the twinkle in his eye beginning to reappear. Jason squeezed his son's hand and watched the world beyond the sliding glass doors play out in silence, like a diorama of vintage Americana: *Young Men Playing Baseball.*

Jason leaned back and Rafe snuggled into the crook of his arm, his head against his chest. Jason began to sing, softly. "Rock-a-bye baby in the tree tops …" He stroked Rafe's chest across the letters of his little Stanford jersey. Rafe picked at the sleeve of his daddy's shirt. Outside, Vuco pitched and Corliss pounded a line drive that streaked past the clubhouse window like a comet. "When the bough breaks, the cradle will fall, and down will come baby, cradle and all."

After a few minutes, Jason looked down and Rafe was asleep.

WHEN PRACTICE was over he strapped Rafe into his stroller, tucked his blue flannel blanket snugly around him and wheeled him outside into the shade of the clubhouse wall. He hurried across the field and caught Vucovich as he was about to step into the dugout.

"How about some infield practice?" He knew Vuco could never turn down a guy who wanted to do more, even one who had pissed him off as much as he had.

"Where's the kid?"

Jason pointed across the field. "He's asleep. We do this all the time."

Vuco grabbed his fungo bat and a couple of balls. Jason stood on the manicured grass between the mound and shortstop and Vuco hit hard groundballs to his right, to his left and straight at him, over and over again. Left right left right, his legs burned but he pushed himself, he wanted to show Vuco that he was serious about the season. Then suddenly the sound of Vuco's bat, the smell of the grass, the slant of the winter sun produced a powerful *déjà vu.* He looked sharply towards the bullpen — Rafe was there, wrapped snugly in his stroller. Every few chances he glanced over, making sure Rafe was still there. Lunge, snatch, throw … lunge, snatch, throw …

Then one time he looked and Vicki was there.

He waved to her just as a ball shot sharply past his knee. "Pay attention!" Vuco shouted. "OK!" Jason said as he watched Vicki pull the blanket tightly up to Rafe's neck and wheel him away without looking back.

HE SLEPT on the couch in his old fraternity that night. He didn't want to see Vicki and have to apologize for throwing the yogurt. Besides, he had meant what he'd said. He was sick to death of their marriage. All he wanted to do was play ball.

The next day was more like winter, a strong wind pushing a procession of dark clouds off the Pacific. But enclosed in the magic land of Sunken Diamond, Jason ran, stretched, sprinted and threw with a passion that inspired everyone. He was determined to wipe out the catastrophe of Day One, to erase the image of him as a Dad and replace it with one of the flame thrower who would lead them to Omaha.

He stayed late again, working on his pick-off move. He was alone, undressing in the locker room when Vucovich appeared in the doorway holding a Coke. A pale ring traced the outline of his shades around his eyes, accentuating the intensity of their blueness. "I probably don't have to say anything, but I'm going to," Vuco said.

"Let me guess: Baptiste thinks I should go out for water polo."

"That thing with your kid isn't going to be the highlight of his year."

"It won't happen again."

"It can't happen again."

Jason peeled off his socks. He wanted to say 'fuck Baptiste' but he couldn't. Vuco had discovered him but Baptiste controlled his fate. They had driven down together from Houston and watched the kid called Heat pitch for the Gulf Coast American Legion. Fast ball and curve, that's all he needed to blow his way through line-ups like a Gulf hurricane. Baptiste had clocked him at 95 and gone to check the radar gun with the Texas Highway Patrol. Most high schoolers didn't throw 95 miles per hour. They had pegged him as a strong, uncomplicated kid ready for molding into a world class pitcher. Vucovich, at least, still believed that.

"You looked good out there today," Vuco said. Jason nodded in agreement. "Milt, Freebie — they know you're the real thing," Vuco went on. "But you're the only one who can make it happen. Prospects don't make it, JT — players do. You've got to work as hard for this as you've worked for anything in your life."

"I know that."

Vucovich tapped his chest. "Heart."

"You don't think I've got heart after what I've been through?" Jason pointed with his chin. "I got heart as sure as you got that caterpillar on your lip."

Vuco touched his new moustache. "My wife says I look like Brad Pitt."

"Brad Pitt doesn't have a moustache."

A loud knock sounded on the clubhouse door. It had started to rain and beyond the streaked glass stood a heavy-set man in a rain slicker and motorcycle helmet, holding a manila envelope. Vucovich slid open the door. "ups for Jason Thibodeaux," the man said in an upbeat voice. Jason signed for the package, the guy handed him the envelope and hurried away. It was from the law firm where Vicki had clerked the summer they were married: Caulkins, Cleary, Wineglas & Huff, 74 State Street, Philadelphia, Pa. "Jason Mark Thibodeaux," it was addressed, "c/o Stanford University Varsity Baseball Team." He stared at the envelope, then at the man pushing through the stadium gate. "United Process Servers," the receipt said.

Vuco sat down and resumed talking. "I've seen guys come through with half your talent try twice as hard ..." Jason tore open the envelope and extracted a thick sheaf of papers. He read the top form but it took him a moment to grasp it. The only legal documents he had ever seen were his mother's death certificate and Stanford's scholarship forms. And, of course, his marriage certificate. He stared at the words as Vucovich's voice receded.

```
PETITION FOR DISSOLUTION OF MARRIAGE:
In the County of Santa Clara, California
Petitioner: Victoria Maria Repetto
Respondent: Jason Mark Thibodeaux
Children: 1. Raphael Jason Thibodeaux
Custody Status Requested:
Primary Legal and Physical Custody to Petitioner
```

Six or seven pages of eye-challenging mumbo-jumbo followed. He felt a surge of giddiness and relief — then rage. Who was she to call it off? But he had said it himself — the marriage sucked. What had Vicki called it? "A sleepover that grew into a tragedy." They'd had great sex at first, but once Vicki was five months pregnant even that went away. They argued about everything and had almost nothing in common — except Rafe.

Jason's heart fell as he realized she was going to take him.

"Baseball," Vucovich was saying with a quiet reverence, "has to be your lover. It has to be your mother, your father, your brother, your best friend … " He turned and looked meaningfully at the man he considered his protégé. "It has to be your *wife*."

Jason walked blindly past him, slid open the glass doors and stepped outside. The rain pelted his chest; he still had on only his baseball pants but it didn't matter — he had to get home. He hadn't seen Rafe for two days. He wanted to fix some dinner and play with his trucks and read him a story and put him to bed. He saw the phony UPS man disappear around the corner on his motorcycle. He began to run with half a mind to catch him and beat the crap out of him. Though what he really wanted to do was take his motorcycle so he could get home before Vicki took off with his son.

HE TOUCHED the wall where a line of faint blue paint had rubbed off Rafe's crib. The little room was as dark and cold as a tomb. The only thing Vicki had left was the poster of Randy Johnson, who looked as ugly and intimidating as she always complained he did.

He slumped to the floor, back to the wall, his hair, shoulders and chest soaked from the rain. He couldn't believe this was happening now, on the eve of his season. He just wanted to play ball. As his eyes adjusted to the gloom something winked at him from the corner — the soft cotton baseball he used to play catch with Rafe. He imagined Rafe toddling towards him, holding the ball out and tossing it gleefully at his face.

Jesus, he thought, how did it ever come to this? The only reason they'd decided to get married was Rafe, and now he was gone. It was right here, lying on the floor searching for the best location for Rafe's crib, where Vicki lifted her blouse and put his hand on her stomach. He could feel the beat of Rafe's tiny kicks. He'd kissed her bulging womb, feeling so surprised and hopeful.

He began to cry, remembering the time he was eight-years-old and asleep in Port Sulphur and the moving van came and started packing everything for the move to Point Barrow. No one had warned him that he'd have to leave behind every friend he ever had and move from the gelid air at the bottom of America to the ice box at the top. His father had been in Point Barrow for five months already — on temporary assignment, his mother said. In the middle of the school year — in the middle of winter — they boarded a bus in New Orleans for the four day trip to Seattle, and five years of exile in Alaska. But no matter how bad he felt about any of that, nothing compared with this feeling of losing his son.

Goddammit, Jason thought, why hadn't he left first? The whole affair should have lasted one night, two at the most. He'd found her standing alone on the porch outside his fraternity house the night of their year-end party. She was so improbably beautiful that he felt emboldened by the fact he had nothing to lose. She was clearly older than him, slim, sexy, reserved, with long dark hair and olive skin and intense black eyes. She wore a black mini-skirt and high heels, a white sleeveless blouse and gold charm bracelet filled with miniature replicas of the Elgin Marbles. She looked as if she had stepped from a European movie.

"Jason Thibodeaux," he'd introduced himself gallantly. "A member of this august fraternity, and candidate for a degree in the Sociology of Humanity." He drew her hand to his lips and kissed it.

"Victoria Repetto," she replied warily. "Second year law."

They danced in a room that literally shook with the vibrations from a DJ's repertoire, beneath a dented National Park Service sign that warned, "ELK RUTTING SEASON. AGGRESSIVE BEHAVIOR. DO NOT APPROACH." He had a surprising gracefulness that was incongruous with his size. She watched wonderingly as people touched or squeezed him as they walked by, as if he were some kind of talisman. "Heat," they called him. He clearly had something that people wanted.

When they finished dancing, Jason grabbed a bottle of champagne and two glasses from the bar and led her back to the porch. They sat in the tiny love seat and shared the outlines of their lives. She was the second of five children — and only daughter — in a big Italian family across the Bay in Fremont. "It was like living in a house of Roman centurions," she said with distaste. "Four guys — five, counting my father — all God's gift to the world."

"You obviously held your own," he remarked. "You got in Stanford Law."

"It was either that or stay home and iron shirts. My father helped my brothers through college, but not me. In my family, girls were for having babies."

He wasn't really listening, though he wished he had. Her anger at her family would figure prominently in theirs — as prominently as the barrenness and isolation of *his* family life had. He watched her thin, lipsticked lips, her earrings dancing in the Christmas lights strung along the porch railings. Everything seemed pointed towards fulfilling that perfect college moment — gratuitous sex on the cusp of summer vacation.

He described the little town he was from — Port Sulphur, Louisiana, on the Gulf south of New Orleans. His father was in the oil business when he'd died eight years before. Jason told her about trying to be "the man of the house," but never coming close to touching his mother's depression. She'd died during his sophomore year, leaving him alone in the world. He'd come to Stanford to get the best education he could, and make a better life for himself than what his parents ever had.

"Why do they call you 'Heat'?" Vicki asked.

"My fastball." He could tell she didn't have the faintest idea what he was talking about. "I'm here on a baseball scholarship."

"You're a jock?"

"Actually, we don't wear jocks anymore." He held his hands as if pressing the sides of a melon. "They have these sports briefs that hold everything together."

She laughed, and he poured her more champagne. Later, they went to his room and made love. After that night, she insisted she'd been drunk. When finals were over he asked her out to a Tom Petty concert at the Shoreline Amphitheater, but they were more courteous than courtly and did not sleep together a second time. It was three weeks before they spoke again, when she called with the news. She had left to clerk for a federal judge in Philadelphia,

"Hey!" he said, surprised. He turned down the sound of the Giants game on his television. "How's life in Philly?"

"I'm at my parents' house," she said. "There's been a change in plans."

"What's going on?" he asked, only half-listening as he watched the game.

"I'm pregnant."

He turned the game off. "I thought you couldn't get pregnant." That's what she had told him, why they didn't use protection — that she had scarring in her tubes from an untreated case of chlamydia that surgery may or may not correct some day.

"Obviously the doctor was wrong."

The next day he drove to her family's ranch house in a suburban cul-de-sac. He'd brought the number for Planned Parenthood, though she'd made it clear on the phone that she was going to have the baby. As soon as she opened the door, he knew what was going to happen. She wore a pair of radiant white shorts and a wine-red blouse with the top two buttons unfastened. Her dark eyes looked at him with a mixture of sorrow, defiance and expectation.

He handed her a large bouquet of mixed flowers with a price sticker still on the wrapper. "You look really nice," he said, kissing her on the lips.

They went for a drive, ending up in a tree-shaded parking lot at Lake Del Valle State Recreation Area. They sat for awhile with their own thoughts, watching a Vietnamese family — mother, father, little girl — fish from a freshly painted pier.

Vicki finally spoke. "My father says I have to get married."

"To who?" Jason asked.

She laughed. "To you — but I know that won't happen."

He watched the Vietnamese father grab the handle of a fishing rod while his daughter excitedly reeled in the line and the mother leaned forward with a net. In a moment a small fish broke the surface and the little girl screamed with delight as the fish flopped in the net. Jason wished he had somebody to tell him what to do. But even if his parents were alive, what could they have offered? Every decision his family had made seemed completely off-the-cuff: go to Point Barrow, to Galveston, to Norway. Nobody discussed anything — least of all with him. Now here was somebody who needed him, who was going to have his child.

"We can do it," he said. "We can do whatever we want."

"We don't even know each other."

"I know that you're beautiful," he said. "I know you're smart, you're sexy, you're a great dancer." Right there, right then, he'd decided he loved her and that anything was possible. And why not? She *was* beautiful — and smart, and sexy. He didn't stop to think at that point that what he really loved was the idea of having a child. He'd never had a brother or a sister, and as often as they'd moved, he'd hardly had any friends. Fate was offering something real here: a choice to stay with this beautiful woman and have a son (he was convinced it was a son), or to leave — like *his* dad had done. And for him, that wasn't an option. He had vowed that he would never do what his dad had done to him.

She looked at Jason, studying his face as if for the first time. "I don't want to make a mistake on something this big."

"Me neither."

"I need to know we can do it right."

He leaned over and kissed her tenderly on the lips, laying his hand on the smooth bare skin of her inner thigh. Then he walked around to the passenger side of the car and opened her door. Kneeling on the asphalt, he took Vicki's hand. "Victoria Repetto," he said with the same gallantry he had shown the night they had met. "Will you marry me?"

She closed her eyes and gripped his hand tightly. It took her several moments to answer, and when she did, tears were streaming down her cheeks.

"Yes," she said, her eyes still closed.

JASON ROSE, slammed the door of Rafe's room and hurried through the apartment. She had taken everything of hers: clothes, vanity, the small card table they shared as a computer table, towels, linens, plates, silverware, pots, posters from the wall. The thoroughness of it was vintage Vicki, but somehow he had never seen it coming.

He found the phone beneath a pile of papers beside the bed. He wanted to call the friends she might have fled to but didn't have the numbers. He thought of calling his own friends, but based on what he'd seen at practice, who'd give a damn? He never felt so alone in his life. Even in Alaska, in the darkest days of winter, he'd had his mother — and the hope, if not the reality, of his father coming home.

He opened the refrigerator and was shocked to see Rafe's food still there. Three jars of half-eaten organic vegetables; a quart of soy milk; a package of Zwieback crackers; a plastic container with tiny pieces of pot roast he had left for Rafe's dinner the day before; a six pack of Juicy Juice; an unopened can of mandarin orange slices. Rafe loved orange food — squash, apricots, yams, cantaloupe. Jason had called the pediatrician, concerned that he was eating too much of one kind of food, but she said it was fine. She suggested that he cook real vegetables and see how he liked them. Rafe not only liked them, he *loved* them: zucchini, broccoli, green beans. He was what moms at the park called a "good eater." In the Stanford clubhouse, they'd call him an animal.

He closed the refrigerator. It was completely dark now but he was afraid to turn on the lights. As long as it was dark, he couldn't see what was missing. The neighbors' voices leaked through the wall, frighteningly clear. Jesus, had they been able to hear all their arguments as easily as this?

The buzzer rang. He lunged across the room and slammed the

31

intercom. "Vicki?"

"It's me, Vuco."

Jason leaned against the wall and gathered himself, then pressed the button again. "I'm sorry about walking out. She took off with my kid —"

"Buzz me in, for Christsakes!"

Vuco carried a six pack of Red Tail Ale and a Round Table pizza. He set them on the kitchen table and peered through the darkness.

"She take the light bulbs?"

Jason flicked on the kitchen light and stood self-consciously by the door, still wearing only his baseball pants. "Vuco, I know you think —"

Vucovich tossed the papers Jason had left in the clubhouse onto the table. "Get dressed, will you?"

When Jason returned he found a bottle of Red Tail ale and a slice of pizza waiting. "My mama always said when you get a shock, you should sit down and eat," Vuco said. He clinked his beer against Jason's. They ate in silence, two large men at a small table that once held a family. "Do you know where she went?" Vuco finally asked.

Jason shook his head. "She took everything. It's like they were never here."

"Makes it easier to move on."

"What are you talking about?"

"She gets the kid, you get to play baseball."

"Jesus, Vuco, she took my fucking kid — you were there!"

"You gonna try and get her back?"

"Get *her* back? I just want my kid."

"Get a lawyer," Vuco said.

Jason looked at him oddly. Having to hire a lawyer seemed strange, after helping his wife become one. "I think we can work it out."

Vuco gestured around the stripped apartment. "Doesn't look like somebody who wants to work things out."

Jason noticed that Vicki had missed the bookshelf wedged beside the refrigerator, full of the parenting books he had collected over the past two years. He took a sip of the beer. "I'm not going to let her do this, Vuco. She can't just take him like that." He studied his coach's face but there was nothing to read. Should he tell Vuco how much he *liked* caring for Rafe? How good it felt to watch his son screw the lid off a jar, pound a plastic peg into his Playskool board, catch and throw a ball, burrow to sleep in the warm folds of his bed? His boy was becoming who he was because of him. He hadn't done what a lot of people expected him to do — run away. How could he ever run away from his own son?

He drank some more and with each sip felt more in control. "Have you ever watched a kid for a whole day — just watched him?" Vucovich shook his head as if he'd been asked if he'd ever eaten a frog or worn a dress. "*Whatsa, whatsa, whatsa?*" Jason jabbed with his finger. "What's a fork? What's a napkin? What's that oil on your pizza? Everything — *everything* — is brand new, like the Earth was created a minute ago." Vucovich watched him, speechless. "Everything's so innocent," Jason continued. "How the fuck do we go from that … to this?" He gestured around the stripped apartment.

"What's your point?" Vuco asked.

"This is my son! Like we were somebody's son. I mean, what are fathers for? My dad wasn't there for me — "

"Christ, man, none of our dads were there," Vucovich bellowed. "*I'm* not there for *my* kids! That's what mothers are for!"

Jason shook his head. That night in Galveston playing catch with his dad came back as clear as a movie on a screen. He wished he had said more to him. Maybe, 'I'm going to miss you,' or 'I hope it's not long.' Or — but that was ridiculous, no one in his family would ever say such a thing — 'I love you.'

His father had left the next morning at dawn in a company van to Houston, where he caught a flight to New York and on to Oslo. He went to work on an oil platform in the middle of the Barents Sea and started to send checks home the size of which they had never seen before. After seventeen years in the field, he finally had worked his way up to foreman. He had the privilege of sleeping in a bigger bed and eating at a smaller table and getting time off on shore. And if he brought in his quota, there would be enough money to buy the liquor store he wanted and make another start and spend that time with his kid, like he promised. But he died first, along with twenty-nine other men, in a spectacular blaze that lit up the Arctic sky for days. For a long time Jason had blamed himself. If his father had had any idea of how much he wanted him to stay, he never would have gone. All that Jack Thibodeaux left behind, besides the money he sent home and death benefit checks from the oil company, was his unspoken promise to be a better father.

Vucovich wiped his hands on his napkin and stood. "Practice at nine-thirty tomorrow," he said. "I'd suggest you be there on time — and alone." Jason nodded. He was vaguely aware of how this looked from the outside, but that's not where he was. It had seemed like the right thing to do, taking the year off. But now it was all gone — his kid, his wife, the respect of his manager. He stood helplessly at the door.

"Get some sleep," Vuco said. Then he, too, was gone.

JASON RANG the doorbell and watched anxiously for signs of life. He wasn't sure what he would say if Vicki answered, then suddenly the front door of her family's home opened and there was Rafe, trying to squirm out of the arms of Vicki's mom.

"Dada!"

Jason smiled, but when he saw the look of fear on Anna Rapetto's face he flushed with shame. Despite the rocky beginnings of their relationship when Vicki's mother struggled to accept the man who got her daughter pregnant, they had become friends, allies. He liked Anna's natural affection and common sense. She had taught him everything she could about raising a child and had fielded dozens of phone calls from him at all hours of the day and night about Rafe. Several times she had driven across the Bay to help him in person when Vicki was pre-occupied with school and Rafe wouldn't eat or sleep. They had become partners in a very real sense, but after the separation and whatever Vicki had said about him, they had clearly become something else.

"I just want to see my son," he said quietly.

She half-turned from him, shielding Rafe. "I'm sorry it's turned out like this, Jason."

"Yeah, me too."

"I don't know what to think. I thought I knew you, then Vicki tells me these horrible things."

"There are two sides to every story, Anna, you know that. Your daughter's not the easiest person to get along with."

Anna smiled ruefully. "I'll have to call her and tell her that you're here."

"Go ahead. I've been trying to call her for a week."

Anna disappeared into the house and returned with a cordless phone. She leaned toward Jason and Rafe slid eagerly into his father's arms.

"Oh God, I missed you!" Jason cried. He inhaled the aroma of his son like a drug. Rafe squirmed and grabbed his father's hair for balance, but Jason didn't complain. He hugged Rafe as he listened to Anna's phone conversation.

"Jason's here, he wants to see Rafe —"

"Don't let him take him!" he heard Vicki shout. "I'll be there in twenty minutes!"

A HALF hour later she burst through the front door, her eyes sweeping the room. Jason rose from his seat at the formal dining room table.

"Where's Rafe?" she asked.

"With your mom. She took him on an errand so we can work things out."

"There's nothing to work out. Please leave."

"I'm not leaving without Rafe. You can't just take him like that."

She faced him across the table. "What are you going to do — hit me?"

"I never hit you. I've never hit anybody."

"You threw things at me! You pushed me!"

"We had an argument. I threw something at the wall. That's no excuse to kidnap our child. You *kidnapped* him, Vicki!"

"I *saved* him! You're a violent man. I'm not going to subject my son — "

"He's *our* son!"

Vicki swept her hand through her long dark hair, her signal of maximum impatience. Then she slowly slipped into a chair; Jason sat down across from her. "Look, you said it yourself — this marriage sucks. We make a clean break, we never have to deal with each other again. No more arguments, no more bickering, no more disappointments — for either one of us. We could pretend we never even met, if that works for you."

Jason stared at her warily. "That's fine with me," he said. "But what do we do about Rafe?"

"It's best that he stays with me. He needs his mother."

"And his father."

"You don't want him to see us fighting all the time. Nobody wants that."

"I checked some books out," Jason said. "We need to work out joint custody."

Vicki shook her head. "That's not going to happen."

"He belongs to both of us."

"Jason, you did what you did and I appreciate that. But this is a full-time job. I mean, it's not a job — it's a commitment, day-in, day-out *for the next eighteen years of your life.* You're not going to be able to do that —"

"He's my son," Jason said firmly. "I'm not leaving without him."

Vicki's eyes widened, more with desperation now than anger. "You can get married again and have as many kids as you want. Rafe's all I got."

Jason laughed incredulously. "Are you crazy? I can't just go out and get a child like a new shirt or something!"

"That's not what I'm saying," she said. "You'll find somebody — so will I someday. And all of this will just be a bad memory."

"It already is."

They faced each other in familiar opposition, their faces hardened. "Please go, Jason. Just leave us alone."

"Screw you," he seethed. "I raised him. I took care of him while you finished school."

"You didn't even know how to change a diaper. My mother did all the work."

"You're so full of shit. You just used me!"

"I don't have to take this." She stood and strode into the kitchen. He was beside her instantly. They had reached that precise moment in a marriage when their dislike for each other became so thorough, so absolute that the desire — let alone the possibility — of ever working cooperatively on any problem seemed to vanish forever. Any restraint that each had employed in the past to avoid disaster was now swept aside.

"Give me my child back." He was almost a head taller than her, and Vicki was not a small woman. She eyed the bank of carving knives beneath the cabinet. "You're threatening me. Get away from me."

"I'll go when you give me my child back."

"Tell it to the judge."

He stepped closer and grabbed her arm. There was only winning or losing and he refused to consider the latter. "Give me my child back!"

"Let go of me," Vicki shouted, struggling to pull away. "Get out of my house!"

He dropped her arm and strode across the living room, yanking open the front door. Far across the bay, the last glow of twilight outlined Mount Montara. "I'll pick up Rafe tomorrow afternoon."

"He won't be here." Vicki slammed the door and locked it.

CONFIRMATION THAT he needed an attorney came in the form of a four page restraining order from Superior Court. He could no longer see Rafe except in a supervised setting. He read it over several times, disbelieving his eyes. The little boy he had powdered, diapered and fed, walked, talked and sung to, carried on his back, bounced on his knee, bathed, bottled and burped now had to be shielded from him as if he were some kind of molester.

He found a lawyer through Graham Nielsen, the Pulitzer Prize-winning head of the sociology department who had gone through a legendary divorce (it seemed everyone Jason consulted on campus had gone through a divorce, legendary or otherwise) with Chilean poet Rosario Lindors. "He's like a Navy Seal," Nielsen described the attorney. "He works in darkness, does the job you ask him to do, and doesn't leave a trace."

But rather than some kind of cold-blooded demolition expert, Robert Marks was a reasonable, soft-spoken man, tall, athletic, with dark brown eyes and a neatly trimmed beard. His office was in a modern suite across from the Fairmont Hotel in downtown San Jose. A plaque on his wall identified him as a twenty-year veteran in the innocuously titled field of Family Law.

Marks listened attentively as Jason related the details of his marriage, how he had left Stanford's baseball program for a year to care for their son while his wife completed law school, and the predictable chain of discord leading to the fight at Vicki's house.

"I was frustrated," Jason said ruefully. "But I never hit her. She took my son, Mr. Marks. I haven't seen him in more than a week."

"There doesn't have to be physical violence to trigger a restraining order," Marks explained neutrally. "The law says any spouse can ask for a restraining order for a 'reasonable *apprehension* of bodily injury to herself or the child.' You made a mistake going there."

"Yeah, well, she made a mistake taking my son."

Marks studied him for a moment. "Did you and Vicki love each other?"

"What kind of question is that?"

"It helps me anticipate the level of rancor. Some of my worst cases are when people were intensely in love — or at least one of them was."

Jason shook his head. "We couldn't stand each other." He stopped, clearly pained. On the baseball field, he knew how to win; his marriage, however, had been a disaster. "We got married because of Rafe," Jason added.

"You're not the first couple that's tried that and failed."

"I don't care about them. I just want to see my son."

"You'll have to undergo psychological testing first, and at least one interview with a court evaluator," Marks explained. "You'll also have to attend an anger management class if the court orders one. You'll have to prove that you're not abusive before you can see your child unsupervised."

"Prove I'm not abusive? But I'm *not* abusive!"

"The court doesn't know that. The burden is on you to demonstrate that you're a loving, kind, considerate father."

Jason couldn't believe the irony. Here he was, the son of a man who never had time for his child, being forbidden to see his. All he could see was the small bundle of his son waving bye-bye from his mother-in-law's car six days ago.

"She kidnaps Rafe and I'm the bad guy."

"I know it's hard. But the majority of these cases are eventually resolved with normal visitation rights for the father. You'll get to see him two weekends a month — "

"I'm his father, Mr. Marks. I want joint custody. I've read about that. I deserve that."

Marks smiled patiently. "Let's work on getting the restraining order lifted first."

THE OPENING game of the PAC-10 Conference found the Oregon Ducks visiting Sunken Diamond, and Jason Thibodeaux pitching for the Stanford Cardinal. He took a 2-2 tie into the top of the seventh, and after his warmups, stepped off the back of the mound and looked around. The barbecues were damped, the concession stands closed, nearly everyone's eyes were on him, number 47. Baptiste had taken the pitchers aside one night and shown films of matadors at work. "Look at their focus, the concentration, the control. He never, ever — *ever* — takes his eyes off the bull. He directs the bull, like you direct the batter.

In, out, up, down, changing speeds, deliveries, looks ..."

Jason stepped back on the mound as the batter settled into the box, and the battle began anew. His cleats gripped the dirt, his fingers squeezed the seams of the leather-bound ball. Ash called for a slider, outside corner — and a slider, outside corner is what he got. Strike one. He loved this feeling, just as the matador must love the feel of a 400 pound bull passing beneath his cape. He was in control. He could hold chaos at bay for as long as he held his cape — the ball — in his hand.

He struck out two men in the seventh inning and got the third to hit a soft liner to Corliss in right. Then everything changed. Baptiste removed him for a reliever, and Jason sat on the bench eyeing the clock. Today was the first day he was going to see Rafe in a month — twenty-nine days, to be exact — his first visit with a licensed chaperone in a court-appointed facility. The game wore on past the ninth inning, until Jason didn't care who broke the tie. Just minutes after Seligman slid home with the winning run in the bottom of the twelfth, Jason took off running straight across campus, still in his uniform. The Palo Alto Family Center was in a large government structure just off campus on Page Mill Road. Sweat streamed down his face as he pushed through the front doors. His appointment was at five and it was already 5:30. He searched the directory for Room 117, then hurried frantically down one, then another corridor before taking a stairway to the right floor.

It was 5:35 when he found the room. A heavy-set woman with a blue denim dress sat behind a reception desk staring at a computer. "I'm here to see my son," he announced, leaning anxiously over the desk. "I'm Jason Thibodeaux — Raphael Thibodeaux's father."

"Just a moment please," the woman said, still staring at the screen. Jason leaned over the desk. "I haven't seen my boy in a month. This is my only chance —"

"Have a seat, *please.*"

She brought him three pages of forms to fill out. It was 5:50 before she led him down a corridor to a large, linoleum-floored playroom at the rear of an office suite. Rafe sat alone on the floor beside a small plastic slide, dressed in a white t-shirt and red cotton overalls. A young man in a blue security uniform sat at a desk just inside the door.

"Rafey!" Jason called out. When he reached him he saw the tears streaming down his cheeks.

"Mommy," Rafe cried. "I want mommy!"

Jason's heart sank. Rafe appeared to not even recognize him. He sobbed and sobbed, crying for his mother. Jason crouched and brushed the tears from Rafe's cheeks, then hoisted him into his arms. Rafe's voice wailed in his ear, his body trembling. "Rafey Rafey Rafey," he cooed. "It's OK, Daddy's here. Do you want to go down the slide? C'mon, let's go down the slide!"

Jason set him at the top of the plastic slide and Rafe just sat there, gripping the handles at the top. "Mommy," he wailed. "Mommy mommy mommy." Jason picked him up again and carried him to the couch. Rafe's crying pierced his heart. Maybe Vicki was right — Rafe needed his mother more than anything. What the hell did he know — he was a baseball player. But then it flashed on him, what was he thinking — it was dinner time! Rafe was probably famished.

"Poor little Buddy," he said, stroking Rafe's back. Then, to the guard, "Is there someplace to eat in the building?"

"Cafeteria on the third floor. But they're closed."

"Vending machines?" The man shook his head. "Soda, juice, candy?" The man shook his head again.

Rafe stopped crying, intrigued by the litany of treats. Jason bounced him once or twice in his arms. "How about we get some ice cream?" Rafe's eyes brightened. "Ice-ceam!" he squealed. Jason laughed and spun him around. It was ten after six. There had to be something in one of the nearby malls that would let them get back by seven.

He headed for the door, holding Rafe in the crook of his arm. The guard stood and positioned himself in front of the door.

"You can't take the child out."

"We're just going for ice cream!" He glowered at the guard, who watched him warily. Jason was a good three inches taller, and in his baseball uniform seemed even larger. There didn't appear to be any gun involved. He imagined a Randall P. McMurphy bust out, bowling over the guard and carrying his child to freedom. As if reading his mind, the guard leaned over and pushed a button on his phone.

"Aw, c'mon," Jason groaned. "The little guy's hungry, that's all."

The guard continued watching him. "Ice ceam!" Rafe shouted. He grabbed his father's nose. Jason carried him back towards the play area. "Ice ceam!"

"I'm sorry, Buddy, no ice ceam today." He slumped onto a low wooden bench and set Rafe on his lap. "Ice ceam, ice ceam," Rafe cried. Jason reached into a trunk full of toys and picked out a purple Nerf ball and began tossing it up and down. "Play catch?" he said. "C'mon, let's play catch!"

"I want ice ceam!" Rafe wailed. Jason tossed the ball a few more times in front of Rafe's eyes. The guard was on the phone, talking to someone in a low, furtive voice. It was probably dark outside, though there was no way of telling in the windowless room. Somewhere, families were gathering around tables and sharing meals, conversations, dreams. Somewhere there was love, affection, trust.

Rafe squirmed away from him and stood up. He pointed to the door, his mouth working with hopeful anticipation. "Ice ceam!"

Jason could see two more people through the wire mesh window — the woman from the front desk, and another uniformed guard. He shook his head, as embarrassed as he was frustrated. Four hours ago when they announced his name, he'd received the ovation of 3,000 people who believed he was the reincarnation of Sandy Koufax. Now, he couldn't even take his own son out for ice cream.

Rafe began crying again. It was so simple — a piece of fruit, a pretzel, a juice box would have made all the difference. He would never forgive Vicki for this. He would never forgive her for taking away his son.

He squeezed the Nerf ball into a tiny wad and tossed it at Rafe. It sprang open and popped against his face, startling him. He began to cry so hard he had trouble catching his breath. Jason held him close and looked over the top of his head to the clock — 6:25. Thirty-five minutes to go. It would be another week before he saw Rafe again. Same time, same place.

THEY WERE gathered at a large conference table in a glass-walled room overlooking the parking lot of the Santa Clara County Courthouse, waiting as Judge Finbarr O'Halloran read, clearly for the first time, from a thick stack of materials. O'Halloran was a tall, heavy-set man with wavy white hair and a droll, irritated manner developed from decades of having the power to control significant portions of other people's lives. Jason sat directly across from him, stuffed uncomfortably into a blue wool suit, white shirt and tie. Beside him sat his attorney, Robert Marks; beside him the Court Evaluator, Bonnie Ripston, in a cherry red pant suit. Vicki sat across from her in a plum-colored Italian suit and white silk blouse, a stack of folders and law texts in front of her. Behind her, seated alone in a row of chairs against the wall, was her mother.

Silence reigned. Then, "How old is the child now?" O'Halloran asked no one in particular, startling everyone. "Two-and-a-half," Vicki replied. The judge flipped through the contents of a blue folder, then began reading from other reports — one from the court-appointed mediator, another from the evaluator, along with depositions from Jason's teammates and Vicki's classmates, from Rafe's pediatrician and baby sitters, and transcripts and recommendations from Stanford Law School attesting to Vicki's character. Jason felt he'd done everything he could to strengthen his claim to joint custody. He'd hired the best lawyer he could find, spending well over half his inheritance on his fees, and as painful as the supervised visits were, he'd managed to make the best of them.

But as the session wore on, he feared it wasn't enough. Marks had warned him that joint custody was a long-shot, but he'd never understood the ramifications of that until now. In baseball, being a long-shot meant you just had to try harder, train longer, pray that your team jelled at the right point — and even then there was no guarantee. The week before, he'd been passed over in the baseball draft. Having missed his junior year, when most top-rated players were selected and sometimes seduced from their last year of schooling, scouts had waited to see how he developed and lost interest when Stanford failed to make the Regionals. Baptiste hadn't helped. He'd developed enough top-notch ballplayers to have scouts trust him when he said he had a live one. But all he would say about Jason was, "What you see is what you get." The skinny was, the kid most people had considered a sure thing had become a "head case" — someone with the physical infrastructure but not the emotional and psychological tools to make the most of it. Not to be taken as one of the 1,498 young men selected in the draft was crushing.

O'Halloran finished reading and looked at Jason and Vicki over the bridge of his reading glasses. "Why can't two intelligent people like yourselves work this out?"

Vicki's voice was calm, rehearsed. "The issue is finding a parenting plan that works for the best interests of my son, Raphael. The record is clear that Mr. Thibodeaux is incapable of providing a sustained and sensitive level of care for a child of this age. It's clearly in the best interests of the child for the court to award primary custody — "

"Your Honor," Robert Marks interrupted. "There are numerous reports before you that attest to the fact that Mr. Thibodeaux is a loving, competent caretaker —"

O'Halloran held up his hand. "Your client has been slapped with a restraining order and his psychological evaluation raises serious questions about his relationship with authority. Why should I award custody of a two-and-a-half year old boy to such a man?"

Jason looked at the judge and felt a rising sense of dread. He was in some kind of nightmare — trapped in the legal system, in a full-fledged fight with a lawyer. He was going to lose his son.

He leaned forward. "I'm not sure how to say this," he began, his voice tight and nervous. "My father wasn't there for me when I was a kid, and I always wondered why. I used to think, he's not around because he doesn't like me … he doesn't love me." Marks set a hand on Jason's forearm, whether in restraint or consolation it was hard to tell. Jason went on. "I felt that no matter what happened in my life, I would never hurt *my* son like that, but that's exactly what's happening. I can't even see him except two hours in a childcare center, with people staring at me like I'm some kind of child molester. Every day he's growing, changing, discovering things and I want to be there —"

"Thank you!" O'Halloran said with brusque sarcasm. He leafed through several other folders, his brows knotting as he tried to get his mind around something that eluded him. "Have you ever struck your son?" he asked Jason in a matter-of-fact voice.

"No sir," he answered firmly. "And I never will."

Robert Marks rose. "Your Honor, we have here a man who has been willing to make extraordinary sacrifices to fulfill his responsibilities as a father. This kind of behavior needs to be rewarded. We're only asking for joint custody, the presumption under the law —"

Vicki rose from her chair. "Your honor, if I may address the court—"

"You may not," O'Halloran said. He closed the last of the folders and rose abruptly. "The decision of this court will be rendered within twenty-one days."

THE CALL came eight days later. '*Robert Marks*' the phone displayed. He didn't want to pick up. Marks had warned him that the best he could expect was 'visitation rights' — every other weekend, every other Wednesday, and two weeks in the summer.

"I never had a chance, did I?" he said, before Marks could speak.

"Like I said, it was a longshot."

"Can I appeal?"

"You could," the lawyer replied. "But I wouldn't take your money."

Jason hadn't felt so helpless since he'd heard about his father's death on the oil platform. That seemed so ferocious in its details, it had to be an act of God. This felt more like something from hell. For a moment he understood the stories he read in newspapers about parents who took their children hostages, or used guns, machetes, knives or their bare hands to lay waste to those who denied them access to their own children.

He called Vuco. "I lost my court case."

"Jesus, I'm sorry."

"You don't sound sorry."

"I just got some really good news," Vuco said.

"About what?"

"The Reds want me to manage their team in Billings, Montana — the Mustangs, Single A. Their GM's a Stanford guy."

"That's great, Vuco," Jason said, trying to sound enthused.

"Yeah, it is," he said. "Why don't you come with me?"

"Come and do what?"

"Pitch, you asshole. But you've got to work your ass off or I swear to God you'll be Exhibit A of what a tough son-of-a-bitch Bill Vucovich is."

With the choices slim or nothing on the home front, he took nothing and left for Montana the next day. He shoved the few things he had of Rafe's into a garbage bag — his small plastic tricycle, stuffed animals, picture books, water colors, a miniature golf set and some plastic trucks — and set them by the curb. The only things he took to remind him of Rafe were some photographs.

His whole life he had looked forward to playing professional ball, but when it finally happened, he couldn't enjoy it. He spent the entire summer missing his son — his smell, his feel, his laugh, his walk, the sound of his voice when he said "Daddy," the way Rafe followed him around the apartment as he put away laundry or got dinner ready. No matter what town he was in — Idaho Falls or Great Falls, Butte or Helena — when he passed playgrounds with their mazes of ladders and slides he imagined Rafe scampering to the top of a jungle gym or arcing into the sky on a swing. At night, lying awake in swayback beds in the cheap cowboy hotels where the Mustangs stayed on the road, he imagined hearing his son's soft even breathing, or the muffled percussion of his feet across the bedroom floor. He wavered between shame and anger with himself for giving up on Rafe, the same way his father had given up on him.

Then after the Mustangs' last game, he knew what he had to do. As Marks had told the court, his son needed him, and he needed his son. Vicki was working in San Francisco for Morrison & Foerster, one of the city's largest and most prestigious law firms, as an associate in their Trademark and Patents Division. He reached her on the phone at her office.

"Hi, I'm back in Palo Alto. I want to see Rafe."

She snorted with disbelief. "The court said every other weekend, not every three months. This is exactly what I was talking about, Jason—"

"My schedule says I get Rafe Friday at five o'clock. Tomorrow's Friday."

"It doesn't work that way," Vicki said. "You can't just walk out and walk back into his life."

"Sure I can. I just did."

THOSE FIRST weeks back were some of the longest and loneliest in his life. Vuco was gone. He didn't want to look up any of the old coaches and players and admit he was losing another round to his ex-wife. He went to movies, worked out, watched baseball in the boarding house on California Street where he stayed. One morning he picked up a copy of *Bay Area Parent* from a sidewalk box to look for fathers' support groups. He thumbed through it a half-dozen times and found two-and-a-half pages of listings for mothers' groups — and not one listing, not one phone number, for fathers.

The only relationship he could count on was with his lawyer, at $275 an hour. They filed a motion claiming obstruction on Vicki's part, countering her claim of abandonment with a notification that Jason's custody schedule was made obsolete by his obligations as a professional baseball player. They requested a new schedule consistent with the rhythms of the season — every other weekend and every Tuesday-Thursday during the off-season, and vacation time in the winter rather than summer. The new request meant more responses and counter-motions from Vicki — and more delays.

It took seven weeks and another $4,700 in legal fees before he could get the court to order Vicki to abide by the original custody schedule.

It was mid-November before he saw Rafe — the first time since July. They arranged for Vicki's mother — "Gramma Anna" — to bring him to West Campus Playground at Stanford, where they had played during his year off from baseball. Rafe exploded from the back seat of Anna's Cadillac.

"Dada!" he cried, running as fast as he could towards him. He looked gigantic, nearly 3½ now and more like a miniature version of Jason than ever. Rafe buried his face in his father's chest, circled his neck with his arms and squeezed. It was Jason, not Rafe, who broke down and cried. Rafe stared at him, alarmed.

"Don't cry, Daddy," he said with his small, sweet voice.

"It's OK, Rafey. Sometimes people cry because they're happy." He turned to Anna. "Thanks," he smiled. His right to see Rafe didn't begin until 5:00 PM, but Anna had agreed to bring him over early so they could have some extra time — and she could have some time off.

"Have a wonderful time," Anna said. "Call if you need anything." She handed over a bag of cookies she had saved from lunch, and tucked a perfumed handkerchief of her own into the pocket of Rafe's overalls. "So long, Rafey," she said, kissing her grandson loudly on the cheek. "Have fun with your daddy."

They stayed at the park until twilight. He chased Rafe up and down the ladders and slides, amazed by how agile he was. And strong. His shoulders were thick and already defined — a slugger's shoulders. He could see a lot of Vicki, too — her luminous eyes and hair, her gracefulness and self-assurance. Everything, he hoped, except her stubbornness and hatred of him.

Afterwards they stopped at a Chinese restaurant where they ordered Rafe's favorite dish — *Chow Fun*, tasty rice noodles smothered in black bean sauce and mixed with chicken and beef and shrimp and broccoli. When they finished they went to the Stanford Mall for some shirts and shoes and a cool Gymboree jacket with a rocket ship for a zipper grip. Then to Macy's for the rest — underwear, socks, bathing suit, a bright orange cotton blanket Rafe picked out, and three stuffed animals who would sleep at Daddy's even when Rafe wasn't there. And a camera. Jason started taking photos right away. Rafe with his new shoes. Rafe with his new animal friends. Rafe in his new jacket, posing with the pretty sales clerk who helped him choose the right size.

As they left Macy's, Rafe spied a display of lawn furniture outside the store and went straight for the glider. He climbed on and started

46

to rock. "C'mon, Daddy, take a ride," he called, throwing his shoulders again and again against the plastic cushion. Jason climbed on beside him and they rocked back and forth with delighted smiles on their faces. Jason reached down and covered Rafe's hand with his.

"It's really good to see you." Rafe rocked harder, then suddenly squirmed from the seat. "I want to go home," he said, heading for the doors. Jason smiled as he followed Rafe out. He loved the way he said "home."

During the long legal delay he had found an apartment and furnished it for the two of them. It was a large two bedroom on Junipero Serra in a California-style courtyard complex with two-story buildings separated by a *faux* stream and bridges. It was expensive, but he could afford it. He'd already signed a contract to play next year in the Reds' system. Despite his depression, he'd had some success with the Mustangs. Vuco pitched him out of the bullpen at first, limiting him to games they were either far ahead in or too far out. He was happy with his progress, although the team thought he could do better with a 98-mile-per-hour fastball. But then, teams always thought you could do better, especially at contract time.

He pushed open the door to the apartment. There was a broad open living room with wall-to-wall beige carpeting. The furniture was classic Abbey rents — full sofa with a stiff, blue-patterned cover, matching easy chairs, maple coffee table and end tables, TV/VCR, a round dining room table, and a hanging light fixture with obligatory decorative chain connecting it to the ceiling.

"Wanna see your new room?" He swept Rafe up and carried him across the living room. The door to his room was open and Jason gazed in proudly. He had painted it himself — pale yellow with light blue trim — and hung three Japanese kites he'd bought in an Asian strip mall outside Menlo Park. Each bedpost was carved with the likeness of an animal — a fox, an alligator, an egret, a giraffe — and the bed was covered with a Stanford quilt. There was a half-filled bookshelf, a chest of drawers waiting for Rafe's new clothes, a small writing table and chair with decals of leaping dolphins, and a large wooden box half-filled with new toys he'd spent several afternoons gathering.

Rafe bee-lined for the bed. "Daddy's team!" he shouted, rolling himself up in the comforter. For the first time since the whole mess began nearly a year ago, Jason felt relaxed. No chaperones, no lawyers, no ex-wife. Just him and his boy, in his own home ... *their* home.

"C'mon Buddy," he said. "Let's get you ready for bed."

In the bathroom, Rafe took great care in brushing his teeth, pushing the brush up and down his teeth many times. "Mommy says I have to brush my teeth for free minutes," Rafe said earnestly. Jason nodded, not certain what to say. "Can I say goodnight to Mommy?" Rafe asked when he was finished.

Jason's heart fell. "She's not here, Buddy. You're at Daddy's now." He supposed he could have dialed her number and let him say goodnight; but how many times had she done that for him? None. Not once.

He leaned over and hugged Rafe tightly. "You'll see Mommy tomorrow night," he said brightly. "Come on, let's go read a story."

The next morning he took Rafe to the pool, a small aquamarine rectangle behind their building, and everything seemed fine. "Last one in's a rotten egg!" Jason shouted, jumping feet first into the pool. Rafe laughed, running anxiously in place, waiting for his dad to break the surface. Then, "Rotten egg!" Rafe shouted and ran off the edge into the water. Jason waited for him to surface and when he didn't, reached down and pulled him up sputtering and coughing and laughing all at once.

"Hey," he said. "We have to teach you how to swim."

"OK, Daddy."

The rest of that weekend was like a dream, the nondescript Palo Alto apartment magically transformed into a true home by the addition of his son. Saturday evening Jason grilled hamburgers and steamed frozen vegetables and they ate on the balcony overlooking the man-made stream. After dinner, Rafe discovered the Indian Village of wooden figures and cloth wigwams Jason had bought at Nature's Way. Rafe carefully arranged the Indians around a campfire, along with wooden horses and two plastic rocket ships from a Lego set. While he played, Jason read *Stolen Seasons*, a hilarious and heartening book that Vuco had recommended about life in the minor leagues. He was immersed in the story of Steve Dalkowsky, a legendary lefty whose fastballs tore through screens behind home plate and who once struck out sixteen batters and walked sixteen in the same game, when he heard Rafe speak up.

"What's that, buddy?"

"Indians don't wear underwear," Rafe announced.

Jason smiled and set the book down. "What do they wear?"

"Skin deer."

He pressed his lips to keep from laughing. "Deer skin?" Jason asked gently.

"Yeah, deer skin." Rafe held up the figure of a brave carrying the carcass of a deer over his shoulder. "Why do Indians hunt with bows and arrows?"

"That's how they got their food."

"Is that where you get hamburgers?"

Jason shook his head. "I bought those at the store."

As with any dream, however, it had to end. The next day at 3 PM, forty-eight hours after Raphael had exploded from the back seat of his grandmother's car, they returned to the same playground to say goodbye. When the Cadillac glided to a stop against the curb, Jason picked up Rafe and hugged him fiercely. Legally, he couldn't see him until a week from Wednesday, and then just for the night. "You be a good boy," he said. "Daddy's going to be right here waiting for you."

"Do you want a cookie, Daddy?" Rafe held out a small baggie with half a dozen chocolate-covered graham crackers that he'd brought to share with Gramma Anna.

"No thanks, Buddy," Jason said. "Save those for Grandma."

Then, in a ritual that would be repeated too many times over the coming years, he watched his little boy leaving in the back seat of someone else's car.

STRIKE TWO

Top o' the 10th …

Tobias Barlow USA TODAY

—

In the male bastion of baseball, fatherhood is a large, yet largely unspoken subject. I'm sure it's hard to focus on your littlest fans when thousands of others are praising you night after night on fields of play. But all that changes when those littlest fans don't have the opportunity to see their daddy, or vice versa. Absence makes the heart go ponder.

Kids, ironically, were the subject when I caught up with Cincinnati Reds' lefthander Jason Thibodeaux at the Margaret Adams Strohmeyer Senior Center in downtown River City. On home stands Thibodeaux serves lunches and assists the physical therapy staff with the rehab of elderly patients who have had their hips, knees and other worn parts replaced. He's here, he says, because he can't stand the sight of kids.

After losing a child custody battle, Thibodeaux sees his 8-year-old son, Raphael, only during the off-season — and on the single road trip the Reds make to San Francisco, where Raphael lives. Under a court-enforced formula, Thibodeaux and his son spend an average of six weeks out of fifty-two — every other weekend and every other Wednesday for four months, and that one precious road trip to the Golden Gate.

A lot of ball players work with youth, but Thibodeaux went the other way. "Every time I see a group of kids I think of Rafe and how much I miss him. Plus I get a lot of satisfaction working here. I never had the chance to take care of my own parents, so this is a way of paying them back."

Not that some of his current charges don't act like kids. After lunch, a man rolls up in a wheelchair and thrusts a copy of *Sports Illustrated* into Thibodeaux's hands, who pens 'Best Wishes, Ted' and hands it back. "He says it's for his nephews, but he's got dozens of these in his room," Thibodeaux laughs.

Thibodeaux has struggled on the mound this year — he's 8-11, with a 4.37 ERA. But to the residents of the Margaret Adams Strohmeyer Senior Center, he throws a perfect game every time he shows. The fan he cares most about, however, isn't here to see it.

The remote-controlled big wheels "hot rod" lay overturned on the carpet. There was a tabletop Air Hockey game from Ryan Habbegger and his mom, Sam Trainor's silly "Booger Sculpture" kit, a 10-pound bag of multicolored marbles, a biography of Beethoven, and a dozen or more classical and jazz piano CDs scattered amidst torn wrapping paper and ribbons on the living room floor of Vicki's townhouse on Diamond Heights in San Francisco. There had been pizza and crudités, cake and ice cream and candles, and on cue Rafe's buddies Laslow Samuels and Angel Villanueva from the Aurora Craverro School of the Arts had broken into a version of "Happy Birthday" on a piccolo and kazoo as the two delivery men from Sherman Clay wheeled the shiny new Yamaha upright into the room with a fancy candelabra blazing on top.

The party was over, the guests gone, the methodical plunkings of Rafe's shortened version of Rachmaninoff's Piano Sonata #2 a fast-fading memory. Rafe sat at the kitchen table overlooking Glen Canyon, his fingers speeding along the Acer keyboard playing "Major League Baseball 9.0". The laptop and software from his Dad arrived by DHL just that morning in a big yellow box addressed to *Master Raphael Thibodeaux*. His friends thought it was cool that his father was a Major League baseball player, though that wasn't such an easy thing. His mother said that baseball was for morons, which didn't make much sense as his dad wasn't a moron, but still, it would have been easier if his dad was a musician because that was what his mom loved most. Baseball took his dad all around the country and Rafe hardly ever saw him during the season. He had only seen him play once in person, and never on TV — though that was about to change. The Craverro School didn't allow students to watch television or use computers until they were eight. Today he was eight.

"Rafe!" his mother called from the living room. "Time for bed."

He glanced at the kitchen clock. "It's only nine o'clock."

"Which is your bed time. C'mon."

He wasn't sure who hit it but a single flared through the Orioles' infield and Rafe, pulling the fielders in, threw the runner out at second trying to stretch the hit. It was a great game, the players responded to his slightest touch, flinging fastballs, flying vertically along the grass to spear line drives, reaching above the wall to steal home runs from big-shouldered sluggers like David Ortiz and Ryan Howard.

"Rafe." Vicki stared at him from the living room doorway.

"Mom, it's my birthday!" He was a slim, lanky boy, just half a head shorter than his mother. He had a long trunk and long legs and strong arms like his father's, and his mother's slim graceful face, dark brown eyes and olive complexion. He glanced quickly at the screen. The players waited silently for his commands.

"And you've had a wonderful day," she said gently. "Now turn that off."

He pressed "off" and the world of Major League Baseball vaporized. Vicki put her arm around him and they walked together toward the living room. "Did you have a good time?" Rafe nodded. They stopped beside the piano, its bulkiness a formidable new presence in the townhouse. "How do you like your new piano?"

"Good," he responded. Then, "Thanks for the party, Mom. The pizza was really good." She squeezed his shoulder just as the phone rang.

"It's probably your father," Vicki said, reaching for the phone. "I need to talk with him first."

"You guys'll just fight," Rafe said glumly.

"Just for a second ... Hello?"

"Hi." It was Jason. "Is the birthday boy there?"

"He's here. He's a little tuckered out from his party." She smiled towards Rafe, who shook his head vigorously. "He got a piano for his birthday!"

"I wonder who got him that?" Jason replied. "Let me talk with him."

"Did you ever find that red sweater my father gave Rafe for Christmas?"

"I told you, I have no idea where it is. I've never seen it."

"Could you look for it? He says he left it there."

"It's not here, Vicki. Put him on, will you please?"

"I know I packed it, the last time he went to Cincinnati — "

"You mean the one time you let him come here and visit?"

" — and now we can't find it. It was a special gift from my father."

"Mom, it's not important," Rafe called out. "We can get another one."

"I don't have the faintest idea where it is," Jason said. "Would you put Rafe on? I didn't call to talk to you!"

"Just take a minute and look, will you please? That's not too much to ask."

There was a pause, then Jason's voice, low and tight. "I'm paying you four thousand dollars a month and you're bitching about a fucking sweater? PUT RAFE ON THE PHONE!"

Rafe was already on the way to his bedroom when Vicki hung up. "He'll call back later," she said. "He just needs to calm down."

CHARLIE GIORDANO flashed four gnarled fingers, then 2-2-4-2-2 and set up for a slider, low and inside. Jason gripped the ball along the inside of the seams, stretched his arms slightly away then back to his body, and turned his head to check the runner at first. Ray Burriss leaned towards him, glove open, and over Ray's shoulder he saw the kid. Eight or nine years old, wearing a Giants cap and a white t-shirt and a look of rapturous concentration on his face, his right hand tucked inside his baseball glove, watching, waiting with the man beside him, his dad no doubt, a father and son out on a warm summer evening in Cincinnati for the timeless American past-time of baseball. Maybe the kid was living with his father, or it was visitation day. That was it — tonight was Wednesday! The night that every divorced Dad who couldn't be a Dad got to play at being one with their "visitation rights."

Jason stepped off the rubber and scuffed the dirt, thinking of the last time he had seen Rafe, in San Francisco. He had gotten him a seat in the owner's box with some friends from school, and he would never forget the look on Rafey's face when the public address announcer broadcast "A Giants' welcome to the students of Aurora Craverro School and to Raphael Thibodeaux, son of Reds' pitcher, Jason Thibodeaux. Welcome to the Big Leagues, Rafe!"

That was two months ago.

He rubbed the ball and looked toward the kid. Maybe the guy wasn't the kid's father. Maybe it was his stepfather, or a neighbor, or his mother's boyfriend — some guy he doesn't really care about and his real father was gone, pissed off, hopeless. Jason's eyes swept the stands. He'd been playing baseball since he was four; it had always been his refuge. The bellowing of his father's drunkenness or the silence of his indifference evaporated in a crowd roaring at a called third strike or a bang-bang double play. His mother's sobbing in the ice-bound bungalow in Port Barrow melted in the chatter of infielders calling his name. But now all he could think of was Rafe. What was he doing? What would he think if he were here watching the game? How did he end up two thousands miles away from his son?

"JT."

He was surrounded — Giordano and Burriss and Vucovich, who'd come to the Reds the same time as he, and the shortstop, Carlos Guardell. The umpire hovered impatiently behind Vuco, his mask off. Voices in the crowd shouted for Jason to pitch.

"What's going on?" Vucovich asked. Jason shrugged.

"Is it your arm?"

Jason shook his head. Guardell whacked him on the rear end with his glove and trotted back to shortstop. Vuco leaned in close. "I'm comin' over for breakfast tomorrow," he growled. "And I want pancakes. Now get this guy out."

Giordano signaled again for the slider, low and inside, but Jason shook him off. He wanted to throw heat. He wanted to throw a pitch so fast that even the batter would be giddy with awe as it screamed into the catcher's mitt. Finally Giordano gave in — fastball, outside part of the plate. One more out and he had a complete game. Not a pretty one, 5-4, eight hits, two of them home runs. But the guys had come through and all he needed was one more out and they could go out for some beers and follow the score from LA.

He went into his stretch and checked the runner — and there was the kid again. He kicked and unleashed the fastest ball he could throw, and he knew instantly that he would never see it again. It streamed down the center of the strike zone and just as quickly reversed, taking the most direct trajectory deep into the left field bleachers. He heard the collective groan of the fans and watched his teammates trot towards the dugout.

VUCO SHOOED a yellow jacket off the syrup-soaked pancake, cut off three pie-shaped pieces and speared them with his fork. He chewed for a moment, then pushed the plate away. "I can't believe your kid likes these things. They taste like shit!"

They sat on the broad brick patio behind Jason's four-bedroom house in Park Hills, Kentucky, across the river from Cincinnati's River Front Stadium. An unlandscaped half-acre sloped down to a stream between his house and his neighbor's two hundred yards away. A single tree broke the expanse of weeds and grass. A golf club and a pile of balls sat nearby on an Astroturf mat.

"You're going into therapy," Vucovich said.

"Fine," Jason replied. "But I still want a trade."

"Let me guess — San Francisco?"

Jason pointed at Vuco's plate. "You want some more?"

"Not on your life." Vuco gazed over the enormous expanse of lawn. "Why don't you get some cattle or something?"

"Nobody to take care of 'em."

"Get one of those au pair girls. You can get 'em on the Internet now."

"That'll look great in the papers. 'Thibodeaux Hires Online Concubine.'"

"I've seen worse." Vuco picked up the nine-iron and hooked a ball sharply towards the stream. He tossed the club aside and turned on Jason. "You're gonna kick yourself in the ass big-time for not taking your shot seriously."

"C'mon, Vuco. If anything, I'm taking it *too* seriously."

"Horseshit. You're stuck in some endless re-enactment of the Alamo, losing the same battle over and over again and loving every second of it."

"I don't love it. Do I look like I love it?"

"Then why do you keep doing it?"

"I've had this same bullshit custody schedule for five years now."

"Then you should be used to it."

"Seeing him two times during the season? Fuck that." Jason gazed with a far-away look over the half-finished suburban neighborhood. "I miss him, man. I can't be his father if I'm not playing in the same town."

Vuco shook his head in exasperation. JT was his creation. He was the one who scouted him in Galveston and recommended him for scholarship; who'd brought him to Billings after they passed him in the draft; who'd worked with him hour after hour in the far flung stadiums of the Pioneer league, teaching him a changeup, a splitter, a new pick-off move — and the one who brought him up to the Reds. Again and again he'd put his reputation on the line for Jason Thibodeaux; and now he wanted a trade.

"They can't move you the way you're pitching."

"Then I'll pitch better."

"That's what I mean about taking it seriously."

"I'm sorry, Vuco. I'm just doing what I have to do."

"What you have to do is win baseball games."

"Fair enough."

Vuco's expression grew visibly softer. "We go back a long ways," he said, clearly uncomfortable with what he was about to say. "I respect what you're doing — on the homefront," he added quickly.

"Thanks, Vuco." Jason rose and stepped towards his tightly-wound coach. Vuco raised his hands as if he were holding a runner at third.

"No hugs, man."

Jason hugged him anyway. Vuco didn't hug back but neither did Rafe half the time. That didn't mean he didn't appreciate it.

"I still want you to go into therapy," Vuco said.

"And I still want a trade."

SYLVIA HLUCHAN was a sports psychologist who had once been involved in a highly publicized case in which she was hired to hypnotize the entire University of West Virginia football team before its season-opener. The fact that the team eventually went 2-8 that year did not diminish the fury of the public ridicule around the opening game loss to Ohio State by a score of 55-3. Dr. Hluchan did not take the criticism lying down. "To be subconsciously convinced you are an excellent football team when you are not, no more guarantees positive results than if you are hypnotized into believing you can fly, only to plunge to your death off a cliff," she said in an article for the *Pittsburgh Press* posted on the wall of her waiting room. "The next time I'm recruited for a job like this, I'll be sure to consult a scouting report as well as Las Vegas odds makers."

Her waiting room wasn't much bigger than a closet, with two straight-back chairs, a small table with back issues of various magazines, that morning's *Cincinnati Inquirer*, and a single potted plant that looked just hours from death. Jason picked up the sports section and glanced at the box score from last night's game: Houston 9, Reds 0. Teddy Driscoll, their ace righthander going for his sixteenth win, gave up six runs in the third inning and they never recovered. They were four games out with three weeks to go and had no more games with the front-running Cardinals.

His thoughts were interrupted by the appearance of a small elderly woman with stiff white hair and thick glasses. "Come in, Mr. Thibodeaux," she said in a no-nonsense voice. She led him into a small, windowless room and motioned to a chair beside a messy desk. She leaned forward from her worn blue easy chair and offered her hand. It was surprisingly dry and delicate, as soothing as talc. "I'm Dr. Hluchan," she said. "Why don't you tell me why you're here."

"Why?" He'd never been to a shrink before and didn't know what he was supposed to say. "I pitch for the Reds — the Cincinnati Reds. Bill Vucovich recommended you ... " She stared at him, her blue eyes magnified to startlingly huge orbs by the lenses of her glasses. He tried to adjust himself upward in the chair, as somehow he was sitting lower than the tiny therapist. But no matter how hard he tried, he couldn't get himself up to her level.

"I'm here because I'm a lousy pitcher, I guess," he finally said.

She shook her head. "You're here because you're a fine pitcher but you're not pitching like one. Tell me what's going on in your life."

He took her back to the day Vicki left with Rafe, then told her about their divorce, the custody battle, the rigid visitation schedule — his ex-wife's refusal to exchange the two weeks allotted during summer vacation with Rafe for time at Christmas or Thanksgiving. "On top of that, she's late all the time — an hour, two hours, sometimes more. Or she'll call and say she's got special plans, or that Rafe's sick and needs to stay in bed."

"Is he sick?"

"It doesn't matter, I'm perfectly capable of taking care of him," he said defiantly. "I like taking care of him when he's sick."

Dr. Hluchan leaned forward in her chair. "You gave a very compelling story about why your ex-wife should see a therapist, Mr. Thibodeaux. But what about you?"

"What about *me?*"

"How do you respond to her behavior?"

Jason squirmed. "Like an asshole."

"Examples please."

"She brings him two hours late on a Friday, I'll bring him back two hours late on Sunday. He's sick on a Wednesday and can't make it, I'll claim that he's sick on Sunday and can't make it back to her house. She won't answer her phone when I call for Rafe; I won't answer when she calls for him at my house."

"You really do sound like an asshole," she smiled. Jason looked up in surprise. She was a tough old bird, he liked her. "Do you fight in front of your son?"

He nodded. "I can't help myself. I just hear her voice and it's like the bell in a boxing match."

"A match you absolutely have to win."

"Exactly. That's the way I am — I want to win."

"Win what?"

Jason stared at her, half-smiling in embarrassment. "The battle."

"The battle for what?"

"The battle with my ex-wife! The battle … " his voice trailed off.

"You won that battle, Mr. Thibodeaux. You were convinced your ex-wife thought you'd disappear and you didn't. You stayed to fight another day, except this isn't a fight. You were given the extraordinary opportunity of raising a child and you went about it the best way that you could. You say you read books, you interviewed child development experts, you talked to mothers, fathers, kids about the best way to raise your child. So why did you stop?"

"I didn't stop. When the courts took him away I couldn't —"

"Courts shmourts. You took yourself away. You chose to play baseball and that's OK — you're a baseball player. Like I'm a therapist and your wife is a lawyer and your kid is a kid. Your ex-wife could be a lot more cooperative in this venture, but then she wouldn't be your ex-wife, would she?" There was the smile again — or at least, the shape of one. Jason stared. "Now you have the extraordinary challenge of loving and caring for that child *despite all this*. And what are you doing about it?"

"I'm doing the best I can."

"Are you?"

"Of course I am! What the hell else would I do?"

"Come on, Mr. Thibodeaux, you graduated from Stanford."

"Yeah, well, all the books say cooperate. But when I see her — "

"*Him*, Mr. Thibodeaux. We're talking about *him*." Jason looked at her questioningly. "Do you ever make videotapes or audio tapes of you reading stories or talking to him?" she asked.

"No."

"Do you ever have a pizza delivered to his school for lunch, just to surprise him?"

"No."

"Do you ever send him postcards from cities where you're playing, explaining interesting things you've discovered and asking him what he's doing?"

"I asked for a trade to be near him," he offered.

She waved his words away. "You're a National League pitcher. I prefer the National League because pitchers challenge hitters — strength against strength, fast ball pitcher to fast ball hitter — am I right?" Jason nodded. "But every once in a while you've got to throw a curve," she continued. "You've got to drop one off the edge of the table and leave them standing there with the bat in their hands, wondering what the hell just happened."

Jason arched an eyebrow. He couldn't figure out where she was going, whether they had just switched to baseball or she was weaving some kind of complicated spell that would leave him in the same straits as the University of West Virginia football team.

"Your ex-wife is hitting your fastball," she said. "She's a lawyer, and you're pitching right out over the plate — fast ball fast ball fast ball. You've got something huge that you haven't used yet, a secret weapon that every man has to discover before he can conquer the world." Sylvia Hluchan tapped her chest beside a small pearl brooch in the shape of a chrysanthemum. "Your heart."

The small clock on her desk ticked softly. Jason realized with surprise that the hour had passed. Herds of questions stampeded through his mind. What if Vicki won't let Rafe play the tapes? What if she throws away the postcards? What if Rafe's friends think his Dad is crazy for sending a pizza to school — or worse, what if Rafe does?

They rose together. Sylvia Hluchan's head didn't even reach his chest. "I think the Reds thought we'd talk about baseball more," Jason said.

"We did."

"About my pitching, I mean."

She hooked him by his left arm and led him into the waiting room. "We determined at the beginning that you're a wonderful pitcher. That hasn't changed in the last hour." She stopped and looked up at him. "I want you to come in next homestand and tell me how you're doing."

"Do I have to?"

"Yes." She gave his arm a squeeze before letting him go. "Keep throwing strikes, Mr. Thibodeaux." She smiled her strange smile, her eyes expanding behind the thick glasses. "Just change speeds once in awhile."

IT WAS, as Yogi Berra said, *déjà vu* all over again. A man on first, the Reds up by a run, eighth inning, the count 2-2 and Giordano calling for a slider low and outside. Jason took a deep breath and went into the stretch and there was the kid again with the Giants hat, sitting in the front row beside the same heavy-set guy eating popcorn.

Jason's eyes locked on the kid, then he stepped off the rubber and smiled to himself. Maybe Vuco was right — maybe he was crazy. Maybe at some point next year — next week — they'll be pulling him off the backstop like Jimmy Piersall in *Fear Strikes Out*. Stranger things had happened.

"*Andale, Ya-sone,*" Guardell whistled from shortstop. "C'mon, JT!" Digger Wells called from third. He glanced into the dugout and saw Vuco staring, posed like Baptiste used to be, his hands in his back pocket, his back curved, pelvis thrust forward.

Jason checked the runner, kicked and the pitch was off — a missile headed straight for the heart of the plate. The batter strode forward, his bat seeking the tiny orb but it broke down and away into Giordano's mitt.

Strike three!

He strode to the dugout and accepted a fusillade of high fives. "JT! JT! JT!" player after another barked affectionately. It was a cold Monday night in mid-September and the Reds were still four-and-a-half games out and nobody believed they were going to make it except them. Everyone was playing well — and no one was playing better than Jason Thibodeaux. With two more wins his record would be 12-12. Two wins put at least another zero on his contract, and his agent could move him to San Francisco.

He stopped at the cooler and tossed down a cup of cold water. Vuco came up behind him. "I'm bringin' in Jervey to finish," he said. Jervey was their closer. Jason's face fell with disappointment but Vuco clapped him hard on the shoulder. "You keep pitching like you did tonight, you can go anywhere you want."

JASON SAW the light on his phone blinking as he entered his hotel room after the game. He looked at his watch — Wednesday. He quickly dialed the message box. "You have two messages. To listen to your new messages, press one — "

He punched one. "JT, it's Digger. I met a dish and can't make dinner tonight." Goddamn Wells, he'd stand up the Pope if some babe got to him first. He erased the message, then waited for the other. "Hi Daddy, it's me, Rafe. Are you there? I'm wondering if you're still working or at a party or where you are." There was a long pause, Jason was afraid he'd hung up. Then, "Hello? Are you there Daddy? Um, anyway, I just called to say hello. Mommy and me had pizza tonight and I hope you're having a good time wherever you are. Bye-bye!"

It was like hearing music after a lifetime of being deaf. He had sent Rafe a bunch of stuff over the past two weeks — tapes of him reading stories from the Brothers Grimm — Rapunzel, Hansel & Gretel, The Fisherman and His Wife; a boxed set of musical sound tracks; a photo of himself from the Cincinnati sports pages; a postcard from the Pittsburgh zoo that showed a Kodiak Bear tossing a ball with his nose at some spectators. He had also sent a telephone debit card, a copy of the Red's remaining schedule with his custody days circled, and the phone numbers where he could be reached. This was the first opportunity Rafe had to use the new system, and he'd pulled it off like a pro.

He pressed 1 and listened again. "Hi Daddy, it's me, Rafe … " His voice felt as close and reassuring as a hug. Jason played the message a third and fourth time, then saved it to listen to later.

"I hope you're having a good time wherever you are. Bye-bye!"

VICKI YANKED down the front of Rafe's white vest until the wrinkles vanished, then swiped the cracker crumbs from the corners of his mouth with her plum-colored fingernail. "You look wonderful," she smiled. She ran her hand down the soft sheen of his cheek. "You look like Mozart."

Rafe gripped his jaw but he could no longer fight it. His eyes filled with tears, his mouth opened in a silent howl. "Baby, what's wrong?" Vicki asked with alarm, squatting beside him. It was a cool October night, with a faint stitching of stars above the city. A steady stream of kids, parents and teachers poured through the front doors of Aurora Craverro School of the Arts.

"I don't want to go," Rafe cried.

"But baby, your whole class is in there." She wiped the tears from his cheeks and held his shoulder firmly with her other hand. "You can do this," she encouraged him. "You know the words." He shook his head. "Sure you do, we practiced them over and over again." She flattened his collar, and jerked his red bow tie back and forth. "Let's just straighten this bow-tie —"

"It's a *butterfly* tie!" he shouted, his eyes sharp with anger now.

"Of course," she said, softening in the face of what could become a full-blown tantrum. "It *is* like a butterfly, isn't it?" She tucked in his shirt and centered his belt buckle. "We should go in now. It sounds like everyone's getting ready."

"Daddy said he was going to come."

"Daddy says a lot of things." She wiped his cheeks again. "C'mon, this is a happy night. We'll go to Mitchell's for ice cream afterwards and celebrate."

He let her lead him into the crowded auditorium, where the Fifth Grade Orchestra was warming up. The other members of Rafe's third grade class — or for the purposes of this special evening, *Le Troisieme Chorale* — had already assembled on the stage, the boys in their white tails and red ties fidgeting and weaving like a field of poppies in the wind, the girls lined up single file in their magenta gowns and matching hair ribbons. He was part of the chorus, singing the original fifth grade composition, "Magic at Hogwarts: The Harry Potter Symphony." Next year, as a fourth grader, he would be in the orchestra as either a pianist or cellist.

Vicki squeezed his hand and released him up the steps. "Good luck, my sweet." Rafe took his place in the back line of the chorus, a lost look on his face. He watched his mom linger at the bottom of the steps, then take out her digital camera and turn it towards him.

"Mom!" he whined, trying to wave her away. Suddenly the students began to stir. Rafe's eyes grew big and a smile lit his face. Vicki turned and there was Jason striding down the side aisle, followed by a young man and young woman pushing hand carts loaded with long cardboard boxes.

Rafe rushed to the edge of the stage. "You came!" he shouted. He had left messages for his father in Chicago and Cincinnati but wasn't sure he got them. Jason laughed. "Of course I came!" He grabbed Rafe and swung him off the stage. He could see that he'd been crying.

"What's the matter, Buddy?"

Rafe squeezed his father as hard as he could. Jason squeezed back. "That's OK, Buddy, I'm here," he whispered.

The familiar discord of an orchestra tuning up signaled the imminence of the program. Jason set Rafe back down on the stage. "Knock 'em dead, Tiger," he said, before backing away. There was a buzz in the crowd that Rafe's father had brought baseball bats signed by Giants' players. His helpers unpacked the boxes and leaned the bats near the stairway where the performers would be leaving the stage.

Slowly, the house began to quiet. Jason ended up standing along the wall of the packed auditorium directly behind Vicki. "What are you doing here?" she asked, turning to address him but without looking at him.

"What do you think I'm doing here?"

She exhaled loudly, clearly unnerved by his presence literally breathing down her neck. "You're disrupting everything!"

"Disrupting what? I'm his father!"

"That hasn't done him a whole lot of good up to now."

"It's not for lack of trying."

The opening strains sounded and the chorus stiffened as if they had been struck by lightning. Rafe watched his parents, his two favorite people in the world, talking together and his smile grew. Maybe they'd have pizza together and watch a movie; maybe his father would come on the school hayride in Sonoma.

"It's going to be different now," Jason said into the back of Vicki's head. Rafe was swaying now in unison with his white-suited classmates, who were gathered like pleats in a semi-circle at the back of the stage. His mouth opened wide as the chorus sang out the opening refrains of the Brahms-inspired overture. "I've been traded."

Vicki turned and looked him in the eyes. A set of violins and goofy flute music erupted from the orchestra, then the boom of a kettle drum and the tinkling of a chime.

"What do you mean?" she asked.

He smiled down at her, clearly gloating. "I'm playing for San Francisco now."

JASON RENTED a two-bedroom condo along the waterfront near PacBell Park, in a bayside development called South Beach Harbor.

There was a big picture window with a view across San Francisco Bay to Oakland, and a swimming pool out the back door shared by the other condos in the complex.

Jason's first day there with Rafe was one of the happiest in his life. They rode bicycles along the waterfront almost to the Golden Gate Bridge, and when they returned they set to work preparing Rafe's favorite dinner, spaghetti and meatballs. Side-by-side they stood at the marble-top counter, rolling ground turkey into meatballs on a wooden cutting board. Jason sautéed the meatballs in a large iron skillet while Rafe cut up lettuce, tomatoes and carrots for a salad, his face knotted with concentration.

"You're quite the chef!" Jason exclaimed.

Rafe smiled up at him. "This is fun!"

When everything was done they sat on opposite sides of the table in the small dining room. "How you doin', Bud?" Jason asked.

"Good." Rafe smiled, shoveling a forkful of spaghetti into his mouth. Jason wasn't sure what else to say. He hadn't spent time with his son since July, when the Reds played in San Francisco. Rafe was taller, his cheekbones broader, his eyes set deeper in his face. It happened like this every off-season, returning like some general and having to introduce himself anew to his family. This time, however, there was one huge difference: the general had come to stay.

"You got homework tonight?"

"It's Saturday!" Rafe replied.

"They don't give homework on weekends?"

"Uh-uh. Weekends are for playing!"

Jason smiled and looked out at the ships lined up in San Francisco Bay. As a boy in Port Sulphur he used to watch oil tankers disappearing over the curve of the sea and dream of sailing away. But no more. He had a contract to play baseball in the town where his son lived. There was no better dream he could have.

After dinner they brushed their teeth in the large, mirrored bathroom, then Jason led Rafe up to his bedroom. He had bought a full-sized double bed for his growing son and covered it with Rafe's Stanford quilt and a half dozen of his favorite stuffed animals. A small ship's lamp glowed beside the bed.

Rafe leaped on the quilt and hugged his furry friends. Then he gazed out the window at the blaze of lights in the center of the bay.

"You know what that is?" Jason asked. Rafe shook his head. "That's

Treasure Island." Rafe's eyes danced as Jason pulled the covers back for him to slide under the flannel sheets. When he was settled, Jason held up an oversized book.

"*Treasure Island!*" Rafe shouted. The cover illustration was a gilt-edged painting of a pirate and his parrot, with a triple-masted schooner looming behind them. Jason balanced himself in the miniature rocking chair beside Rafe's bed. "*Chapter One,*" he intoned. "*The Old Sea-Dog at the Admiral Benbow.*"

He looked down at Rafe. "You ready for this? There's pirates and stolen treasure and sword fights — it's pretty rough stuff."

"They have sword fights in *Star Wars,*" Rafe said dismissively. "With light savers."

"Light sabers," Jason corrected him.

"Light *savers,*" Rafe insisted. He looked sincerely into his father's eyes. "It's all make-believe anyway, Daddy."

Jason smiled and set the book across his knees so Rafe could see the illustrations as he read. "*Squire Trelawney, Dr. Livesy, and the rest of these gentlemen, having asked me to write down the whole particulars about Treasure Island, from the beginning to end, keeping nothing back but the bearings of the island ...*"

He paused and looked at Rafe, who smiled back at him with warm, sleepy contentment. Jason took his hand and squeezed it. "I'm glad you're here, Buddy."

"*Read*, Daddy!"

Outside, the lights of Treasure Island twinkled in the center of the bay. Jason returned to the book, reading in a firm, animated voice: "*... and go back to the time when my father kept the Admiral Benbow Inn, and the brown old seaman, with the saber cut, first took up his lodging under our roof ... *"

IN SAN FRANCISCO, nobody argues with a Giant. Despite Vicki's objections, the court granted Jason's request for joint custody on alternating weeks, even during baseball season. Vicki didn't tell Rafe about it until the end of the week, when he was scheduled to begin his first full week with his father. She picked him up early from aftercare and took him to his favorite restaurant, the Sushi Boat, where food sailed by on little wooden barges along a flume filled with flowing water.

"What's that? What's that? What's that?" Rafe cried excitedly as the sushi floated by. Vicki leaned over and swiped a smear of wasabi from the sleeve of his sweatshirt — *Aurora Craverro School: Life Imitating Art.* "You know," she began, her eyes fixed on his face. "Things are going to be different now. The courts have ruled that you have to spend every other week with your father. I won't see you until next Friday — a whole week away."

Rafe squeezed a California roll between his chopsticks and brought it carefully to his mouth. "Did you hear what I said, Rafe? Do you know what this means?"

"I spend a week with Daddy and a week with you," he replied simply.

"You don't have to do it if you don't want to. We can ask the court to keep things the way they were."

"That's OK," Rafe said. "I spent a week in Hawaii with Gramma and Grampa." He watched more sushi boats sailing by with their cargo. He had no idea what most of them were and let them go. Either way, he didn't want to think of the other stuff. As long as he sat here he could choose whatever he wanted; his mom ate the ones he picked that were too strange to eat. The ones he really liked were the California rolls, cylinders of rice stuffed with cucumbers and avocado and crab, but there hadn't been any of those for a while.

"That was vacation," Vicki said. "This will be on school days and music practice days and weekends too."

Rafe's attention was focused on a procession of freshly loaded boats listing with gleaming slivers of fish, rice cones overflowing with roe, and octopus arms trailing in the water. Then a boat loaded with a fresh California roll appeared around the bend. He watched anxiously as it sailed past the other diners, then he reached out and grabbed it.

"Don't you want to try something else?" Vicki asked.

"I like these," Rafe replied.

JASON WAS pacing the sidewalk when Vicki and Rafe returned to school. He loomed over Vicki's Acura as soon as she stopped. "It's my turn to pick him up — I've been waiting since quarter-to-six!"

Vicki glanced at her watch. "We went out for dinner," she said. "What difference does fifteen minutes make?"

Jason yanked open the door of Vicki's car. "C'mon," he said to Rafe. "We're going to be late." Rafe reached for the little overnight bag he had packed — his Sylvester the Cat travel toothbrush, cable car slippers, a black plastic spider ring, his purple platypus Pillow Buddy. "This arrangement stinks and you know it," Vicki said as Rafe got into Jason's jeep. "This is his *life*, Jason. He's got off from school on Thursday — do you have plans for him? He's got music lessons Wednesdays, soccer practice Tuesdays and Thursdays, and play dates worked out for the weekend. You can't handle that yourself."

Jason looked at his watch. He had hoped to get to the Oakland Arena by seven and introduce Rafe to some of the Warriors. He had expected Rafe to be here, ready to go, and be well on their way by now. "Compared to having to deal with you, that's nothing."

"This isn't about you and me, Jason. It's about what's best for Rafe."

"That's right." Jason pressed forward, seeming to swell with self-righteousness. "Do you know the number one reason for teen pregnancy? Drug use? Depression? It's not having a father in their lives."

Vicki stared at him with unmistakable contempt. "He's not a teenager."

"You know what I'm talking about."

"This is too abrupt," she insisted. "We should do this more gradually … two days on, two off, something like that."

He'd planned to be magnanimous in victory, but his lips curled with a contemptuous smile. "To quote the immortal words of Vicki Repetto — 'Tell it to the judge.'"

—

NEW GIANT A FORCE OFF THE FIELD, TOO
B.A. Najarian, SAN FRANCISCO DAILY

Last fall when the Cincinnati Reds challenged the Cardinals for the divisional playoffs, their MVP in the stretch was former Stanford lefthander JT Thibodeaux. Pitching with the power and precision scouts always predicted, Thibodeaux finished the season with four straight victories and helped bring the overachieving Reds within one game of the postseason. Most players would spend the winter plotting a return to even loftier heights, but Jason Thibodeaux is more than a baseball player.

Thibodeaux is the guy who forewent his senior year at Stanford to raise his son. Actually, he almost forewent his baseball career, overlooked in the draft as a head case rather than a heart case. But Thibodeaux eventually found a home in the Reds' farm system, where he earned his way to the Show and compiled a 24-27 record in 2+ years for the Reds. The only problem, the kid he had raised was two thousand miles away — in San Francisco. So Thibodeaux did something that no one has asked to do since their pennant-winning team three years ago — he asked to be traded *to*, not from, San Francisco.

The rebuilding Giants are counting on Thibodeaux's strong left arm and senior-circuit experience to help put them in contention. Thibodeaux, for his part, is counting on proximity to his eight-year-old son, Raphael, to revive his starring role as a father. "I'm really happy to be with this team," he said. "But I have to be honest and say that the main reason I'm here is my son." Thibodeaux's boy is a third grader at the Aurora Craverro School, a private arts school in the city's Noe Valley ("Home of baritones and ballerinas," JT says).

Besides a 98 MPH fastball, JT brings a scholar's knowledge of NL hitters. As a student of Stanford's Walt Baptiste, Thibodeaux kept notebooks on every hitter he faced. He applies the same kind of discipline to child-rearing. In a profession where men drop their seeds with the vigor of a full-grown Valley Oak and nurture them with the diligence of werewolves, this Giant is an oddball.

Thibodeaux challenges those in the league who say they spend quality time with their kids. "How many know what their kids' favorite foods are? Their shoe size? The name of their favorite stuffed animals? That's the kind of knowledge you only get by putting in the time."

Maybe the Giants will win more games this season, maybe not. A twelve-game winner with the Reds last year, Thibodeaux most likely will replace twelve-game winner Rick Lambert in the starting rotation. But whatever happens on the field, the number of Giants pulling full-time duty on the homefront just went from zero to one.

—

THE GIANTS' facilities were state-of-the art compared to the moldy basement the Reds skulked around in. The selection of new treadmills and Cybex machines, stationery bicycles, Stairmasters and Beaman weights inspired Jason to work out almost as much as his desire to make good in the city that housed his son. Living near PacBell Park, he became a regular at the Giants' training facilities.

The Monday before Thanksgiving he came in for his workout as usual after dropping Rafe at school. His locker was two spaces away from the famous corner belonging to Isaac Sands, the premier slugger in the National League. Voted Most Valuable Player three times by the sportswriters he publicly disdained, Sands had negotiated an entire corner of the dressing room for himself, comprised of four lockers. The regulation lockers were already luxurious affairs, cherry wood cabinets with two polished shelves, a lock box for valuables, a compartment for street clothes on one side and baseball gear on the other, and a hand-carved wooden shoe rack. The dividers in Sands's lockers had been removed to make room for a CD and DVD tower, a 47-inch television, and a water cooler holding a ten-gallon jug of PowerAde.

Jason was surprised to find Sands himself sitting on his black leather couch, watching what looked like a highlight film of his own exploits, mostly a parade of images of his powerful left-handed stroke pounding balls over walls in various ballparks in rapid strobe-like succession. He was a tall, broad-shouldered man with a full handsome face, and the charisma of someone one hundred percent certain that the millions of people who thought he was the greatest ball player of all time were absolutely correct. He wore black slacks, a black turtleneck sweater, black shoes, a small diamond earring in his left ear, a thick gold-banded watch on his right wrist, and a heavy gold necklace with a crucifix.

Jason changed into Giants sweats, tied on his cross trainers and locked away his wallet and watch. He wasn't sure what to do. Sands was notoriously uncommunicative, known for his loud home runs and one word answers to the press. But seeing that Sands's highlight reel was finished, he stopped in front of the couch.

"I'm Jason Thibodeaux," he announced, sticking out his hand. Whatever he had expected from the slugger, it wasn't what he got.

"String cheese, Pop-Tarts and artichoke hearts," Sands said, without looking up.

"Pardon me?"

"Godzilla, Superfly and Lambchop."

Maybe it was some kind of hazing, gibberish for newcomers particular to the Giants' clubhouse. "I'm with the team now — I came over from the Reds," Jason offered.

"I know who you are," Sands said. "You're the guy who says I don't

73

know my kids' favorite food. Or the names of my kids' animals."

Jason stared, mouth open. "The morning paper," Sands said. "Read it and weep."

It wasn't difficult to find Najarian's column. Someone had posted it on the bulletin board outside the manager's office. He had let B.A. Najarian spend a morning watching him work out, talking about the trade, his pitching philosophy, his custody struggles. But he was mortified when he read the article. It was hard enough being traded to a new team. Loyalties and affection that get built up only through combat have not yet been formed. And most guys are traded to fill some need of the team — replace an injured player, help the team meet the salary cap, rebuild for the future, back up a valuable veteran — rather than the needs of the player. He was a less-than-.500 pitcher with a reputation for flakiness — and now this.

Jason pushed through the double doors and up the ramp to the field. It was a soft sunny day, a Northern California autumn classic. He did a series of warmup stretches and ran two perimeters of the field, then more stretches and windsprints across the outfield before heading back to the weight room. Sands was there, jerking and pressing unimaginable amounts of weights. Jason went through his own regimen, self-consciously adding plates to his normal amounts but acutely aware that he was lifting nothing close to Sands's limit. There were a couple of other guys there as well — Darryl Brooks, a backup second basemen, and Felipe Colon, a centerfielder trying to make his way back from shoulder surgery. No one said a word to him.

After an hour, he made his move. He found Sands between reps, hunched forward on a bench, rolling his shoulders like locomotive wheels.

"As lame as it sounds," Jason said, "I was misquoted."

Sands didn't look at him. "If you don't talk, they can't misquote you."

Jason chuckled. "I'll remember that." He paused. "I admire what you're trying to do — what you're doing with your kids." Jason, along with the rest of the world, knew that Sands was going through a bitter divorce and custody battle involving his two daughters, eight and five, and his three-and-a-half-year-old son, as well as the most judicious way to divide up his six-year, $160 million contract. In an argument over money, Sands had pushed his estranged wife and called her a whore in front of their children. It cost him more than six months away from his kids, mandatory enrollment in an anger-management class and the opprobrium of millions. He had completed the twenty-six week anger-management class and now was awaiting the court to assign a custody plan.

Sands rose from the bench. He was an inch shorter than Jason, but by his bulk and sheer power of presence seemed a foot taller. He grasped Jason's hand in an old-fashioned soul grip, pulling him closer. "I admire what *you're* doing, man. You are the Nina, the Pinta and the Santa Maria."

Jason was shocked. Sands continued to hold his hand, staring into his eyes. "You got a kid whose favorite food is artichoke hearts?" Jason finally asked.

"My boy eats them like potato chips," Sands grinned, dropping Jason's hand. "He calls them okes. '*Okes, okes, okes*,'" Sands said in a baby voice as he strutted back to a set of weights that Jason estimated at 340 pounds. "He eats any kind of vegetable." Sands lay on his back and grasped the bar. "If it's green," he said, pushing the massive weights above his head, "it's good."

Jason smiled knowingly. "My kid loves salad."

"Salad is cool," Sands grunted, lowering the weights. He gathered himself, then pushed the weights up again. "But mostly my kids love baseball."

After Sands broke the ice, the other guys started talking. It was baseball now, and nutrition, who was playing winter ball, who was hurt, who was a comer. Sands held court in the weight room for nearly two hours, quietly sharing insights about pitchers in their division, what they threw, how to beat them. At two o'clock, Jason lowered his last weight. "I've got to pick up my kid at school," he announced.

"You do that," Sands said. "Tell him Isaac Sands says hello."

Jason grabbed a falafel from Tunisia at 20th and Valencia and double-parked his Jeep behind the row of SUVs and foreign luxury cars outside Rafe's school. He sat at the wheel wolfing down the sandwich, wondering what to fix Rafe for dinner. He had wanted to take him to the library but there were so many other things to do. Rafe needed new shoes and underwear, and his hair was out of control. Vicki was leaving more and more of these things for his weeks with Rafe. Fathering wasn't just Saturdays at Waterworld or a weekend in Disneyland anymore. It was a week-long job, showing up every day at the schoolhouse door, fixing dinner and cleaning up, helping Rafe with homework, drawing a bath, herding him to bed, reading a story, tucking his tired body beneath the blankets, giving that last hug, the last back scratch, the last reassuring word. But all that was fine, really. It took Jason back to the year he cared for Rafe when he was a toddler. What he was having trouble with was Rafe's total indifference, even hostility, towards baseball.

Rafe climbed into the car without a word.

"Hi Buddy."

"Hi."

"How was school today?"

"OK."

"Just OK?"

"Yeah."

Rafe stared silently from the window. His remoteness unsettled Jason. He'd cut short his workout, interrupted his new rapport with Isaac Sands, sped across town and this was his reward? He decided to blow off the errands. A mood like this usually meant Rafe was tired, hungry — or both. Vicki could get him new shoes and a haircut during her week.

They drove home in silence. Jason pulled into the parking lot behind the condo and cut the engine. Seagulls swirled in the wind above the masts in South Beach Harbor. "Isaac Sands says hello."

Rafe looked up in disbelief. "To me?" Jason nodded. "He said his children love baseball ... you want to play some catch?"

"No."

"We've got time before dinner."

"I don't want to," Rafe said glumly.

Jason walked ahead, clearly perturbed. Rafe didn't know what to do — either way he couldn't win. 'Baseball is for jerks,' his mother had said. 'Your mother's a jerk,' was his father's response. The weeks he was with his mom, he could never mention sports; the weeks with his father, he was afraid to bring up his music. They both always seemed so angry, and their anger always seemed to be about him.

Jason turned at the steps leading up to their house. "You used to play," he said light-heartedly. "I used to toss the ball to you in your playpen ... remember?"

"How can I remember — I was a *baby!*"

"You were a *ballplayer*," Jason said with some regret. "It's an American tradition, you know, to pass along the game to your son. My father taught me, his father taught him — all the way back to the

76

Pilgrims." His father hadn't taught him, *per se*, though he had bought him his first glove, which he almost never took off. But baseball was a huge part of his father's life. There was always a game on the radio, the announcer and chorus of fans competing with show tunes on his mom's portable stereo. It was Nolan Ryan vs. Gordon McRae, Joe Buck vs. *The Music Man*, Phil Rizzutto vs. the cast of *Cats*.

"The Pilgrims played baseball?"

"They played a game like baseball," Jason replied. "It's called cricket."

"*Cricket?* What's cricket?"

"You play it with a wicket instead of a bat."

"A cricket wicket," Rafe smiled. "Let's play that!"

"OK. We'll play some after dinner."

Jason broiled salmon with a maple syrup-ginger sauce that Rafe liked, and served it with steamed broccoli and rice. Rafe ate quickly, eager to begin playing.

It was a soft autumn evening with stars glowing warmly above the Bay. Jason brought along a softball, a three foot long plank from the building's utility room, and a potholder glove from the kitchen and set up under the lights of the parking lot. He put home plate in front of the gate to the trash cans and stood between fifty and sixty feet away with the ball — he wasn't sure of the dimensions in cricket. He had never played a minute of the game in his life, or even seen it played. "OK, here's how it works," Jason explained, holding up the softball. "I pitch — or *hurl* the ball to you on one bounce. You try to hit it with the wicket, then run."

"Run where?"

Jason spied a large plastic garbage can beside the neighboring Java House, dragged it over and positioned it approximately where second base would be on a baseball diamond. "You hit it and run to the can here — the *cricket* — and try to get back to home plate before the ball."

"Cool," Rafe said, his eyes flashing. This wasn't like baseball at all, his mother couldn't object. The first hurl came in on the bounce and Rafe swung the heavy board and missed. The ball rolled back to the shed. "Go get it," Jason shouted. "There's no catcher." Rafe retrieved the ball and tossed it back to his father; the softball was bigger and heavier than he expected. The wicket was heavy too, and rough on his hands. Jason hurled a second pitch even slower, but Rafe missed this one as well. He retrieved the ball, slouching discouragedly, then tossed it wildly over his father's head. "C'mon Buddy, throw it *to* me." Jason ran to retrieve the ball beyond the arc of light. When he returned, Rafe was standing without the wicket.

"Get ready," Jason called out.

"I don't want to play."

"We just started! Pick it up and try." Rafe picked up the board half-heartedly. Jason threw a fat one-bouncer and Rafe waved at it, missing it seemingly on purpose. "Focus!" Jason shouted. "It's just you and the ball, you and the ball …" The same thing happened on the next three pitches. He'd seen Rafe hit a ball before; he knew he could do it, and the fact that he wouldn't even try pissed him off.

Jason stepped in closer. "I know you don't care but this is important to *me*, OK? C'mon, just try to hit it. Hands up, eye on the ball, OK? Just you and the ball … "

He sent another pitch Rafe's way, fairly wishing the bat against the ball, a crisp hit, a run to the cricket, a laugh or two — or at least a smile. Instead, Rafe swung half-heartedly, just waving at the ball, his face a mask of glumness. He dropped the board again. "This is as stupid as baseball," he whined.

Jason whirled and heaved the ball high over the light stanchions, into the Bay. "You sound like your goddamned mother!" He kicked the garbage can over, sending containers, styrofoam cups, wrappers, coffee grounds and other detritus from the Java House spilling across the pavement. Rafe began crying, tears streaking his face. Jason stopped and stared at the garbage strewn across the parking lot. He walked over to the can and righted it. Then he walked back to Rafe and threw his arms around him.

"I'm sorry, Buddy, that was wrong of Daddy to do that."

Rafe stood stiffly in his father's arms, uncertain whether the storm had passed. The tears still came, but his sobbing had stopped. He desperately wanted everything to be normal. He wanted to please his father, so something like that would never happen again. "I'll do better, Daddy. I'll learn how to play baseball."

"You don't have to learn baseball if you don't want to," Jason said. He felt overwhelmed with shame. The garbage lay spread across the parking lot. Somewhere a new softball bobbed on the waters of San Francisco Bay. His anger had torn a hole in the fabric of Rafe's universe, and he wasn't sure how to sew it back together. The only thing he could think of was to keep squeezing him.

"DADDY?"

"Yeah, buddy?" Jason glanced across the hall to where a nightlight glowed just inside the door to Rafe's room.

"Is it morning yet?"

"No, it's not morning yet. Go to sleep." There was silence, but Jason knew it wasn't over yet.

"Is it a long time till morning?"

Jason looked at the clock — 4:20. "Long enough to go back to sleep."

"Will I sleep a long time?"

"Till morning. Why?"

"I don't want to miss breakfast."

"You won't miss breakfast," Jason laughed. He slid out of his bed and into Rafe's room. Only Rafe's head showed above his comforter, Winnie the Pooh beside him on the pillow. Jason cradled his son's soft cheek in his hand.

"When I wake up, will you be here or in Arizona?" Rafe asked.

"I'll be right here, Buddy." He kissed him on the forehead. By the time he reached the stairs, Rafe was asleep.

AT 7:30 Rafe dragged his blue blankie and Pooh Bear into Jason's bed, snuggling against him and waking him with his squirming. "Happy Birthday, Daddy!" Rafe shouted as soon as Jason's eyes opened.

Twenty-eight years old — old enough to know better, and young enough to pull it off. This was going to be his year. The Giants wouldn't win the pennant, but they'd turn some heads. He was going to be the fourth starter in a rotation with two righthanders — Julio Flores and Rick Tarkanian — and the lefthander he most wanted to be like in the National League, Kirk Darwin. He was living in the same town as his son. He was working towards a Master's Degree in sociology at USF in the off-season. He couldn't think of a better set-up for his birthday.

Jason hugged Rafe as hard as he could without crushing him. "What are we having for breakfast? I'm starving!"

"Pancakes!" Rafe cried.

"Aw, those are your favorites."

"You love pancakes. You told me."

"Waffles," Jason said. "Waffles are *my* favorite."

Rafe's face fell, it was impossible to miss his disappointment. "But today," Jason added quickly, "I want the best *pancakes* you can make.

It's my birthday."

"Deal!"

This day, after all, was going to be hard enough. It was a transition day, always fraught with the possibility of drama. Rafe went back to Vicki's, then before the week was up Jason left for two months of spring training in Scottsdale, Arizona. He wanted today to be as easy as he could make it. He wanted to eat breakfast and take Rafe to the aquarium and stop for pizza and drop him off at his mother's house with Rafe convinced that nothing was out of the ordinary and never would be.

They threw on their matching Giants bathrobes and hurried downstairs to the kitchen. While Rafe mixed the ingredients for pancakes — eggs, milk, Bisquick, blueberries — Jason clomped down the front steps to get the morning paper. The first pancakes were on his plate when he returned. Rafe looked proudly at the next batch bubbling in the pan. "Go ahead, Daddy — eat!" But Jason stacked the pancakes onto a plate in the oven while Rafe cooked the rest. When they were ready they sat at the dining room table and smothered the pancakes with butter and syrup and devoured them all. As soon as they finished, Rafe disappeared up the stairs and returned with a flat package wrapped in pale green paper and tied with a gold ribbon.

"Happy Birthday, Daddy. I made it myself."

"I see you wrapped it yourself, too. Should I open it?"

"Yeah!" Rafe cried. "It's your birthday!"

Jason tore open the package to reveal a hand-drawn picture mounted on a piece of blue construction paper. A tall figure on the left labeled "Dad" was throwing a ball to a smaller figure with a bat on the right, labeled "Rafe." The sun shone between several dark clouds in the sky; huge smiles graced the faces of both father and son.

"That's us, playing baseball," Rafe said. "You can take it with you when you go."

Jason reached over and folded Rafe in his arms. "It's perfect, Buddy. Thank you."

"Are you coming back?" Rafe asked.

"Of course I'm coming back." They had talked about it so much, Jason was surprised it was still an issue. "It's only spring training. I'll be back in eight weeks."

"Eight weeks is a long time."

"Not really," Jason said, but it didn't sound convincing to him either.

Good God, he didn't want Rafe to miss his father as much as he had. He didn't want to subject him to that sadness. He didn't want to be one of those guys who leaves his kid. Why bother having kids if you weren't going to be there?

"Look," Jason said, taking hold of Rafe's arm. "I'll always be there for you. That's why I asked to be traded — to be with you. I'm your Dad no matter what."

"You and mommy used to live together. You never came back to her house."

"That's different. That's an adult thing. Married people split up all the time, they get tired of each other —"

"Maybe you'll get tired of me."

Jason gathered Rafe in his arms again. "I love you, Rafe. More than anything or anybody in the world. I don't know what your mother's told you, but I'll never get tired of you. I'm here for you. I'll always be here."

Rafe squeezed back.

"Now you wait here," Jason said. "I've got something for *you*."

Rafe was surprised when his father returned with a gift-wrapped box almost four feet tall. "In some countries it's a tradition for everybody in the family to get presents on birthdays," Jason fibbed. He had ordered it for Rafe months ago, but the shipment had been delayed by a longshoreman's strike.

"I know what it is," Rafe said.

"What?"

"A baseball bat."

"Open it and see."

Rafe tore off the wrapping paper and studied the sturdy cardboard underneath. "FRAGILE HANDLE WITH CARE," the box said. "MADE IN GERMANY." Rafe picked futilely at the tape-sealed seams. "It won't open."

Jason grabbed a paring knife from the kitchen and guided Rafe's hand along the seams. The flaps opened like French doors, revealing a nest of German newspaper strips. Rafe dug through until he felt something, then withdrew his hand and looked questioningly at his father.

"When I come back," Jason said. "I want a private recital."

Rafe pulled the handsome Conrad Gotz cello from the box and

held it between his legs. He drew the horsehair bow expertly across the strings, coaxing a low moan that sounded as if it were coming from the center of the earth.

Rafe looked at him eagerly. "Can I take it to Mommy's?"

"You can take it wherever you want — as long as you take good care of it."

Rafe ran his hands along the pale, polished wood of the body, the carved ridges of the neck, the tuning pegs. He looked up and smiled at his father with pure satisfaction.

"This is the best birthday I've ever had."

OPENING DAY is the New Year's Day of professional sports, when last year's misfortunes are forgotten, transgressions forgiven and resolutions made to make the coming year a winning one. On Opening Day, pundits remind the most cynical fan, every team begins at 0-0; every team starts with dreams of the pennant flag flying over their field at season's end; every team takes the field with the hopeful certainty that all the errors, miscues, strike-outs, missed signals and misjudged fly balls of spring training were simply lessons learned on the path to glory. Opening Day is wedding night, inauguration day, the first day of school, the first kiss of a romance, the first brush stroke on a blinding white canvas. It's a day of birth, rejuvenation, resurrection, hope, as enduring a rite of spring as the first robin singing on the lawn after a March storm.

Jason's heart swelled as he walked with Rafe up the dugout steps and onto PacBell Park's lush green carpet of grass. He had ordered a special kids uniform with his own number — 52 — and his name, "Thibodeaux" sewn on the back — and a new glove for Rafe that half a dozen Giants had autographed.

Mounds of gray clouds scudded over the stadium, but not even the threat of rain could dampen the spirits of the crowd. It was the Giants versus the Arizona Diamondbacks, rivals who had battled down to the wire for the pennant three seasons ago. More than forty-two thousand noisy fans held vigil around the sacred altar of the perfectly groomed field, hoping, through their collective lust for success, to propel their heroes towards the Holy Grail — the National League Pennant and a shot at winning the World Series.

"What do you think?" Jason asked. "This is where Daddy works!"

Rafe's eyes darted nervously. It was overwhelming for a player, let alone an eight-year-old. The steeply banked stands filled with eager spectators, the awesome expanse of grass, the mythically-sized men with bulging forearms and long sunburned necks. Coaches, club officials, dignitaries, photographers, grounds crews, a retinue of symphony musicians preparing to play the national anthem, a dozen kids playing catch with their fathers all helped create what appeared to be a ten-ring circus. The noise was a steady roar, like the sea, punctuated by laughing children and the loud talking of adults.

Rafe gazed out towards left field at his favorite part of the park — the giant sculpture of the baseball glove he could see from the balcony of his condo, and the huge replica of a Coca-Cola bottle with two long slides inside it.

"Can I go down the slide?"

"Maybe later. C'mon, let's play some catch." He stuck a baseball in Rafe's glove and strode ten yards away. Erik Nyles was playing a spirited game of pepper with his son Carter; Gordon Dragicevich pitched an oversized plastic ball to his two-year-old boy; Ron Ehrlich and Brett Fortson tossed baseballs with their daughters.

Rafe stared uncertainly at his father, then down at the ground, his face hidden beneath his Giants cap. He was deathly afraid of throwing the ball wrong, or dropping it when it came back. He was afraid that his father would get mad at him again and yell, this time in front of everyone.

"Just throw it," Jason called with strained patience. Two, three, four times the ball passed back and forth — then Rafe dropped it. He stood, frozen. "Pick it up" Jason shouted, but Rafe just stared at him. Jason started towards Rafe, but Isaac Sands got there first. "You must be Raphael," Sands said in a soft, friendly voice. Rafe stared up at the broad-shouldered man with the diamond earring. "Your daddy tells me you're a great cello player," Isaac Sands said, picking up the ball in his huge hand. "I play a mean maraca."

Rafe glanced self-consciously at his dad.

"What do you think?" Jason asked. "Can Isaac play maraca with you sometime?"

"Sure," Rafe responded shyly.

"What kind of music do you like?" Sands asked.

"At school we mostly play classical."

"But what kind of music do *you* like?"

Again Rafe glanced at his father, who nodded for him to go ahead. "You can tell *me*," Isaac said. He took off his hat and leaned his clean-shaven head close, listening to Rafe's whispered response. A smile lifted his face. "My man," he said, slapping high fives. "That's my favorite too."

By the last of the fifth inning the Giants were down 5-1. "Come on come on come on let's get some runs!" third base coach Wade Lymans shouted as he passed through the dugout on his way to the coach's box. The crowd, pumped up with beer and the joy of an afternoon off from work, began to stir as the organist struck up "Charge!"

Isaac Sands sat down beside Jason on the bench. He held a new ball in his right hand and a Sharpie in his left. "How do you spell Raphael?" he asked.

Jason turned to him, surprised. Sands was notoriously stingy with autographs, even refusing to attend Fans' Fairs where players were paid to sign. "R-A-P-H-A-E-L." Sands wrote, "To my friend, Raphael — Isaac Sands," finishing with his own name written so ornately it more resembled musical notes than letters. He handed the ball to Jason. "At least he's here." Sands's custody case was still tied up in the courts, though the restraining order had been lifted. He was seeing his children two weekends a month and every other Wednesday. Today, unfortunately, was neither.

Jason held the ball reverently, letting the ink dry. "She can't keep them from you forever. It's not right for the kids."

Jason's friendship with Isaac Sands was as surprising to him as it was to the rest of the team. The thirty-four-year-old African-American from Pt. Richmond, California and the twenty-eight-year-old lily-white pitcher from Port Sulphur, Point Barrow and Galveston, Texas. Jason felt strangely protective of the slugger. While Sands's lawyers helped him through the legal process, he didn't have a clue how to handle the emotional side of his custody battle. Sands sought out Jason behind the batting cage, shagging fly balls, in the weight room after the other guys left. What's the best way to stay in touch on the road? How could he keep his kids from forgetting him? ('They never will,' Jason advised.) How do you handle the feeling of remoteness when you haven't seen them for weeks? ('Oreos.')

"What'd Rafe tell you his favorite music was?" Jason asked, tucking the autographed ball into his glove. Sands watched impassively as pinch hitter Gordon Dragicevich led off with a sharp double into the left-center field gap. The rest of the players erupted into shouts, whistles, applause.

"That's our secret, man."

Jason saw a hint of a smile behind Sands's eyes. "C'mon, he's *my* kid!"

Sands popped a handful of sunflower seeds into his mouth and spit out a fusillade of shells. "Musicals. *Oklahoma, Annie, The Music Man!*"

Jason wasn't surprised. Rafe could sit for hours and listen to the tapes he had kept from his mother's Broadway collection. But Sands was notorious for blaring hip hop from his powerful sound system, especially after bad games when he wanted to keep reporters at bay. "Those aren't *your* favorites!"

"I used to go to shows when I was with the Mets," Sands explained. The catcher, Bobby Diaz drew a walk. Jaz Walters was up next, then Nyles, then Sands. The crowd was on fire now. The manager, Artie Phleger, was swiping signals across his chest, tugging on his earlobes, clapping his hands, spitting streams of tobacco juice beyond the dugout steps.

"You know how I got the name Isaac?" Sands asked. As he talked, he watched the pitcher as intently as a lion sizing up his dinner on the Serengeti Plain.

"No."

"My mother was gonna have an abortion and my father found out," he said matter-of-factly. "He ran five miles to the doctor's office and stopped him just as he was about to suck me out."

Jason took a sharp breath. "Jesus Christ."

"I only saw him four or five times in my life. He didn't have shit to do with raising me; my grandmother did most of it. I thought for years he didn't come around because he didn't love me. And then I found out he saved my life."

Walters slapped a low outside pitch just inside first base. Two runners came home, making it 5-3. Sands rose, picked up his helmet, drew his bat from the rack at the end of the dugout, took his shin and elbow guards out of the cubbyhole marked "Isaac" and slowly strapped them on at the top of the dugout steps. He turned to Rich Tarkanian, who had given up five runs in the first two innings and then settled down to pitch three scoreless innings before leaving the game. "Consider yourself off the hook," he said. Tarkanian leaned forward and gave him five.

Erik Nyles followed with a ground ball to second for the first out, the runner advancing to third. Isaac strode to the plate with his half-speed saunter mimicked by a million inner-city kids. He stood outside the batter's box and bathed in the delirious accolade of forty-two thousand fans. He surveyed the field, then narrowed his focus to the sixty feet, six inch corridor between the pitcher's mound and home plate. He took his stance in the batter's box and slowly waved his bat back and forth with the menacing languor of a lion flicking his tail.

Jason joined the other Giants at the top of the dugout steps. He turned and looked towards the box seats but with everyone standing he couldn't find Rafe. He moved over a few steps and craned his neck and there he was, standing on his seat between Grampa Andy and Gramma Anna, his glove on, his Giants cap clamped over his ears, watching Isaac Sands step up to the plate.

"Rafe!" Jason shouted, though he knew he'd never hear him. "Hey Rafe!"

He saw him turn to Grampa Andy as the umpire called the first pitch a strike and a thunderous "boo" shook the stadium. A collective sigh of relief followed when the next pitch, an inside fastball, was called a ball — then a growing restiveness that a second ball would lead to a third and a fourth and Sands would be issued a walk. But the Diamondbacks had their premier pitcher out there, who wasn't going to back down. This early in the season you pitched to the batter; you challenged everybody and tried to set a tone for the season.

With the count 3-1 the pitcher brought in a slider low and away — a strike, but virtually unhittable. Except this was Isaac Sands. With a flick of his wrists he drove the ball deep into the left field bleachers for a two run homer. His teammates beat each other on the shoulders and back. Jason watched Rafe turn to Grampa Andy and ask a question, then turn back with his eyes shining, watching his new friend circle the bases and trot towards home with a hard, far-away look on his face. As Sands stepped on the plate he pointed to the sky and blew a kiss to his God, then held up three fingers that stood for the three fans he really cared about, but who, like God, were nowhere to be seen.

THE YOUNG blonde glanced at the doors at the top of the stairway. "Are you sure he can't hear us?"

"I'm sure," Jason said. "But even if he could, what would he hear but the sound of your beauty meeting my desire?"

"You talk funny."

"I am funny." He caught her arm and pulled her to him and gently grasped her lower lip with his. He could smell soap and the heavy overlay of perfume on her soft white skin.

"Where do you sleep?"

"I don't. I'm a werewolf. I play baseball by day, and devour women at night."

She laughed but looked nervously out the windows for the moon, which was hidden by the summer fog. "On nights when my boy is here, I sleep down here." Without breaking his hold on her, he stooped and reached under the cushions of the couch and pulled. A fully made bed with a colorful spread appeared at their knees. Jason gently lowered her onto the bed, cupping the firm edge of her buttocks in his hand.

"Any other requests?"

"How about some music?"

The controls of his CD player happened to be on the edge of the couch. He reached for it and smoothly introduced Tim McGraw's newest CD to the scene. She pressed eagerly against him. "Oh yeah!" he moaned happily.

They had met just hours before, after the first of a four game series with the Braves. She sat directly behind the bullpen in what the players called the Beaver Box. Blonde, wearing tight jeans and a black satin blouse, she had made clear by her glances that an approach by him would not be unwelcome. He had sent a note via one of the batboys. "Mr. Jason Thibodeaux requests the honor of your presence for a drink after the game." He took her to Bacar, a stylish wine bar and restaurant four blocks away. Her name was Cindy Matheson. She was a sales rep for Brita, responsible for replenishing the filtered water supply of Northern California from Monterey to South San Francisco. And fortunately for Jason, like so many young women on the cusp of the millennium, she was convinced that sex was a prerequisite to friendship rather than a result.

They didn't even make it across the parking lot to the door of his condo before falling on each other, stopping to see if the lips they had studied across the candlelight tasted as good as they imagined. The walk upstairs to his home was giddy, anticipatory, triumphal. "This is so cool!" she cried when she saw the view of the bay from his living room. She loved it. Most women did. A professional baseball player making millions a year — or about to — living by the sea with his eight-year-old boy. And that wasn't all. He was a careful, attentive lover. He worked women like he would a hitter with men on base — slow at first, nibbling at the edges, then hard pitches straight into the power zone until the batter succumbed.

When it was over, Cindy excused herself to the bathroom. Jason could hear the ghostly melody of ropes slapping the yacht masts in the nearby harbor. He pulled the covers tight to his chin, recalling the wind outside the house in Pt. Barrow, the smell of his mother's cigarette smoke as she sat at the kitchen table listening to musicals and drinking beer deep into the night.

Cindy reappeared, ready for bed in one of his Giants t-shirts. She leaned over to kiss him, her breath smelling of toothpaste. "You're somethin else," she grinned. He liked her; she was sweet, funny, sexy. But then, Vicki had seemed that way too.

His hands gripped the top of the blankets. The longest relationship he had had since his marriage was about six dates. He couldn't trust women after Vicki — especially anyone he really liked. She had stolen years of his life, then tried to steal his child. He had to do everything he could to protect himself — and Rafe — from that ever happening again. "I'm sorry," he said. "You're not going to be able to stay." She stared at him, not understanding. "I don't want my son to wake up in the morning and find somebody here he doesn't know."

It could have been endearing, a tender demonstration of how devoted and protective a father he was. But it sounded cold and rehearsed, as it always did. The fact was, Rafe wasn't upstairs. He was on his way back that very night from Hawaii, where he and Vicki had gone to visit one of her brothers. But to pretend that Rafe was upstairs worked on many levels. If it wasn't Rafe, he would have had to make up some other excuse — early batting practice, a six a.m. flight to New York, training rules, insomnia. The more beautiful and alluring the woman, the more comfortable he felt with her, the more determined he was never to allow the relationship to work. Because when all was said and done, the most important criteria in a woman for him was that she leave before any damage could be done.

EVERY TEAM has some point where it finds a rhythm, a gelling, an intangible buzz that lifts it above the fray and gives it at least a glimpse of the Promised Land, if not a ticket to enter. Every team except that year's Giants. They were doing as poorly as everyone figured they would. One of the few bright spots was Jason Thibodeaux. Through the fourth week of July he was 10-6, with an ERA of 3.97 and two complete games — including a shut-out against the Rockies in Denver. He was putting together a "career year," establishing a baseline from which future judgments — and contract negotiations — would be figured. And therein lay the source of his problem.

They were in Tampa Bay, several hours before an interleague game against the Devil Rays, when the manager called him into his office. As usual before a game, Artie Phleger was shirtless. He was a short, middle-aged man with a huge gut and cheeks perpetually bulging with chewing tobacco. He had come up through the Giants farm system as slowly and inexorably as quartz squeezes to the surface of the earth, becoming the Giants' manager after twenty years of loyal service more by default than decision. Columnists were demanding to know why the mighty Giants kept a dog like Phleger at the helm. His vulnerability only made the players want to do better; they knew their shitty season wasn't his fault.

"What's up, Skip?" Jason asked. "I was just getting ready to take some whacks."

"What for? We got the DH."

"Yeah, but we got the Diamondbacks next week. I wanna take Tirado long."

Phleger grimaced and looked away, then turned and stared Jason straight in the eye. "You've been traded to the Rockies. They want you in Milwaukee tomorrow night." Jason could only stare back. He knew there wasn't a damned thing he or anybody else could do. It all happened upstairs with the guys who wrote checks talking with guys who wrote bigger checks. It was like working for some corporation and getting moved — to Galveston or Port Barrow — or Norway. Only it was baseball.

"Why the hell are they trading *me?* I've done everything except park cars."

"They figure they won't be able to afford you next year. They want to use the money on prospects."

The word "prospect" pierced Jason like a dagger. He'd been a prospect once. "We could have worked something out. I didn't come here for the money, for Christsakes."

"I'm sorry, JT," Phleger said. He leaned over and spit a thick brown stream into the bucket beside his desk. "You keep throwin' like you are, you'll be able to buy a lot of plane tickets for your kid." He reached out and shook Jason's hand. "Be easy on us when we play you."

DUST FLEW from beneath Rafe's tires as he sped across the worn meadow. His bathing suit flapping, his thin chest naked in the sun, sandals strapped to his feet — he was the model of an American boy free on a summer day. His mom sat on a blanket in another meadow half a mile away, swaying to the sounds of the High Sierra Music Festival. His dad would be back from Florida in three days. The forested hillsides surrounding Camp Mather seemed to lean in with a protective embrace. His bike, a silver and black Haro Revo with shiny mag wheels and trick pegs, sped him on his quest for a rainbow popsicle at the General Store.

He leaned his bike against the steps, checking several times to make sure it wouldn't fall, then lunged up the steps two at a time and pushed open the creaky screen door. He knew exactly where it was, in a freezer halfway down the first aisle next to the Slurpee machine. He slid open the glass door and dug through the frost-rimmed boxes. The one he wanted was right on top — the rainbow popsicle with purple, blue and yellow swirls — but he wanted to see what else they had before he made up his mind. His wrists began to throb from the cold. The Nutty Buddies looked good but they cost $1.25. He looked at the girl behind the counter, a teenager with long hair and red lips, and thought about asking her for a discount. As if in answer, she threw him a suspicious look. He grabbed the popsicle and set it on the counter along with his dollar.

"Close the freezer, *please*." She used the magic word but in a tone that sounded like she didn't mean it. Rafe shuffled back to the freezer and on his way saw a single San Francisco Chronicle left in the news rack. He slid the door closed, then grabbed the paper and flopped it open to the sports section. They always ran a box profiling that night's starting pitchers. He was sure it was his father's turn, but there was Rick Tarkanian's photo, with his record of 5-9. "Giants Drop Series Opener to Marlins," the adjoining story said. He flipped the page to read more, and there, below the box score for last night's game was a small article headlined, "Diaz, Thibodeaux Dealt to Rockies."

"Excuse me, that's fifty cents!" the girl called from the counter.

> The Giants beat the trading deadline with a deal that sent
> former All-star catcher Bobby Diaz and left-handed pitcher
> Jason Thibodeaux to the Colorado Rockies for two minor league
> prospects and an undisclosed amount of cash. Diaz, 38, played
> with the Giants for three seasons after a twelve-year career with the
> Padres. He was hitting just .228 with 4 home runs. Thibodeaux, 28,
> came to the Giants from Cincinnati in the off season. He was 10-6
> for the Giants with a 3.97 ERA, his best year in the majors. Coming
> over from Colorado is Steve Henman, a former #8 draft pick from
> Arizona State.

Rafe ran from the store clutching the Sports section. "Your popsicle!" the girl called, but he was gone. He pedaled blindly along the meadow trails he had been riding all weekend with posses of kids. He branched off on the trail that went past the staff residence — shirts, jeans, underwear, bathing suits hung over the balcony railings — then turned onto a narrower trail that rose into the National Forest. The higher he climbed, the louder the music seemed from the nearby meadow. He shifted into gears he had never used, pumping, pumping, pumping. He couldn't go back and tell his mother. She'd just say how bad his father was and that it was OK he was gone. She hated his father. And now, more than ever, Rafe hated her for that.

He rode until he passed a fork in the trail, then stopped. He couldn't hear the music any more; he didn't recognize the land around him. A huge granite wall studded with gnarly trees ran off to his right. To his left was thin forest interspersed with manzanita and laurel. He laid his bike down and leaned against the granite. The sun was sinking, but he didn't care. The only thing he wished was that he hadn't left his popsicle. Sweat poured from his face, the roof of his mouth was caked with dust. He took out the newspaper he had shoved in the band of his bathing suit. A broad crease of sweat ran across the fold, smudging the newsprint. *Diaz, Thibodeaux Dealt to Rockies.* He knew it — he knew he would leave.

He tossed the paper into the bushes and picked up his bike. He plunged recklessly back down the trail, but when he got to the fork and saw the sign he realized he had no idea where he was. He took the trail to the right, along a flat, grassy stretch through some trees. Several hundred yards further the trail angled sharply upwards between some boulders. He backtracked to the fork, aware of the rapidly retreating light in the west. The other trail cut sharply to the left, but that didn't look like the right way either.

He dropped his bike to the ground and stared, his bare chest streaked with sweat and dust. The only sound was the gasps of his own breath — and then his sobs.

"Mommy," he cried. "Mommy, mommy."

An hour later he heard voices coming from the canyon below and saw the sweep of flashlights. Shivering, hunkered against a rock, he didn't return their calls right away. He wasn't sure he wanted to go back. As long as he was here, no one could confirm what he had read. But he knew he couldn't stay out here. He had never been so hungry, so thirsty, so scared — ever.

"Rafe!" his mother called, her voice tight with fear. "Rafe, where are you?"

"Mama!" he called. "Mama — over here!"

He hurt inside far more than out. His dad was leaving and he was sure it was his fault. It was probably about baseball — because he couldn't play it, he wouldn't play, he wasn't a batboy like the other kids. His father didn't love him, he was sure that was it, and his stomach hurt so bad that he felt he was going to throw up.

"Rafe! Rafe!" His mother's voice became even more hysterical once she heard him. "Rafey, are you OK? Where are you?"

"Over here, Mama! I'm over here!"

He wiped his tears and picked up his bicycle. When the lights picked him out he was poised on his seat, a look of scared and uncertain bravery on his face. "Oh baby, baby!" Vicki cried, hugging his shivering body and smothering him with kisses. The others in the search party stood respectfully off, lighting the scene with their flashlights. Rafe cried too — from sadness, not relief. What he wanted to hear was, "Hey Buddy." He wanted his father to explain that the newspaper was wrong, that he wasn't leaving, that he'd be back in a week and everything would go on like before. Except for one thing different, Rafe thought. This time he would learn how to play baseball. He would learn how to hit and field and catch and throw. He'd get his homework done early and come to the park for home games and be a batboy. He would do all that if only he could hear that his father wasn't really leaving, and never would.

Day and night Jason called, but no one picked up the phone. At first he left long heart-felt messages for Rafe on Vicki's answering service, explaining his own frustration at being traded from the Giants. Then he'd put his energy — and thousands more dollars — into mobilizing his attorney to file motions allowing him to talk to Rafe, a battle he thought he had won long ago. It was expensive, time-consuming torture and he had to do it all from a distance; the Rockies weren't due to play in San Francisco for six weeks.

"How can she do this?" he yelled at Robert Marks one night before a game in Pittsburgh. "This is a direct violation of our custody agreement."

"Enforcement is one of the flaws in the system," Marks explained. "If somebody doesn't want to do something, there's not much the other party can do."

Jason missed Rafe's voice, the feel of his hand, the sound of his feet on the floorboards when he passed on his way to the bathroom. He missed him grinding away on his new cello, plunking the piano at Momo's when they dropped in for French toast and smoothies on Sunday mornings. He missed reading to him, tucking him in at night, hearing his sleep-softened voice sighing sweetly, "Goodnight, Daddy." He still hadn't been able to explain the trade to Rafe — that it wasn't his fault, that he'd be back in San Francisco after the season, that he still loved him. All Rafe knew was what Vicki had told him, and he could only imagine how bad that was.

Finally in late August, the Rockies came to San Francisco. Jason called from the pay phone across from the condo complex so Vicki wouldn't see his number on caller I.D. The phone rang three, four times and he braced himself to hear her voice. Miraculously, Rafe answered. "Rafe!" Jason cried. "It's Daddy — I'm in San Francisco."

There was a pause, then softly, "Hi Daddy."

"I'm at South Beach, getting the rest of our stuff. I want to come over and see you, I miss you, man. Did you get my letters?"

"Why did you leave?" Rafe's voice was suddenly shrill, accusing.

"The Giants traded me, Rafey. They move players around, you know that. I have to go wherever they tell me —"

"You said you'd never leave."

"I didn't leave, Rafey, I was traded. It's just for the season, I'll be back —"

"I hate you!" Rafe shouted, and hung up.

He called back immediately and Vicki answered.

"That was great," Jason seethed. "You've really helped him deal with the situation."

"I can't let you do this to him, Jason."

"Do what to him? I was traded!"

"He's devastated. It's better for everyone if you just leave him alone."

"Leave him alone, what the hell are you talking about? I'm coming over to see him."

"I can't let you do that. I can't let you hurt him again."

In retrospect, he never should have gone. He should have been patient and called his lawyer — but he felt as far from patient as a man could be. Every minute he wasn't there he feared that Vicki would turn Rafe against him. Why else would he say he *hated* him? He had to see Rafe before he lost him forever.

He had a 7:35 game, but he wasn't pitching and seeing Rafe was far more important than shagging fly balls. He climbed the twenty-four steps to the front door of Vicki's townhouse and rang the bell. He was in full Rockies uniform, clutching a copy of their custody agreement. *'Now going insane, number forty-seven, Jason Thibodeaux!'*

He rang the bell over and over again. He knew they were there, he could smell cooking — a pot roast or some kind of stew. He tested the railing that surrounded the stoop, protection from the twenty-foot drop to the driveway, then clambered up and supported himself by grasping a light fixture mounted on the side of the house. Leaning over the driveway, he pulled his head and shoulders across the front window and peered into the living room. He saw a small table in the corner with a blue vase, a coffee table stacked neatly with magazines, a beige leather couch — and beside the couch, a pair of frightened eyes belonging to his son.

"Rafe!" Jason called. Rafe began to back up, a look of terror on his face. "For godsakes, open the door!"

Rafe began to cry. Vicki hurried up behind him and put her arm around him. She held a camcorder in her other hand, pointed directly at Jason. He knew he should go, but he was too far along to back off. It was battle time, and though she had the upper hand, if he tried hard enough he could always find a way to win.

"Let him go Vicki. I'm his father."

"Get out of here now!" Vicki shouted, "or I'm calling the police."

He shook the papers. "You're the one going to jail! You're in contempt of court!" He squeezed the papers and pounded his fist on the glass. "I want to see my son!" The window trembled like jello and he could hear Rafe's wailing through the glass.

"Rafe — open the door NOW!" Jason shouted. "I'm your father! Everything she's told you is wrong. Open the door!"

Through it all, the camcorder kept running.

LOW AND AWAY

THE FIRST TIME HE GOT drunk after losing Rafe was at a bar in Atlanta. He was jet-lagged and desperate to sleep and with each glass his problems miraculously slipped away — the memory of losing control at Vicki's house, his son cringing in the corner of her living room, his lawyer informing him that the court had responded to Vicki's petition by rescinding his custody schedule and imposing another restraining order. This happened near the end of his mediocre half-season with Colorado, his record just 2-5 and his spirits even lower. As a condition for resuming contact with Rafe, the judge ordered him back to supervised visits and into a twenty-six week anger management class. He also ruled that Jason undergo psychological testing and a minimum of fifteen hours of psychological counseling. It was in the midst of all this that he made two amazing new friends — Alcohol and Marijuana. His big league salary allowed him to afford big league friends — forest-fresh sinsemilla from the southern Rockies, the amber opalescence of Courvoisier VSOP and Martell Blue Ribbon. He discovered that if he got really tight enough with his new friends, they could even help him forget the videotape Vicki made of his visit to her house, which she threatened to release to the press if he tried to defy the court order and see Rafe on his own.

On the Tuesday before Thanksgiving he left in a taxi cab for the Denver Airport to catch a flight to San Francisco. His shame over facing Rafe in another supervised setting was so overwhelming that he smoked a pipeful of weed before the cab arrived. He had lost, and he hated losing. Even worse, he hated the idea of his son seeing him as a loser. As they neared the airport, a string of billboards promised worlds free of care and self-reproach. Singapore, Paris, Rio. "Ixtapa — wish you were here." When the cab lunged to a stop in front of the terminal, Jason didn't budge.

"Southwest, right?" the cabbie asked.

"Ixtapa," Jason said.

"That's AeroMexico, man. It's all the way on the other side — "
"Mexico! I want to go to Mexico!" he shouted.

THREE BEERS and four cognacs later, Jason followed the stream of tourists into the harsh Mexican sunlight, still sporting the blue cotton sweater and sport jacket he'd brought for autumn in San Francisco. He grabbed a pair of wraparound shades from a sidewalk vendor and walked along the crumbled shoulder of the pot-holed roadway. He hadn't gone more than ten yards before he heard a whistle.

"*Señor — taxi!* Where are you going?"

Jason trudged ahead, his Rockies duffel bag slung crookedly over his shoulder. "Ixtapa!" he shouted.

The cabbie laughed, keeping his taxi even with the very large, very drunk gringo. "Ixtapa is a thousand kilometers away. This is the road to Mazatlan." Jason stopped. "You want a ride now?" the cabbie asked.

Jason set down his duffel bag. "Do you know who I am? *Sabes quien soy? Soy lanzador famoso!*"

The cabbie looked closer. He knew almost every major league pitcher by sight, but this one didn't ring a bell. "*Como se llama?*"

"*Me llamo Whitey Ford!*" Jason shouted.

"*Bueno Blanquito, venga. Hay muchos kilómetros de aquí y la ciudad. Hay solo coyotes aquí.*"

Jason resumed walking, his face shiny with sweat. The cabbie inched along beside him. "Show me your stuff!" the cabbie called.

"What stuff?"

"Show me your fastball."

Jason stopped and looked back towards the airport. The control tower loomed against a row of pale purplish mountains. "Fuck you," he said and resumed his pilgrimage. After a few steps he heard the sound of a car trunk closing. He turned and watched the cabbie spill fifteen or twenty hardballs on the ground, unfold a three-legged table and set up a pyramid of wooden bowling pins. He walked off twenty paces, then drew a line with his boots in the dirt. "Sixty feet, six inches, just like *los Grandes*," he called. "Come on, *Señor Lanzador*, show me your stuff."

Jason stumbled back and peered closely at the cabbie. He was a medium-sized man in his early-to-mid-thirties, with a rough, handsome, pockmarked face.

He handed a ball to Jason. "Let's see you knock down those pins."

Jason peered at the carnival set up, gripped the ball in his left hand and released a pitch that sailed four feet above the pins. He picked up his bag and started walking again. The cabbie took a ball, wound up with a slow, exaggerated motion and let fly a pitch that wiped all three pins cleanly from the table.

Jason turned and stared at the pins on the ground, then at the grinning Mexican. He started walking again — this time back towards the airport.

"Where are you going?" the man called.

"To get a drink."

"Wait, I'll go with you!"

THE FOLLOWING morning Jason woke next to Barbie, her blonde hair like corn silk though she wore the white cotton blouse and black knee-length skirt favored by young women of Mazatlan. A half dozen of Barbie's friends lay scattered on the floor of a room that was painfully pink — pink walls, pink curtains, pink and white lamps, pink purses hanging from the posts of each of four pink-blanketed beds. His head pounded, his eyes felt as if they were trying to separate from their sockets. He saw his feet sticking beyond the end of the bed and for a moment wondered whose they were. He recalled going to a bar with the cabbie where a mariachi band was playing, and drinking shots of tequila in honor of Pedro Martinez, Manny Ramirez, Alex Rodriguez, Mariano Rivera, Vladimir Guerrero, Omar Vizquel …

He groaned, pulled on his pants and shirt and shuffled out to a small living room littered with piles of folded blankets and pillows. He heard voices and followed the smell of tortillas through a doorway to the kitchen. A row of small round faces turned to greet him. A short woman in a blue cotton dress stood over the counter with her back to the door, rolling dough into circles.

"*Buenos días*," he said in a deep, tequila-singed voice. The girls looked at each other and giggled. "*Buenos tardes*," the woman replied, eyeing him suspiciously. "Willie went to the ballpark. He wants you to meet him there."

Jason looked around the kitchen and into the eyes of four of the most beautiful girls he had ever seen. They ranged in age somewhere from three to seven and each wore identical white cotton dresses; they looked like a row of kitchen canisters. "You wouldn't happen to have a beer, would you?" he asked the woman hopefully.

"Orange juice or coffee," she replied.

"Just point me to the ballpark."

THE MAZATLAN Venados played in a rust-stained concrete stadium on the southern edge of the seaside city. Surrounding it was a hard-packed dirt field littered with broken glass and pieces of brick, separated from the neighborhood of cinderblock and frond-roofed homes by a sagging chain link fence. It was four hours to game time but already vendors were building charcoal fires on sliced-open 50-gallon drums, or waiting patiently behind hand-built wooden carts lined with plastic jugs of pastel *licuados*.

Jason pulled Willie's rattling Volkswagen up to the gate. A guard wearing a military-style uniform and a Florida Marlins cap waved him through. He parked where the guard directed him, in a small section beside the stadium marked "*No Estacionamiento*" — No Parking. While on the outside the run-down ambience of the stadium was unlike any ballpark Jason had ever seen, inside it was like every other. Centered between rows of sagging, unpainted benches was a baseball field, comfortingly symmetrical and astonishingly green. A single groundskeeper pushed a small seeder by hand across the outfield grass.

He found Willie beside the visitors' dugout, talking with a slim, mustachioed man wearing the uniform of the Culican Tomateros. "This is the man I told you about," Willie said proudly. He put his hand on Jason's shoulder and steered him towards the Tomatero. "This is my cousin, Roberto Sanchez. He was named after Roberto Clemente, but he can't hit worth shit!"

"I can hit my cousin though!" Roberto laughed. He shook Jason's hand. "*Mucho gusto*," he said admiringly.

Willie turned to Jason, a gleam in his eye. "How did you sleep last night?"

"I should have stopped with our toast to Clemente."

Willie laughed. "My friend wanted to honor all the Latinos in *los Grandes*. There isn't enough tequila in Mexico!"

It was close to five o'clock and the Tomateros were preparing to take batting practice. Jason walked with Willie across the field to the Mazatlan dugout.

"Why didn't you tell me you played professional ball?" Jason asked.

Willie frowned. "This isn't professional ball."

"Bullshit. Look what you got here."

They watched the Tomateros take BP, hitter after hitter pounding balls to the deepest parts of the field and some over the wall. Other players shagged balls in the outfield in a pre-game ritual familiar from the jungles of Venezuela to the plains of North Dakota. Jason recognized a couple of Americans among the players — Gil Dominguez, who played with the Cardinals on their last playoff team, and Rudy Parfitt from the Braves. He wondered what they made in the Mexican Pacific Coast League. By the looks of the rundown stadium, it couldn't have been much, but as they used to say on the bus to Cheyenne or Pocatello — "It's baseball." Jason felt totally at home.

A short, stocky boy wearing sandals, tattered brown slacks and a faded Dodgers t-shirt dragged a heavy duffel bag towards them. He was the spitting image of Willie, without the pocked skin. If Willie had told him he had a son, he couldn't remember it.

"Carlos," Willie called out. "Come and meet a real baseball player." The boy looked shyly away. "Shake his hand, *hijo*. He plays for the Colorado Rockies."

Jason grabbed Carlos's hand tightly. "How old are you, big fella?"

"Seven and a half."

"I have a boy who's eight," Jason said.

"I'm going to be a pitcher, like my father," Carlos beamed.

Jason glanced at Willie, who nodded proudly. "*Better* than your father," Jason said softly. "You always want to be better than your father."

He watched the game a few steps away from a little wooden stand where a man sold iced cans of Tecates with wedges of lime. He was on his fourth beer by the seventh inning when the Venados removed the screwball throwing lefthander, "*El Churro*," named after the twisted sugar-coated Mexican pastry, and brought in his new friend, Willie Herrera. He looked taller on the mound, and with his hat pulled low over his eyes and the menacing glare of a backroads *bandito*, the equal of any hitter he would face. The Tomateros had put men on second and third with two out, the home team leading 5-3.

The first man Willie faced was former major league outfielder Kobe Parks. He started him out with two sliders low and away that Parks didn't bite at, then a fastball up and in that Parks started to swing at but stopped as it hit him on his inside shoulder. Parks took a couple of obligatory steps towards the pitcher but Willie had already walked off the back of the mound. His fight wasn't with Parks, it was the next batter, who now knew that Willie wasn't afraid to pitch inside. It was a major league move.

Sure enough, Willie started the next batter on the outside and got two quick swinging strikes. His third pitch was in the dirt and blocked expertly by his catcher. Jason was impressed. Willie had good stuff and knew how to pitch. His next pitch was a shoulder-high fastball that the batter really wanted to swing at but didn't, taking it for a ball. Then a slider low and away — another good pitch, except the batter didn't bite.

The count now was 3-2, bases loaded. Willie had to come with heat, Jason thought; so did the batter and everyone else in the stadium. A walk meant a run, and any mistake after that would tie the game. Willie had to bring heat. Any pitcher would.

Willie began his slow, unorthodox windup, his left knee jerking against his chest, then a long stride forward as he brought his arm in a full over-the-top motion. Jason waited for the ball to pound into the catcher's mitt, leaving that sweet signature pop that was every good fastball's calling card: "Sorry you missed me." And he waited and waited and waited. The ball seemed caught in the heavy Pacific air like a pearl in honey, heading toward the plate but hardly moving, a slow arching changeup that had the most astonishing quality of hesitancy and buoyancy that Jason had ever seen. It was *mañana*, it was Mexico, it was a *mariposa* floating on the breeze. The batter swung so early it seemed he almost had time to reload and swing again. But it was over. The umpire's right arm was in the air, the catcher flipped the ball back towards the mound, the fans shouted deliriously, "*El Loco! El Loco! El Loco!*" Willie Herrera's changeup was so renowned, it had a name.

Jason hurried downstairs for another Tecate to celebrate.

Riding back to Willie's house, Carlos excitedly relived the heroic feats of *El Loco*. His pride in his dad and his love for baseball threw Jason's dismal record as a father into stark relief. "How 'bout stopping for some beer?" Jason asked as Willie steered his rattling cab out the nearly empty boulevard. "The stores are closed, Yasone." He looked across the seat at the big major leaguer and his long, sad face. "I have El Presidente at home."

"What's El Presidente?"

"Brandy," Willie replied, and a smile appeared on Jason's face.

The girls were awake when they arrived, camped out in the dim light of the living room. "No no no," Jason insisted. "Go back to your room — I'll sleep on the couch." Ixchel, Maria Emma, Guadalupe and Ana scurried back to their room, dragging their pink blankets and stuffed animals with them. When they were settled, he watched from the doorway as Liliana went from bed to bed, tucking in each girl and giving her a hug and a kiss on the forehead. The room was warm and smelled of children. He took man-sized sips of El Presidente and smiled at the simple beauty of children going to bed. Liliana turned out the light and brushed past him. A small voice called sweetly from the darkness, "Goodnight, Yasone!"

Carlos's room was in the rear of the house, a homemade addition with a low ceiling and a single window looking out over the beet field in back. Willie was re-wiring the plug of a lamp he had made from the barrel end of a baseball bat. Carlos sat up in bed poring over a two-year-old Dodgers program Willie had brought back from a trip to Los Angeles. He wore the same Dodger's t-shirt he had worn all day. On his walls were pictures of Jesus Christ and Tommy Lasorda and a drawing of a baseball player throwing what looked like a fistful of stars.

Carlos's eyes lit up when he saw Jason. "Papi said you played in Dodger Stadium!" Jason sat on the edge of a small desk, his glass freshly filled from the bottle in the Herrera's kitchen. He was right where he needed to be — standing on the shore of a sea of alcohol with his feelings ready to sail. "What was it like?" Carlos asked. Jason took a long drink of the Mexican brandy and nodded.

"There is no better place to play baseball," he said. "Every game there are fifty thousand people, many of them Mexicans, cheering like mad. It is always seventy-two degrees and the Dodgers are always in the hunt."

"Did you hit a home run?"

"I'm a pitcher!" Jason laughed loudly. The memory of circling the bases in PacBell Park on a night when Rafe came to watch him slipped through his shield of alcohol. "I hit one," he said. Carlos watched him, hanging on his every word. It was a fast ball he had timed perfectly, driving it towards the Coke bottle slide where Rafe spent most of his time at the ballpark. He should have known it by the feel in his hands, the deep vibration of wood to bone, though he thought it was just going to be an out until the cheers broke over the field. It was a wonderful memory for anyone to have, and Carlos waited anxiously to hear it. But before Jason could speak, he dropped his glass and leaned slowly off the desk. Willie lunged and caught him as he fell.

"What's wrong, Papi?" Carlos asked. "What happened?"

"It's time to go to sleep," Willie said.

THE BASES were loaded, the entire stadium was waiting but he couldn't find the ball. He stepped off the mound and signaled for a ball, then the umpire pointed at him and he saw he wasn't wearing pants! He turned towards second base but his teammates turned away. He turned back towards home plate and the batter was shouting at him. He needed a ball; with a ball he could shut him up, shut the umpire up, shut everyone up. But he needed pants too. He looked into the stands but no one seemed to notice he was naked from the waist down. "*Andalé, Yasone,*" a voice called out. "*Andalé, por favor.*"

He glared in towards home plate, but everyone was laughing. He felt something grabbing at his shirt and he pulled back with all his might. "No!" he shouted. "Leave me alone!" He awakened to his voice and saw little Maria Emma standing beside the living room couch, a look of horror on her face. Jason's bare chest was exposed, the sheet pulled down to just below his belly button. At home he slept naked, but in deference to Willie's daughters he wore his bathing suit to bed.

"Maria," he said more softly. "You scared me. What are you doing?"

Details of his dream trailed through his mind, alongside memories of drinking at a seaside restaurant called Chava's until 2 AM. It was his fifth day staying with the Herrera's, each one pretty much the same — baseball by day, drinking by night. But now a different reality stood before him, a three-foot-tall girl in a crisp white blouse, black skirt and shiny black shoes, tears running down her delicate brown face.

"It's OK," he said. "I was having a bad dream. *Qué pasa?*"

"Mommy is sick. You have to walk us to school."

Jason threw on a t-shirt and hurried into the kitchen. Carlos and Ixchel sat quietly at the table, finishing their breakfast. Liliana was scrubbing the countertop with a brush.

"Good morning," Jason called out, Maria Emma trailing behind him.

"You're up early," Liliana said, without turning around. Jason knew that Willie's wife did not share her husband's — or her children's — affection for him. He imagined that his unscheduled presence, along with his appetite, his hangovers and his sadness probably wouldn't endear him to most households.

"Maria Emma said you were sick. She says I'm supposed to walk her to school."

"*Hija!*" Liliana scolded the girl sharply. Maria Emma's eyes widened with innocent denial. "I told you not to bother him."

Jason noticed Carlos and Ixchel watching him with the same expectant expression as their little sister. He also noticed the tall glass of fresh squeezed orange juice in front of Carlos. "I'll get dressed," he smiled. "Save me a glass of that juice."

The 'walk to school' was just to the end of their street, where the kids caught the school bus for the two mile ride to Francisco Madero primary school. Jason hadn't seen this end of the day in a long time. The sidewalks were crowded with kids walking to the same bus stop. Ixchel and Maria Emma gripped Jason's hands as tightly as candy, while Carlos walked ahead with a proud swagger. A cluster of kids goofed at the bus stop while their mothers talked in small groups at the edge of the sugar beet field. The Herreras beamed as they approached with their prize, their Big League companion towering over everyone like a Macy's Thanksgiving Day balloon.

Then Carlos, Maria Emma and Ixchel ran off to play with their friends and Jason stood off to the side. His head hurt. His mouth was dry. As a student of sociology, he had to marvel at the irony of a major league ballplayer with a $2 million contract, lost, hung over, essentially living on the couch of a poor Mexican family. But Mexico worked for him. The smells, the heat, the language, the daily cacophony of the culture enhanced the wonderful job alcohol was already performing, helping him forget his shame.

The old blue school bus squealed to a stop and the children clambered aboard. Carlos and Ixchel waved goodbye. Maria Emma blew him a kiss and ran up the steps. "See you later, alligator!" she giggled. As the bus roared off, Jason felt something giving way inside him, like a wall beginning to crumble. If Willie's children could love him, then maybe someday his son could, too.

HE STAYED into the new year, working out with the Venados by day, drinking brandy by night. But the drinking became less of a compulsion as the weeks wore on. He wanted to be able to get up and walk the kids to the bus stop, which became a daily ritual as important to him as it was to them. He bought ball gloves for the kids in the neighborhood.

He was able to make peace with Liliana, especially after she saw how devoted he was to her children. He studied Willie's barbecue technique, and when Willie left on road trips, he filled in as the backyard chef. The one thing he could not help Liliana with was her fear that Willie would leave for *El Norte* and try to make it in *Los Grandes*. "I'm no model for resolving conflicts between family and career," he told her.

The night before Jason left for spring training at the end of January, Willie grilled mounds of chicken and *carne asada* and *cebollas* on his home made grill fashioned from a sliced-open 50-gallon drum. Liliana and a half dozen women from the block cooked huge pots of beans and served rice, tortillas and salad to dozens of neighbors and members of the Venados who turned out. Everyone brought something for Jason to sign — calendars and church bulletins, posters of players they'd had on their walls for years — Tony Oliva, Rod Carew, Fernando Valenzuela, Dennis Martinez ... even a photo of Bill Clinton. They brought presents for him — papayas, mangos, statues of the Virgin of Guadalupe, onyx and jade figurines, hand-painted vases, serapes, a framed picture of the Pope, bottles of tequila and mezcal. Jason had something for them, too. He had bought hundreds of dollars worth of toys — plastic tricycles, push cars, plastic bats and balls, toy kitchen sets, dolls, baseball gloves, soccer balls, and bags of dark sugar candies from the huge indoor market in Mazatlan, and before dinner he passed them out like Santa Claus to the kids.

By eleven o'clock the neighbors had gone. Liliana was in the house putting the children to bed. A mound of coals shimmered in the grill, throwing a faint red glow over Jason, Willie and two other players from the Venados sitting on folding chairs. Joaquin Salazar, a Venezuelan outfielder trying to work his way to *Los Grandes* through the Mexican leagues, waved off the bottle of mezcal. Jason took it and raised it to his lips.

"How many games will you win this year?" Salazar asked, his tone more a challenge than a question. Jason passed the bottle to Paco Lopez, the Venados' catcher.

"Depends. I'm the number four, I won't get as many starts —"

"Why number four? Why aren't you number one?"

Jason stared at Salazar across the fireglow. He could hear the tinkling of mezcal flooding from the neck of the bottle as Paco lowered it. "We've got Doornbos," he said, referring to their number one starter, Alex Doornbos, who had gone 19-11 last year. "The best I could hope for is number two."

He knew how weak it sounded and so did everyone else. The bottle returned and he drank again. Then Willie spoke from the darkness, where the odor of marijuana mingled with the smell of charcoal. "You have a gift, *amigo*," he said. "The Lord doesn't give everyone a fastball that goes 98 miles an hour."

"The Lord giveth," Jason shrugged, "and the Lord taketh away."

"You have a family to take care of now," Willie said, watching his friend's sad face in the fading light. Jason looked up; Willie jerked his head towards his sprawling house. "We are your family now. And as your family, we would like you to stop drinking and be the best fucking pitcher in the world."

Willie took his plastic bag of marijuana from his pants pocket and gestured towards the fire. "I will say goodbye to Mary Jane, if you say goodbye to Don Pedro."

Jason glanced across the darkness. He knew why Willie wanted to quit pot, and it had nothing to do with his drinking. Willie's fantasy — and Liliana's greatest fear — was to one day play in *los Grandes*. "That's your choice, Willie," he said. "I'd quit drinking right now if I could have my son back."

"That's bullshit, *hermano*. You can't have him now, you know that."

"Exactly."

Willie moved into the light. The sound of the girls squealing playfully came from the house. "Everybody here goes north to work. They leave their wives, their kids … you can't always have everything you want, *sabes?*"

No one said a word. Paco was half asleep, lost in Mezcal dreams. The vulpine Salazar watched, his eyes reflecting the glow of the coals. Jason knew these guys didn't have shit, but somehow he felt less than them. He had a Major League contract, they had families — who was ahead? The imminence of his return to the States pressed on him. He wanted to get drunk with the locals again, sleep late, pitch batting practice to the Venados tomorrow and the next day and the next. But his flight left at 9:30 AM, direct to Denver. A new season was about to begin. There was no more hiding.

The bottle came back, warm from Paco's hands. The stars floated above them with a vast indifference. The fire whispered the last of its heat to the darkness.

Jason set the bottle on the ground and stood. "Good night,

gentlemen," he said. "Thanks for the party."

Willie leaned forward and tossed his baggie into the fire. The plastic wrinkled then burst into a snaking blue flame, spreading the distinctive odor of marijuana across the yard. He wrapped Jason in a hug, squeezing him hard. "*Buenas noches, amigo.* I don't know who I'm going to miss more — you or Mary Jane."

JASON CALLED his housekeeper from the airport and asked her to remove every drop of alcohol from his house. "Have a party," he told her when she asked what to do with it. "Just don't tell me where." He enrolled in the Rosemont Clinic's alcohol dependency outpatient program. He got a schedule of AA meetings for the greater Denver area.

No one expected much from Jason Thibodeaux that year, which was fine. He had nothing to live up to except his own expectations, which were set as high as his hopes. He found scouting charts the Rockies had used for him. He watched films and analyzed his technique. He consulted with catchers, coaches and trainers in camp about situation, strategy, conditioning. These were the things he had control over — the *only* things he had control over. Not his drinking — he admitted he was powerless over alcohol, that his life had become unmanageable. Not his son. And certainly not his ex-wife. Baseball was what he knew best, and it was what he wanted to do, with all his heart. He knew that on the field he was a winner, not a deadbeat. That was where he belonged.

By the end of spring training he dropped twelve pounds, upped his bench press to 280, and put another notch on his fastball — to 99 mph. He went 14-9 that year for the Rockies and 16-9 the following year under Joe McNamara, brought in from the Angels. McNamara was a player's manager. He respected the men and let them play, and supported them with solid decisions and a minimum of crap. Inspired by two straight second place finishes, the front office picked up closer Jay Petrajic from the Marlins and lead-off hitter Darnell White from the Royals. They signed slugger Toronto James to a three-year deal, which filled the hole in the lineup when Jamaal Greene left as a free agent. And on Jason's recommendation, they gave a try-out to Willie Herrera, who worked for half a season in the minor leagues before he and "El Loco" were brought up to become part of the Colorado Rockies' surprising run for baseball immortality.

STRIKE THREE

Top o' the 10th ...

Tobias Barlow USA TODAY

—

If they grill it, they will win.

On most Colorado Rockies home stands JT Thibodeaux and owner of the trademarked "El Loco," Willie Hernandez, throw open their home on the west side of Denver to teammates for the grilling of meats, vegetables and opponents' reputations. A sliced-open 50-gallon drum, tubs filled with beer, sodas and *licuados*, and hip-popping Mexican *corridos* on the stereo provide the infrastructure of what is now a hallowed Rockies tradition.

Baseball players being the superstitious lot they are, it will remain a tradition for as long as the Rockies occupy first place in the West. While a barbecue in Denver is hardly unique, the Rockies in first place any time past Tax Day certainly is. But there they are, five games up on the Dodgers with just five months to go.

The team batting average is in nosebleed territory, nothing unusual for mile-high baseball. But this year they may have the pitching to back it up. Alex Doornbos is fresh off a 19-11 year — and freshly signed to a four-year, $24 million deal. Jason Thibodeaux has begun his contract year 4-0 and hasn't given up a run since Opening Day. They've got Gil Petrajic and the Forty Saves, and possibly the division's best middle relief corps, led by El Loco himself.

The barbecues are family affairs, with kids talking baseball and grown men acting like kids. The one I went to didn't last long. With a day game following the Saturday evening fest, the Rockies and their families were gone by ten, fed, watered and stuffed with cholesterol and camaraderie.

It's way too early to start talking about playoffs, but there was a quiet confidence that first place was just the place for a Rockie to be. You can save this column and hold me to it later. But if these Rockies continue to believe in themselves — if they dig, shove, and dish it out as well as they can take it for the next 130 games, the nation may be treated to a rare spectacle indeed — a World Series a mile above sea level.

Rᴀꜰᴇ's ᴄᴏᴀᴛ ꜰʟᴀᴘᴘᴇᴅ ɪɴ ᴛʜᴇ fog like the flag of a losing empire. Danny Bright sliced past him on his skateboard, aimed directly toward the bench bolted with the O'Hearn Mortuary poster at the corner of Portola and O'Shaughnessy. The clack of plastic wheels on the sidewalk ended with a crash against the concrete bench and the thud of Danny's palms on the bus shelter's shatterproof glass.

"What the hell was Whopper talking about today?" Sal asked. He leaned toward Rafe, mimicking their history teacher, Matthew Burgermeister, aka the Burger Man — or Whopper. "*The tragic confluence of historical and familial trajectories, played out against the background of blah blah blah.*"

"I thought the Civil War was about slaves," Claudia Zeno said with bored exasperation.

"Whopper's always addin' shit," Danny piped in. "Those essay questions ... I mean, he always wants you to write, like, you know ..."

"*Words?*" Sal cracked. "Whopper just wants quantity, man. That's why he's the Whopper. Put anything down — a recipe for chocolate cake, why I love my dog — he loves it. He thinks he's put here by *God* to bring out our natural ability." He squeezed the shoulders of Kim Ayashi — 'Kim Chee, my geisha girl,' Sal called her. "The Whopper," he announced solemnly, "is the Messiah."

"The Whopper is whack," Kim replied.

"The Whopper's a *buster*," Danny shouted. He crouched on his board and sped down the sidewalk curving towards Sal's street. Raphael trudged, unseeing, though acutely aware of Claudia walking behind him in her black pants, black t-shirt, black cotton thrift store jacket, black shoes, black eye shadow, black lipstick and long black hair braided into ropes. She'd started tagging along the past couple of days; he was sure she was along for Sal. Sal's father was part owner of Southwest Airlines and his oldest son was expected to become a high-flying executive like his dad. The girls thought he looked like Johnny

Depp: they called out "Johnny!" at school and he blew them kisses in response. Sal already was 5 feet 10 and weighed about ninety pounds. His real name was Peter D'Alessandro but his friends called him "Sal" — short for Salad, as he rarely ate anything besides lettuce. He had long stringy black hair and penetrating black eyes and a full sensuous mouth that girls at the San Francisco Middle School for the Arts (MISCA), or MISCUE, as they called it — considered crucial.

The D'Alessandro house was a gray European manor in St. Francis Wood, three stories high with giant Monterey pines soaring over its slate roof. Danny leaned his skateboard outside the back door. Sal pulled out a huge ring of keys and unlocked the door. "Kicks off," he ordered. They left their shoes in the hallway and followed him into the large kitchen, where a short middle-aged woman and two young Latinos rolled out sheets of pastry dough.

"*Bonjour, Madame Gilbert,*" Sal sang, pronouncing her name *Gee-Bare.*

"*Bonjour, Pierre.*"

"*Est-ce qu'il y a quelque chose à manger?*" he asked.

"*Bien sûr.*" Sal motioned with his eyes for them to go ahead. Rafe took the lead up the back stairs to the intimate, slope-ceilinged third floor. He passed the bedroom belonging to Sal's sister, who was away at college, and another on the left where Mrs. Gee-Bare slept. At the end of the hallway Rafe opened a door to a spacious, thickly carpeted studio with cork-lined walls on three sides and a set of double-paned windows facing the ocean. Pages of musical notes covered a large desk set against the window. A half dozen Ottoman pillows were strewn across the floor. A cello, violin, three flutes, a clarinet and a guitar leaned on low shelves against the wall, beside a sound system connected to powerful speakers in each corner of the room.

Danny went straight to Sal's desk and pulled a half-filled Ziploc bag from a drawer, along with a blue alabaster pipe shaped like a cobra. Claudia watched as he packed the bowl and flamed a Bic to the bulging mound of weed. He took a huge inhale, then exhaled a fragrant cloud of smoke that circled the room like a spirit. Rafe reached for the pipe and sucked in the harsh, sweet smoke, then held it out to Claudia.

She looked at him uneasily. "I've never smoked." Danny's laugh sliced between them, his voice singed. "Ganja, dank — the Blessed Sacrament!" She looked at him again, uncomprehending. "We're not tweakers, dude. It's just marijuana."

Rafe held the pipe up to Claudia's black-painted lips. She flashed a quick 'whatever' smile as he lit the Bic. The bud turned red and Claudia's eyes wavered. Her chest convulsed and she coughed, spewing smoke and spit across Rafe's forearm. She grasped his shoulder and began to laugh hysterically.

"She's keyed!" Danny cried.

Rafe took another hit and offered the pipe to Kim. She waved it away and turned back to reading *The Last of the Mohicans*. "Kung Fu woman saves west from scourge of drugs," Danny teased. Kim raised her middle finger without looking up. Rafe held the pipe to Claudia's lips again as Sal burst through the door carrying a silver tray laden with lady-finger sandwiches, chocolate chip cookies, bottles of Snapple and a large bag of Hawaiian-baked potato chips.

"Greetings, fellow psycho warders!" He set the tray on his desk and grabbed the pipe from Rafe and sucked it with comic desperation. As he exhaled, he stared straight into Claudia's eyes. "Is it true your father's in the Argentine secret police?"

Claudia moved closer to Rafe. "He's an asshole, but he's not a cop."

Sal smiled and lit the pipe again. It was a typical afternoon at Sal's, minus the bottle of Starfire Gin and mixers from the parental pantry Sal sometimes provided: orange, cranberry, passionfruit juice, lemonade or Squirt. Rafe had been coming here for almost a year and he'd seen Sal's parents in person just a handful of times, usually Mrs. D'Alessandro prepping for some party or a night at the symphony. 'Parents should be neither seen nor heard,' Sal said, a statement that always raised mixed feelings in Rafe. He hadn't seen *his* father in six years.

Rafe switched on the CD player. A Haydn string quartet began and he shut it down. "Classical Sal," he teased. "Where's Ludacris?"

Sal slumped on the floor and snuggled against Kim's shoulder. "I don't ace Haydn next week it's ludicrous."

Rafe found Ludacris's *Back for the First Time* and replaced Haydn. *Yeah yeah, yeah, yeah give it to me now, give it to me now, give it to me now, give it to me now* ... He felt Claudia beside him and turned and looked into her dark eyes. She had impressed him as someone who didn't care much about anything, which he had learned wasn't true when Mrs. Wrinklestein — the name MISCUE students gave their annoying Dance and Human Expression instructor, Mrs. Wallerstein — began ripping her mid-winter dance piece. Claudia had tried to portray migration across the Mexican border, but she wasn't the most graceful dancer and without music it appeared even clunkier. Rafe picked up a flute and began playing the opening of "Winter" from Vivaldi's *Four Seasons*. Claudia lurched into a wild, writhing dance, Rafe playing faster and faster with the other kids clapping in rhythm until Mrs. Wrinklestein shouted, "Stop!"

Claudia thanked him after school, then tagged along with the entourage in her black masquerade, a sweet Italian-Argentinean girl rebelling for whatever reason against her family, who ran a restaurant called Pampas in the Mission District.

I wanna li-li-li-lick you from yo' head to yo' toes
And I wanna move from the bed down to the, down to the flo'

"What's supposed to happen?" she asked. Rafe looked at her quizzically. "The marijuana," she said. He shrugged and slumped to the carpet, leaning against one of the Ottomans. His thrift store trench coat opened to his gray sweatshirt and faded black jeans. He was as tall as Sal but without Sal's emaciated vulnerability. His shoulders were squared and powerful, his neck as rippling and graceful as a race horse. He had a long, handsome face, with his mother's aquiline nose and well-spaced, olive-dark eyes, his father's broad forehead and short, sandy-colored hair, which he hated. Three months ago he had dyed it jet-black, but his mother kept him out of school until he went to a hair-stylist and changed it back. But it turned a dull bronze rather than back to its original color, so he shaved his head and had worn a hat until the hair grew back. It was virtually shapeless now, a uni-length 'do' that looked like something Huck Finn would wear.

"You don't talk much," she said, sitting cross-legged on the floor beside him.

Sal leaned backwards over his pillow, his long hair falling to the carpet. "Raphael is a man of mystery. He talks with his cello."

"I thought you played the flute."

"Sometimes. Sometimes piano."

I wanna get you in the bathtub
with the candle lit, you give it up till they go out

Their legs touched and she did nothing to move away. "And you changed your name. Who does that?"

Rafe shrugged. "Eminem, Ludacris, Ja Rule ..."

"His dad's a famous baseball player," Danny chimed in, thinking he was helping Rafe in what looked like an impending conquest. "He pitches at PacBell Park."

Rafe stood and grabbed Sal's cello; he ran the bow across the strings and the cello moaned like a grieving old woman. He bent his head and drew long, sorrowful notes contrapuntal to the snare and organ pumps of Ludacris. Claudia stood and began to dance, her eyes closed. She slowly removed her black cotton jacket, revealing a broad torso and a horizon of creamy flesh between her t-shirt and pants. She moved in a small circle, flowing with smooth languorous sweeps of her arms. Kim continued reading. Danny chased villains across the miniature screen of Sal's Game Boy. Sal rose, stuffed the pipe full of weed again, and after loudly inflating his own lungs, held the pipe to Rafe's lips — and, after him, to Claudia's.

The notes from Rafe's cello became hard and insistent, rising with the hip-hop beat into the corners of the room. It was Rafe's piece now, something ancient and contemporary at once. Claudia exhaled and swayed exaggeratedly. She raised her arms and pulled her t-shirt off, revealing a black brassiere encompassing full mocha-colored breasts. Then her shoes, socks, pants were off and she wore nothing but a brassiere and black underpants. She passed close to Rafe and he didn't even pretend not to look. She leaned over and kissed him, and after a moment Rafe lay the cello down. He never noticed Danny, Kim and Sal leave the room, as he had so many times when Kim and Sal were about to get it on.

She was in his arms, then they were on the floor, Claudia draped over one of the Ottomans. Rafe had always sworn he wouldn't do it like this. This was how his parents had gotten in trouble. He didn't want to have to get married and raise some fucked up kid. But holding her, tasting her, feeling himself inside of her, how could anything bad come from this? He wanted it to go on forever, to make his body part of hers, his mouth part of hers. He wanted to disappear inside of her ... just disappear.

We can do it in the white house
tryna make them turn the lights out
in the back row at the movies
you can scratch my back and rule me

After he was spent, they rolled apart, like a melon cleaved. The CD player had gone silent. A cold wind blew through Sal's window from the sea.

"We should have used a jimmy hat," Claudia said. Rafe shrugged. "Fuck," she said, grabbing her clothes. "Where's the bathroom?"

He watched as she hurried naked out the door. Fuck is right, he thought. Fuck I'm late for dinner. Fuck she might be pregnant. Fuck who gives a shit. He pulled on his pants, threw on his gangster overcoat and ran down the stairs two-at-a-time. He grabbed his shoes from the back hallway and disappeared into the fog.

THE NEXT day after school Rafe burst up the back stairs into Sal's cork-lined room, not bothering to knock. Sal was in an uncharacteristically studious pose at his desk, hunched over his algebra workbook. A small circle of light from his desk lamp illuminated a page of hieroglyphic-like equations. It never occurred to Rafe that Sal had a life separate from the dissolute wisecracking that consumed their time together.

Rafe snatched away the workbook. "Two words," he said to a frowning Sal. "Hip-hop opera."

"That's three. Gimme back, got a test tomorrow."

Rafe took the bottle of gin from the shelf in Sal's closet and mixed huge shots with Orange Slice in plastic Southwest Airlines cups. "How would you like to win first prize at Performance Day?"

Sal peered at him before taking a sip of the strangely sweet and bitter drink. "That's usually given to people who give a shit."

Rafe's eyes smiled as he drank. He loved the knife-like flavor of gin as it cut through the Slice. It tasted like something good for him and dangerous at the same time.

"You're serious about this," Sal stared.

"MISCUE's first, last and only Hip Hop Opera," Rafe said. "We'll be legends."

Sal took another sip, then reached into his desk drawer and pulled out the bag of marijuana. "We're already legends. But that should seal the deal."

THEY SPILLED off the bus onto Fourth Street and headed towards the neon portals of the Metreon, Sal shouldering his saxophone case,

Rafe cradling his cello, Claudia wearing her all-black ensemble and a mounded black backpack. They followed a Hobbit-sized friend of Sal's named Spunky D who looked like any kid who just jumped off a skateboard — oversized faded jeans, high-top red sneakers, a Giants sweatshirt with the 's' blacked out, cancer patient haircut. He had a jittery, insistent manner that Rafe disliked immensely, but Sal said he had rehearsal space so he was willing to play along.

Rafe walked several steps behind Claudia, watching her buttocks moving beneath her pants as they crossed the lawn at Yerba Buena. Spunky D herded them behind a curtain of water at the Martin Luther King memorial and pulled a huge wooden pipe the shape of a Playskool hammer from his jacket. He touched a red plastic lighter to the contents and inhaled deeply.

"Get *baked!*" Sal whooped. The pipe made the rounds several times. A small group of Asian tourists fled as smoke spread across the ceiling of the concrete underpass. Rafe read the words carved into the marble behind the waterfall.

We will not be satisfied until justice rolls down like waters and righteousness like a mighty stream. I have a dream. It is a dream deeply rooted in the American dream that one day this nation will rise up and live out the true meaning of its creed — *We hold these truths to be self-evident, that all men are created equal.*

Here was a guy who had nothing, and now he had a fountain named after him — and a holiday. King's words tumbled through Rafe's mind like notes seeking a melody. Martin Luther King, *Jr.,* he noted. So he had a dad. Wasn't that a kick?

He followed the crew into the Metreon, a noisy catacomb of tiled corridors filled with foreign tourists and bored teenagers. Sal led them into the Star Wars Lounge, where he fed tokens into a Jedi starship and blasted enemies off the screen.

"C'mon," Rafe whined impatiently. "We got work to do!"

Sal squeezed off a final burst of fake electrons, then followed the group across Mission Street to the Marriott. Spunky D led them through the lobby onto the express elevator to the 44th floor. Rafe hugged his cello and watched the numbers speed upwards, ignoring Claudia as he had since that afternoon at Sal's.

They walked down a silent, thick-carpeted hallway to a door marked

"Pacific Rim Suite." Spunky D swiped an electronic card through the keypad and the door opened to a spacious suite with plush, padded furniture, a gleaming coffee table, a full dining room complete with crystal chandelier, fireplace, wet bar, writing desk and grand piano. Rafe wasn't sure how they got there, but it was a perfect place to stage a rehearsal of his opera, *The Merchant of Menace*.

Spunky D raced to the window and drew the curtain back, unveiling a vertiginous view north across San Francisco Bay. Rafe removed his cello from the case as Spunky D pulled two bottles of Doc's Vodka Lemonade Cooler from the refrigerator, divided them into four cocktail glasses, then poured half a Vodka miniature into each of the drinks and passed them around. Sal sprawled on the couch and lit a joint. Rafe hurried around the room, passing out the music. "Let's get going!"

"Going, going — GONE!" Sal cried, as he waved the joint at Rafe. "Enjoy the spoils of your toils, maestro. Our man Spunky D has procured this righteous space —"

"Then let's use it!"

Sal passed the joint to Claudia, then pulled his saxophone from its leather case. It shone in his hands like Moctezuma's gold. Spunky D flipped open the Steinway and ran the keys. Rafe poised his bow above his cello's strings. Claudia removed her shoes and jacket, shoved the chairs against the wall and waited in the center of the room.

Sal nodded. Rafe pulled the bow across the cello at the highest octave possible while Sal spit an impudent cry through his saxophone. Claudia jerked her shoulders sideways, Spunky D followed with a disjointed, arrhythmic riff on the piano. It went like that for several minutes, a premeditated cacophony designed to strip the protective shield from every spinal column in the house.

Then Sal's saxophone stopped. His high-pitched voice wailed over cello and piano. Claudia began doing sinuous pushups on the floor.

This is the way the world works
vibe revealed revolved spinning on a plastic CD
everyone trying to confiscate what I communicate
its ancient gift of the lip steady creating
activating passion vocal vibrations
to the blind plus the seeing human
being doesn't mean just being
alone with your dreams —

Rafe threw his bow across the room. "This sucks!"

"What sucks?" Sal shouted back.

"Everything."

Rafe grabbed one of the cocktails and drank half of it before realizing how strong it was. He could still hear the cello's moans, feel its trembling between his legs ... but the words were nonsense. *The Merchant of Menace* was about a man who made a fortune selling tickets to watch the end of the world, then had to watch his own children die in the show he was making a fortune from. But it wasn't working. Everything would have to be changed, and Performance Day was just two weeks away.

Spunky D skittered into the bathroom and in a moment the thunder of running water could be heard. He emerged after a few minutes wearing only his underpants. "Hot tub!" he shouted. Sal hurried in, then Claudia. Rafe finished his drink, stripped to his underwear and joined them in the bathroom. Spunky D was sitting immersed up to his hips, with the water rumbling in like a mighty stream. Rafe slipped in beside Claudia, who was down to her underpants and black t-shirt. Sal passed the pipe while Spunky D dispensed miniature liquor bottles from the room's well-stocked refrigerator.

In a few moments they were happily high. Spunky D slid from the tub and called room service, ordering Giant Shrimp Cocktails, burgers for everyone, hot fudge sundaes, cherry cokes — and a bottle of champagne.

"Who's paying for all this?" Sal asked.

"You just sign the room number!" Spunky D laughed.

A miniature bottle of Courvoisier started around and they all took sips. Then, "COME IN!" they shouted and laughed when the buzzer sounded. They were ravenous from the weed, and eager for the food they'd ordered. Then three men walked into the bathroom. One wore a security guard's uniform, a gun strapped in a holster on his hip; the other two wore suits. "You have the right to remain silent," the taller suit said. "Anything you say may be used against you in a court of law."

"What's the charge?" Spunky D cried. "Enjoying our room?"

The other suit, a thin older man with wispy gray hair, pulled a well-worn booklet from his jacket and began reading. "Breaking and entering!" he shouted, pointing an index finger at each of the four in turn. "San Francisco Penal Code 34-dash-98, unlawful entry into a private establishment and the commission of crimes therein."

"We have a key!" Spunky D shouted back.

"Sure you do," the other suit said, as the guard gathered up empty bottles and Spunky D's pipe and put them into Ziploc bags. "Except it's not yours."

A SMALL fire crackled in the black marble fireplace, its flames reflecting like melting wax off the polished hearth. Vicki Repetto, wearing a lush burgundy sweater and black slacks, her long hair pulled back in a pony tail and face still flushed from an afternoon in the mineral pools at the Calistoga Spa, sipped a glass of Chardonnay at a table for two. Across from her, Rafe stared sullenly at the fire. He was wearing unwashed black chino pants and an Alcatraz Psycho Ward sweatshirt. They had come to Calistoga several times a year to play in the hot pools when Rafe was in grade school, and their new therapist had thought it a good idea for them to come here to talk things out. The therapist had spent an entire session teaching them a technique called 'active listening,' which might have been useful if Rafe would say something.

Their waiter brought salads and Vicki ordered another Chardonnay. When he left, Vicki leaned in and spoke in a confidential tone. "All that time we worked on decision-making. Do you think you made the right decision?"

"What do you think?" Rafe replied sarcastically. He had gotten three years probation as the ringleader of the hotel break-in (Sal got a suspended sentence), a three-day suspension from school, and though it was mostly a threat, the judge had warned Rafe that further transgressions of the law could land him in Juvenile Hall.

"What could you have done differently?"

"I told you, Sal's friend had a room with a piano; we needed a place to practice," Rafe said, his sandy hair flopping over his forehead.

"We have a piano at home."

Rafe exhaled and looked away with disgust. The waiter set Vicki's Chardonnay on the table and took away her empty glass. She took a sip and looked at him longingly. "Rafey, you don't want to get caught up in this system. I see cases at our law firm ... they don't care about helping you, they just want to scare you. It's brutal." Rafe sipped his Coke and glanced indifferently at the small salad in front of him. "I blame myself," she said. "Maybe if you had a little brother or sister ..."

"What difference would that make?"

"Somebody to hang out with," Vicki smiled. "Somebody who looked up to you. That can be very empowering."

Rafe shrugged. Familiar words moved through his mind, as much his own now as they were Eminem's: *It's so scary in a house that allows no swearing/to see him walkin' around with his headphones blaring/Alone in his own zone, cold and he don't care/He's a problem child ...*

Vicki leaned closer. "Are you stoned?"

"Now?" Rafe laughed. "No."

"Because I don't think you're listening. Do you have any idea what it feels like to bail your own child out of jail?"

"What do you care?"

She stared at him, her eyes welling with tears. "I trusted you, Rafe. I gave you freedom. I thought you could handle that."

"The freedom to do what you want me to do."

"That's crap," she said sharply. Diners nearby pretended disinterest, but some had at least one ear cocked towards them. "You come and go when you want. You have your own key. I never had that kind of freedom when I was a kid."

Rafe watched her lips, barely listening. Usually she was giving some sort of order. Practice your cello. Do your homework. Sit up straight. And then she'd go upstairs and work or talk on the phone or get dressed to go out. They didn't even own a TV. "Mozart didn't play video games," she joked once, though she was at least half-serious and he knew it.

Little Hellions, kids feelin rebellious/Embarrassed their parents still listen to Elvis/They start feelin like prisoners helpless/'til someone comes along on a mission and yells BITCH!!!

"Big deal, I have a key."

The waiter brought their dinner — chicken for her, pasta for Rafe. The interruption allowed her to shift their conversation from their familiar dynamic to something different. "It's obvious that you're really unhappy," she said. "Do you have any ideas what we can do about it?"

"I want to go live with Dad."

Vicki's response was instantaneous, unthinking. "You don't have a dad. He left."

"It's different now," Rafe said angrily. "I'm old enough to do stuff with him."

"You haven't seen your father in six years. This is just some fantasy."

"It can't be any worse than this."

"Thank you," she said with wounded sarcasm. She took a sip of wine, trying to calm down. "Why are you so angry? Can you tell me what you're angry about?"

"Me?" he scoffed. "You're the one who's always angry."

He's a problem child, and what bothers him all comes out/When he talks about his fuckin dad walkin out/Cause he just hates him so bad that blocks him out/If he ever saw him again he'd probably knock him out ... "You and Dad, fighting all the time, every time he calls. It's whack." Rafe shoved two or three quick forkfuls of pasta into his mouth.

"What's whack?"

"That. Fighting. You and Dad —"

"What does that word *mean*," she asked with a steely insistence.

"Bad, awful ... fucked. Why don't we live together, like other families? You guys are so angry you can't even see straight."

She smiled with a kind of grim hopefulness. "That's not what it's about. Your father and I married too young. It didn't work —"

"Yeah, well, this isn't working either."

She set her fork down and leaned across the table with an open, entreating look. "Rafe." He was staring at the candle flame arcing over the top of the fluted glass. "Sweetie." She waited until he looked at her. "I can't do this without your help." He looked away again. "The next time, they'll send you to jail."

You know like in the movies when it ends with a scream/Well fuck face I got news this is the real world and I did things ...

"I don't care," he said.

"Yes you do, Rafe. You have to care."

SAL PEERED from the wings and quickly withdrew. "It looks like the Titanic," he whispered. "Everybody's dressed in tuxedoes." Ari Mittal's quartet was wrapping up Albonini's *Adagio in G minor*, playing with painful precision. The sixth and seventh graders had already ground their way through their performances, a series of by-the-book recitations of Mozart, Brahms and Bach. Rafe, dressed in a 1950s-style sharkskin suit, with a white shirt and thin black tie, sat quietly on a stool just inside the curtain, nervously massaging the neck of his cello.

"They're going to put everybody to sleep," he said.

"Not for long," Danny Bright grinned.

Performance Night used to take place in the auditorium at MISCUE, until the local NPR station proposed broadcasting the work of San

Francisco's fledgling musical geniuses and they moved it to the Herbst Theater, a baroque auditorium where the UN charter was signed in 1945. Nearly a third of the house had left, but the teachers were still there, as were Sal's parents in celebratory black tie, Vicki in a black business suit and white silk blouse, and Vicki's parents. The D'Alessandros sat a row back and a few seats away. Neither family acknowledged the other; they hadn't talked since the arrests, and didn't look as if they had any plans to.

The Albonini piece halted abruptly, followed by the fervent clapping of the quartet's family members. "C'mon Mittal, get off!" Rafe muttered as they took a series of bows. Then they scurried past, giddy with the weight of their months-long project lifted from their shoulders. "Good luck," Ari called. Rafe nodded. Luck would be OK. So would an earthquake or a fire. But Mrs. Janes had already begun her introduction.

"Thank you for that lovely rendition of my favorite Albonini adagio," she gushed with practiced cheerfulness. "Now last, but certainly not least, we present an original composition for voice and instrument by Raphael Repetto, accompanied by Daniel Bright on the pre-recorder and Peter D'Alessandro on cello. The piece is entitled," she read, pausing either for effect or disapprobation, "*Die Rappeur*."

Rafe led his group on stage, handsomely retro in the suit he had bought on Haight Street for the occasion. They took their positions — Sal seated with Rafe's cello between his thighs, Rafe holding the microphone stand in his right hand, his left arm arched over his head like a rock star. Danny stood behind them with the boom box on his shoulder. The overture from *Die Walkure* escaped from the box, an ominous stalking of strings.

Vicki glanced proudly at her mother, and beside her, her dad. "I thought he played the cello," Anna whispered. "He does," Vicki replied, patting her mother's hand. Suddenly Rafe's voice boomed from the speakers, harsh and insistent:

"You gotta listen to me, listen to me, listen to me
You gotta listen to me, listen to me, listen to me
You gotta listen to me, listen to me, listen to me
Tonight we're going to the opera, *honnnn-eeeey*."

The overture sped to its finale, violins and base violas pulling like runaway horses. As Wagner faded, Danny's boom box produced a syncopated anthem of hip hop snares, the two-four beat of a hipster's roll down a gum-smeared liquor-stained street and over it, the sardonic moan of the cello.

We must die for our country, that's what the game is
But they don't even care what the hell your name is
You got a mother a father a country a school
but nobody asks you they just think you're a fool
fighting and strutting and sockin away dough
honey put your clothes on we're goin to the sto
Wait let's roll a banger and smoke it 'fore we leave
Put the rest of it in a holder and stuff it up your sleeve
You got nuthin to live for the rules are all made up
The only choice you got is to just chalk it all up ...
(All three) TO EXPERIENCE!

Die Walkure reappeared, like Jack the Ripper slinking through the London fog, and over it Rafe's refrain. Vicki stared straight ahead, a bewildered smile frozen on her face. Two seats away her father squirmed while faces in the audience swung this way and that, looking for someone, somewhere, to do something.

In the land of the blind the one-eyed rapper is king
He sees your innies your outies and all your nasty things
How can you rule if your own house is not in order?
This would be cute if it were all just a dream
But every time I peep it I starts to scream
Rules without rulers, schools without schoolers
If you can make the grade well you got it made
But nobody wants to listen to what's in *your* head
Until you're dead, or dying
And you can die trying, try flying, die flying
Some of us got airplanes, some are just crying
For something new to come along and make us buy it.

You gotta listen to me, listen to me, listen to me
You gotta listen to me, listen to me, listen to me
You gotta listen to me, listen to me, listen to me

Tonight we're going to the opera, *hon-nnn-eeeey.*

It ain't right living without rights
Listening in our rooms to endless fights
You're a fucking asshole, well you're a cunt
There's nothing you've ever done right, not even once
We're not dying for our country, we're already dead
Everything that's happy happens just in my head
Why are you so angry, everyone wants to know
You might as well ask why I'm a Negro
Shanking up the night with the hip hop opera
Winning the game in the bottom of the ninth
But that's not all there is to it uh-uh, uh-uh
You can chew it you can spew it
You can spit it out the side
You can study what you got or just ...
(All three) IGNORE IT!

The refrain began again, each boy shouting into their microphone. Vicki's father leaned towards her. "What the hell's going on!" he growled. "This isn't music!"

The song ended and two teachers moved towards the stage. Rafe turned to ashen-faced Danny Bright and nodded. If they stopped now, everything would be OK; except it wouldn't, because it would still be the same. "Go!" he whispered. Danny hit the play button. From the speakers came the soothing clippity-clop opening of the *Oklahoma* stalwart, "The Surrey With the Fringe on Top." The teachers halted their advance. Bodies in the audience relaxed. Vicki looked over at her father and smiled.

"Chicks and ducks and geese better scurry
When I take you out in the surrey,
When I take you out in the surrey with the fringe on top!
Watch that fringe and see how it flutters
When I drive them high steppin' strutters
Nosey pokes'll peek thru their shutters and their eyes will pop!"

The cheery strains of the musical faded and Rafe's voice took over. This time Sal sawed the cello furiously, his long body arched over the instrument like Zeus over Leda.

I was doing time in the wine of my womb
when the doctor's knock came, 'it's time to make room
the rest of your brothers are comin in behind
this isn't your call you're flying blind
it's simple really, you'll be raised by wolves
we'll fix you up with pimps and whores
with juice and mota and all the stores
you're gonna be a man by the twenty-first span or else.'

(All three, Chorus):
Breaking and entering, that's what they did!
took me from the oven and made me a kid
without instructions or a how do you do
unauthorized entry to a business or home
you got a key — whose boy are you?
Were you assigned this room, or the room assigned to you?
Whose name did you use if you didn't use your own?
Where you gonna go — cause you can't go HOME!

Rafe saw his mother's frozen expression, his grandparents in silent
shock beside her. He turned and signaled again for Danny to hit "Play."

"I can see the stars getting blurry,
When we drive back home in the surrey,
Drivin' slowly home in the surrey with the fringe on top!
I can feel the day getting older,
Feel a sleepy head on my shoulder,
Noddin, droopin close to my shoulder, till it falls kerplop!"

I've got a funulator, a syncopator, a spongeulator, a 'ho,
A dialator, anihilator, a moculator and mo
I didn't ask to come into this world
Nobody showed me how to give it a whirl
you sit on your wallet and tell me to dance
I'm out in the streets looking for romance
right outside there are pimps and gangsters
women with muffballs spinning on their wangsters

Breaking and entering! Whose boys are you?
Breaking and entering! Whose toys are you?
Take me to Paris and show me the sights
keep me singing on long summer nights
I'm a simple dimple pimple boy
a number one package, your number one joy
take me to heaven, don't show me your fights
take me anywhere, just turn out the lights.
I can't handle this shit, can YOU?

As soon as Sal lowered Charlie's bow, Mrs. Janes grabbed the microphone while Mr. Daniels, the phys-ed teacher, pulled Rafe from the stage with a pincer grip on his arm. But he had pulled it off. Four or five kids applauded; a parent shouted, "shame on you!" Rafe waved his free hand like a cartoon character leaving the stage.

"Thank you," he shouted. "Thank you very much!"

RAFE COULD feel the room shaking from the wind as he sat on the bed with his back to the wall. The moan of the foghorn leaked through the thick frosted windows. Some nights it sounded close by, as if they were at sea. It reminded him of life with his dad on the waterfront, a time he could barely tell was real or just a story he recalled.

The Sunday sports page was spread across his knees, the final stats from the regular season. "Statistics don't tell it all," his father once told him. But they were all he had. The Rockies had won their division, finishing six games ahead of the Dodgers — and 22½ games up on the Giants, he noted happily. Their pitching staff had been superb, led by Alex Doornbos with a phenomenal 23-6 year — and Jason Thibodeaux, 17-8, 3.41 ERA. Innings pitched, 221. Strikeouts, 197.

Rafe carefully folded the paper along the edges of the Rockies' box. The light from the single steel-caged bulb cast a dull glow around his shadow as he pressed his thumbnail up and down the creases of the paper. He tore out the box and taped it to the last empty patch on his Wall of Fame. *Thibodeaux's two-hitter Skins Braves. Rockies Vault to Division Lead. Ex-Giant Tames Former Mates. Rockies Clinch Postseason Slot.*

The door of his room swung open and he turned, flexing his hands in anticipation. It was Halley — "Halley's Vomit," they called him —

Dr. Jeremy Halley, assistant superintendent of the San Francisco Youth Guidance Center. He was a short, heavy-set man with a half-halo of badly dyed hair encircling his freckled head. His face was shiny and clean-shaven, as if he'd just showered. He glanced at Raphael with small, unreadable gray eyes, then closed the door behind him. He was carrying a manila folder and a small cup sealed in plastic.

"You're very proud of your father," Halley said softly, studying the wall.

Rafe had heard of Vomit's visits. They were, some of the older guys said, as predictable as diarrhea follows all-you-can-eat taco night. But having served half of his six weeks without a Halley visit, Rafe thought he'd been spared somehow.

Halley sat on the edge of the bed. Rafe stood quietly near the Wall of Fame. The foghorn sounded again with deep, mournful moans. Halley shook one of the cups like a bell. "We need a urine sample."

"What for?"

"To test for drugs."

"I don't have any drugs."

"Then you have nothing to fear."

Rafe took the cup reluctantly. "We're not supposed to leave the room …"

"You can do it here," Halley smiled. "It's just us guys."

Rafe turned to the wall. *Thibodeaux Bests Bosox.* He opened the plastic cover and removed the opaque cup. "You'll need to turn around," Halley said.

"What for?"

"I have to make sure you're not adding anything to the sample."

Rafe turned, his expression wavering between fear and disgust. Getting thrown out of MISCUE was a game. Getting busted for selling dope to an undercover agent outside Washington High was a game. Getting locked up in Juvenile Hall for six weeks and becoming a bonafide member of the elite club of San Francisco's juvie offenders was a game. But this didn't feel like a game. This was bullshit.

He lowered his zipper and held the cup in front of him. Time stood still and he felt if he stood still with it, nothing bad would happen. The foghorn sounded again and he closed his eyes and the ship's lamp in his bedroom at his dad's apartment came into view as big as life. He heard his father's voice reading from *Treasure Island,* the end of the fateful chapter where Jim confronts Israel Hands, after the Hispaniola has run aground and Jim's life is on the line.

One more step, Mr. Hands, said I, and I'll blow your brains out! He thought about strangling Halley, or bashing his head against the bed frame. Then Halley's voice came to him, inches away. "You have to take it out." Rafe took his penis with his left hand and pointed it towards the cup. From what he'd heard about Halley's visits, he was getting off easy.

It came out first in nervous spurts, then a thin soprano stream. Then his father's voice grew more animated. He liked to dramatize what he read, making up accents and peculiar ticks for individual characters. *I was drinking in his words and smiling away, as conceited as a cock upon a wall, when, all in a breath, back went his right hand over his shoulder. Something sang like an arrow. I felt a blow and then a sharp pang, and there I was pinned by the shoulder to the mast.*

He finished peeing and started to fold his penis away. Suddenly Halley's hand grabbed his. "Jesus Christ!" Rafe shouted. He leaped back. The cup flew into the air and sprayed urine across Halley's jacket. Rafe stared at him, terrified. Halley leaned close to his face. The smell of his own pee on Halley's wool jacket was overpowering. "It's OK," Halley said. "We won't tell anybody what happened."

When he was gone, Rafe curled on his bed, too drained to even pull back the sheets. Again, he heard his father's voice, reading: *Without hesitation, I fired my pistol and a second later I heard a choked cry. The coxswain loosed his grasp upon the shrouds, and plunged head first into the sea.*

When he finished reading, his father always used to lean over and pull the comforter up to his chin. He would push the hair back from his forehead and hold his hand there for a second, then lean over and kiss him on the cheek.

"*Good night, big boy,*" he would say. "*I'll see you in the morning.*"

"*Good night, Daddy. I'll see you in the morning, too.*"

GRAY SMOKE billowed above the roof of the two-story townhouse, spreading the aroma of roasting chicken, ribs, eggplant, corn, peppers and potatoes around the suburban neighborhood. Jason watched from the balcony overlooking his spacious yard as the two Mexican chefs tended the banquet-sized barbecue. Willie Herrera, wearing Colorado Rockies jersey number 47 with "Thibodeaux" on the back, patrolled the buffet line making sure everyone had silverware, drinks, napkins, a pat on the back. The late-afternoon shadows angled across the rented tables, the barrels full of soft drinks and beer, the muscular guests and their families in sharp autumn relief. In the distance loomed the Rocky Mountains, an apparition of greatness.

He glanced at his watch — 3:50 ... 5:50 New York time. It was good to be home. They had their fans now, their air, their intimate knowledge of the ballpark ... and no designated hitter. Tomorrow he would pitch the sixth game of the World Series, against the New York Yankees. He had never wanted a win more in his life. He wanted to be able to read through the books and turn to the World Series rosters and find a "W" beside his name. Plus, his contract was up after the season. He had finished the regular season with four straight wins, including the game that clinched the division. He was 3-1 in the postseason, with a no-decision in Game Two of the Series. If he won tomorrow, his agent assured him a four-or-five-year deal worth forty million at least, taking care of him for life and letting him finish with a team, in a town, that felt more like home than any place he had ever lived.

He walked slowly down the stairs to the yard, careful to avoid any domestic tragedy famous in baseball lore — George Brett breaking his toe doing laundry ... Bobby Ojeda slicing his hand with hedge clippers. He crossed the lawn to where third baseman Julio Marrero sat at a table with his wife, Guisela, and their two children. "*Hola, niños,*" he smiled, placing a hand on their shoulders. "*Les gusta la barbacoa?*"

"*Si, claro,*" Guisela replied when her six- and four-year-old children failed to respond. "Thank you so much for this lovely party, Jason."

"I just want to make sure everybody got together before Sunday," he replied, squeezing Julio's powerful shoulder. The message of unspoken confidence was that there would be a game Sunday — that the Rockies would win and force a seventh game. He wanted to bring them together, take their minds off the game, make it seem like an everyday occurrence that they were two wins away from being World Champions.

"You guys going somewhere afterward?"

"Las Vegas," Guisela replied, wrinkling her nose. "He loves to gamble."

"How about you, *amigo?*" Julio asked. "Going to Mexico again?"

"*Como no? Si Colorado es casi un paraíso, Mexico es lo verdadero.*" Jason filled his plate and joined the bachelors' table at the far side of the yard. He noticed more neighbors than usual on their balconies. A few had hung banners — "Go Rockies!" "Beat the Yankees!" And Jason's favorite, "Buena Park 4, New York 3." Buena Park was the name of their neighborhood.

He dug into a mound of potato salad and looked around the yard. He caught Eric Lavalle's eye and smiled. Eric was a slim African American man, just twenty-four and one of the hottest players on the team. The whole team was a bunch of kids, except for Jason, Willie Herrera, and their temperamental first baseman Toronto James. Jason was thirty-four. Willie Herrera never told his age, but Jason guessed he was at least that. Toronto was thirty-eight.

"You keep smilin', JT," Lavalle nodded. "You want a beer or somethin'?"

Jason shook his head. He pointed at the half-finished Corona in front of Willie. "We're in the World Series and you're sucking down Coronas?"

"*You're* in the World Series," Willie laughed. "The only way I get in is if you fuck up."

Omar Ortega, whose uniform was the eponymous "00," laughed. "You guys are like a married couple or something," he said. "You sure you're not a couple of *maricones?*"

Jason wrapped his arm around Willie's shoulders and kissed his cheek. "Willie is the best goddamned cook in the world," he said. "But man, do his feet stink!"

The tables rang with laughter. Some of the players shared houses, apartments, and in one case a trailer, but Willie and Jason shared lives. During the season they lived in Jason's townhouse. Off-season, Jason took a week to drive through northern Mexico and join Willie's family for the winter in their new house on the outskirts of Mazatlan. For Willie, the arrangement gave him a place in Denver where he could focus on his surprising major league career away from the demands of his family. For Jason, it gave him companionship, and the joy of a loving family during the darkest months of the year.

Willie took a sip of beer. "I don't think they can do it in our yard."

"It's the Yankees," Jason muttered.

Despite his efforts, Jason couldn't hide how nervous he was. "You should dedicate this game to something big," Willie said. "In Mexico, we offer everything up to Our Lady of Guadalupe."

"And we know what a great success Mexico is."

"Hey, things are better than before she came."

"That was like 1870 or something!"

"You gotta admit, things have gotten better since then."

Jason high-fived his friend. He couldn't have felt any more alive than he did right then — surrounded by friends and neighbors, his belly full of good food, ready to do battle with the New York Yankees on sports' biggest stage. There was only one thing missing.

Willie turned towards the tables and held up his Corona. "To my roomie. I can't think of anyone I would rather see on the mound tomorrow." Cheers erupted from the yards around them. "Rockies! Rockies! Rockies!"

The warmth of the day drained away as the sun sank behind the mountains. Jason stood at his front door squeezing hands, shoulders, stooping to bid goodnight to the children. It had been just another meal, a way to acknowledge a special day without making anything special about it. It was just another game tomorrow, the same way June 6, 1944, was just another day in northern France.

That evening he and Willie watched *Lethal Weapon IV*, dubbed in Spanish. A half hour into it Willie said, "You look a little like Mel Gibson."

"You look like Danny Glover."

Willie glanced at him, then at the clock. It was close to ten. "How you doin'?"

"OK," Jason replied. "For some reason I've been thinkin' about Rafe. It's been six years, man."

"That's a long time."

"Maybe I should dedicate the game to Rafe."

"That's a good idea," Willie nodded. "Win the fucking thing for Rafe."

"And Our Lady of Guadalupe. Just to cover my ass."

"That's an even better idea. I'll say something to her too."

Jason rose and clapped Willie on the shoulder. "You sleep well, *hermano*."

"You sleep too, *hermano*. *Sueña de los Yanquis vencidos*."

THE DEN mother of every baseball team is the clubhouse manager, customarily a well-seasoned fellow who has been with the team since shortly after Abner Doubleday sewed his first cowhide around a ball of string. The "clubbie" oversees the whole off-the-field operation — uniforms and equipment, pre- and post-game banquets, clubhouse ambiance, medical supplies and special requests by players for out-of-town car rentals, comp tickets for friends and relatives, calls screened from wives and girlfriends, customized bats, NASCAR tickets, appointment with a special trainer. The clubbie, as they say, "knows everything, and tells nothing."

The Rockies' "clubbie" was Skeedy Olmstead, a short, round, fist-hard man who had started as a bat boy with the Denver Zephyrs in 1955 and never left the clubhouse. His entire life was dedicated to the well-being of players in his charge. The first player in the clubhouse found Skeedy in his office; the last player out said goodnight to him. Skeedy had a family, though no one ever saw them. His passion was baseball and the men who played it.

Forty-five minutes before game time, Jason sat on the stool in front of his locker, studying his book on the Yankees' hitters one last time. The room was the same ditzy chaos it was before every game. Right fielder Alex Heredia polished his shoes while listening to merengue and salsa on his Walkman. Darnell White jerked to hip hop banging from his boom box. Second baseman Chuck Pfeiffer read the Bible; Eric Lavalle, Toronto James, and Bobby Davis finished a game of Cutthroat, one eye on the TV monitor showing sexy music videos on BET.

Jason closed his eyes and took a deep breath. How was he going to get through this lineup? They were hitters coming to a hitters' park at a time of year when Yankees became as invincible as gods. It was the sixth game of the World Series. A Yankee could smell the ink drying on the winners' checks.

Skeedy hurried across the clubhouse and laid his beefy hand on Jason's shoulder. "You have a phone call." Jason looked up, surprised to be interrupted. He saw anxiety haunting Skeedy's eyes. "It's your son."

Jason followed Skeedy to his office with the large window looking out into the clubhouse. Posters of all-time Colorado greats graced the wall, along with the one Rockies' pennant and photos of old Zephyr teams. A button on his multi-line phone blinked. "Line two," Skeedy said, watching him anxiously.

"It's OK, Skeedy," Jason said, indicating he'd like to be left alone.

He picked up the receiver with numbed detachment. The last time he had talked to Rafe six years before hadn't exactly made *The World's Most Touching Father-Son Moments,* when Rafe said he hated him.

Jason held the receiver up to his ear and stared at the flashing light, half-expecting it to blink off before he pressed it — and half hoping it would. The distance between them, for years the source of so much pain in his life, had developed into a margin of comfort. This was too sudden, too real. Rafe would be fourteen now. What was he like? Why was he calling?

He took a deep breath and pressed the flashing button.

"Hello … Rafe?"

"Hi Dad." It didn't sound like his child's voice. He could hear other people in the background, talking loudly in an enclosed space.

He didn't know what to say. "Where are you?" he finally asked.

"San Francisco," Rafe replied. "I just wanted to wish you good luck. I hope you beat the Yankees. Everybody here's rooting for you."

"Thanks, Buddy." Then he heard another voice, urging Rafe to "wrap it up."

"Rafe — wait!" He turned and saw half a dozen faces watching him from the clubhouse. He knew what they were thinking — it was roll-back-the-clock-and-lose-his-nerve time. Maybe so. Even he didn't know what was going on. His son, calling *him*.

"Why don't you fly out for the game tomorrow? It's the World Series —"

"I gotta go, Dad. Can you save me a ball or something?"

"Rafe, what's going on? Where are you?"

"Fuck the Yankees!" Rafe shouted. And the line went dead.

IT WAS a cool clear night, 51 degrees at game time with the sky a solid arch of indigo blue. As soon as he stepped on the field he could feel something was different, and it wasn't just the force of 54,447 fans waiting for the game to start. Why had Rafe called after all these years? It was the World Series, of course — how many kids had dads pitching in the World Series? He saw a camera focused on him, silently prying. What would they see, he wondered? What did it all mean?

Then the game began, and he entered what athletes called "the Zone." He didn't remember a thing about the first six innings. It was like playing catch with Wells — he threw what he was told, exactly where Wells held his glove. When he watched the video later he saw a man wearing his number mowing down Yankee after Yankee in one of the most efficient World Series games in history. He took a no-hitter —

and a 1-0 lead — into the seventh inning. Then Larry Manouso banged a lead-off double off the right field wall and the fans rose for a standing ovation. It was like waking from a dream. He walked off the back of the mound and rubbed up a new ball, glancing over to Section 128, Row G, seat 9, directly behind the Rockies' dugout. When he'd first arrived in Denver he had bought a season ticket for that seat, planning for Rafe to be there at least half the games. He used to tip his cap to the seat at the beginning of every game. Then after the season, he let it go. Rafe had never come — not once — and never would until his Dad returned to San Francisco and faced the courts for his outburst at Vicki's. He never had. Cast as the villain, Jason assumed the villain would never win so he never tried. And by leaving it that way, he had given his ex-spouse the ultimate rationale to say to Rafe, "see, he doesn't love you," even if it wasn't true. He loved him too much.

Sitting in Rafe's seat today was a gangly girl with long brown hair and a Rockies windbreaker, maybe twelve years old. Jason stared at her and their eyes met. She broke into a smile and turned excitedly to her father. "Go JT!" she shouted, the stadium lights gleaming like sparklers off the braces on her teeth. The people in her box, some of whom knew the story of her seat, picked up the chant, "Go JT! GoJT!" Soon the whole section, then most of the packed stadium was shouting, "Go JT! Go JT! Go JT!"

He stepped back to the pitching rubber and stared in for the sign. He knew what it was without looking — cleanup hitter, runner on second, one run game — intentional walk. He tossed four outside pitches to Wells, his second walk of the day. Two men on, the go-ahead runner on first, nobody out. He watched their number five hitter dig in and thought again about the call from Rafe. "I just wanted to wish you good luck." The casualness of it heartened him. They could just pick up where they left off. There wouldn't have to be any wrenching soul-searching. What a surprise … what a gift!

He stared in for the signal, then went into his stretch. Everything was going to be alright. Which was only his point of view, of course; Juan Altasierra, the Yankees' batter, had his. He fouled off two sliders trying to bunt, then worked the count to 3-2. Now Jason had to come in; he couldn't walk the tying run over to third with nobody out.

Suddenly he felt the possibility of the whole game coming undone. Julio Marrero trotted over from third. "Get it to me, great. Otherwise Big Cat's waiting." He nodded towards Toronto James at first. Jason appreciated the break. Most times the mound felt like a fortress that only he was expected to defend, which most times he felt perfectly capable of doing. Other times — like now — it felt like a desert island.

What happened next would become part of World Series lore, filling highlight reels and the memories of people who never even saw the game. The Yankees sent the runners on the 3-2 pitch. Altasierra got a fastball on the outside part of the plate and drove it over the hole between third and shortstop where no one should have been. But to protect their one-run lead, the Rockies were still playing for the bunt and a force out at third. On his way to cover third, shortstop Eric Lavalle threw up his arm and the ball found his glove, spinning him around face-to-face with the runner heading to third. He tagged him and fired a perfect throw to second baseman Chuck Metheney covering first, doubling up the runner and completing the first World Series triple play since 1920.

It wasn't the end of the game, but it felt like it. The stadium, the city, baseball fans in a dozen nations celebrated the speed, improbability and finality of the feat. Jason pitched a 1-2-3 eighth, then the Rockies scored an insurance run in their half. But when Jason gave up a walk to open the ninth, Joe McNamara walked slowly out to the mound. Wells, Lavalle, Metheney, Marrero and Toronto James joined him.

The manager put a hand on Jason's shoulder. "You've brought us to the Promised Land."

"But like Moses, I won't be entering."

McNamara shook his head. "Moses didn't pitch a one-hit shutout."

His teammates whacked him on the butt as the manager signaled for their closer, Gil Petrajic. But when McNamara reached for the ball, Jason squeezed it inside his mitt.

"Get him a new one, Mac. I got plans for this one."

THE FOG swept across the roadway, misting the tinted windows of the rented Cadillac. Jason pulled off Portola Boulevard and checked the San Francisco street guide: so this *was* it. He looked up at the row of reinforced windows in the Youth Guidance Center and wondered which one was Rafe's.

My God, he thought, how did it come to this?

A tired, white-haired man in a security uniform waved Jason through the metal detector, then pointed down a dimly lighted corridor.

"Through the double doors to the left." He found seven or eight men in brown uniforms, milling around a guard station. "I'm here to see Raphael Repetto," Jason said quietly. Several of the guards looked at one another. A heavy-set young man with a small gold earring spoke up. "Good game the other night," he said. "We were pulling for you — National League and all." Jason glanced from face to face. Angry, insecure men who spent their lives pushing kids around. Had any of them ever hit Rafe? Had they tried to help him? Though who was he to judge — what had he done to help his son these past six years?

"Thanks," he said. Several guards lingered, hoping for some manly banter. Another guard pushed a clipboard towards him. "Fill this out," he said. "We'll need to see your driver's license too." He examined the contents of the plastic bag Jason brought. *The Rolling Stone History of Rock and Roll*, the most recent issues of Sports Illustrated, Baseball Digest and Baseball Magazine, a Colorado Rockies sweatshirt — and the baseball from Game 6, signed by the entire team. The guard put everything back in the bag except the baseball.

"You can pick this up on your way out."

"That's for my son. It's from the Series." The other guards glanced at the ball, then up at Jason. The one clearly in charge didn't flinch. "Not allowed," he said. "It could be used as a weapon."

Jason grimaced and took the bag. It was supervised visits all over again, only this time Rafe was the bad guy. He followed a guard into an octagonal room with plastic straight-back chairs against the walls. Along one wall was a low table set up with a Day of the Dead altar — sugar skulls, photos of relatives and offerings of corn, beans and M&M's scattered among them. It was nearly 7:30 PM. Visiting hours were over at eight. A young, heavy-set Latina with a tiny girl dressed up in a red and white frilly dress sat with a sulking teenage boy. An elderly, well-dressed black woman sat alone with her hands folded on her lap. Jason took a seat and glanced around self-consciously. This wasn't really happening. He wasn't really sitting in jail waiting to see the son he had once raised, the son he had fought for, the son he had loved more than anything in the world. Yesterday he was front and center on the world's stage, signing autographs for legions of fans. Today he was filling out security forms to visit a juvenile delinquent.

He watched as a guard escorted in a tall teenager with light, short-cropped hair. He wore a gold earring in the shape of a cross in his left ear, a sagging green jumpsuit and tattered white sneakers. His shoulders were slumped, a wary, distrustful expression on his face. Rafe stopped and looked across the room. He couldn't miss the disapproval on his father's face. The guard plowed into Rafe from behind. "C'mon, Repetto!" he snarled, shoving Rafe forward. Jason rose, uncertain what to do.

"You got twenty-five minutes," the guard said, and closed the door behind him.

Rafe nodded quickly at his father. "You pitched awesome."

"You saw the game?"

Rafe nodded. "They should have saved you. You would have won Game Seven easy."

"Not without runs," Jason replied, recalling the painful 4-0 loss in Game Seven, the feeling of helplessness watching from the bench. But this felt much worse. He never imagined it would be this difficult. His fantasies about reuniting always had them smiling and hugging and confiding things closest to their hearts. But he didn't want to know what was in Rafe's heart. There was something toxic and off-putting about him, like kids he saw on street corners in Denver and Chicago and LA — aimless, angry kids he wanted to kick in the ass and shout, 'Why aren't you in school? Why aren't you at least *trying* to make something of your life?'

He smiled anyway. He had to see it through for twenty minutes at least. He held out the bag. "They took the ball I brought you," he said apologetically. "They're pretty strict about what they allow."

"They're assholes," Rafe said. He set the bag on the floor without looking at it. He wanted to be appreciative but looking at his father — the tanned, self-assured face, the expression of superiority, the clear desire to be somewhere else — only depressed him.

"I guess this isn't very easy for either one of us," Jason said.

"Yeah," Rafe replied sardonically. "Except you get to leave."

"Why didn't you call me? Why didn't you let me know?"

"What difference would it make? You never wrote or anything."

Jason stared, incredulous. "I called a hundred times and nobody picked up the phone. I came to the house and you wouldn't answer the door."

It was Rafe's turn to stare with disbelief. The gap between what his father was saying and what his mother told him was too big to get his mind around. His father didn't love him, she said. His father was too busy to care. His father was selfish and self-centered and thought only

142

about baseball and money.

"The last time I saw you, you were hanging from the side of the house like a madman." Rafe made a face like a man being hanged, his head to one side, tongue lolling. "Mom said we were lucky we weren't killed —"

"I never hurt you," Jason said firmly. "I couldn't possibly be as bad as your mother made me out to be. She hated me so much she didn't care about the consequences — for anyone."

Rafe looked at him with unmistakable contempt. He was supposed to believe that his father, a major league baseball player making more than $10 million a year was helpless in the face of his mother — the same woman he'd stood up to himself! "Just tell her she's full of shit!" he exploded. "You just let her beat you like that, without even fighting?"

Jason studied him — the broad shoulders, the prominent forehead, the strong, big-knuckled hands — unmistakably his son. Except his son was only eight-years old, bright-eyed, trusting and sweet, in love with his father and the world. This was someone altogether different. He glanced at the clock. How could he explain this in fourteen minutes? He grabbed a chair, intending to slide it closer but it was bolted to the floor. He leaned towards Rafe. Somehow it had become a contest between him and Vicki again, something he neither expected nor wanted. "What your mother and I did had nothing to do with you. It was a mistake, a huge mistake."

"What was a mistake?"

"The way we handled ourselves. The way we handled the divorce. Your mother made things so unpleasant it seemed the best thing ... all I wanted to do was get out of there." Rafe shook his head. Jason despaired of ever being able to explain the corrosive, unclean feeling of knowing that someone in the world — someone he'd had a child with — hated him with her whole being. He had chosen to not be around someone who hated him that much. But the price he'd paid now sat in front of him — a sullen, angry kid with a bad haircut and a faded prison jump suit. His son.

"You were gone six years," Rafe said.

"I'm here now. All we can do is move on and try to make things better." He looked hopefully at Rafe. "We can do that, can't we?"

Rafe shrugged. "Why not? I mean, you just signed a forty-two million dollar contract — that could make things better."

"Money seems like the least of your worries."

"You owe me, man. You're my father!"

If this were someone else's child, it would be tragic, but all Jason could feel was shame. He pulled four twenty dollar bills out of his wallet. "I'll send you more when I get home." Rafe looked at the bills without expression, then stuffed them into his jumpsuit. The din of the Youth Guidance Center was growing louder as families rose to say their good-byes. Guards moved towards the reinforced doors, signaling the end of visiting hours. Rafe's eyes suddenly darkened with fear.

"You've got to get me out of here," he whispered urgently.

"How am I supposed do that?"

"I could live with you. They'd let me out for that."

"Who told you that?"

"You're a star! They'd go for it for sure."

Jason smiled nervously. "That's between you and your mother. She calls the shots until you're eighteen."

"You could if you wanted to," Rafe insisted. Jason shook his head. The last thing he wanted was hand-to-hand combat with Vicki again. He had a good life, a busy life. He was the featured guest at a Boys & Girls Club banquet when he returned to Denver. Then he was off to Mexico, to work out with the *Venados* in Mazatlan as he did every winter. Then, Spring Training. "We'll talk about it when we have more time."

Rafe scoffed. Talk — that was all his father was good for: I'll always love you. I'll always be there. Let's move on and make things better. I'll never leave.

"Mom's right. You don't give a shit about anybody."

"No she's not," Jason shot back. But before they could discuss it, the guards were in the room. The other inmates slouched towards the door, Rafe following with his head down. Jason wanted to call out something, but he didn't have the faintest idea what.

THE FIRST call came at the end of January. Liliana was putting the kids to bed, he and Willie were on the patio behind the house, drinking lemonade. "*Ya-sone*," Liliana called from an upstairs window. "*Una llamada de teléfono — es la madre de Raphael.*"

He took it on the Herrera's kitchen phone, dreading every implication of the call. Vicki would never call with good news. The last time they had talked was after he had discovered Rafe was in jail, and he confronted Vicki about keeping something so monumentally important from him. It went downhill from there. It was his fault for leaving; it was her fault for driving him away. They both felt like failures, and it was essential that the other take the blame.

He picked up the receiver. "What can I do for you?" he asked coldly.

"We need to talk about Rafe."

We needed to do that ten years ago, he thought. But something about her voice made him not say it. "What's going on?"

"I don't know what to do, Jason. I don't know whether it's me or Rafe or you —"

"What do you mean me? How can it be me —?"

"—that's setting him off."

"—when I'm not even there."

"Jason, please. Just *listen* for a minute." Rather than angry, Vicki sounded frightened. "He got out of Juvenile Hall last Sunday. I took him to Macy's for some new clothes and he shoplifted a shirt right in front of me! He called me a bitch when I made him take it back. On Tuesday I found out he flunked both of the courses he took at Juvenile Hall. He's going to have to repeat them —"

"And this is my fault?"

Jason waited for the sound of the click, for Vicki to hang up. That's the way they had always done it before. To his great surprise, she was still on the line and obviously fighting back tears. "I don't know where else to turn. Some nights he doesn't even come home. I don't know where he is, I'm worried out of my mind."

"I didn't know things had gotten this bad."

"He says he wants to come and live with *you*," Vicki said exasperatedly. "He says he wants to be a baseball player," she added with some disbelief. "Maybe that's the right thing, I don't know. I don't know what to do anymore."

Jason stared out the window into the dark Mexican night. He recalled the slouched, angry young man posing as his son in Juvenile Hall. The old feelings of anger and shame rose inside him again. Why had Vicki pushed him away? Why had he let her? He wanted to see her pay for what she had done to him, but who would really pay?

Then suddenly he realized what she was saying. This call was clearly a white flag and a cry for help, and he feared what that could mean: Spring Training started in two weeks. Where would Rafe go to school? Who would take care of him when he was on the road eighty, ninety nights a season? How the hell was he supposed to raise a teenager by himself? "I don't know either," he said numbly. "Can't you handle this until the season is over?"

"No," she said. "I'm scared, Jason. One more offense and he goes back to jail."

A stillness came over the line. They were all that Rafe had, and until now it clearly hadn't been enough. They both knew that the situation called for them to do something completely different to save their son; both of them were still convinced it was the other one who should start.

"I don't know what he's like. I haven't even *seen* him in six years, except in jail."

"I don't know him anymore either," Vicki replied, clearly saddened. "I think I'm in way over my head."

Jason feared that he was about to go in way over his head too. The pressure of his new contract and his son's need collided in his heart. He started to retreat into the familiarity of anger. "This is so unfair, Vicki. I tried for so many years and now —"

He felt a tug at the bottom of his t-shirt. "*Tio Ya-sone.*" He turned and looked into the eyes of little Ana, eight years old now and wearing the pink Powerpuff Girls pajamas Jason had brought from Denver. She squeezed him around the waist. "You forgot to say goodnight."

Jason hugged her back and kissed the top of her head. "*Buenas noches,* sweet one," he said, then shooshed her upstairs.

Vicki sighed. "I'm sorry to disrupt your life like this."

"No, don't worry," he said quickly. "He's our son, we have to do something." Neither of them had used the word 'we' since before the divorce. Another silence settled in, this time filled more with promise than pain.

"Do you really think this will work?" he asked.

ONE THURSDAY night after the first home stand he was making love with an avid Rockies fan when the front buzzer sounded. "Excuse me, gorgeous," Jason said, disengaging himself. He wrapped himself in his white bathrobe with the Rockies insignia and strode to the front door. "This better be good!" he said, jerking it open.

Rafe was wearing black slacks about four sizes too large and a t-shirt that depicted a skateboarder swirling around the edge of a toilet bowl. His hair was still close-cropped, the crucifix still in his left ear, his skin still had the sickly indoor glow of a prisoner. He carried an ugly green duffel bag over his shoulder.

He stared at Rafe and sincerely tried to conjure some feeling of happiness or at least appreciation, but it wouldn't come. This kid didn't look like his son. He didn't even have the same name. Jason heard a door closing behind him — the sound of his bachelor life walking out.

"You weren't supposed to be here until next week."

"I had to get out of there," Rafe said, brushing past him.

JASON WOKE in the middle of the night and heard the TV in the living room. He had set up Rafe there after reluctantly seeing his date-of-the-night off. Then the next thing he knew, his alarm went off. He ate breakfast, read the paper, showered, dressed and made three phone calls and Rafe never stirred. Before he left he walked through the living room one last time. Rafe was sleeping with his right leg, smooth and unmuscled, hanging off the edge of the couch. He remembered when Rafe was little, he would adjust his blankets and watch him sleep and smile with joy. Staring at his gape-mouthed teenager crashed on his couch, all he could think of was running.

Rafe. We're playing the Cubs at 1 and you're welcome to come. Call a cab (777-1919) and tell him "Hi Corbett Field." If not I'll be back by 6.

He put a house key on top of the note along with a twenty dollar bill. He picked up Rafe's airline ticket. 'Raphael Repetto. San Francisco to Tucson. One Way.'

That night he drove them to his favorite restaurant in Tucson. Rafe stared out the window as they exited at New Mission Road, cruising past new car lots and a field full of cemetery stones for sale. He wore his standard black garb, and a Rockies "National League Champions" hat backwards on his head. At one point Jason shot a panicked glance his way. What would they talk about? How would they get started?

The parking lot of Emiliano's was packed with battered, dusty pickups and old Japanese cars held together with wire and prayers. Inside, horn-laden *corridos* and *baladas* blasted from the jukebox. Though it was mid-March, strings of Christmas lights criss-crossed the low-ceilinged restaurant. As friends of Willie, they were seated in a prime booth at the front, beneath the mural of the Mazatlan waterfront — white sand, palm trees, thatched *palapas*, the furl of Pacific waves. The restaurant's namesake, a slim, mustachioed man in his late-thirties, hurried over with menus.

"*Es tu hijo?*" Emiliano asked excitedly, smiling at Rafe. Jason nodded, putting his hand on Rafe's shoulder. "This is my son, Raphael," he smiled.

Rafe shook Emiliano's hand with surprise. He thought they were going someplace fancy where he'd be completely out of place. Instead, he felt instantly at home. "Emiliano's everybody's friend," Jason explained. "He takes care of people."

Rafe noticed patrons looking their way, smiling and pointing at his father. "You're famous!" Rafe said proudly.

"I come here a lot," Jason replied, though clearly pleased that his son was impressed. They sat across from each other at the formica table and studied their menus. Jason glanced from time to time at Rafe, hoping to see into the mind of the fifteen-year old. The only thing he had to go on was his own experience of being fifteen, which didn't offer many clues. He couldn't remember what he had wanted his father to be like, other than there. But if he had been there, what would they have talked about?

"It's good to see you," he finally said. "I'm glad you're here."

Rafe didn't look up. "What's a *chimichanga?*" he asked.

"Order one. If you don't like it you can get something else."

"Really?"

"Sure. Go ahead."

Layers of music and chatter filled the room. Rafe ordered *chimichangas,* along with *quesadillas,* guacamole and chips, and a vanilla Coke. Jason ordered *chile colorado* and a pineapple *licuado.*

"Your mother tells me you want to be a baseball player," Jason began.

"You guys talked?"

"Of course we talked," Jason replied, though he wished that Vicki hadn't told him as much as she had. Knowing how far off the tracks Rafe had strayed was heart-breaking. He didn't know who to be mad at more, Vicki or Rafe — or himself. "I think we need to put the past behind us and focus on where we're going," he said hopefully. Rafe nodded, then smiled as Emiliano's pretty twelve-year-old daughter Regina brought their drinks and set a platter of tortilla chips, salsa and guacamole on the table. Rafe hungrily began stuffing chips in his mouth as Jason watched, feeling the full weight of what he was confronting: the responsibility — no, the opportunity — of providing his son with a father. It suddenly became clear to him that he and only he could save him. Wasn't that why Rafe was there?

"You know, this isn't going to be easy," Jason said.

"What's not going to be easy?"

"I've got a hundred and sixty-two games to play, half of them on the road. Even when I'm here I've got to be at the ballpark for ten or eleven hours a day. I'm going to need you to step up to the plate and take some responsibility."

Rafe nodded. "I can come to some of the games. Or watch you on TV."

A spark lit between them and fanned into smiles. Neither one knew what to say about it, but the fact that they were comfortable saying nothing was some kind of affirmation all to itself.

Their dinners arrived, along with another vanilla Coke for Rafe. "So what's a *chimichanga*?" Jason asked.

Rafe picked at the large cylinder on the bed of rice, buried beneath a blanket of red sauce and cheese. "Like a burrito, but it's fried or something."

"You don't have to eat it."

Rafe looked at him distrustfully. "Mom makes me eat everything on my plate."

"Your mom's not here."

Rafe's eyebrows rose. "Can I still get dessert?"

Jason laughed. "If you eat everything else."

As they ate, Emiliano removed his apron and hauled a classical bass into the center of the dining room. His eight-year-old son, Eric, hung a guitar nearly as big as himself around his shoulder. Regina hurried to finish serving a table and joined them to the opening strains of *El Canto de las Palomas*. Rafe paused in mid-chew as Regina sang the mournful *corrido* in a sweet, pure, innocent voice that brought everything in the restaurant to a stop.

"When my papa comes back from the campo, he smells of sweet oranges and love; when we sleep under stars in the desert, we wake each morning with the doves."

Watching Rafe, Jason suddenly felt like crying. The lights, the music, the warmth — the presence of his son — filled him with an unfamiliar sense of completeness. Emiliano's family played two more songs and the patrons erupted into applause. Jason left two twenties for their $26 check and waved goodnight to Emiliano. Outside, it was pitch dark. A broad swatch of stars swept across the moonless desert sky. Rafe climbed into the suv and leaned back against the seat. Jason started up the car and headed back up New Mission Road towards the lights of downtown Tucson.

"I thought we were going to have dessert," Rafe complained.

"You like ice cream?"

"Yeah."

"There's a great ice cream place on the way home. That work for you?"

"Yeah."

WHEN CAMP broke, McNamara let him go back to Denver to set up Rafe for school. They spent the afternoon getting the house in order and settling Rafe into Willie's old room. Willie was renting a single room in a house near Coors Field and had left behind his stationary bicycle, some sealed cardboard boxes, a set of free weights and a *piñata* in the shape of a burro.

On his second trip to the garage with Willie's stuff, Rafe noticed the entire back wall lined with unpainted plywood cabinets. He opened the first one and found the shelves already full of boxes, each one marked "Rafe" in the upper right hand corner with a black felt-tip pen. He took down a box and unfolded the flaps. Inside was an Easter Bunny coloring book, half-finished, a children's astronomy book, a kaleidoscope, Chutes and Ladders, Candy Land, a sheaf of drawings he had done in second grade, a jar full of marbles, a bag of plastic insects, and picture frames made from hand-painted popsicle sticks. He took down another box and found Blueberry, his stuffed blue whale, and a dozen other animals he had shared his bed with at his father's house. In another box were Legos, electric race cars, plastic dinosaurs, an indoor miniature golf game, his Game Boy. Another box held the children's books his father had collected, including his much-turned copy of *Treasure Island*. Another held a collection of framed photos of himself — flying a kite at Crissy Field, celebrating his birthday at PacBell Park … him and his dad with their arms around each other, standing in front of the South Beach Marina.

And there was Charlie. He snapped open the spring-loaded clasps and the smell of polished wood rose like perfume from the velvet-lined case. Charlie — that's what he had named the cello his father had given him — Charlie the Cello. Charlie was the closest thing to a best friend he'd had for a long time. Charlie had come back and forth between his mom's house and his dad's. Charlie was something both his parents liked — but ultimately that didn't matter either. He had left Charlie out for the garbage man one morning, but somehow he had ended up here.

He stared, dumbfounded, then took down another box with his name. It was filled to the top with neatly wrapped packages, addressed to him. He took out the top three or four. Further down were stacks of envelopes addressed to him, all of them stamped and unopened. He tore one open and found a handmade birthday card with the number nine drawn with a red marker pen. "9 Reasons Why I Love You." He opened the card and a fifty dollar bill fell out. "1," it said, in bright red marker: "You're a great artist; 2: You're a great cook; 3: You're a great musician; 4: You're a great comedian; 5: You're a great runner; 6: You're a great student; 7: You're a great friend; 8: You're a great bike rider; 9: You're a great son. Happy Birthday, Love Dad."

He opened one of the packages and found, wrapped in tissue, an illustrated edition of *The Count of Monte Cristo,* inscribed, "Merry Christmas Rafe, Love, Dad." Another package contained a boxed set of John R. Tunis's youth baseball series, another a Game Boy Advance with Major League Baseball action. Another contained CDs from the Classical Young Masters competition in Prague, and a card containing a hundred dollars.

He didn't hear his father come down the stairs. Jason stopped, a look of concern on his face. He had almost forgotten about these boxes, packed away so long ago.

"I guess I knew you'd be back," Jason said quietly.

Rafe turned, his face pinched with confusion. "Why are these *here*?" He held up an envelope that had never been mailed. Jason rummaged through the packages and found one with its stamps cancelled, an index finger pointing to the return address. *Addressee Unknown … Return to Sender.* Looking at them brought back the anger, the remorse … the shame.

"Your mother sent them back." He looked at the pile, not believing it himself. "I just stopped sending them. I didn't see what good it did."

"Why did she do that?"

"You'll have to ask her." He sat down beside Rafe. He had never realized that nearly all the cabinets were filled with Rafe's stuff. It was all out now and something about it made him afraid. The connection between who they used to be and who they were now was present somehow in this confusion spread across the garage floor.

Rafe resumed picking through the boxes: a folder of drawings he had done — a smiling round face with a baseball cap and the caption, "Dada." A tree, a flower, a smiling sun; a small square of white paper with a single red heart pasted on it and the words, "I love you Dada." A tiger confronting a little boy who says defiantly, "This is not my tiger!" Jason watched, wondering what was going through Rafe's mind, wanting to reach out and hug him.

Suddenly Rafe stood. "Where's your phone?" Jason handed him his cell phone. Rafe dialed quickly and ascended the stairs two at a time.

"Why did you send all these things back to Dad? Those were my things!"

"Rafe?" Vicki said in surprise. They'd talked only once since he'd left San Francisco, a brief conversation of hellos and uncomfortable lulls. "I'm in the middle of dinner, can I call you back?"

"I found all these cards and presents that Dad sent to me when I was a kid — dozens of them. Birthday stuff, Christmas presents ... why did you send them back? What's that all about?"

There was a pause before Vicki spoke. "You were so upset when he left. I did it to protect you —"

"Those are my things!"

"I know that, Rafe. But there was a lot more going on than what you know about. You were devastated. I was trying to keep you from —"

"They were addressed to me!"

"I didn't know what to do, Rafe, so I —"

He threw the phone as hard as he could against the wall, pushing an indentation in the plaster board of the living room. After a moment, Jason appeared. He picked up the phone and flipped it open. "Still working — score one for AT&T." He started across the room and stopped when he saw the tears in Rafe's eyes. "People do things wrong sometimes even when they think what they're doing is right. All you can do is stop doing the wrong things and make up for them somehow."

Rafe wiped his eyes. "Why did you leave San Francisco?"

"I was traded. Everybody's traded at some point in his career."

"Mickey Mantle wasn't traded."

"Those were different times. He was a superstar. I'm not a superstar."

"You pitched in the World Series!"

"Hey, I could get traded tomorrow. But the big difference is, this time I get to take you with me."

THE NEXT morning his father was gone — the Rockies opened the season in Houston. Rafe walked the route they had practiced the day before, and arrived alone at his new school. Everett F. Stokes High School was a dark, neo-classical structure built in 1962 and gone to seed. An equestrian statue of Don Quixote at the center of a long semi-circular drive, marred with graffiti, had its placard altered to read, "Don Corleone." Rafe lingered alone on the sidewalk, then merged at the bell with the stream of mostly African-American, Chicano and Southeast Asian kids crowding through the front door.

The morning was a blur. The steam heat from the old radiators made it feel as if someone was holding a dusty rag over his face. Lunch time was even worse. Tables were lined up in rows in the old gymnasium; the high windows and dingy light reminded him of Juvenile Hall. He escaped to a bench outside, alongside the asphalt schoolyard. The snow-capped peaks of the Rockies loomed in the distance, a bank of gray clouds boiling above them. Everything seemed so different — the light, the weather, the air. He worried that he had made a mistake coming here. His father was gone but what could he do — go live with his mom again? That wasn't an option he wanted to exercise.

He took his lunch out of his bag — a roast beef sandwich he had bought on the way to school, a bag of chips, an apple — but didn't touch it. The other kids spilled from the gymnasium, taunting, teasing, tossing balls. They passed him as if he weren't there, which he wished he weren't, except he couldn't figure out where else he wanted to be.

AT HOME everything was different too, including the smells. Instead of barbecue, on his first afternoon back from school the house had the dense, steamy odor of a locker room. Two large chickens were boiling in a pot, along with potatoes, carrots, celery and onions. A squat, heavy-set woman with short brown hair and a broad, plain face smiled as Rafe walked in. "I hope you are hungry," she said brightly. "I'm making *caldo de pollo,* a typical *plato colombiano!*"

His father had hired the middle-aged Colombian to stay at the house when he was on the road, and to cook and clean on game days.

Teresa Otero had raised five children of her own and had no interest in life except children. Jason thought she would be perfect for Rafe, who had been inordinately fond of the Nicaraguan woman he had hired to baby-sit in San Francisco. He figured this would work out just as well: in his book, a teenager was simply a larger version of a kid.

Rafe opened the refrigerator and stared inside. Mrs. Otero had bought enough food for a family of six, but Rafe recognized almost none of it. He pulled out a row of attached plastic tubs filled with bright yellow, green and red gels. "What's this stuff?"

"Dessert," she said. "*Pastel de cereza!*"

He tore open one of the foil tops and stuck in a finger. It had the consistency of pudding and tasted like a Slurpee. He grabbed a spoon from the drawer and slouched upstairs. He threw his backpack on the floor of his room, flipped on his CD player and stood at the window eating the goo as the room trembled with the relentless staccato laments of Eminem. A half hour later Mrs. Otero called him from downstairs, but Eminen drowned her out. She climbed the stairs and knocked on the frame of his open door. "Dinner is ready!"

He sat at his desk in the twilight, nodding to the harsh lyrics. "I'm not hungry."

"You have to eat something." Rafe ignored her. "It's a *comida especial,*" she pleaded. "My children love it." Rafe continued to ignore her, and she left.

Around eight o'clock the phone rang. Rafe knew it was his dad. He had called last night at this time, and the night before. He picked it up before Mrs. Otero could.

"Hello."

"Hey Buddy," Jason said. "How's school going — any better?"

"Yeah," Rafe said.

"Yeah? You makin' some friends?"

"Yeah."

"That's great," Jason said. "How's everything going with Mrs. Otero?"

"Good."

Jason had lost sleep obsessing what to do with Rafe while he was on the road. The fact that they opened with a ten day trip — Houston, St. Louis, Chicago — didn't help. He was ecstatic when he found Mrs. Otero — and even happier to hear that Rafe was taking to her.

"What'd you have for dinner?"

"Some kind of chicken thing."

"That's great. You got homework? You getting your homework done?"

"I'm doin' it right now."

"Thataboy."

Rafe gripped the phone tightly in his hand. He missed his father but didn't know how to say it. He wanted to ask him to come home but he didn't want to ask him that, it was way too dangerous. The last time he had missed him like this he hadn't come back for six years. He thought it would be different, coming to live with him, but it wasn't working out the way he had planned. Spring Training in Tucson was all baseball, all the time. Jason said he would try to get home but he never did until nine-thirty or ten, when Rafe was deep into his music and resentful that his father had spent the whole day doing something other than being with him. The night at Emiliano's was nice, and their first night in Denver. But that was it. Now it was just phone calls. It was happening again.

After a painful silence, Jason said cheerfully, "OK Buddy, keep up the good work. I'll call you when I get to St. Louis."

"OK," Rafe said, and hung up.

The next day was the same, and the next, right on through the weekend. On Monday morning Rafe went through the garage and took fifty dollars from one of the envelopes with his name on it. It wasn't difficult finding the guys with drugs. They hung behind the gas station near the northwest corner of campus, where they managed to ingest an array of illegal substances a few yards beyond school boundaries. For weed, Rafe was steered to a short, floppy-haired kid called Lo-Jack, who offered three classes of marijuana — super, stratospheric and space station — with corresponding prices. Rafe sprung for an eighth of an ounce of the Stratospheric, a zip-locked trio of dark green buds that smelled like pineapple. Lo-Jack threw in a package of E-Z Wider rolling papers, which Rafe used to roll a pencil-thin joint that transformed his day from schoolhouse blues to Elysian Fields in two inhalations.

"JB's don't usually hang here," Lo-Jack informed him.

"JBs?"

Lo-Jack studied him with jumpy brown eyes. "Jail Birds. Your PO finds out, you're back in Alcatraz, Jack."

"Nobody knows who the fuck I am." Rafe watched as the baseball team ran laps around the far edge of the athletic fields, several dozen kids in matching sweatshirts and hats. It was too late to go out for the team; they were already three weeks into the season. He would learn from his father next year and be better than all these guys.

"Your Dad's on the Rockies, right?"

"What the fuck's it to you?"

"They're on the tube tonight. Wanna watch the game?"

"Where?"

Lo-Jack zippered his backpack and motioned to follow him. They crossed Colfax Boulevard to the edge of a huge parking lot beside the Mt. Airy Mall. "Wait here." Lo-Jack waded into the sea of autos and disappeared. Five minutes later, a Ford Expedition pulled up beside Rafe, by all appearances driverless. The window lowered and Lo-Jack's voice called out — "Get the fuck in!"

Rafe climbed into the huge vehicle and Lo-Jack gunned it onto Colfax. He held up a carton of Marlboros. "There's a case of Corona in back!" Lo-Jack lit up a cigarette and scanned the horizon like a pirate at the helm of his corsair. Rafe watched the landscape go by, row upon row of suburban homes, the streets empty of all visible life. He had assumed that Lo-Jack's name was for his small stature. But he discovered it was for his daily practice of visiting one of the area's many malls, and borrowing a car for the afternoon. "I love these fucking things," he said, peering over the wheel of the Expedition. "If the cops ever caught me, I'd just roll 'em."

After an uneventful ride into Lakewood, Lo-Jack swung the Expedition into the day-use parking lot of Alameda Park, turned off the engine and left the keys in the ignition. "The owner gets a ticket for leaving the keys!" he laughed. He stuffed the Marlboros into his backpack along with six bottles of Corona, dumped the groceries onto the floor and repacked a bag with frozen pizza, tortilla chips, a six pack of Mountain Dew, Pop Tarts, Honey Nut Cheerios, and a half-gallon of ice cream and thrust it into Rafe's arms. "Follow me."

They cut through the small park to a neighborhood of rundown one-story ranch homes. Lo-Jack's older brother was on the couch in the messy living room making out with a small brunette and completely ignored them as they passed through to Lo-Jack's room. If Rafe had to guess, he would say an adult had not set foot in the room in ten years. It was beyond cool — it was whack. The carpet had disintegrated into what looked like a thin covering of topsoil. The bed, a single mattress on top of a wooden platform, was covered with an oily-looking sleeping bag and pillow that looked like they had been dragged through a coal mine. Candy wrappers, t-shirts, free weights, comic books, plastic toys, empty cigarette packs, soda and beer cans littered the floor. And on a table, rising like an icon above an otherwise destroyed civilization, was a 35-inch television set that turned on like magic as they entered the room. And miraculously, the first image that appeared on the screen was his father.

Lo-Jack noticed the resemblance immediately. "Is that *him?*"

Rafe nodded. It was like watching *Star Trek* and his dad was running the Enterprise. He suddenly realized he had never watched him play when he was loaded. He sat down, transfixed by the televised face he lived with every day — the broad, flat forehead, the piercing green eyes, the intimidating gaze. His father's eyes peered over his glove like a member of a firing squad. 'Hitters sense weakness,' he'd told him. 'I try to convey one thing and one thing only: I'm going to get you.'

"That your Dad?" Lo-Jack asked again.

"I told you, *yeah!*"

His father's next pitch hit the batter squarely in the back. The hitter sprinted towards the mound, but never got there as Rick Wells, the Rockies' catcher, tackled him from behind. His dad watched impassively as the brawl proceeded around him, a shield of players protecting their pitcher who had, under the code of 'hit and be hit,' the announcer explained, retaliated for one of their batters getting plunked earlier.

So that was it, Rafe thought. It was all an act, like pro wrestling. Like saying he was going to be there, then not being there. Even his mother was in on it, sending back his father's cards and presents for years. Things were not what they appeared to be; but what they really were, he had no idea.

Lo-Jack rolled a spliff, lit it and passed it to Rafe — this one for free. It passed between them once when the bedroom door burst open and his brother strode in, grabbed the joint out of Lo-Jack's mouth and left without a word. Calmly, as if nothing had happened, Lo-Jack began rolling another one.

"What's it like, having your dad be a baseball player?"

"I don't know. I don't see him much."

"Me neither. My dad works for the fuckin' railroad." Lo-Jack lit the second joint, this one considerably thicker than the first, and passed it to Rafe. "You must be a pretty good baseball player."

"Not really."

"Why the fuck not?" Lo-Jack asked.

Rafe continued watching the game, the THC making him lighter, dizzier, more numb. He blew a stream of smoke against his father's face on the screen. "What do you know about drivin' a fuckin' railroad?"

Lo-Jack looked at his new friend and shook his head. "You're a trip, man."

They watched the game for another few innings, immobile on Lo-Jack's greasy bed. The Rockies scored two runs in the top of the fifth. It was 3-1 in the seventh when they pulled Jason and brought in Willie Herrera with men on first and third.

"I gotta get going," Rafe said. He was supposed to have been home hours before. His father would call again after the game.

"You can stay here."

Raphael looked around at what could have been the aftermath of nuclear war. "I'll take a raincheck." It took three busses and he didn't get home until after twelve. Mrs. Otero lost control, waving her arms and yelling at him in Spanish. From what he could tell, his father had called and would call again in the morning. She kept talking as he piled cold chicken, roast potatoes and tortilla chips on a plate. For some reason the projection of his father on the television set kept coming back to him, a presence to be seen but not touched. Nothing had changed, he realized. His dad didn't give a shit and neither did his mom, shipping him out here. All he had was this squawking cleaning lady and some new fucked up friends in place of his old fucked up friends in Frisco.

"*Hiciste tu tarea?*" she asked. "*Tu padre quiere que yo te ayude con la tarea.*"

"Yeah yeah," he squawked back. "Take a dumpo, por favor." He climbed the stairs and shut the door to his room.

IT RAINED the second day in Chicago and the next day as well. The forecast was for more rain but the League wanted them to wait until mid-afternoon before letting them leave. The manager instructed everyone to stay in their hotels until a decision was made whether to play or go.

A gray, rain-swollen sky hung over the city. For Jason, it was one of the longest days of his life. He paced in front of the window on the seventh floor of the Lakeside Marriott. Willie flipped through the cable stations, stopping at every Spanish language channel. "Jesus, Willie, what am I going to do? I'm doing everything half-assed."

"You beat the Astros. That wasn't half-assed."

But here he was, sitting out a rainstorm in a hotel room a thousand miles from home, wondering whether his kid was even in school or not. The other night when he called, Mrs. Otero didn't know where Rafe was. He'd called at seven the next morning knowing he'd catch him in bed.

"Where were you last night? We had a deal!"

"I was watching you play the Astros."

"That's where I was — where were *you*?"

"Over at a friend's house."

"What friend?"

"A friend from school."

"What friend from school?" Jason shouted.

"Jesus, Dad, you're not going to know who it is."

Jason had glanced around the generic lobby of the generic hotel, feeling helpless. He *didn't* know any of Rafe's friends. He *didn't* know any of his teachers, what courses he was taking, what his interests were. He had been on the road now for more than a week and it was driving him crazy.

"C'mon, Rafe, you promised me you'd help. All you gotta do is come home after school and do your homework. If you go out, be back by nine o'clock. Is that so hard?"

"No."

"It's either that or you don't go out at all. You hear me?"

"Yeah."

But he wasn't there the next night he called, or the next. "You need a *novia*," Willie counseled.

"I'm not going to find a girlfriend in two weeks," Jason replied. He stared out the window. He had faced batters hitting .400, sluggers with more than 500 home runs, pitched out of late inning jams with the success of an entire season on the line — but he didn't know how to pitch out of this one. Memories of Rafe came to him, his happy boy pedaling his bicycle full speed down the Embarcadero, practicing his cello, reading a book. *That* was his son, not this sullen imposter.

"You get home and kick his ass, he'll come around," Willie counseled.

The league declared a rainout at 5 PM and the team's chartered flight got them to Denver by 9:55. Jason sped home from the airport, wondering what he would do if Rafe wasn't there. Or what would he do if he *was*. A month ago he'd been living the rarefied life of a bachelor ball player, concerned mostly about the break of his slider and passing notes from the bullpen to blondes in the stands. Now he envisioned his son marauding through the streets in a Rocky Mountain remake of West Side Story.

Mrs. Otero was asleep before the gaudy blaze of a Latino variety show. Canned laughter and mariachi music filled the living room. He set down his duffel bag and took the stairs two at a time. Inside Rafe's room was the chaos of a boy's world — papers, books, magazines, CDs, clothes on the floor — but no boy. He thought briefly of searching for drugs, condoms, goth CDs, but he didn't really want to know.

He was on his way down the stairs when the front door opened. He stopped and listened as lids were lifted and lowered on pots, the refrigerator door opened and closed, and heavy, insolent steps thudded down the hallway towards the stairs.

"Get something to eat!" Mrs. Otero called out from the living room.

Rafe started up the stairs. His backpack was slung over his shoulder, a chicken leg in his hand. He stopped when he saw his father looming at the top.

"I thought you were in Chicago."

"I thought you were doing your homework."

"We were watching the game."

"What game?"

"Your game — the Rockies game."

"Let's go," Jason said. "We've got to talk."

THEY SAT on opposite sides of the kitchen table with bowls of Mrs. Otero's *caldo de pollo* in front of them. The house was immaculate, though it felt as unoccupied as when he and Rafe had opened it after spring training. Rafe pushed the chicken and vegetables around the bowl. On the table beside him was a new cell phone and instruction book.

"How did your meeting with your parole officer go?" Jason asked after a long silence.

"Good."

"Probably was from your perspective," Jason said, "seeing you didn't go." Rafe looked up, surprised. "Jefferson called me."

"I didn't have any way to get there."

"Bullshit. I gave you cab money." Rafe looked into his bowl, as if searching for answers. "What did you do instead?" Still, no answer. "Look," Jason continued, doing nothing to disguise his frustration. "You came here because you fucked up in San Francisco and you wanted another chance. But the whole idea of another chance is it's not supposed to look remotely like the ones you just blew. Do you follow me?" Rafe nodded. "You're lying to me. You're lying to your parole officer. You're lying to your teachers and blowing off most of your classes. And this is just the first week of school!"

Jason rose abruptly and yanked open the refrigerator, the bottles in the doorway rattling together. He could see it now — the father who asked for a trade to be with his son, escorting him back to jail. He'd be the laughing stock of America.

He slammed the refrigerator door. "And you reek of marijuana." Rafe's eyes darted. "It's a question of character, Rafe. I know it's hard adjusting to a new school, a new town. I had to do it myself. You can be like every one of those angry fucks you were locked up with — or you can make something out of your life. It's up to you."

Rafe stared at the table. The threat of violence had passed. It was just words, his father listening to himself talk — like The Whopper, like most adults.

"From now on, you come home directly from school. Mrs. Otero will help you with your homework —"

"I didn't come here to live with Mrs. Otero."

Rafe's words singed Jason's heart, but what could he do? There wasn't any time — wouldn't be any time — until the season ended. Didn't this kid appreciate anything? Mothers, fathers everywhere balanced careers and commitments, just like he was. They were there for their kids. He was there ... he was *here*.

"It's the best I can do, Rafe. And I need you to do the best you can. Come home and do your homework, that's all."

"Are we done now?"

"You got something better to do?"

"Yeah."

"What?"

"Homework."

His FATHER met him at the players' gate, larger than life in his Rockies uniform, his spikes scraping like armor on the concrete. "C'mon," Jason said, holding the gate open. "You can meet some of the guys before you get started."

The clubhouse was a wide, soft-carpeted room with dark stained wooden lockers and the smell of medicine, cologne and sweat. Jason stopped beside a man with square, powerful shoulders seated on a stool in front of his locker reading a magazine. "Alex, I'd like you to meet my son, Raphael."

Rightfielder Alex Heredia swung around, smiling broadly. "Great to meet you," he said, offering his hand. "I've heard a lot about you." Rafe shook his hand but couldn't muster a word. They moved on — Eric Lavalle, Chuck Metheney, Rick Wells. He was astonished at how much bigger they were than on TV. They were giants, his father among them. But what did that make him?

Jason led him into Skeedy Olmstead's office. A cluttered desk faced the wall opposite the window that looked into the clubhouse. "When you're finished you can come up and watch the game," Jason said. The plan to do his homework with Mrs. Otero had bombed. Now, every afternoon that Rafe didn't have music club, he was to do his homework at the stadium. Theoretically, it took care of many things. He'd be sure to get his work done, he'd be exposed to the atmosphere of a major league team, and Jason would know where his son was. Theoretically.

Rafe opened his Algebra book to two pages of quadratic equations, the numbers and letters jumbled as if some prankster had arranged them on the page. Players shuffled soundlessly by the clubhouse window like predator fish, huge muscular men returning from whirlpool baths with towels wrapped around them, others getting dressed, listening to music, reading, playing cards. A couple of batboys scurried around oiling gloves, wiping down bats, helmets, shin guards, elbow pads.

Rafe stared earnestly at the page, but the material refused to make sense. What difference did any of this make? How many of these guys knew the value of 'x'? Would it help him learn how to do anything real, like play baseball?

Jason popped in a half hour before game time. "How's it goin?"

"Good."

He peered over Rafe's shoulder. "You haven't done anything!"

"I don't understand this stuff."

Jason rolled his eyes. "C'mon Rafe, what have you been doing in school?" Rafe looked around nervously, certain the other players could hear. He didn't know Skeedy's office was soundproofed.

"Why do I have to do this here?" Rafe asked in a whisper.

"Because you won't do it at home!" He noticed a pile of papers spilling from Rafe's backpack. There was a bulletin about upcoming events at school — an overnight camping trip with parents and students, a concert by the music club, parent-student movie night. There was an application for Eagle Scouts, a flyer about Earth Day activities, a reminder about parent-teacher's conferences in two weeks, a request for chaperones for an upcoming dance. A rush of panic seized him. Who was going to see that all this stuff was taken care of? Plus, Rafe needed a haircut, new shoes, a new jacket ...

"Maybe somebody can help me," Rafe said hopefully.

"This is *your* job," Jason growled. "Start paying attention in class!"

His dad left and Rafe stared at the book for another half hour, then gathered up his things and left. The broad corridor beneath the stands echoed with sounds of the crowd. He wandered for ten minutes before realizing he was lost. He backtracked past a row of unmarked doors, then to huge forty-foot high doors mounted on hinges the length of his arm. "Caution: Sound Alarm Before Opening." He backtracked again and yanked open a metal door. A short set of well-lighted steps led to another door. He found himself in a large, dimly lit room with a huge piece of machinery — a furnace or generator — taking up most of the space. On the opposite wall was a narrow rectangular slit about four feet from the ground. He crossed the room and peered through the opening. No more than sixty feet away was the classic tableau of batter, catcher and umpire, poised in anticipation of the pitch. To the right were the pitcher and the left side of the infield — third base coach, third baseman and shortstop — and the visitors' dugout.

Rafe stooped and pressed his chin against the bottom of the opening. There was the pitch, the flex of the bat, the recoil of the catcher's glove, the umpire turning slowly to his left and signaling "Ball!" Rafe's heart raced. He could smell the dirt on the first baseline, the chalk, the fertilized turf. The little window was for ventilation, perhaps, the line of sight waist high with the batter. The guy up to bat was crouched over the plate, the number 2 stitched on his gold and black Pirate's uniform. He leaned back on his left leg, his body coiled. Rafe had never watched a game this close up. He could see the mechanics of the swing, the powerful turn of hips and shoulders, then WHACK! — the ball flashing low across the right side of the mound and the crowd cheering as the Rockies' second baseman dove into sight, speared the ball in his glove, scrambled to his knees and threw to first. The crowd yelled as the umpire called, "Out!"

Then the next batter stepped in, his hips squarely facing Rafe, legs wide apart, a slow pendulum of warm up swings as he waited for the pitch. It was so beautiful, the field lighted by high white lights, the bright green grass, the power, balance and grace of the hitters, each one as unique as a separate species at the zoo.

He left at the beginning of the eighth inning, marking the door number down before finding his way out of the stadium. He ran most of the two miles home, excited by his discovery. He lay on his bed reading *The Count of Monte Cristo* until he heard the garage door open. He turned off the light and listened to his father's heavy step on the stairs, the cascade of pee in the toilet — then the door of his room opening. He squeezed his eyes shut so tightly they hurt.

"You asleep?" Rafe kept his eyes squeezed shut, fervently hoping his father would leave. He remembered waking several times when they lived together and finding him standing in his room in the dark. It had felt comforting and protective then, maybe what God was like when he appeared to people. This didn't feel like God though. God wouldn't rummage through the papers on his desk. God wouldn't take his algebra workbook and inspect it. He knew there would be a lecture at breakfast tomorrow, and the next day, and the next — until his dad was on another road trip and he was free.

RAFE SCANNED the traffic and saw a silver Mercedes pull into the "NO STOPPING ZONE" directly in front of the main entrance. Lo-Jack stepped out, dressed in baggy black pants and a powder blue t-shirt — Rockies' colors — and strode directly towards him. Rafe turned and pressed the buzzer on the inside of the railed gate.

"Go Rockies!" Lo-Jack cried. Rafe watched anxiously as a cop and a security guard inspected the brazenly-parked Mercedes. The cop leaned over the driver's seat, staring at the keys. Rafe turned and saw Herman Riles, the elderly security guard assigned to the side entrance, smile as he pulled open the gate. "Thanks, Herman," Rafe said.

He led Lo-Jack down the familiar corridor past the clubhouse to a set of doors that led onto the field. Trainers, secretaries, publicists and sportswriters scurried up and down the wide hallway. Lo-Jack grabbed his arm; his eyes had a strange intensity. "I gotta find a bathroom," he said. "Are you stoned?" Rafe asked, but Lo-Jack only laughed. In the bathroom inside the 'Mile High Club' Lo-Jack pushed Rafe into a stall and bolted the door. He pulled a small plastic case from his pocket and held out a pale green capsule. Rafe looked at him questioningly. "Ecstasy," Lo-Jack grinned.

"What's it do?"

"Makes you happy."

"I'm already happy."

"Bullshit," Lo-Jack said. "I mean *happy* happy."

Rafe stared at the capsule. A little happiness wouldn't be a bad thing. The home stand had been a disaster, almost as bad as his dad being away. They saw each other briefly in the morning before school, and a few minutes at the ballpark before he started his homework. As soon as the game began he slipped into the generator room and watched from his ringside window. It was the closest he had ever come to understanding baseball. He could now distinguish a slider from a fastball, mimic the batting stance of every player on the Rockies, and understand the intricate interplay of the hands and shoulders and hips as they turned on a pitch. But the decisive battles of the French and Indian Wars, the geographic highlights of South America, or the principal theme of *Huckleberry Finn,* forget it. Each night his father inspected his homework and got more frustrated. And after tonight's game he was leaving on an eight day swing to California — San Diego and LA. More Mrs. Otero, no father.

He swallowed Lo-Jack's pill. "C'mon, my dad wants to meet you."

But they were too late. Jason had already begun his warm-ups. Larry Birns, Skeedy Olmstead's ancient, sunken-chested assistant, showed them to their seats near the corner of the dugout where they could see most of what went on inside — and vice versa.

"This is so cool!" Lo-Jack exclaimed. "Let's get a couple of brews!"

"Keep it down, will you?" There were two other people in the box — a white-haired man about seventy quietly watching the field, sitting with a man who was clearly his son, reading the *Wall Street Journal.*

"There's your Dad!" Lo-Jack pointed. The older man turned and smiled at them. "His dad's Jason Thibodeaux. Number forty-seven. He's the greatest," Lo-Jack boasted. "One-two-three strikes YER OUT!"

Rafe had never seen Lo-Jack like this. He resonated with motion, even sitting still. Then he felt a shift in his stomach and remembered the capsule he had taken. A strange luminescence appeared at the edge of his vision. He watched as his father finished his warm ups and walked towards the dugout with his game face — gaze straight ahead, shoulders squared. But before reaching the dugout, he detoured to their box. Their eyes locked, and Rafe knew for sure his father could tell he was on drugs.

"Hey Buddy," Jason smiled. "Is this your friend Steve?" Rafe just stared. He had forgotten Lo-Jack's real name. Lo-Jack lunged forward and shook Jason's hand. "Glad to meet you, sir. I'm your biggest fan. Well, not the *tallest* but the biggest, you know what I mean — *grande*, man. I watched you beat the Astros, whamm! It was incredible the way you pitched —"

Jason thrust a ball into Lo-Jack's hand. "Come down after the game and I'll get the guys to sign it." He looked quizzically at Rafe, then vanished down the dugout steps.

"That was so cool!" Lo-Jack sang, brandishing his ball for the others in the box. There were more people with them now — an elderly couple with a boy around six, two guys in their thirties — one talking on his cell phone — a man in his fifties with a pretty woman half his age. The young man not on the cell phone high-fived Lo-Jack. "You got a ball!"

"You get us a couple of beers it's yours," Lo-Jack said. The man started to laugh, then realized Lo-Jack was serious. He shook his head and turned away.

The Ecstasy took over by the third inning. He felt at the center of some kind of force field, as if he were a magnet and everything else a compatible metal. His skin was tingling, his stomach churning, his jaws clenched, his eyes locked on his father like radar to a target. It was incredible to watch, the grace of his powerful body, the flow of the pitch to the plate, the batter pirouetting like a dancer. Why had his mother kept him from this? Had she ever even *been* to a game? Didn't she see the beauty of a ball fielded deep behind third and thrown clear across the diamond on a rope? Didn't she feel the surge of a crowd ignited by a batter swinging through his father's fastball?

He knew now he could play this game. He knew now he could hit against his father. He watched the ball leaving his hand, the seams rolling end-over-end for a fastball, diagonally into a curve, and reversing, like wagon wheels in an old western, for a slider. He could see each pitch come to the plate like a comet, pulling its own parabola.

And he could see there was one Diamondback who had his number, a skinny guy named Craig Counsell. He had a stance unlike any of the ones Rafe studied from his secret window — his body high and straight, his hands above his head like a man ready to lower an ax. It looked incredibly awkward, but the first two times Counsell faced his father he drilled the ball into left-center field for doubles. The first time he died at second; the second time he scored the only Diamondback run.

In the bottom of the fifth Lo-Jack went for hot dogs and sodas. "You alright?" he asked when he returned. "You haven't said a word." Rafe shrugged. Lo-Jack talked enough for both of them, commenting on the plays, the strategy, the girls in section 123, the characters in the dugout, his desire for beer. Rafe felt too strange to talk. He took a bite of the hot dog and watched the Rockies run onto the field for the top of the sixth.

Jason strode out and scraped the area in front of the pitching rubber with his spikes, then looked at the box behind the dugout. His son, finally at a game. All the fighting, all the legal bills, all the anguish and disappointments and there he was, eating a hot dog and sipping a coke, watching his old man play the great American game.

He started the first batter with a curve that dropped over the edge of the plate for a strike. He was on, and his teammates could feel it. They chattered and whistled, the crowd cheered, the vendors shouted. It was baseball on a sunny Sunday afternoon, it didn't get any better than this. The batter bounced to second for an easy out. Jason took a new ball and rubbed it up. He stepped beside the rubber, then glanced again over to the box where his son and his hyperkinetic friend were sitting, but they were gone.

HE CALLED the next night from San Diego and got Rafe's voice mail. "Rafe, the whole purpose of having the cell phone is so we can talk. It's about quarter to ten, your time. Give me a call as soon as you get this."

Rafe never called, and Jason never slept, even after taking a sleeping pill at two and another at four o'clock. He lay awake, rigid with anger. Where the hell was Rafe? Why hadn't he showed up in the clubhouse after the game yesterday? He threw off his covers and slid open the door to the balcony. Willie was splayed on his bed snoring softly, the sleep of a man who had successfully compartmentalized his work and home life as billions of parents did the world over. Jason leaned against the railing and stared at the lights of San Diego's port. The sweet morning breeze off the ocean troubled him for some reason. The world was good, it seemed to be saying, but to him it felt anything but. His son had already been expelled from two schools, arrested three times and jailed, ran away from his mother and was hardly making progress in Denver. What chance did he have of making anything of himself with that kind of foundation?

The first light of day seeped over the city. He thought of calling Vicki, but dismissed it. He knew she would ask for Rafe to come back. And as painful as it was to have him, it would be far more painful to admit that he had failed. But that is exactly what he seemed to be doing.

He slipped back inside and closed the door. He looked at the rumpled bed and despaired of ever sleeping. Then he noticed the hum in the closet — the mini-fridge with its tiny bottles of gin and vodka and scotch, any one of which would help him sleep.

He crawled into bed and covered his head with a pillow. It wasn't unusual to think about drinking. Every bar he passed, every beer he smelled after the game, every shimmering cognac in a restaurant made him think of it — and just as quickly dismiss it. What was uncommon was his absolute conviction that it would be OK to have one, just this once, because he deserved it.

THE AFTERNOON began like all others — blow some weed at the Citco station behind school, a lift to Lo-Jack's house where they copied each other's homework in the chaos of his room. Afterwards they cruised in another loaner to City Park for a rendezvous with the rest of the crew — Sherry Stockler, Diane Buttaglia and one of the strangest kids in their class, Charles Noyes. Noyes was a chemical wizard who had few friends at school except Raphael and Lo-Jack, and that was only because Lo-Jack knew — which no one else did — that Noyes had friends in the chemical industry who manufactured Ecstasy, which he could get for two dollars a hit when everyone else was paying ten.

They dropped at City Park and the Ecstasy came on a half hour later. It was the fourth time Rafe had done it since his messy maiden voyage at Coors Field, where he'd spent the last three innings in the bathroom regurgitating his dog and soda. He was careful since then to not eat anything before or during. Ecstasy was nourishment enough.

They were cruising down Colfax in some obliging salesman's Toyota

Land Cruiser, the back filled with drapery and upholstery samples, when Rafe spied the giant cutout of Don Baylor holding a massive bat on his shoulder. There were about thirty cages, fenced-in rectangles on acres of what just months ago was probably pastureland or winter wheat. The place was deserted except for two people at opposite ends of the complex, bathed in light from towering high intensity lamps.

"Lo-Jack Lo-Jack Lo-Jack we gotta go there," Rafe shouted. Hip hop pulsed from the Cruiser's state-of-the-art sound system, which allowed Lo-Jack to ignore Rafe's request. "Lo-Jack," he cried again, jumping up and down like a five-year-old. "Come on man, pull over."

Lo-Jack swung the wheel and docked the Land Cruiser at the edge of the complex. The ping of a metal bat hitting hard balls rang from the far end. Rafe walked towards the small yellow shack beside the parking lot, with a lighted sign that said, "Twelve swings $3."

He bought two tokens for five dollars, picked out a bat with Isaac Sands's autograph and walked to the cage marked 86 mph. He took a few practice swings to cheers from the Land Cruiser. Rafe mimicked the high, exaggerated stance of Craig Counsell, the guy who had hit his father so easily. He waited, knees flexed, hands gripping the bat high above his shoulders, watching as intently as a cat waiting for a mouse to emerge from a hole. But nothing happened. Suddenly the gate swung open and the attendant strode in. He tapped the large black letters on the box inside the door. "You gotta put the token in."

Rafe handed him a token. He could hear laughter from the car and he started to laugh himself. Then suddenly a dense "thwump!" sounded beside him. He turned and saw a ball being fed into the spinning cylinder and heard the sudden expulsion of air as an 86 mph fastball came his way straight from the machine. "Thwump!"

"Holy shit," he muttered. This was only 86 mph — his father threw 99. He stepped to the plate and raised his bat just in time to hear another ball thud into the backstop. Thwump! He had never even seen it. He gathered himself, watched the ball feed into the wheel, settled into his stance and suddenly the ball was there and he swung just as it hit the rubber behind him.

He barely nicked one of twelve pitches, topping it into the fake grass at his feet. He yanked open the door and hurried down to the cage marked 72 mph. He put in his token and retreated quickly to the left side of the plate and planted himself, knees flexed, hands high, the bat waggling above his left shoulder. This was an older machine with a long mechanical arm that circled slowly and picked up a ball, then came over the top and slung a pitch that looked just like the other but it stayed up long enough for him to meet the ball in front of his body and drive it like he saw the guys at Coors Field do. His first hit was only a ground ball, but he hit it solidly and he could feel it in his hands, as if his bones and the bat were connected.

There was no time to savor it, however. The mechanical arm circled to pick up another ball. Again, he settled into his stance, preparing to crush it this time — when suddenly the lights in the complex went off. "What's going on?" Rafe shouted.

"They're closed!" Lo Jack called. "Let's bounce!"

Rafe started towards the token booth, carrying the bat like a club. He wanted nothing more than to feel that solid contact in his hands, and see the ball arc towards the top of the net. "You owe me a token," he barked at the attendant. "I only hit one."

"You wouldn't hit another ball if we stayed open till Christmas," he sneered, and slid the window shut.

WHEN THINGS were right Jason went to another plane when he pitched, a place of quiet, though not silence. It was more white noise, like being alone with the sea. But when he took the mound at Dodger Stadium, he knew he wasn't going there tonight.

He took the game ball and turned his back to the plate. Half the guys out here were playing with some kind of handicap. Some had fought back from major surgery, some were playing with more pharmaceuticals in their veins than a transplant patient. Omar Ortega — ACL, eight months rehab; Toronto James, achilles tendon; Dave Metheny, shoulder and neck surgery in the off-season. Just last month, reliever Lan Christiansen's father was found murdered by his best friend in Denmark over the memory of a girlfriend they had competed for forty years before. Ariel Moreno had lost a brother and a friend to death squads in Colombia. Rick Wells's wife had left him, Alex Heredia was fighting a palimony suit, Jay Petrajic was suing his financial adviser who couldn't account for nearly $3 million in investments, Eric LaValle's wife just had a miscarriage. And what was his excuse? He was worried about his kid.

His first pitch was a slider that didn't slide. The Dodgers' leadoff hitter lined it hard — but directly at Darnell White in left. The second batter jumped on a curve and smashed it down· the first base line; Toronto speared it over the line and simply laid his foot across the bag for out number two. The third batter jerked two fastballs into the left field seats just foul, then looked at a changeup for a called third strike that was a strike thanks only to the largesse of the home plate umpire.

Sometimes such miracles were all that he needed to settle down — but not tonight. The first three batters in the second inning doubled, sending in two runs. Then he walked the next two and gave up a single to the pitcher. Pitching coach Ed "Stormy" Weathers strode to the mound. Eric Lavalle, Chuck Metheney and Rick Wells joined them.

"What's goin' on?" Stormy inquired.

"I don't have it today."

The coach gazed towards the bullpen. The reliever was six pitches into a twenty-four pitch sequence. "Any idea where 'it' is?" Weathers peered through the catcher's mask into Wells's eyes. "Everything's coming in flat," the catcher reported. Then he stared at Jason, who shrugged. "My arm feels dead."

"You didn't say anything beforehand."

The home plate umpire hovered beside the mound. "C'mon Stormy, make a move." The coach hated to pull a starter this early. But the mound was no place for intensive psychotherapy with a faltering pitcher, nor was a 4-0 deficit with no outs the right time. "Hold the runners 'til Tree's ready."

Three pick-off throws later, they brought in their spot starter, Lucas "Tree" Maples, but it was too late. Tree let in both of Jason's runners, and the Rockies eventually lost the game 7-3. By the end of the cool spring evening in LA, Jason's record stood at 1-3, his ERA at 7.87, and his spirits the lowest they had been in years.

He was on his cell phone the minute the game was over. 'Hi, leave a message," Rafe's voice said. Jason slammed down the phone. He showered and left in a cab with Willie, Alex Heredia and Julio Marerro to their favorite restaurant in East LA, *La Playa Escondida*. They had lost again but no one was panicking. Losses this early in the season were learning experiences, not harbingers. Leaving a game in the second inning with nobody out was certainly a learning experience for Jason, though he didn't know what he had learned except that for one evening he sucked.

Alex ordered a pitcher of Negra Modelo and the waitress brought four mugs. Willie shoved his glass aside and gently laid a hand on her arm as she started to pour a glass for Jason.

"*Esta bien*," Jason nodded at the waitress. He held his thumb and index finger about three inches apart. "*La mitád.*"

Willie stared with disbelief. Jason slid the mug from his left hand to his right and back again before raising it to his lips. Just the smell made his heart race. It was the smell of excitement, of forgetfulness … of failure.

"I gotta get some sleep. You were snoring like a goddamn freight train last night."

The other two laughed. They didn't know, however, what Willie knew. "*Qué pasa, hermano?*" Willie asked. Jason sipped the beer delicately, as if testing it for poison, then closed his eyes and drank it down. Willie grabbed his arm as he reached for the pitcher. "We had a deal."

Jason yanked his arm back. "You're not my fucking mother."

BACK IN the hotel room he went straight to the little refrigerator and pulled out the miniature Courvoisiers. They were like toys, charms for a bracelet — replicas, not the real thing. "Ya-sone," Willie said. "*Hace siete años.*"

"Didn't help me today." He poured one of the bottles into a cocktail glass. Willie slumped onto his bed and turned on the TV to a Spanish language station. Immediately he was immersed in a World Cup broadcast from Buenos Aires. Jason sat in a chair at the window sipping appreciatively, wondering why he hadn't done this earlier. This was more like it — the rock rolled away from the gravesite, his dreams resurrected. Everything was going to be alright, as soon as Rafe learned to behave.

He finished the little bottle and poured another. "Who's winning?" he shouted. Willie ignored him. "Fuck you, Willie. I mean, what the fuck do you know about raising a kid?" Willie turned up the volume. The frenzied voice of the Mexican announcer filled the room. Jason looked outside but saw only his own reflection in the glass doorway. All the injustices of his life suddenly lined up beside him, like soldiers waiting inspection. His steel-assed father lighting a Camel as he pulled away in a van. Coach Baptiste at Stanford calling him a diaper-changer. Vicki tossing her mane and sneering across the courtroom. Artie

Phleger lamely explaining his trade to the Rockies. His mother yoked to the kitchen table in Port Sulphur, Point Barrow, Galveston, a beer at her elbow. Rafe slouching at the table, refusing to do his homework.

Jason raised the drink to his own reflection — and to his ghosts. "Fuck you," he growled. He downed what was left in one swallow, the taste warm and promising. Everything was going to work out fine. He'd get a good night's sleep and pitch again tomorrow. He'd only lasted an inning plus, he could throw on one day's rest. He had what it took. He was a pro.

He lurched into the bathroom and stood over the toilet. "Hey Willie, remember that time I threw a no-hitter in Mazatlan? Willie?"

An hour later Mexico scored, securing a victory over the Ivory Coast. Willie found his roomie asleep on the floor, his head against the bottom of the toilet bowl. He straddled Jason's body, peed, brushed his teeth, and turned off the light.

"Hi, i'm JT and I'm an alcoholic." His head felt heavy, his legs stuck in cement. The second day of a Midwest road trip and he knew he would drink eventually, if only to sleep. In sleep, he couldn't think about what a lousy father he was.

"Hi, JT."

"I don't know where to start. I hadn't had a drink for seven years and then a couple of weeks ago …" He took a deep breath and looked at his hands. There were 16 meetings in Chicago that evening and he'd ended up at one with a dozen people just a few years older than Rafe. He had listened for nearly an hour, absorbing their pain. The boy whose father left when he was five. The girl whose father left when she was two and never spoke to anyone in the family again. The boy whose father worked twelve hours a day and drank the rest of the time. The girl who compared the time her father spent with his dog and with her each week, and came out on the short end, thirty-five hours to two. Mean fathers, neglectful fathers, drunken fathers. Fathers without jobs. Fathers without consciences. Fathers without hearts. He had read all the studies, spoken about them on talk shows and with reporters. Now he was hearing it from their children. The runaways and drug abusers, the dropouts and drunks. The girls who got pregnant or attempted suicide, who ate incessantly or never ate at all. All of them, every last one of them, were tied as tragically to a faulty parent — usually their father — as a suicide to a concrete block. Somehow he had to let these kids know that he wasn't one of those fathers.

"I tried to call my son — he's fifteen, he's back in Denver, that's where we live. And when he wasn't home I went ballistic. He's having trouble in school ... he's been in trouble with the law — drug charges, breaking and entering. I've got a job that takes me out of town for weeks at a time ..." They had beaten the Cubs that afternoon. The team was on a roll. He wondered — he worried — how many of these kids knew who he was.

"Anyway, I'm rambling. I don't know what's wrong. He came to live with me ... his mother and I are divorced. It was a painful divorce. I don't think we did it very well but it's over now ... he's living with me and I'm trying to stay involved but it's really difficult with my job. I feel like I'm not doing right by him or with my job. When I call him from the road I want there to be a connection but I can't get any feel for him at all. Sometimes after I hang up I feel like throwing the phone as far as I can. And that's when I want to drink ... I *have* been drinking."

He paused and took another deep breath. Then he began to cry. He didn't want to, but others had already cried so it didn't seem so bad. Besides his own pain, he could feel Rafe's too — leaving his mother ... his friends ... his dreams. "I don't know who he's with. I don't know what he's doing. I wonder why he came to live with me, because he doesn't seem happy at all." A few of the young people watched him intently. This was the hard part. This was the part even he didn't want to hear. "What really bothers me the most is, I don't think I love him anymore. It's just too hard."

The secretary glanced at Jason, then at her watch. She waited a moment, then smiled. "Thank you," she said. "Would everyone who wants to please join me in the closing prayer?"

Afterwards, Jason folded his chair and leaned it against the wall with the others. It was only 9 PM and he was wondering what he would do in Chicago for the rest of his insomnia-extended night when a long-haired, heavy-set kid who had spoken hatefully about his father came towards him, carrying a couple of chairs. He had condemned his dad as a man who worked obsessively at a construction business, then left him and his sister and his mother and moved to Michigan, where he made a fortune and began another family. "Thank you for your share," he said, setting the chairs down. Jason smiled uneasily. "It meant a lot to hear there's fathers out there trying."

A strange chill came over Jason. He had been praised for his fastball, his slider, his command with runners on base, but no one had praised him for being a father in a long time. "I am trying, though I don't know what good it's doing," he said.

"That's all you can do." The young man moved closer, as close as Wells got when he came to the mound to talk. Jason wasn't sure what to do. He hadn't been to an AA meeting in five years. He knew what the young man was looking for, but it was awkward; he knew what he needed for himself, but that felt awkward too. Finally, he threw his arms around the young man's shoulders and hugged him.

"Thank you," Jason said.

The young man squeezed back, then stepped away. "Your son doesn't care if you love him," he said. "That's just the icing on the cake."

BY EARLY August Jason was 6-9 and the Rockies were nine games out of first place, a symmetry that was not unnoticed by analysts trying to determine why their beloved Rockies had relapsed to mediocrity. There were others on the team whose numbers didn't match last year's, but no one had anything as visible as a teenage albatross around his neck. And the albatross only got heavier as the season wore on. Rafe had ended up in summer school, but rather than use it as an opportunity to advance his academic standing in Everett F. Stokes High School, he continued his downward spiral. Notes sent home two weeks and four weeks into the summer session identified Rafe's work as "unsatisfactory." He seemed about to achieve the impossible — flunking summer school.

Jason's final road trip before Rafe finished summer school took him to Milwaukee, Cincinnati and St. Louis. They dropped the second game of the Milwaukee series 3-1, after pounding out a 10-2 win the night before. As soon as the game was over he called Rafe. As usual, he got his voice mail. As usual, he hung up.

"Hey," Alex Heredia called out when he got off the phone. "*Vístete. Las chicas nos estan esperando.*" The Latino Caucus, as the Spanish speaking players called themselves, were going to Lupita's, a salsa place on the south side of Milwaukee, but he declined. He wanted to walk. He loved this time of year, when every town in America felt like Port Sulphur. Two blocks from the hotel he strode into a boisterous neighborhood that appeared to be some kind of eastern European enclave — Polish, Bulgarian, Czech, he couldn't tell. There were smells of cabbage, cinnamon and beer, old country music mixed with rock and roll lingering on the warm humid air. People moved on and off their front stoops as if they were rafts, drifting to neighbors' homes, the corner store, into the house for a beer. Families — brothers and sisters and grandmothers gathered in noisy pods ... but where were the fathers?

He felt ashamed of himself. He pictured his son walking the streets of Denver, clothes hanging like laundry from his body, a sullen slouch inviting the spotlight from passing Denver PD. What good was he doing anybody? This is the way his father did it, and his father before that, and all the fathers missing from this neighborhood. He was following in their footsteps — footsteps that didn't lead anywhere.

He stopped in front of a pet store and punched Rafe's number on his cell phone. He stared into the eyes of a tiny Labrador puppy watching him through the window. "Leave a message," Rafe's voice said. He hung up. The puppy ran back and forth across the window front, yapping with delight as he tapped on the window. Maybe he should get a dog. Give Rafe a companion, teach him to be responsible about something. Or maybe, he thought, it was time to send him back to Vicki.

He led the puppy back and forth across the window with his finger, watching his excited, trusting eyes. What was he thinking? Rafe was just fifteen, he didn't know what he wanted. His mother had given up on him and now his father wasn't there either. How could he believe in himself if his parents didn't believe in him?

His hand had drifted away from the window and the puppy was watching, waiting, a look of eager anticipation on his face. Jason thought of himself as a kid and the thousands, the tens of thousands of hours he'd spent playing baseball since then. Out of everything he'd ever tried — school, marriage, drinking, drugs — baseball was the only way he had found to escape who he was destined to be — the son of a hard-luck oil worker — and become something altogether different. And now, he was going to have to give it all up — the sound, the feel, the glory of baseball. He had no other choice.

He put his hand back to the glass and the puppy leaped at it. "Good night, little guy," he said sweetly. "Somebody'll give you a home real soon."

THE DAY summer school ended Lo-Jack picked Rafe up in a golden

Lexus. He was waiting at the corner of his street wearing baggy gray shorts, a faded blue t-shirt with the logo of late-night eatery impresario Johnny Reno — three pot-bellied men eating from a garbage can with the caption, *Johnny Reno's World Famous Garbage Plate!* His hair was sculpted into some kind of medieval cut, the top longer than the sides and back, the hair falling off to the side and into his eyes.

"Where we going?" Rafe asked, sliding into the cool leather seat. The two girls and Noyes were along as usual, riding in back to give Rafe the honored shotgun seat.

"The Don Baylor Pro-Tech Batting Cages!" they sang in unison.

Lo-Jack handed him his capsule of Ecstasy and he swallowed it with Sherry's Diet Coke. Rafe smiled. Tonight he'd go for 86 mph. He'd come back to the cages again and again, working on his swing: hands up, weight back, turn the hips and shoulders, extend the arms. On Ecstasy it all made exquisite sense, a harmony of desire and deed. He owed it to Lo-Jack for getting him out there at least twice a week. Sometimes they left him there and Rafe would hit for an hour on his own. The attendant found out his father was Jason Thibodeaux and some nights gave him a handful of tokens for free. He thought Rafe would get him tickets to the Rockies sometimes, but he hadn't.

At one end of the cages was a small crowd celebrating a birthday. Two of the cages were decorated with pink and purple balloons, and a barbecue grill smoked behind the tailgate of a pickup truck. The only 86 mph cage open was one with an old fashioned mechanical arm. Rafe selected a bat and shoved a token in the slot. The gears began whirring behind the metal mesh and he felt the Ecstasy speeding through his body, destined to make him stronger, quicker, more alert. He saw the arm swinging around, the ball cradled in the metal cup, the seams trembling from the machine's motor, then suddenly — Thwump!

He glowered at the machine and set himself again, his hands high, legs flexed. This time he saw the ball clearly, but he missed it completely — Thwump!

Twelve more pitches and he missed every one. Something was wrong. He should be ready; he'd practiced for weeks. He'd hit 72 and 80 mph, so six miles an hour couldn't make that much difference. He stormed over to the Lexus and tapped on the window. The tinted glass lowered, releasing a cloud of marijuana smoke.

"More E," Rafe demanded.

"Wait for the kick," Lo-Jack counseled.

177

Rafe raised the bat. Lo Jack gestured "*no mas*" and reached in his shirt pocket. The others watched warily. None of them had ever gotten uptight on E, except for when Lo-Jack mixed it with LSD and the single malt scotch he had found in the *car du jour*.

"You OK, Rafey?" Sherry called from the back seat. He tossed the capsule into his mouth, ignoring her. He'd failed summer school but he wouldn't fail this. Eighty-six wasn't even a fastball. Ninety-five, ninety-eight — those were fastballs. Eighty-six was nothin'. Eighty-six was whack.

He slid another token in and leaned over the plate. Lo-Jack, Noyes, Sherry and Diane were out of the car now, lined up along the outside of the cage. "Go, Rafe!" they shouted. The mechanized arm picked up the ball, jerked slowly around then swiftly flung it low and away across the plate where it thudded, untouched, into the backstop.

"Rafe, Rafe, he's our man," Sherry and Diane sang, "if he can't hit it, nobody can." Rafe blinked, recoiled and waited for the extrasensory powers the additional Ecstasy would bring. The machine delivered again. He swung and missed — again. Thwump!

And then, miraculously, everything changed. The long metal arm began moving in slow motion, turning as gracefully as an underwater plant. The ball nestled into the hollow of its metallic hand and rose slowly towards its release point. Rafe settled eagerly into his stance, certain of himself now, ready to pounce. He was a player, a slugger, the son of a Major League star.

Thwump! The ball was past him before he even swung. He strode the length of the cage and brought the bat down as hard as he could on the arm as it circled to pick up another ball. The machine groaned, emitting a whining sound as the gears strained against the twisted metal. He pounded the arm again, then the metal mesh protecting the nest of gears. He couldn't tell how long he was at it. It could have been minutes, hours, days, anything would have made sense. The others watched dumbfounded as the machine collapsed, its belts and springs intertwined like drowning lovers.

Then he saw the po-po lights spinning behind the Lexus and figured they were finally on to Lo-Jack. He resumed his pounding with renewed fury. He had to work on his swing no matter what. He had to get it right so he could show his father he could hit an 86 mph fastball. Hell, he'd show him he could hit a 100 mph fastball — a *1,000* mph fastball. But not with a net over him. Not with three cops wrestling him to the ground. Not with a set of handcuffs on him.

"Let me hit! Let me hit!" he cried. "I've got tokens!"

As soon as the plane touched down at Denver International the cell phones appeared. Jason noticed that he had one message — a voice mail from Rafe. He was surprised, Rafe rarely called him. Maybe this was some kind of turning point.

"Hi Dad," Rafe began. Just the sound of his voice, like when he was five, seven, eight years old, made him smile. "Uh, they told me I got one phone call and this is it so, uh … I'm at the Denver Police Station and I need you to come and get me."

He heard Rafe turn away from the phone and ask, "Do I leave a number?" and someone say, "Just hang up."

There was a click and he was gone.

STRIKE FOUR

Top o' the 10th ...

Tobias Barlow USA TODAY

—

What's a father-son relationship worth — two million dollars? Ten? How about $42 million? That's what Rockies' pitcher Jason Thibodeaux gave up last week to lay claim to his troubled teenage son, retiring from a solid major league career at the beginning of a four-year, $42 million contract.

That's some chunk of child support. But Thibodeaux not only walked the walk, he talked the talk. "I wanted to be a baseball player since the time I could walk," he told a press conference at Coors Field. "But those who know me also know that a big part of my life is family. Recently, my son Raphael came to live with me in Denver. But as a single father and a Major League baseball player, I wasn't able to provide the attention or guidance he needed. That was my failure, not his.

"A professional athlete knows when it's time to retire. But for me, it's not that anything's wrong with my arm. I can't pitch any more for the simple reason that my heart's not in it."

Thibodeaux's sixth game victory in last year's World Series is the stuff of legend. So should his eleventh hour retirement from baseball. Some critics say he's cutting out on his team, but the Rockies aren't going anywhere with or without him. Watching Thibodeaux at his farewell press conference, I got the feeling there were simply more important things in his life.

"One of my problems has been the pull between the world of baseball and the world of parenting," Thibodeaux said. "I think my son needs to know that I'm only going to do one of those things."

I've covered Jason Thibodeaux since college — he a pitching phenom at Stanford University, I a literary prodigy with the now-defunct San Francisco Examiner. Announcing his retirement, he looked absolutely serene. The long battle between father and ballplayer has come to a close, and it looks like the right man won. Final box score: *no runs, no hits, no errors, two men left.*

T HE ENTIRE CAMPUS OF Holy Innocents High School shimmered with a kind of anticipatory energy in the autumn afternoon. A crisp Pacific breeze polished the most mundane details of the surrounding streets into vivid relief — hand-painted Chinese letters on the wall of a laundromat, a row of pastel stucco homes, a streetcar lumbering down Taraval Street to the sea. A bell sounded and a boy in a blue sweater and tan slacks burst through a door and rushed along the sidewalk. Then another boy, three girls in tartan uniforms, and a riot of sophomores emerged, hurrying to the parking lot.

Raphael watched from the top of the bleachers overlooking the broad athletic fields. He could see the stoners slinking out to the moss-covered stairwell at the edge of the adjoining park, and for a moment thought of joining them. He'd gone out there a couple of days into school and smoked, but rather than escaping anything he ended up riding home stoned on the streetcar, mentally replaying his Greatest Fuckups tape: in de la Salad's attic wearing his stupid trenchcoat, pretending to practice music and wasting the better part of two years — the expulsions, the time in Juvie, the Ecstasy blow in Denver, his father quitting baseball.

BTDT — been there, done that. He closed his eyes and stretched beneath the sun's warmth. When he looked again the stoners were gone and the wide green fields filled with soccer and lacrosse and football players. He swung down from the bleachers and slipped through the side door, walking quickly down the corridor. HI's lofty ceilings, carpeted classrooms and music rooms with real instruments still made him feel out of place. "*Magis.*" That was the motto of Holy Innocents — *More. Better.* "We believe our students can always do better," the admissions officer said. Better than what? Rafe had wondered. He had no base to work from.

He turned down a bright corridor with glass walls. On either side were courtyards with palm trees, a maze of English hedgerows, clusters of flowering shrubs. He felt vaguely unnerved; there was something disturbing about this place, something indefinably *right*. He was deathly afraid that everything was going to work out.

HE KNOCKED lightly on the familiar door of Room 319. Father Giacamo Baldassare, a psychology teacher and HI's part-time counselor, sat behind a huge desk with the sun slanting through the window behind him. He was a short, round-shouldered man in his mid-forties with a large nose, dark intelligent eyes and a sagging, sympathetic face. He wore a black, short-sleeved cleric's shirt with white Roman collar, plain black slacks, and a watch with a simple black band on his left wrist.

"Sorry I'm late," Rafe muttered.

Baldassare rose to shake Rafe's hand. "Please, sit down," he said with his surprisingly deep voice. He gestured to one of two leather chairs in front of his desk. Rafe's father sat impatiently in the other. Father Baldassare watched, waiting for the two to greet each other. The silence in the room was palpable.

"Thank you both for coming," Baldassare finally said. "I've wanted to meet your father for a long time — and not because of his fame as a baseball player. As you can tell from my build, I'm more fit for Elysian Fields than athletic ones." He smiled, but neither Thibodeaux responded.

"I've asked for this meeting for preventive reasons more than anything else. Single parenthood puts special pressures on a family, and I'm aware of all the other pressures in your situation," he said, glancing sympathetically from one to the other. "But there are also some fundamental principles we need to keep in focus. Raphael, when you were accepted at Holy Innocents, you made a commitment to abide by the rules and perform at the required academic level. We're more than two months into the school year and it's our assessment that you need to start living up to that commitment."

Rafe stirred in his seat, avoiding his father's gaze. "So what happens now — are you going to throw me out?"

Baldassare's head jerked in surprise. "We don't give up on our students unless they've given up on themselves," he explained. "The basis of our education is student responsibility. You're the only one who can do what has to be done."

Rafe looked up at the swarthy priest. "Do what?"

"Doing your homework would be a good start," Jason interjected.

Baldassare smiled. "What is it about Raphael's homework that concerns you?" he asked diplomatically.

"That he doesn't do it! I tell him over and over again to do it, ask him to do it, beg him to do it, but he won't. He just won't."

Rafe slumped deeper into his chair. Two afternoons of drug counseling per week. Two afternoons of community service. Monthly visits with his parole officer — and monthly drug testing — and it still wasn't enough. He had to get better grades, join the school band, make the baseball team, be a star.

"The first thing we counsel, Mr. Thibodeaux, is simply *trying*."

"That's an excellent idea," Jason replied with obvious sarcasm.

Father Baldassare turned to Rafe. "The juvenile court has ordered you to maintain at least a C average. I'd like you to leave here today with a plan for how you're going to do that."

Rafe looked down at the floor. "I'd like to go live with my mother."

Jason stiffened, stunned.

"Why do you say that, Raphael?" Baldassare asked.

"I made a mistake, going to Colorado."

Jason threw up his hands. "*You* made a mistake? I threw away my career —"

"I wish you'd stop talking about that," Rafe said.

"It's the truth!" Jason turned expectantly to Baldassare. He had come an hour before Rafe and told the counselor everything — his love for baseball, how his own father had left him, how he'd cut himself off from baseball to be with Rafe. He described an average day of his new "life" in San Francisco … his daily six a.m. run out to Ocean Beach and back. His solitary breakfasts, tossing the sports section so he couldn't see where the Rockies were in the standings; his afternoons at the gym, shopping for dinner, cooking for his unappreciative son. He had never had much of a social life and he certainly didn't have one now. Baseball had been his life. Now his life's work was Rafe's rehabilitation. And Rafe's job, it seemed, was to thwart him.

Baldassare clicked on the lamp behind his desk, sending a comforting glow over the room. "I'd like to make a few suggestions that might take us down a different path." He turned to Jason. "Your son's homework is our job, Mr. Thibodeaux. You should stick with yours."

"I don't have one."

Baldassare nodded. "I recommend that you not express any concern directly to Raphael about the performance of his homework — whether he brings it home, whether he does it or not, whether he brings it back to school or anything in between. Secondly, I highly recommend that you take a job, either on a paid or volunteer basis, in an area of compelling interest to you. You have undergone a huge change in your life with your retirement from baseball. It's important that you fill that vacuum as quickly as possible." He smiled at Jason's surprise. "I know for a fact our Junior Varsity team needs help. Coach Shannon's wife is about to have their first child."

He turned to Rafe. "I recommend that you call the cable company and cancel your service. Put your television in some out-of-the-way place and limit your viewing to two hours a week."

"Two hours *a week?*"

Baldassare smiled and nodded. "And I want you to call your mother."

Rafe's eyebrows flew towards the ceiling. "And say what?"

"I'm sure you'll think of something. She's your mother."

THAT NIGHT Jason made his favorite comfort food — roast chicken rubbed with olive oil and garlic and coated with herbs, roasted in a pan with carrots and potatoes and turnips. He liked to cook. It gave him the satisfaction of providing something tangible for Rafe, even if he never showed any appreciation for it.

At seven o'clock he called upstairs but there was no response. He ate by himself, glancing from time to time at the doorway and growing angrier each time when Rafe didn't appear. When he finished, he went into the living room and dialed the number Father Baldassare had given him.

"I'm glad you called, Mr. Thibodeaux," the priest said. "What can I do for you?"

Jason stared blindly at the wall. Raise my son. Let me play baseball again. "I don't know," he said. "I'm kind of raw from our session this afternoon."

"I'm sure you are."

"I mean, I gave up so much. And now he wants to go back to his mother. Maybe it's for the best. I don't see what good I'm doing anyway."

"Where is Rafe now?"

"In his room."

"Did he cancel the cable TV?"

"Yeah."

"Good," Baldassare said. "I know how painful this is, especially after everything you've gone through. But what you heard this afternoon wasn't disapproval or hatred. It's fear."

"Fear of what?"

"Fear that he can't live up to your expectations. Fear you won't love him and go away again."

"But I gave up my *career* to be with him."

"That's made it harder for him in some ways."

"I'm having trouble getting my mind around that one."

"Try to look at it from Rafe's point of view. You're a major league baseball player — a mythical figure for a kid. Rafe sees himself as an outsider, which isn't surprising. Huge decisions have been made for him his entire life without his input. Who he lives with, where, when ... what school he goes to. He's been incarcerated, the ultimate loss of autonomy. Now he's mortified that you quit baseball because of *him*, and he thinks you hold it against him. He desperately wants to please you but doesn't have the faintest idea how."

Jason heard a noise and peered into the kitchen. Rafe, CD headphones planted in his ears, was cutting off chunks of chicken and piling potatoes and carrots on his plate. "I do hold it against him," Jason said quietly, edging away from the door. "But that doesn't mean I'm going to run out on him. How do I get him to believe that?"

"I would start by creating some kind of working relationship with your ex-wife."

"What!?"

"Rafe doesn't have a safe place in the world," he explained. "He's starting to believe in us at school, but the two people he loves most appear to hate each other —"

"We *do* hate each other."

"Think about that, Mr. Thibodeaux. How is Rafe supposed to believe you'll never give up on him, when his mother and father have given up on each other?"

"Oh Jesus —" Jason began. Then, "Excuse me, Father. All these other things, OK. But asking me to have anything to do with the woman who took away my son —"

"You won't get anywhere as a family unless you do."

"We're not a family. We've never been a family."

"That's not the way Rafe sees it."

HIS MOTHER'S house didn't feel like any place he'd lived before. It was too small, too neat; Rafe's memories of rage and frustration didn't fit the orderly normalness of it all. In the dining room, two places were set for dinner. The moist smell of roasting meat permeated the house.

"I made Gramma's pot roast," Vicki said cheerfully as she led Rafe into the kitchen. "That was always your favorite."

"Can I put my stuff upstairs?"

Everything in his room seemed the same — desk, bed, chair, curtains, bedspread — but without the whacked out chaos of his CDs strewn across the floor, posters of Eminem and Ludacris and Michael Myers from *Halloween*, rug stains and half-empty cups, twisted sheets, scattered papers and the familiar dankness of mildewing laundry. This was somebody else's room, some boy he never was but his mom wished for. It was as clean and characterless as a hotel room, and on one level that was fine with him. He could always check out if he wanted to.

He dropped his piece of luggage on the floor and stood before the shelves full of books he had pretended to read or never even looked at. *Broken Arrow. Wizard of Oz. Huckleberry Finn. The Diary of Anne Frank. While the Clock Ticked.* He pulled *White Fang* from the shelf with a derisive snort, recalling the book report he'd turned in to his teacher at Juvenile Hall: "It's about a big dog with white teeth."

He stretched out on top of the bedspread and began to read. Twenty pages later his mother's voice sliced up the stairs. "Dinner time!"

"Not hungry!" He was mesmerized by the muscular world of the Yukon and its total lack of phoniness — and embarrassed that the book wasn't about a "big dog with white teeth" but a tense drama of two men fighting off a pack of desperate wolves. He read to where the one surviving man was rescued, then hurried downstairs.

The dining room table was cleared. Vicki was in the living room reading *San Francisco* magazine.

"Did you eat it all?" Rafe asked.

"I put yours in the oven."

He found a plate mounded with Gramma Anna's famous pot roast, carrots and mashed potatoes and took it to the table. Vicki set down her magazine and joined him.

"I was hoping we could eat together your first night back."

"I was reading," he said somewhat triumphantly.

"Some other night," Vicki said with a resigned smile. She looked on as the food rapidly disappeared from Rafe's plate. "I really missed you," she finally said. "Is there anything you want to talk about — maybe about what happened over at your father's?"

"Not really. He's just a hard-ass about homework and stuff."

"That's your father," she said. "But you know, I'm not going to be any easier about that sort of thing. It's important to start out — "

"You're not supposed to interfere," Rafe cut in. "Father Baldassare says my homework's between me and my teachers."

"Who's Father Baldassare?"

"My guidance counselor."

"And how's that working out?"

"Good."

Rafe mopped the last of the mashed potatoes from his plate with a forkful of beef. "Would you like some more?" Vicki asked.

"Is there more? This stuff's great."

Vicki microwaved another plateful and set it in front of Rafe. "I'm really hopeful we can make it work this time, Rafe. But we need to talk about the schedule you've worked out."

"What about it?" He'd worked it out so he'd spend weekends with his dad and weekdays with his mom.

"I want to propose switching. Your father has more time during the week — "

"I'm keeping weekends open for baseball."

Vicki's face fell as if it had been deflated.

"There you are, pissed off as usual."

"I'm not *pissed off*," Vicki replied. "I don't care what you do —"

"Great. You don't care."

"Rafe." Vicki leaned across the table. "I don't know what's going on over at your father's, but we're not going back to the way things were over here. We're just not."

"Fine with me!"

Vicki's eyes moved over Rafe's face with pleading tenderness. "I've had a lot of time to think about us. I'm willing to do this your way, but whatever we do we have to love and respect each other and accept our differences — "

"Like the fact that you want me to be a musician and I don't?"

Vicki nodded. "That's one thing."

"Then it's all bullshit — "

"I'm not saying you have to *become* a musician," Vicki added. "I mean, I get to have my wishes, don't I? But this is clearly *your* life, Rafe, I know that. You have to figure out what it is you want to do, based on what's inside you. I can't tell you, obviously. Your teachers can't tell you. Maybe your father can tell you, I don't know. But whatever it is, it has to be what *you* want."

"And then I make the wrong choice and I'm some fucked-up kid you don't want anything to do with."

Tears streamed down Vicki's face. "I'm sorry for what's happened, I really am. I love you so much. I know I made a huge mistake pushing you into music. You probably did the exact opposite of what I wanted just because I'm your mother."

"No," Rafe replied. "I just wanted to play baseball."

Vicki nodded, as if confirming something with herself. "Then that's what you should do," she said. "If that's really what you want."

JASON EXPECTED to dislike coaching high school kids. After the Majors he figured that the fumbling of pubescent boys would be so aesthetically unpleasant that he wouldn't be able to take it. But from the opening minute of the HI Fall Baseball Clinic, he was glad to be there. The feel of the grass, the ringing of bat against ball, the enthusiasm and respect of the boys for what used to be the only American sport that mattered brought him back to the thing that he loved most — baseball.

"Ladies and Gentlemen," Len Frawley, the varsity baseball coach at Holy Innocents, called out facetiously to the all-male cast assembled behind the school. "One year ago Mr. Thibodeaux was mowing down Yankees in the World Series. Today, he's here to kick your butts and show you how baseball is really played."

Jason was startled when Frawley simply turned the boys over to him. He'd volunteered to help, not run the show, but Frawley was eager to learn some new tricks himself after twenty-three years on the job. The boys gathered around him. "I can't really teach you how to play," Jason confided, "but I can teach you how to prepare. We'll start out with running. Then we'll run some more — and then," he smiled, looking from surprised face to surprised face, "we'll run some more. Baseball is for athletes and you need to be in shape. You have to eat right, sleep right, work out on your own and abstain, absolutely, from drugs and alcohol."

He had them stretch first, then they ran — five perimeters of the field and a series of wind sprints between the leftfield and rightfield lines. Then he had outfielders field hits into the gap and throw to a cutoff man. Infielders took grounders and brought their throws home, then took the throw from the catcher at the nearest base.

They called him "Mr. Thibodeaux" and looked upon him with the same reverence Jesus must have commanded during the Sermon on the Mount. *Blessed Be the Agile, for They Shall Turn the Double Play. Blessed Be the Fundamentally Sound, for They Shall Commit No Errors.* He watched for that special spark in any of the kids — the quick step, the vacuum glove, the mitt-popping throw. Most teams had at least one whose skills quickened the blood of the others. But during that first week Jason didn't see one. They were earnest and attentive kids, eager to work hard. It would have been a perfect setting for Rafe, but he couldn't make it because of his rehab visits, his community service, his appointments with his probation officer.

Then suddenly, it all changed.

That Thursday night Jason was wandering from room to room like he used to in Cincinnati, missing his son. Rafe had been at his mother's since Monday and he wasn't due back until Friday evening, after community service. He sat on Rafe's bed and gazed around the darkening room, imagining him there surrounded by school books, magazines and rumpled clothes, headphones clamped over his ears. It had been a hard week — losing Rafe, or at least feeling he had. He was alone again with a house full of regrets, remembering the feel of a ball in his hand, the thrill of a fastball blowing past a flailing slugger, the roar of a crowd. He was wondering if this was all he got — eight tough months of fatherhood, then the brush-off. Then the phone rang.

He hurried down the hall to answer it. "Hi Dad."

"Hey Buddy, how are things going?"

"OK. You watchin' the game?"

The game? Ah, the World Series, the Reds and the Angels, tied at two apiece. Vuco had finally made it — and here he was, running a high school clinic. "No," he replied. He hadn't watched a game since he left the Rockies. "How about you?"

"A couple innings," Rafe said. "Then I gotta do my homework."

"Thataboy." There was a long pause, but not an uncomfortable one. They were both glad the other was on the line. "So what's up?" Jason finally asked. "You just call to talk?"

"Sort of. I want to see about coming out for the baseball clinic."

"Really?" Jason's mind raced. The other boys had busted their butts all week. If it wasn't his own son, he would have to tell him to wait for Spring. But it *was* his son. "What about your counseling?"

"The judge let me off for the week."

"How did that happen?"

"We called her and asked."

"We?"

"Me and mom."

"That's great, Buddy," he said, studying Rafe's cluttered desk, his CD stack, his calendar with "Mom" written the length of every week, and "Dad" on the weekends. "There's some good ballplayers out there."

"I'm a good ballplayer."

IT STARTED on Monday. Rafe was issued an HI practice jersey, gray flannel with blue trim and high blue socks that filled in the leg space on the three-quarters length pants. It was the first uniform he had put on since the Giants' opening day when he was eight. Jason almost didn't recognize him when he walked onto the field. The cut of the uniform and the spiked shoes made him look taller, more poised. Jason's heart quickened; he remembered Rafe's little Stanford uniform with the number "1½" that Vicki's dad had bought, but this was different. He wasn't a mascot — he was a player. At least he looked like one.

"Gentlemen," he said, leading off the session, "this is my son Raphael." Most of them looked him over closely. Rafe's sullen countenance was familiar around campus, but nobody messed with him because nobody really cared. If Rafe wanted to avoid everyone, that was one fewer kid for everyone else to bother with. Word was, Rafe was a tweaker, with all kinds of drama that any sane kid preferred to stay away from. Rafe nodded and half-smiled at a few of the guys as if he knew them, which he didn't.

After stretching and calisthenics, Jason sent them running two perimeters of HI's athletic fields and watched with JV Coach Mike Shannon, who had come out to participate in the second week of the clinic. The first time around Rafe stayed close to the middle of the pack, but fell quickly to the rear when they started the second lap. "C'mon, Tupac, you can do it," Enrique Tai encouraged him as he loped beside him. Tai was a burly half-Japanese, half-Filipino kid who had played freshman ball and was trying to make it as the team's catcher.

"Tupac?" Rafe asked.

"You're the hip hop man — up from Juvie," Tai explained. They were bringing up the rear, both of them happy someone else was there to keep from appearing last.

Tupac. It could be worse. One kid who transferred in was 'Cinderella,' because he worked weekends cleaning houses with his mother. There was Smell Man, Pizza Face, Big Ugly's Brother, Deuce, Chops, Waffle. Tupac was alright. He could live with Tupac. Of course, Tupac was dead.

By the time they straggled back, the squads had been formed. Rafe was placed with the Quails, made up of mostly freshman players, under the tutelage of Coach Shannon. His father coached the Hawks, mostly sophomores and a few upper classmen who had come to learn from a pro.

"Thibodeaux, what position do you play?" Shannon called out.

"DH," Rafe responded. The kids laughed. Designated Hitter was a privilege, not a given. Shannon looked Rafe over — tall, lanky, left-handed. "Fourth inning go to right field."

The Quails were down 7-0 when Rafe trotted out to right, and he prayed that nobody would hit the ball to him. Which, of course, the very first batter did — a line drive that sliced over the second baseman's head. He started backwards, then stopped. The ball shot past him and by the time he reached it, the batter was crossing home plate.

The Hawks exploded in cheers and laughter at the easy run. Rafe's fellow Quails turned to face the next batter, keeping their opinions to themselves. Then the next batter lofted a pop-up in back of second base. Eddie Flanigan turned and sprinted into right field. Rafe, racing towards the ball, stopped when he saw Flanigan heading towards him. The ball fell about fifteen feet in front of him, nestling into the uncut grass. The runner was steaming into third base by the time Flanigan picked up the ball and fired it in. He turned and cast a look of unmistakable contempt at Rafe.

"Alright, alright," Shannon clapped from the sidelines. "Let's get this next guy and get our ups."

Every major leaguer dreams his son will some day follow in his footsteps; Jason was hoping only that his son get off the field alive. It was a reflection on him, of course. But even worse, he was afraid it would destroy Rafe. He knew that if it weren't for his passion for baseball Rafe wouldn't even be out there, and it broke his heart. For years he had watched kids five, six, seven-years old at clinics sponsored by the Reds, Rockies and Giants, their faces glowing with pride for just being there. That was the time to have exposed Rafe to baseball; there was far too much at stake now. Jason wanted to call him in, take him out to dinner, talk him into pursuing music. He wanted Rafe to forget baseball; he was sure he would by the summer.

Rafe was the first batter scheduled in the last of the fifth. Jason watched with dread as he stepped into the box and assumed his curious stance. Coach Shannon looked Jason's way and when he didn't respond, stepped forward and grabbed Rafe's hands and pulled them level with his cheekbones. He moved him a half step further back from the plate and stood back to watch his handiwork.

The Hawk's pitcher sent a fastball low and outside. Rafe flailed at the pitch and missed. Jason turned away, his insides churning, and saw Vicki watching from fifteen feet away. She didn't acknowledge him, staring intently at her son. Jason turned in time to see Rafe miss another pitch, readjust his grip on the bat, then step back into the batter's box with the same goofy stance he had used before Shannon adjusted him. Jason started forward, then stopped. If he was supposed to leave him alone at school, then he probably should here, too.

"Hold it!" Shannon called. He walked towards Rafe. "You really think you can hit the ball like that?"

"Yes sir." Rafe stood defiantly in the box, his hands gripping the bat handle so hard his knuckles were white. This was the stance of the man who had successfully hit against his father. It was his stance now.

Shannon shrugged and walked away as if to say, 'have it your way.' He shot a glance at Jason that was equal parts bewilderment, resignation and dismay. To have some *prima donna* kid and the major leaguer who had quit to pamper him mucking up his clinic was not exactly the kind of help he had in mind when Jason volunteered. Coaches had to stick up for each other, and Jason's silence spoke volumes.

Jason watched, seemingly impassive, his shoulders squared to the woman behind him. He couldn't help thinking how different this scenario might be if she had allowed Rafe to play as a kid. He would probably be a prodigy by this point, steeped in his father's knowledge of the game. But now, driven by demons Jason couldn't begin to fathom, Rafe seemed determined to humiliate himself — and his parents. He wanted to turn and say, 'see what you've done?' But he didn't.

Rafe waited in his Giacometti-like stance, his bat waggling above his head, his right foot tapping the ground, his weight back until the ball flashed from the mound and his hands dropped, his weight moving forward into the swing. Jason realized that despite the unorthodox stance, there was harmony to it as Rafe followed through with a powerful arc of extended arms and rotating hips and shoulders. It made him think of pelicans he had seen on the coast, so clumsy on land but so graceful in their flight over water. Somehow they got the job done.

But not Rafe. He swung at a pitch that was neck high and unhittable. It was strike three but he stayed in the batter's box, as if the rules somehow didn't apply to him.

"OK OK OK!" Shannon clapped. "Last inning, let's look sharp."

THE RIDE home was only ten minutes but it seemed like an hour. There were a dozen things Jason wanted to say about fielding, throwing, dealing with coaches … about humility. But he knew Rafe well enough to know this wasn't the time to say them.

Rafe went straight to his room. Jason filled the rice cooker and marinated two salmon steaks in lemon juice, olive oil, thyme, garlic, salt and pepper and set them aside. "Dinner's in forty-five!" he called upstairs. "You got salad tonight."

Jason showered, dressed in slacks and a Holy Innocents sweatshirt and came downstairs expecting Rafe to be well into the salad; the kitchen was empty. He fired up the gas grill on the patio and slapped on the salmon, reading snatches of Richard North Patterson's *Balance of Power* while the steaks cooked. He'd gotten hooked on legal potboilers — Patterson, Grisham, Baldacci, Iris Johansen. He loved their self-contained worlds of cause-and-effect, with reasonable solutions to even the most unreasonable crimes. Bad guys were bad, good guys struggled with virtue but won out in the end, within a system governed by indisputable rules.

He ate alone at the kitchen table, reading his novel and listening to the local jazz station. When Rafe appeared Jason had long since finished eating. He watched as Rafe put a salmon steak, a pile of rice and some salad on a plate and shoved it in the microwave. Jason didn't say a word, but he was boiling inside. When the food was heated, Rafe sat across from him and began forking rice into his mouth. Lettuce leaves and slices of carrot were lasered to the plate like pottery designs.

"If you want to make the team you're going to have to do what your coaches tell you to do," Jason finally said.

"I don't want to listen to those assholes."

"If you think you're going to play baseball without listening to assholes, you might as well quit now."

"I want *you* to teach me." Rafe looked up with a sour expression. "Why didn't you say something out there?"

Jason stared at the angry boy at his table. He knew that Rafe didn't have the faintest idea what he was getting into — the days, months, years it would take to reach the pinnacle he thought was his by virtue of genetics. The best thing for Rafe right now was submission to someone who could cut through his self-absorption and appeal to whatever inner strength he had. Jason didn't want to be that person. He was willing to teach him what he knew, but not at the risk of losing him again.

"You need somebody to be tough on you," Jason said. "I don't want to be tough. My father was tough — that's what all men think they're supposed to be. It's bullshit."

Rafe squinted, uncertain what his father was saying. "I don't want Mr. Rogers," he said. It was a joke between them. Rafe couldn't stand Mr. Rogers. He thought he was creepy and refused to watch him. "Juvenile Hall was tough. I saw a lot of shit."

"I'm sure you did," Jason nodded. He was also sure Rafe didn't have a clue about what he had just told him — any more than he knew what Rafe was talking about. Tough to Rafe was something on the outside, something to be endured. To Jason, toughness was something inside — the stuff that helped you endure.

He pointed at Rafe's plate. "You want tough? Eat that — everything."

Rafe stared at his plate. The possibilities were many. 'I'm not hungry.' 'I don't like salmon.' 'I want a burger.' He took a forkful of salmon and examined drops of lemon and oil and seasoning clinging to the pink flesh. His father wasn't a bad cook. Rafe couldn't think of anything his father made that he didn't like — except the hot cereals he was brought up on in Alaska — Cream of Wheat, Cream of Rice, Malt-o-Meal.

Rafe ate everything on his plate, down to the last grain of rice. "OK?"

Jason nodded. "You've still got to pass your courses. And complete your community service. And show up for your parole meetings. Baseball is just one thing you do. All of it," he said, molding the air with his hands, "is who you are."

"That's between me and my teachers, remember?"

Jason gazed at his son, who now wanted to learn baseball, the one thing he was probably qualified to teach him. "You just made me one of your teachers."

"As long as you don't sing the Mr. Rogers song."

"I'd never do that to you," Jason smiled.

WILLIE MET them at the Mazatlan airport in the same cab he'd picked Jason up in seven years before. Except now it had a lavender paint job, with new trim that made it shimmer like a hologram. On the driver's door was the insignia of the Colorado Rockies. On the passenger side was Willie's old logo, but freshly painted — *"Taxi a Todas Partes."*

"Hermano — qué tal!" Willie exclaimed as he embraced Jason in the brassy seaside light outside the terminal. He broke away to look at Rafe, then smiled and offered his hand. "You look like a ballplayer," he said. Rafe blushed and muttered hello. Willie hustled them into the cab. A handsome young man sat behind the wheel, salsa music blaring. Jason looked at Willie and raised his eyebrows. *"Qué hombre!"*

"You should see him throw the ball, *Ya-sone*," Willie said proudly. "He makes his daddy look like a tired old man."

"His daddy *is* a tired old man."

'Little Carlos' greeted Jason with a warm handshake. He had grown a foot in the year since Jason had seen him, nourished on the protein of Willie's major league salary. Willie had also grown since Jason had left the team in June: his stomach hung over his trousers in the classic repose of many of his neighbors. To look at the two of them, one would be hard-pressed to choose Willie Herrera as the active ballplayer.

Willie pointed out signs of progress on their way into town: a new elementary school that was half completed, reinforcement rods sticking out of a hoped-for second floor; a glass office building that Willie boasted was full of computers; a new KFC. Then, Willie's new house. It looked like it had been airlifted from a Denver suburb, a broad, two-story structure with faux Tudor beams between top floor windows. "Six bedrooms," Willie said proudly. He showed them upstairs to the guest room, with twin beds and an old fashioned roll-top writing desk. On the wall between the beds was a team photo of the Colorado Rockies, with Jason towering in the back row.

Rafe threw his duffel bag on the bed. "Is that the field you're always talking about?" he asked, staring out the window at a sun-baked ball field with a sagging chain link backstop behind home plate.

"At least it's not raining," Jason said. "Let's get something to eat and work out."

"We ate on the plane!"

"OK then — suit up!"

They marched down the stairs carrying their gloves, hats and cleats and confronted the embracing gazes of Ixchel, Maria Emma, Guadalupe and Ana, now fourteen, twelve, eleven and nine, and Willie's wife, Liliana. "*Tio Yasone!*" shouted Ana. She had Willie's round friendly face and twinkling eyes. "Did you bring presents?"

Rafe had heard about the sisters but he wasn't expecting their obvious devotion to his father — and their beauty. Ixchel, as tall as Carlito but with a narrower face and full lips, stepped towards him.

"Hello, how are you?" she said proudly, in perfectly accented English.

"Hello," Rafe responded, stunned.

Jason clinched Liliana in a big hug. "*Buenas tardes* — you look wonderful," he said. "So do the kids."

"*Igualmente*," she responded. She turned to Rafe. "Welcome to our home. We are very happy to see you."

Rafe shook her hand and nodded. Jason clapped him on the shoulder. "Rafe is dying to play baseball. It's been raining for months in San Francisco."

"Of course," Liliana smiled. She was used to yielding to baseball.

They laced on their spikes, grabbed two bats and a bucket of baseballs from the garage and stepped onto the field. It was dry, heat-baked, lumpy, but it was a diamond. Jason smiled. People had basketball courts, tennis courts, putting greens — how many had their own baseball fields? Willie had even added chalk marks down the baselines, bases bolted to the ground, a vinyl home plate.

They jogged the periphery of the field, passing the backsides of small stucco homes at the far end. "How you feel?" Jason asked. "Fine." Jason never knew what that meant. Academically, Rafe was keeping up his end of the bargain, though little more. He had finished his drug counseling, and had another month of community service before he was free. He was getting C's at HI, doing most of his homework and working it out with his teachers when he didn't. He had few friends, but he didn't seem to care. Whatever demons had driven Rafe before had transferred their obsessions to his father's sport. He wanted to play baseball all the time. They had discovered a field behind a shuttered middle school in their neighborhood and every weekend, weather permitting, Jason banged out balls to Rafe. Pop-ups, grounders, line drives, bunts ... followed by running and calisthenics, then more grounders. In three months, his clumsy, tentative son was replaced by the graceful chrysalis of a boy in love with his mastery of motion.

They finished running and Jason began banging grounders to Rafe. He was quicker and more fluid than Jason ever was, with an almost effortless grace and ability to anticipate where the ball was going. Over and over they repeated the drills — grounder to the right, grounder to the left, step on first base, throw home. A dozen neighborhood kids appeared, drawn by the news that Willie's big league friend was back.

"Focus!" Jason shouted when Rafe missed a ball; he said nothing when he speared it. Sweat poured down Jason's face. It was well over ninety in the Mexican sun. Carlito and Willie joined them with their ball gloves, and stood on the side watching.

"He looks good, *hombre*. Can he hit?"

Jason handed the bat to Willie.

"Not yet."

THE BIG grill smoked with steaks and half-chickens, peppers and zucchini and roasting eggplant. The picnic table was crowded with bowls of tortilla chips, pickled radishes and carrots, fresh homemade salsa, baskets of warm tortillas, plates, glasses, silverware, napkins. The girls were all eyes on Rafe, who pretended he could care less. The youngest one, Ana, sat next to him and flirted shamelessly, putting corn on his plate, handing him warm tortillas, refilling his glass. The others passed plates of grilled meat and vegetables, mingling their English and Spanish in an attempt to find a combination their handsome guest was comfortable with.

At one point, driven by necessity, Rafe asked Ixchel, "could you pass the chicken?" Ixchel spoke English the best of them, but she was also the most worried about making a mistake. *"Como?"* she asked. Rafe looked questioningly towards his father, who shrugged with mock helplessness. Willie leaned forward, smiling. *"Pasela por favor,"* he said, pointing to the platter. Ixchel handed it to Rafe and quickly looked away.

"Say thank you, Buddy," Jason reminded him.

"Thank you."

"You're welcome," Ixchel replied quietly.

After dinner the men retired to chairs at the edge of the yard. Willie's kids and some of the neighbors mingled on the field, chatting in the twilight. Rafe had gone up to his room after dinner, as he did at home, to read and listen to music.

Willie produced a bottle of Don Pedro and some heavy crystal. "No thanks," Jason said. Willie poured himself a glass of the powerful spirit. "We really missed you this year, *Ya-sone.* Not just your arm but your shitty jokes."

"I missed you guys too."

"You doin' alright? You seem really pissed off at something."

"I can't bullshit you, Willie. I miss playing really bad. The money too." He had started listening to games during the World Series, thinking as long as he didn't watch it would be OK. But the familiar, unhurried voices of the announcers caught him like an old song. Five minutes into his first broadcast, he was hooked. Who's up next? What's he hitting? How's the matchup — lefty vs. righty? Fast ball pitcher to fast ball hitter? How many runners on? Are they going with the pitch? It was like old friends, old teammates, an old love. It was baseball.

"I can imagine," Willie said. "But Rafe, he's gonna be a hell of a player."

"I don't think so, man. He doesn't listen to shit." The first star appeared above the Eastern horizon. Mars, Jason was pretty sure — solitary, arrogant. "He plays to his own drummer, and there's nobody else in the band."

"He's only fifteen," Willie said. "Kids got a lot of strange things in their head."

"Yeah. And I don't know what's in there. He never talks to me — about anything."

"Did you talk to your father?"

Jason watched Willie's kids horsing around with their neighbors, playing bursts of 'tag,' slapping hands, laughing in the warm night air. "I mean nothing, Willie — *nada, nunca, ningun.*" There was a long pause. The happy sounds of children surrounded them and Jason's lament was lost in the music of their voices.

"I'm sorry to hear that." Willie lit up a joint and exhaled the smoke straight above. "They let me go, *Ya-sone*."

"What do you mean?"

"The Rockies are paying me $600,000 not to play this year."

"Ah Jesus, Willie. That sucks."

Willie took another toke, held it for a few seconds, then let it out. "Hell, if you told this Mexican he would make $600,000 for not playing baseball," he laughed, "I'd say you were smoking too much *mota!*"

Jason clapped him on the shoulder. "They don't know shit."

"I felt it as soon as you left. I pitched six fucking innings the rest of the year."

"What're you gonna do?"

"Spend time with the kids. Play Mexican ball, if anybody wants me." He took another drag. "What about you?"

Jason shook his head. "I don't know."

The next morning at 5 AM Liliana rose and prepared a breakfast of eggs and salsa, beans, tortillas, bacon, strong black coffee and fresh-squeezed orange juice and had it on the table by six. Rafe wolfed his down, then waited for his father by the edge of the field. At seven they started stretching, then ran. Willie and Carlito joined them. "I might as well start getting in shape now," Willie said. "It's going to take me longer, now that I'm a *viejo*."

Running with Willie, Jason couldn't help thinking back to the year before, at the beginning of his new contract before Rafe came to Denver. This was the first time in twelve years he wouldn't be getting ready to play professional ball. Spring training started in three weeks. *He* wanted to be fielding. *He* wanted to be hitting. *He* wanted it to be somebody's job to be telling *him* what to do.

The word went out and the neighborhood kids started showing up, many with the gloves Jason had given them years before. Jason gathered them and chose a batting order that included everybody from big to small. It was the only chance these youngsters would ever have to play with two bonafide major league players, and he wanted to give everyone a chance.

"I thought we were going to have batting practice," Rafe complained.

"We're going to play a game first," Jason said. "Maybe you'll learn something."

"I'm not going to learn anything from a bunch of Mexicans!"

Jason grabbed Rafe by the arm and pulled him to bleachers. "You sit here," he growled, "until I tell you to get up."

They played three innings of silly, chaotic ball with as many outs as they needed for each kid to get up to bat twice. Willie pitched blooper pitches to everyone except Carlito, who looked like he could handle whatever his father threw. Carlito hit one past Jason down the first base line that would have been a double, and another over the little kid's head who was playing a hopeful, though ineffective, left field. "Way to go, Carlito!" Jason applauded. "*Estas listo por los Grandes!*" Carlito beamed.

After three innings, Jason pulled Willie aside. "Catch for me, will you?"

Willie put on the equipment and settled behind the plate. There was the familiar rocking motion, the high graceful kick, the sweet sound of the ball slamming into the leather mitt. Jason threw half a dozen pitches, then yelled to Rafe, "Put on a helmet!"

Rafe rose and walked slowly towards the bats and batting helmets leaning against the backstop. He hadn't hit in a month — or rather, tried to hit. They had taken a bag of balls to their field, but before throwing Jason had explained all the ways that facing a pitcher was different from hitting against a machine. A pitcher changes speeds, location, direction … coming in sidearm or over the top … throwing down, up, out, in — and outside the strike zone. Jason's perspective of hitting from a pitcher's point of view was not an inconsiderable advantage. But Rafe just didn't seem to get it. When the ball was in the strike zone, he hit it as hard as any kid his age. But if the ball was out of the zone, he swung and missed every single time, no matter what Jason said. Twenty, thirty pitches he would throw off the plate; twenty, thirty times Rafe would swing and miss it.

"*Swing at strikes!*" Jason would shout.

"*Then throw strikes!*" Rafe shouted back.

This was Rafe's first trip to the batter's box since that day. Jason stared at him, expressionless. There were perhaps a thousand major league ballplayers, and tens of thousands more at the minor league, college, high school and Little League levels and there couldn't have been a half dozen with the bullshit batting stance his son insisted on using. He had tried to modify it, but Rafe wouldn't change. It had to be his way.

He threw a major league fastball right down the middle of the plate and the ball smoked into Willie's glove before Rafe knew what had happened. Rafe dug in and hiked his hands even higher. The next time he swung but he was swinging more at the motion of his father's arm than the ball, which passed untouched into Willie's glove, a perfect strike. It went like this for five, ten, twenty pitches and neither Jason nor Rafe said a word. "Step deeper in the box," Willie advised him at one point, but Rafe stayed put. He could hit his father. He knew he could.

The kids cheered the first few pitches, then watched silently, unable to understand what they were witnessing. After about thirty pitches Jason turned away from the plate. His heart was pumping, his arm pulsed with a feeling of strength. Good god, how he missed this. He turned back and there was Rafe in the batter's box, waiting. What he first thought was sweat streaming down his son's face, Jason could unmistakably see were tears. He worried that he had gone too far; and if so, he wondered what the way back was. Rafe had asked him to be tough, but up to now he really hadn't been. Not tough the way he had seen people be tough. Not major league tough. Maybe this is what Rafe needed all along. Maybe this is what he had been asking for. Or maybe not.

"Alright!" Jason called out. "Three strikes you're out."

He threw a decent major league fastball, nothing extraordinary but still 87, 88 mph and Rafe took a beautiful swing and fouled it back to the screen. Jason had to give him credit: he hadn't given up. The second pitch was much the same. The third one Jason upped to 90 and Rafe swung above it by a foot. Strike three. He stood uncertainly in the batter's box, then started to walk away.

"One more," Jason called. "Four strikes you're out."

Rafe settled back into his stance, but this time he took Willie's advice and stepped back in the box. Jason unleashed a pitch maybe 85 miles per hour — faster than any pitch Rafe would see from his own peer group until he got to college. It flew off Rafe's bat far out to right field, where it bounced with a ringing crash against the tin siding of a chicken coop. Five or six chickens flapped squawking from the coop, followed by the frightened crowing of a rooster. The kids laughed and applauded.

"Good going," Willie said. Rafe waited for the next pitch with grim determination. Once again, Jason threw three solid fastballs — Strike One. Strike Two. Strike Three. Then, a fourth, softer pitch that Rafe pounded with powerful precision.

They continued like this for twenty minutes, the neighborhood kids shagging balls and Willie catching the ones Rafe missed. Finally, after a line drive that carried deep into center field, Jason walked in towards home plate. They had been at it for three hours. He felt warm, lubricated, spent. It was a good feeling, surprising after the way the morning began, and testimony to the healing power of baseball.

Rafe leaned over the plate, rubbing the blisters at the base of his fingers. He looked up at his father proudly. He had stood in and taken his father's best stuff. He could still feel the vibration in his hands from balls he'd hit solidly.

"I want you to apologize to Willie and Carlito for what you said," Jason insisted.

"That's OK, *Ya-sone*," Willie said, halfway out of his catcher's equipment. But Rafe knew better. There'd be no more fielding, no more lessons until this was done.

"I'm sorry Uncle Willie," Rafe said. "I'm sorry, Carlito."

Willie leaned over and clapped him on the shoulder. "That's OK, *hijo*. You just keep practicing, you're going to be a great ballplayer." Then he looked over at Jason and smiled. "But your daddy," he whistled. "He's still got it."

Rafe turned and gave his father a wondering look.

VINCE LASKY wore a blue and white checkerboard sport coat and light blue golf shirt, a pair of white slacks and white shoes with baby blue socks. He was in his mid-fifties but looked seventy, with a ring of badly dyed hair circling the sides and back of his head, a round fleshy face, and a complexion surprisingly unaffected by the sun — perhaps because the sun rarely penetrated the perpetual cloud of cigarette smoke surrounding him.

"I got a radar gun in the car," Lasky said. "The arm works, you join them tomorrow in New York. You always pitched good against the Mets."

Jason didn't know what to say. Lasky's call to the house two days ago from West Palm Beach had shocked him. He was sitting in his kitchen in San Francisco, trying not to look at the headline on the sports page, which shouted "Play Ball!" There was a jumble of dishes in the sink, balls and bats leaning in the wooden box by the back door and he was wondering what the hell he was going to do. He had taken a job as assistant coach at St. Frances de Sales High School in Burlingame, in a different league from Holy Innocents. He and Rafe had argued for a week about it. Rafe wanted his father as his coach and couldn't accept the fact that he wasn't offered a job at HI. Jason thought it was best for both of them that he not be there, so Rafe could have exposure to other coaches and learn to stand on his own. "*You* have to swing the bat, *you* have to catch the ball," he told him. "There isn't anything more for me to do." What Jason was more upset about was not being able to play himself. And then Lasky called.

"Which one's yours?" Lasky asked, jerking his head towards the field in Golden Gate Park. Jason spotted Rafe at the end of the bench, apart from the line of teammates standing on the bench cheering their teammates on. "Number seventeen," he pointed. *The kid with the chip on his shoulder*, he could have added.

"He's not starting?" Lasky observed.

"It's a long story."

Rafe had made the team, but only because the coaches were too embarrassed not to include him — especially after Jason gave $15,000 to the Spring fundraising drive and the school's trustees assumed there would be more. But Rafe's education on the diamond was painful to watch. He had the firm conviction that he knew more than anybody else about baseball, despite never having played a minute of organized ball in his life. Through the first six games, Rafe was hitting .089. He'd hit two electrifying triples — and struck out eleven times.

"You look like you're in great shape," Lasky observed, returning to his reason for being there.

"Tell you the truth, Vince, I'm in the best shape of my life." Lasky grabbed a fold of his own flesh beneath his golf shirt and pulled, extending it like taffy. "If I didn't smoke three packs a day I'd be bigger than Tony Soprano."

Jason smiled. Lasky had been third base coach when he broke in with Cincinnati. He had played for the Astros, the Angels and the Phillies as a hard-hitting third baseman, then ended up as DH with Toronto. He was one of the last breed of old-timers who never lifted a weight, ran a windsprint, or met an all-you-can-eat smorgasbord he didn't take literally. He was a scout now with the Phillies. They were short a left-handed reliever and had asked Lasky to check out Jason Thibodeaux.

Rafe's team erupted as Matt Cibotti bounced a single over second base, scoring Ed Flanigan with the game's first run. The Hawks were especially pumped up. It was their opening game in the city's Catholic league, against their archrival, St. Ignatius College Prep. There they all were, kids he had coached during the Fall Clinic: Red. Lopey. Chops. Walrus. DZ. Waffle. Deuce. Big Ugly's Brother. Good kids, outgoing and cooperative. And then there was Rafe.

"Willie Herrera says you're throwin' good," Lasky said.

"Why don't you give *him* a shot?"

"Not unless he's throwin' lefty."

St. Ignatius carried a 3-1 lead into the top of the fifth when Rafe trotted out to right field. "The Phillies are a good team for you," Lasky pressed him. "They're ready to talk three, four years, depending what the Rockies want for compensation."

Jason watched intently. Maybe this was the day Rafe put everything together. Ran down every ball, hit his cut-off man, backed up plays at first base, cheered on his teammates, laid down a bunt when he was asked, took a pitch, hit behind the runner ... "That's him out in right," he pointed. "Do me a favor and tell me what you see."

Nothing came Rafe's way that inning. He trotted in nonchalantly and took his place at the end of the bench. Lasky lit cigarette after cigarette, looking impatiently from his watch to the field and back again. The sky had clouded up and as it did most afternoons, a cold Pacific wind pushed the fog in from the coast. "Jesus Christ," Lasky exclaimed, "what is this, the fuckin' Tundra League?"

Rafe finally strode to the plate with two outs and runners at second and third. Both runners had walked and moved up on a wild pitch. The obvious strategy when facing a pitcher struggling with control would be to wait him out for a walk, or at least for a good pitch to drive. Rafe took his stance; Lasky turned and looked at Jason.

"I know, I know," Jason said. "Just watch him, will ya?"

The first pitch was low and away, an obvious ball, but Rafe swung and squibbed it off the end of his bat towards the opposing team's dugout. The second pitch was too high for even Rafe to swing at; it sailed over the catcher's head and hit the backstop so hard that it bounced directly back to the catcher, freezing the runners. With first base open Rafe was even more certain not to see a pitch to hit; in fact, the next pitch came in high and tight, impossible to hit in any situation. Rafe strode into it and swung a good foot beneath the ball. A few voices from the Hawks' bench cheered him on, but most of his teammates sat quietly. Rafe had cultivated few friends on the team; almost no one had any affection for him, let alone faith in his abilities.

The count was 1-2 and the pitcher hadn't come close to throwing a strike. Jason fought the impulse to close his eyes. He knew what was going to happen. Hours of throwing to him day after day and it wasn't going to make a dime's worth of difference. While every parent in the world would be squeezing for their son to hit the next pitch a country mile, Jason couldn't — he couldn't stand the disappointment.

The pitcher went into his windup, the runners walked off their bases, Rafe waggled his bat, his right foot tapping the earth in anticipation. The pitch came in high and outside. Rafe flailed at the ball and the catcher had to lunge to trap it in the webbing of his glove. "Stee-rike! Batter's out!" the umpire shouted.

"He wear glasses?" Lasky asked.

"No. Why?"

"Maybe he can't see the fuckin' ball."

Lasky pulled out a pen and wrote a number on the back of his business card. "Give me a call. We'll set up a time to throw."

"WHAT WOULD you throw here?" Rafe asked.

It was the last of the fourth, the A's and Indians at Oakland's Coliseum. Jason was surprised by the question; surprised, in fact, by Rafe's demeanor the entire evening. He was alert, attentive, inquisitive about players, situations, strategies. They were seated in the players' Family Box behind home plate. From this angle they had the same view as the home plate umpire. They could see how fastballs hop and curve balls break, the downward dart of sliders and the sharp trajectory of hits as they jumped from the bat. Rafe was enthralled. It was the first time he had been to a major league game with his father as a fellow fan. The stadium, half-full and flooded with powerful light, the players strong and self-composed, his father by his side — he couldn't remember being happier.

"Depends," Jason said. "You work with a scouting report, the pitcher's and batter's strengths. But you start with the situation. Men on first and third, one out, the count 3-1, the number eight hitter up to bat. In the National League I can throw a breaking pitch because I can afford to walk a guy with the pitcher up next. But here in Wiffle Ball

League you've got the DH and a real hitter coming up next, so he'll probably come in with a fastball — unless he's got a killer change-up or slider."

Rafe followed a pitch that began in the center of the plate and broke in on the batter's hands. "What was that — a curve?"

"Slider."

Rafe scanned the field — the positioning of the players, the coaches rubbing signals like sunscreen into their arms, necks, earlobes, the catcher looking to the dugout for signals — it had never seemed so alive to him, so complex, so accessible. They had to go to more games; this was the coolest. Bases loaded, one out. The Oakland batter dug in at the plate. He could see the muscles in his forearm, his hands gripping the bat, the umpire squatting over the catcher, the pitcher staring in for the signal.

"Whoa!" Rafe shouted, after a huge looping curveball dropped over the plate for a strike.

"You see the strike zone there," Jason said, shaping a vertical rectangle with his hands. "Picture a refrigerator. Anything inside the refrigerator is a strike. Anything outside, you let it go."

"Got it," Rafe said eagerly.

Jason suddenly saw what was going on and he was mortified. Father and son at the game — why hadn't he thought of this before? His own father had never taken him — and in a strange and unconscious coincidence, he'd never taken Rafe until today. Before he'd never had a chance — he was a player. And since retiring, he'd avoided contact with Major League baseball as thoroughly as an alcoholic avoids a drink. Now, three games into the new season, he had unlocked a hidden door in his relationship with his son — just as he was preparing to walk out through a different one.

The A's got a run on a sacrifice fly, then ended the inning with a double play. Rafe watched the Indians leave the field, his eyes snapping with interest.

"Pretty cool, huh?" Jason said.

"The ball moves like a laser."

"Now you see why you have to focus." Jason stood. "You want anything? I'm going to the bathroom."

"Could I have a lemonade?"

When he returned, Rafe was leaning forward in his seat, following every pitch as intently as if it were a video game. Jason took his seat and watched, waiting for the right moment. This was the hardest thing he'd ever done — at least since the last time. But what difference would it make? If he stayed there would be pain. If he left there would be pain. He didn't seem to be making any difference in anybody's life — at least until tonight.

Then miraculously, Rafe created the opening. After a hard smash to third, a dive across the line, a throw across the diamond to beat the runner by half a step, he turned to his father with a wide-eyed admiring look. "I can't believe you did this!"

Jason smiled. "I may have a chance to do it again."

"What do you mean?" Rafe asked.

"The Phillies want to make me an offer. It's nothing definite yet. They need a left hander." Rafe turned away. With a runner on third and one out, the score 1-0, a conspiracy of signals flashed around the field. The pitch came in low and skipped in the dirt, but the batter swung anyway. What a waste, he thought — swing at strikes!

"But I'm not going anywhere without talking to you about it."

"Talk about what?"

"Whether it's all right with you. I'm not going anywhere if it's not all right with you."

Rafe spoke still facing the field. "What differences does it make what I want? What do *you* want to do?"

"I want to play. But I don't want to screw things up again." He paused, trying to catch Rafe's eye. "I don't want you to think I'm abandoning you, because I'm not. It would only be for a year, two at the most. You'd be with your mom — you're there all week anyway. I'll be back in the off-season, we could see each other as much as we wanted then. Plus you could come to games when we're in San Francisco, sit in the dugout ... "

Some kind of pitch — Rafe couldn't tell what it was — headed towards the outside half of the plate, then darted a foot off. The batter checked his swing — Ball One.

"But it's got to be OK with you."

"Sure. It's OK," Rafe said.

"I mean OK. Not just saying OK, but really OK."

"It's OK, Dad. You should play ... really."

Jason patted Rafe's shoulder in appreciation. The count was 2-2 now, the runner still at third. Rafe studied the pitcher, saw his arm come around and the ball head for the plate. He imagined himself hitting, sending the ball on a laser-like trajectory over the scoreboard in center field for a game-leading homer. But the pitch was just off the outside corner of the plate and the batter took it for a ball. It was 3-2 now. The field became a blur in front of him.

Rafe stood up, grabbing his jacket. "Can we go?"

JASON BROUGHT up the big suitcase he used for road trips from the garage. The house was disturbingly quiet. It was a Wednesday night, Rafe was over at Vicki's. He would see him one more time before he left the next day and remind him this wasn't about him. It wasn't about them. It was about baseball.

He lined the bottom of the suitcase with his cotton boxers. He remembered looking in the bedroom when he was a kid and seeing his father packing for one of his trips on some oil rig off the coast of Bahrain, Venezuela, Norway. He would study maps and imagine his father on the sea, extracting oil with something that looked like a vacuum cleaner. He never knew how long he'd be gone for. He never got a call or a card. Then one day seven or eight months later, the battered suitcase would reappear in the hallway, and he knew his dad was home.

He plopped in a pile of t-shirts, his travel alarm, a handful of condoms. Then the phone rang. It was Vicki. "Rafe said you're leaving."

"Philadelphia offered me a contract. It's just for this season."

"You're not going to do this again. You're not going to run out on him again."

"I didn't run out the last time, if you'll recall the details. You threatened to expose me as a child abuser if I tried to see him." He hadn't initiated a call to her precisely because of this. Conversations with Vicki more often than not descended into sniping, sniping into battles, battles into wars. While they finally had accepted that they had to talk to each other, they still didn't know how to do it effectively.

Vicki's voice softened. "He's devastated, Jason."

"No, he's not. He's disappointed. He'll get over it as soon as he realizes I'm not running out on him. He can come visit any time. I'll fly him there."

"I can't do this by myself," she said. Jason stopped, surprised. It was one of the most direct statements he had heard from her in years.

"Aw, Vicki, it's just one season ... maybe two — I'm thirty-six years old! He doesn't give a shit whether I'm here or not anyway."

"You're wrong, Jason. He's getting good grades now. He cares about things ... about baseball ... about *you*."

But she was too late — fourteen years too late. "It's gonna be OK, Vicki. We're gonna do it right this time, I promise."

THE NEXT morning Rafe climbed into the Pathfinder and stared straight ahead. "Why do I need to go to the eye doctor? I can see fine."

Jason held up his right hand. "How many fingers?" Rafe rolled his eyes. "C'mon, how many fingers?"

"Five!" Rafe shouted.

Jason shook his head. "Four — the other one's your thumb."

"Hilarious, Dad."

The offices of Dr. Mordecai Byrne, one of the top eye specialists in the country, were on the top floor of the Stanford Medical Center. Jason sat in the waiting room while Rafe went through a battery of vision tests. The walls in the waiting room were filled with team photos of the Oakland A's and San Francisco 49ers, and autographed portraits of sports stars from other pro and college teams in the region. Jason took out his cell phone and pressed through to his phone book. He was supposed to call his agent and give him an answer to the Phillies' offer — $1.4 million for the year, with $3 million to the Rockies for compensation. "They want to know today, Jason," Springer had said. "Don't fuck this up."

Seated across from him was a kid, maybe five or six-years-old, his shoes dangling above the floor. He wore a set of thick glasses, one lens covered with a beige eye patch. Jason smiled at him and the kid snuggled shyly into his mother's side. At that moment, Jason realized that he didn't have the faintest idea what to do. He put the phone back into his pocket.

It was an hour before the nurse called him in. Byrne's private office was lined with beautiful watercolors of California landscapes, signed *Mordecai Byrne*. Rafe sat quietly in front of the desk, then Dr. Byrne came in clutching a manila folder. He was an athletic, middle-aged man with a full shock of Kennedy-esque hair and an open, friendly manner. He shook both Thibodeauxs hands, then stared openly at Rafe. "When you're hitting, when do you see where a pitch is going?"

"What do you mean?"

Byrne pulled a baseball from his bookshelf, signed by Mark

McGwire. He went into a windup, bringing his arm down slowly. "Here?" he asked. He continued until he threw the ball into the couch against the back wall. He did it a second time, and Rafe pointed to the very top of his motion.

Byrne nodded and turned to Jason. "Our tests show your son has extraordinary eyesight. Twelve/20 vision in his right eye — his lead eye as a left-handed batter, and 20/20 in his other." He turned to look at Rafe. "That means he can identify an object from twenty feet that a person with 20/20 vision sees from twelve. But even more extraordinary is his depth perception." Rafe stirred and watched Dr. Byrne closely. "I've examined thousands of people and I've only seen two with eyesight like this," Byrne said. "Tony Gwynn and Barry Bonds. If you wanted to create a formula for a gifted baseball player, you would start with this."

Jason shook his head. "Except one of the reasons we're here, a friend of mine — a pro scout — thought he wasn't seeing the ball at all."

"I don't think so." Dr. Byrne turned back to Rafe. "The ball probably looks as big as a grapefruit to you sometimes."

Rafe shrugged. "It looks like a baseball."

Byrne smiled. "Can you see the rotation of the ball?" Rafe stared uncertainly. "The way the seams move when it's thrown." Again, he simulated a throwing motion. Rafe nodded. "Yeah, sure."

Byrne turned to Jason. "He's got it — if he wants to use it."

THAT AFTERNOON Eddie "Fanagain" Flanigan was feeding the Monster at the end of the batting cage, holding the ball up to let Rafe know it was coming, then dropping it into the spinning wheel. Foomp! It shot straight towards the plate where Rafe was standing. *Crack!* — the ball crashed into the upper corner of the netting, then dropped to the ground like a felled bird.

"Bingo," Rafe muttered smugly. Fanagain held up the next ball, then fed it into the machine. Again, Rafe smoked it into the highest corner of the netting. "Bingo." The next ball and the next and the next all met the same fate. A college level fast ball, a college level pounding. And this was just the beginning, he knew. He had a special power, and these guys didn't have shit.

"Gamer!" Flanigan called, signaling the last ball in the bucket. Rafe crouched, his eyes zeroed like radar on the dark opening where the ball would appear. Then, foomp! Crack! — and it was gone.

"Nice hitting, Juvie," Octavio Lopez called from outside the cage, where he was warming up with Enrique Tai. They were the closest thing Rafe had to friends on the team — the lone Latino and the half Thai, half-Japanese second-string catcher. Rafe walked towards the door of the cage, still wearing his official Rockies batting gloves.

"Don't call me Juvie anymore, OK?" he asked Lopey. He never liked the name. He didn't like remembering Juvenile Hall or anything that had happened there.

"Whatever you say … Juvie," Lopey grinned.

Other players warming up outside of the cage overheard Rafe's request. "Juvie's not a juvie any more," Bobby Turlock called out. "He's going to need a new name."

"How about Whiffer!" Jerrod Manes shouted.

"Fan Man!"

"The Holy Braille!"

Rafe stepped outside the cage. "You guys are full of shit. I'm going to be in the Big Leagues while you're still chasing dog pussy around the Sunset."

"Oh! Oh! Juvie has spoken!" Turlock shouted. "He addresses the mortals from the heights of Mount Bullshit."

"I got a name," Fanagain chimed in. *"Big League."*

"Maybe just *Big* for short," Turlock laughed. "Or Big Asshole."

Rafe was on him like a panther. He pinned Turlock's shoulders and drove him against the portable backstop. Ferociousness and speed were key, he knew from fights he had seen in Juvenile Hall. He pressed the pitcher to the ground and pounded two quick punches to the face. He wound up for another blow, his gloved hand poised above Turlock's shocked face when Coach Shannon pulled him off.

"You're so gone, Thibodeaux," the coach growled.

IT WAS 5 o'clock when Jason pushed open the front door of Holy Innocents and held it for Rafe, who passed in front of him, head lowered, his hair falling across his forehead. Jason had seen a hundred fights like the one Baldassare described, the confluence of testosterone, competitiveness and insecurity flaring up as naturally as grassfires in the Sierras. Not that he was excusing it, but this wasn't any time to pile on. Rafe already was suspended from school, and his place on the team in jeopardy.

Rafe waited beside the Pathfinder. "Let's go hit some," Jason said.

"Hit what?"

"Baseballs."

Rafe looked up, surprised. "I thought you were going to Philadelphia."

"We'll talk about Philadelphia. Let's play some ball."

He parked at the curb in front of their house and pulled a bulging duffel bag from the back of the vehicle. Rafe followed him across the street, toward the two-square block reservoir their house looked over. Jason pushed through the thick row of oleanders and stepped through a hole in the chain link fence. He had never given the space much thought, until he came home one afternoon and saw a file of kids parading from the bushes with baseball bats and gloves. He found the hole, and inside a convex asphalt surface the size of several football fields. There was an old futon wired to the fence as a backstop, a regulation home plate with a batter's box drawn on both sides — and sixty feet, six inches away, a pitching rubber painted on the tar.

"What is this place?" Rafe asked. Jason dropped the duffel bag. The metal bats rang like chimes. He unzipped the bag and handed a bat to his son — a heavier one, 32-ounces, to help him keep his hands back. "The Raphael Thibodeaux All-Star Memorial Batting Cage," Jason smiled.

"You're not pissed off?"

"What good's it do for *me* to get pissed off? Your coach is pissed off, your teammates are pissed off — even *you're* pissed off."

Rafe swung the bat hard four or five times. "I am pissed off. I'm pissed off you're leaving. I'm pissed off I can't go with you."

"You should be pissed off. I'd be pissed off too. But you know what?" Jason said. "I'm not going to Philadelphia."

"What are you talking about?"

"I'm not going. I'd rather be here with you."

Rafe gazed wonderingly at his father, then a look of fear crossed his face. "Oh no," he said. "I don't want you to quit because of me again."

"I'm not," Jason said. Not totally anyway. It was all about not doing the wrong thing twice. He'd run out on Rafe once; what kind of man would do it again? Rafe had special talents, special needs, and he was his father. "I'm doing what a father's supposed to do — be there for his kid. It's what I want to do."

"But then you'll get all depressed and blame *me* for not playing."

"You might be right," Jason nodded. "I might regret it. But it would never come close to the regret I'd feel if I left now."

Rafe didn't know how to respond. It was too much — going from losing his father, his spot on the team, his place in school, to this.

"C'mon," Jason urged. "Let's get in some hacks before it gets dark."

Rafe approached the plate with uncertainty. Everything had changed. This place, right across the street from his house — a kid's paradise, the horizon stretching forever. His father, waiting to throw him pitches. He half-smiled and took his stance. His dad threw half a dozen pitches, some of which he hit but most he didn't. The balls began to line up along the fence beneath the futon and Jason wondered how somebody with Rafe's eyesight could miss the ball so consistently. His next pitch came over the outside part of the plate. It was a good pitch, probably in the mid eighties, and Rafe powered it deep to left center where it hit the pavement and rolled out of sight. He threw the next one low and inside, off the strike zone, and Rafe hacked at it awkwardly.

Jason walked in towards the plate. "Can you tell me what's going on, right there?" he asked, pointing to where the pitch had passed Rafe's ankles.

"I'm trying to hit the ball!"

"No," Jason said patiently. "Just tell me what you're seeing. Because now I know you *can* see it."

Rafe looked at him, confused. He thought his dad was going to be angry again, but there he was, talking with him, calmly asking him questions. "I follow it and I try to hit it," he replied.

"Down there, outside of the strike zone? Why?"

"Why?"

"Yeah — why?"

"Because it's there. Because I can see it. Because I want to hit it."

Jason took a deep breath to calm himself. Six months they'd been practicing. Six months he'd tried to teach Rafe where the strike zone was, how to wait for a pitch to drive. Six months.

Rafe watched, waiting for the inevitable explosion. Jason stepped closer. "When you walk into a department store to buy a pair of pants — just a pair of pants — you see hundreds, maybe thousands of other things they're trying to sell you. Underwear, wallets, jewelry, ties. If you buy any of these other things, you're not going to have any money left to buy the thing you came for."

Rafe nodded. This beat the hell out of his father yelling, "swing at strikes!" Or throwing harder and harder until he couldn't even see the ball. "My job as a pitcher is to make you buy all that other shit before you get to the one thing you came for — a pitch you can hit." A surge went through Rafe, goose bumps stood up on his neck. "Remember the box we saw at the Oakland game," Jason continued. "Chest to your knees, the outside of your shoulder to the other, the width of home plate. Anything outside that box is bullshit. Anything inside — it's yours."

Jason walked back to the pitcher's mark. Rafe settled into his stance, envisioning balls trailing away from him like asteroids. He was always so anxious about showing his father he could hit, he was never able to do it. But something felt different. His game belonged to both of them now.

The first pitch came straight down the middle and Rafe froze. "That was yours," Jason said. His next one was way outside and Rafe flailed at it helplessly. "That was mine." His next pitch was a good high school fastball down the middle. Rafe smashed it to straightaway center, where it hit the pavement and rolled against the fence hundreds of yards away. Rafe smiled and set himself again. Jason threw a pitch the same speed two feet off the outside part of the plate; Rafe strode forward but checked his swing.

"Thataboy!" Jason shouted. "Save it for that pair of pants!"

By the end of the second bag as many balls lay against the backstop as out against the fence, but they were balls Rafe hadn't swung at rather than ones he'd missed. The others he'd crushed straight into the teeth of the afternoon wind, dozens of hard drives any hitter could be proud of.

They circled the field and gathered the balls into the duffel bag. When it was full, Rafe zipped the bag and turned eagerly to his father. "Can you hit me some grounders?"

"You got homework, Buddy. You got a whole week of schoolwork to cover."

"They suspend me and expect me to do *homework?* That's bogus!"

Jason shook his head. He had forgotten how clueless a teenager could be. "If I were you, I'd make it easy for myself and follow their rules."

"Ah, it's Mr. Rogers time."

"Hey, you owe me some Mr. Rogers time after what I went through," Jason said, alluding to the painful meeting with the school's principal, Father Riordan, and Coach Shannon. "Any other father would have whipped your ass, or grounded you for the summer. But I'm not going to do that. I'm just going to put on my sweater, pull up an easy chair ... and sing you the Mr. Rogers song!"

"No!" Rafe cried.

Jason sat and leaned against the futon hanging behind home plate. There wasn't any place to be except here — for either one of them. This was it. This was their life.

"Reach in the bag there," Jason said. "There's a couple of beers."

Rafe pulled out a cold Kleisthauler from a plastic bag full of ice and handed it to his father. "The other one's for you." Rafe pulled out a second beer and sat down, holding the bottle uncertainly.

"The top twists off."

"I *know*," Rafe said, removing the cap. Jason held out his beer and clicked it against his son's. "Cheers."

"These aren't real beers," Rafe said knowingly.

"Real enough for me." He looked at Rafe as if for the first time. Baseball was transforming his son, as it once had him. He saw a different kid, eager, trying to excel. He saw himself. "We gotta learn how to do this better somehow."

"Do what?"

"How to talk to each other — about everything." Jason watched a horizonful of faint gray clouds spreading over the city, backlit with a flare of gold as the sun sank towards the sea. Rafe tipped his bottle and drank, then brought it down.

"Sex?" he asked.

"Sex."

"Drugs?"

"Drugs."

Rafe watched the sky along with his father. "I'm sorry about the fight."

"I know you are," Jason replied. "You know, Rafey, I had no idea what I was doing when I was your age. I was scared shitless. Most guys are, but no one admits it. We piss and moan and fight and pose ... I think that's what happened with me and your mom. I was so goddamned scared. I had this scholarship and you were a year old and somebody had to take care of you. I used to walk into your room when you were crying and I didn't have the faintest idea what I was supposed to do. I felt like that astronaut when he took his first steps on the moon."

"*You* were scared?"

"Lost in space. And I didn't like feeling that way so I got angry."

"I didn't think you ever made mistakes."

Jason laughed. "How many games did I lose?"

"One hundred eleven."

"Hey — a hundred and eight!" Jason stared towards the ocean, the sky as big as the sea. Then he turned to Rafe, gripping his neutered beer, and began to sing. "It's a beautiful day in the neighborhood, a beautiful day for a neighbor. Would you be mine? Could you be mine?"

Rafe shook his head. "That's even worse than I remembered it."

A comfortable silence surrounded them. Then, after another long pause, "I'm glad you're not going away," Rafe said.

"Me too."

"But I wish you could still play."

"Me too."

THAT NIGHT they set up a schedule for the rest of his suspension week: school work from 8:30 to 11:45 AM, lunch, then hitting and fielding drills from 1-3:30, schoolwork from four-to-six, dinner, reading and homework, bedtime at eleven. But when Jason popped into Rafe's room at ten, he caught him hiding a magazine beneath his *Anthology of Great American Writing*. "C'mon," Jason groaned. "We had a deal."

Rafe held up the new edition of *Sports Illustrated,* with Isaac Sands on the cover.

"Because it's baseball you think I don't give a shit? You've got work to do!"

Rafe closed the magazine. "I forgot to thank you this afternoon."

"Thank me for what?"

"For bailing me out at school. And only singing one verse of Mr. Rogers."

JASON MADE it to the next Holy Innocents JV game just in time. He knew Rafe wouldn't start; there was a high probability he wouldn't even get in the game, but it was important to be there. He knew Rafe was counting on him.

As usual Rafe sat alone at the end of the bench. Bobby Turlock, his cheek discolored where Rafe had slugged him, sat at the other end. The Hawks played dispiritedly. They didn't hit and they committed three errors by the fourth inning. Jason could tell the dynamics off the field had distracted from the spirit on it. He knew Rafe had to do something positive or his days at Holy Innocents were probably numbered.

He looked up and down the bench — Turlock, Flanigan, Marnes, Davids. Sons of lawyers, engineers, businessmen, kids who played baseball for exercise, character and skills they could apply to other parts of their lives. How to roll with the punches, psych out an opponent, stay within yourself … how to set goals and achieve them … how to win. Poor Rafe had never won anything. He'd lost his father. He'd lost his way at school. He'd lost his mother's respect. He'd lost the respect of his teammates and coaches. He wanted to win, but he had no idea what winning was.

The Hawks were down by five runs in the seventh inning when Coach Shannon called down the bench. "Thibodeaux, get a bat." Rafe squeezed past his teammates. No one said a word — except Bobby Turlock. "He's throwin' everything outside," he said quietly. Rafe glanced back, then strode to the on-deck circle. "Deuce" Twombley had singled sharply to the right side, then stolen second. "Fanagain" walked on five pitches and was leading off first as Rafe approached the plate. He glanced down the third base line for his signal. A pull on the right earlobe, a rub of the forearm, a pull again on the earlobe, a clap of hands — bunt. Rafe's heart sank. He didn't want to bunt, he wanted to slug a home run, wipe three runs off the lead and electrify the crowd. They were five runs down — what good would a *bunt* do?

He stepped out of the box and adjusted his helmet, then watched Mr. Gant flash the same signal. Rafe took his stance, what Coach Shannon said looked 'like a sprinkler in the middle of a beet field.' He watched the pitcher go into his stretch, check the runners, then wheel to the plate. Rafe squared to bunt but kept his bat back. The pitch was well wide of the plate — Ball One.

He looked hopefully at the coach but there was the signal again. Again, the pitch was off the plate — and again Rafe took it. Ball Two. The Hawks were on their feet now, smelling a break in a game that had looked out of reach. Another walk, a couple of hits and they'd be right back in it.

"C'mon Rafe, get a hit!" Vicki called out. Jason didn't know she was there. He turned and she smiled at him; he missed the next pitch which came in on Rafe's fists, forcing him away from the plate. "Ball Three!" the umpire called. Jason couldn't be prouder of his son. He was showing he understood the strategy of baseball, not just its muscle. The next step was a no brainer. There had to be a 'take' sign on; the pitcher hadn't been close and the way he was throwing, probably never would. Rafe didn't have to think of a thing, just follow his coach's order.

But Rafe never looked at his coach. He settled into his stance, waiting for the juicy 3-0 pitch down the middle. He cocked his bat, his right leg twitched, his weight shifted forward as the ball headed to the plate.

Jason watched, his throat tightening. It looked like Rafe was going to defy baseball logic and swing away. But then, at the last moment, he stopped and the pitch sailed wide.

"Ball Four!" Rafe flipped his bat and glanced at Bobby Turlock, who was on his feet applauding with the rest of his teammates.

"Way to go, Big League!" Octavio Lopez called out.

Jason rose to his feet, applauding with the others. The sight of his son trotting down the first base line with a base-on-balls was one of the most gratifying of his life.

MEN ON BASE

RAFE AWOKE TO THE SMELL of barbecue smoke curling through his window. He stretched and looked at the clock — 7:29. The novel he was reading for his English final was splayed open on his desk: *A Canticle for Liebowitz*, about society after a nuclear holocaust. He imagined the chaos, confusion and pain after such a cataclysm, and amidst the charred frames of houses, the stumps of highrises, the smoldering strips of crumbled boulevards he saw his father standing over his Weber grill, slathering marinade on steaks and listening to NPR.

Jason heard the shade rise on Rafe's window. "Hustle up!" he called from the yard. "Training table in five."

THE PATIO table was set — a large tossed salad, two huge glasses of milk, a basket of sourdough bread, dinner plates weighted down with steaks in pools of their own juice. Rafe's profile loomed against the inside of the screen door. "What do we need?"

"Nothing. Come and eat." Rafe emerged onto the patio wearing what he had slept in — blue and white HI gym shorts and a Rick Wilders t-shirt with the song title, "Love is for Losers." Six-foot-three now, his legs long and muscled, shoulders broad, his large handsome face slimmed into the refined Italian profile, long dark eyelashes and dark eyes of his mother.

"How'd you sleep?" Jason asked.

"Good."

"Wish I had."

They dug into their steaks and were well into their unorthodox breakfast before either spoke. "You know who's pitching today," Jason said.

"Ridenour."

"You know what he throws."

"Junk."

"It's more what he *doesn't* throw," Jason said, watching his son eat. "He doesn't throw strikes."

"I know, Dad." He tapped his forehead just above his right eye.

"There's gonna be scouts there. Giants, A's, Reds, Dodgers, they're all gonna have people. And USF — they want me to coach."

"Stanford?"

"I don't know," Jason lied. He knew Rafe's grades would never get him into Stanford. The heart-warming story of the boy raised on campus by his baseball-playing father, returning to make good on his legacy wasn't going to happen, no matter how badly Rafe wanted it. But the story they'd made was still a good one. Rafe had taken to baseball with an astonishing single-mindedness, a devotion so intense that on at least two occasions the school declared him ineligible to play because of low grades. Rafe's advantage, however, was having a father who could teach him as much baseball as his coaches could while he pumped his grades up. Jason loved that job. It kept his hand in baseball, and it led to Rafe becoming what Jason had long ago dreamed of him becoming — a player.

Jason watched Rafe eat. "You're going to be nervous, that's only natural," he said. "Just stay within your game. It's all right if you walk four times."

"Then nobody sees I can hit!"

"They can see you play the field, back up your teammates, run the bases. There's a hundred things a scout looks at." He could see Rafe's lack of enthusiasm about milking the intangibles, and he didn't blame him. He too wanted him to wow the scouts, go high in the draft, sign for $2 million and start his professional career next week. Then he could play ball himself.

"They've got tryout camps all over the country," Jason explained. "There's nobody they can put up against you at your level."

Rafe polished off everything on his plate and stood up. He saw George Owyang striding across the backyard, carrying a large potted plant wrapped with a red ribbon. "Good morning gentlemen!" Mr. Owyang sang out. He was a short, broad-boned man in his early eighties, who didn't look a day over sixty-five.

"Hi Mr. Owyang," Rafe smiled.

"Lilian and I are sitting there with our simple pork bows and tea, smelling this delicious feast. We'll have to try one of these power breakfasts sometime," he laughed.

"Way too much cholesterol for you, George," Jason said. "We're getting Rafe ready for the city championship today."

Mr. Owyang smiled and set the plant on the table. He was a retired grocery store owner and avid baseball fan who owned season tickets to the Giants since they moved to San Francisco in 1959.

"It's Chinese tradition to wish friends good luck with a new business," the old man said, pointing to the Chinese letters emblazoned on the red ribbon. He reached forward and shook Rafe's hand, his eyes sparkling behind his glasses. "*Hoy jeong dai gut* — Good luck, Rafe. I look forward to cheering for you in the Major Leagues."

A COUPLE hundred fans were scattered over the bleachers beside the University of San Francisco's Benedetti Field, huddled in down parkas and blankets to ward off the cold of a typical June afternoon. Rafe warmed up along the third base line, playing catch with Enrique Tai. It wasn't difficult to spot the scouts in the crowd, tanned men in shirt sleeves straining not to shiver, clutching clipboards and pens. Most were there for Rafe, though HI's challenger for the crown — Junipero Serra High — was where Barry Bonds had gone to school, and there was always hope it would produce another like him.

Jason watched his son throwing and marveled at how far he — *they* — had come. In three years playing varsity for Holy Innocents, Raphael Thibodeaux had set almost every schoolboy hitting record in the history of San Francisco: most doubles, most home runs, highest average, highest slugging percentage, most runs batted in, highest on-base percentage ever. He had also developed into a fine fielder, exploiting the same gifted eyesight that blessed his hitting. But mostly, he worked harder than anyone else on the team. He studied books, tapes and hitting techniques in his spare time. Most evenings he could be found with his father on their secret field atop the reservoir, hitting baseballs until the sun sunk into the ocean. Evening after evening, across the windpacked sands of the Sunset district, the sound of Rafe's metal bat could be heard ringing in the damp air. The payoff for all that work was today.

The teams gathered along opposing base lines for the national anthem. Jason watched Rafe standing literally head and shoulders above his teammates. He had discovered that the joys of living vicariously through your offspring were vastly underrated. He had never before experienced the depth of happiness he felt watching his son develop. What he had accomplished himself was always tempered by the hard work it took to get there. This was an outright gift — earned through someone else's effort.

HI took the field first and their nervousness showed immediately. A single, an error and a double steal put runners on second and third with no outs. Jason heard Len Frawley clapping and telling his players to pull together. It was only the first inning but you never wanted to get in a hole, but that's exactly what happened. Bobby Turlock walked the next batter, and the next batter brought home two runs with a bloop single to left. Rafe charged the ball, then foolishly threw to the plate. The ball sailed over the catcher's head into the backstop, allowing the runners to reach second and third.

It was 4-0 before the Hawks left the field — and 4-0 when they went back out. The first inning went 1-2-3, leaving Rafe, their clean-up hitter, waiting in the on-deck circle. The second inning wasn't much better. A walk, a stolen base, a fielder's choice, an infield hit, an error and a two-run double made it 7-0 before the best hitter in San Francisco high school baseball even got up to bat. Jason could see a number of scouts in the stands fidgeting. They were probably wondering, as Jason would if he were scouting the game — if this kid's team was so bad, how good could he be?

He stepped into the batter's box and took up his signature stance — back straight, knees slightly bent, bat hoisted high above his head. The wind blew in hard from center field, pushing dust runners across the infield toward the mound. The conditions for Ridenour's off-speed pitching couldn't be better.

Rafe watched the first pitch off the outside corner called a strike. The second one was in the same place but he swung and fouled it off. He stepped out of the batter's box and looked up at his father, who quickly tapped his forehead just above his eye. 'See it, wait for it, swing at strikes,' the gesture meant.

Rafe stepped back into the box. He knew Ridenour was going to throw the same pitch — he'd gotten him twice, why wouldn't he do it again? He watched the arm come around and the ball emerge from Ridenour's hand. He started his stride before he saw it wasn't headed for the outside corner but inside, a curve ball spinning down towards his knees. He tried to hold up but couldn't. His bat passed over the ball by half a foot.

Strike three!

In the top of the fourth, Jason heard a familiar voice. "How's he doing?" Vicki sat down beside him, the lapels of her suit jacket pulled tightly up to her neck.

"They're down seven-to-nothing. Rafe struck out."

They watched as Turlock walked the first batter, then deftly picked him off first. He could tell Vicki had something on her mind; from experience he knew better than to ask. When the teams changed for the bottom of the inning, he found out anyway.

"What are we going to do about college?"

"We don't do anything. He'll do whatever he wants."

"You've got to talk to him."

"You can talk to him. You know him as well as I do."

"He listens to you — you've got this *guy* thing." He knew she meant it as a compliment, but the tone of her voice instantly raised his defensive shield.

"C'mon Vicki, not here. Not now."

Vicki ran her hand through her hair and stared out to left field, where Rafe tossed the ball with another player. "He's got to go to college, Jason. How many make it — one, two percent?"

"About that," Jason nodded. "And even if you do make it, an injury, a couple of bad months ... before you know it, you're out driving an ice cream truck."

"Have you told *him* that?"

"Of course. But he's convinced he's the real deal."

"What do you think?"

"You never know for sure until you try."

Rafe was up third that inning. HI was down 7-1 and it looked like the best thing for him would be to salvage something for himself. With a six run lead, Ridenour should be throwing strikes, though he started off nibbling around the plate like before. Ball one ... Ball two. Jason didn't blame him. If he were the kid's coach he'd advise him to keep the ball away from a guy hitting .642 too. Just as he'd advise Rafe to wait him out until he got something to hit. Which is what Rafe did. "Ball Four!" the umpire barked, and Rafe trotted dejectedly down the first base line with a walk.

"Way to go, Raphael!" Jason shouted as Rafe took his place on first. Vicki stared dully at the field, her mind clearly elsewhere. Jason clapped as Rafe stole second base, though he died there as the next batter struck out.

Vicki dug her hands deeper into her pockets as the Hawks took the field. "Maybe it was my fault for fighting it so long," she said glumly. "It's like my father, he didn't want me to become a lawyer. It just made me more determined."

"It's not anybody's *fault*, Vicki. He just wants to play baseball."

"He should go to college," she said. "Then if this baseball thing doesn't work out, he's got an education at least."

"I agree with you one hundred percent. Except it's not what *he* wants to do."

"He'll play for you at USF."

Jason looked at the fog-shrouded buildings of the hilltop campus. He could see himself coaching here — but not for another three or four years. He was only thirty-eight. He had seen too many coaches who were coaching because they couldn't play, but he knew he still had something to give. Plus, he didn't want to spend the next four years coaching his son, and he didn't think Rafe wanted it either — or needed it.

"He says he's going pro unless he gets into Stanford."

"He's not going to get into Stanford," she snapped.

They both could feel it then, something large, almost monumental coming to an end. The eighteen years of pain, hatred, misunderstanding and animosity slowly began to recede in their rearview mirror. Rafe had grown up. He was going off on his own. He was free and so were they — of each other.

"He'd do it if you pushed him," she said, giving it one last try. "He'd do anything you told him to."

Jason turned and looked at Vicki's tense, pretty face, her elegant suit, her driven manner and marveled at how fate had brought together two such totally different people. "He has to find his own path, just like we did."

She shook out her hair, then reached in her pocket for a tissue and blew her nose, pretending she had a cold and wasn't crying. "It's amazing, what you did," she said. "Quitting baseball. You've been a good father."

Jason stared towards left field, uncertain how to respond. She had never said anything like that, ever. "I'm sorry it's been so hard," he said quietly. "I'm sorry I was such a pain in the ass."

"I'm sorry too." She stared at her son in left field, her eyes filled with tears. "I thought I was doing the right thing."

Jason put his arm around her shoulders. "Somehow this was all meant to be."

"What's that supposed to mean?"

"We slept together once, and here we are eighteen years later."

They gazed together at the boy who had entwined their fates. The apple of their eyes, the fulfillment of Vicki's motherhood, the bane of his career, throwing the ball across a vast expanse of grass as he warmed up for the next inning.

"It wasn't about us," Jason said. "It's about him." He felt a gentle squeeze at his waist as Vicki put her arm around him. It was the first time she had touched him in many years. "We got him this far," she said.

Jason squeezed her back.

BY THE top of the sixth inning the Hawks had whittled the lead to 7-3. Then Bobby Turlock retired the first two batters, but walked the next two and faced the Padres' clean-up hitter, a huge Filipino kid named Marco Edora. The wind had stopped and the field was draped in a curtain of fog. The Padres could smell the kill; another hit would finish off the Hawks.

Turlock checked the runner at second, then delivered the pitch, a fastball belt-high over the outside half of the plate. Edora sent it screaming towards the far reaches of left center field, well beyond where Rafe was positioned. Except Rafe wasn't there. From the instant the ball left the bat he broke to his left, gripping his cleats into the thick grass and propelling into a full run in several strides. The Padres' fans shouted with glee, certain Edora had crushed a homer. The second base umpire hurried into center field, running like a man trying to catch a trolley. Rafe ran at the fullest capacity of his body, his eyes following the flight of the ball over his right shoulder. He was deep in the gap where the wall angled outwards. As the ball shot towards the earth, Rafe threw himself parallel to the ground with his glove outstretched, then felt the cold swipe of turf sliding down his shirt.

He lay there for a second, his right hand held in the air. He had felt the ball hit his glove, but didn't know if it was there or not. The umpire huffed up behind him and glanced into the glove. His right hand shot up in the air. "Ooooouuut!"

Rafe's teammates mobbed him as if they'd won the game. Even Vicki got into the swing, jumping up from her seat and clapping her hands.

"That's good, isn't it?"

"It's unbelievable!" Jason grinned.

As fate always has it in these circumstances, Rafe was due up that inning. There was some concern about his shoulder but after examination by a trainer and a few practice swings, he was allowed to bat. The Hawks were fired up now. The first batter, Charlie Musgrove, smoked a double just inside third base. Oscar Dane drew four straight balls, putting runners on first and second. Then up stepped Raphael Thibodeaux.

Jason knew right then that Rafe was gone. The scouts had come to see a hitter and witnessed an outfield play that few kids could have pulled off at any level. Anything now would just add zeroes and commas. He began to wonder how Rafe would react to the incredible loneliness of being an eighteen-year-old kid on the road as a professional athlete. How he would respond to the inevitable tinkering with his stance by self-appointed experts in the pros.

The Padres had to pitch to Rafe. A walk put the tying run at the plate with no outs, a no-no in any coach's book. But the first pitch was in the dirt, and only a major league block by the catcher kept the runners from advancing. The second pitch was down the middle but just under Rafe's chin, and he let it go.

Jason knew what would happen next. He had seen it a thousand times, and if he lived long enough he hoped he would see it a thousand more. The Serra pitcher fired a fastball on the outside part of the plate, thinking he was safely away from Rafe's power. But Rafe, recognizing the trajectory the moment it left the pitcher's hand, kept his hands back and pushed his weight through the ball, driving it into the left-center field gap — the gap he had just filled with his own miraculous catch. The ball rocketed between the two fielders, bringing in two runners and leaving Rafe standing on third base, clutching his fists at his teammates on the bench.

Whether or not the Hawks went on to win the game would be irrelevant to Rafe's future. The scouts would file reports that would inspire a parade of executives to his door, some of whom Jason would know and several he had played for. They would interview Rafe, review his stats and videos, talk to his coaches, his teammates … his father.

And in two weeks time Raphael Thibodeaux would be drafted, and leave home to pursue his dream of succeeding at the game his father had given up for him.

It was only an hour's drive, but it felt like a journey backwards of twenty years. Stompers Stadium was tucked into a neighborhood of run-down one-story homes with a reliquary Fosters-Freeze on the corner and a Big-4 Rents storage yard beyond the left field fence. Rusted fleets of dump trucks and backhoes sat baking in the mid-July sun, surrounded by dry grass and patches of hard-packed dirt. The stadium featured three light towers and a set of mobile office trailers parked inside a cyclone fence. There was a covered grandstand that held fifteen hundred fans, and a bleacher area down the right field line for another three hundred. A huge hand-painted sign arched over the padlocked gate, spelling out the team's name, "Santa Rosa Stompers."

An attractive, friendly young woman showed Jason through a side gate into the first trailer, which contained a row of offices with windows facing the ball field. "Mr. Hatcher will be right with you. He's busy — "

Suddenly an eight-foot tall stuffed animal wearing a Stompers jersey lurched through a doorway. "Jesus Christ!" Jason yelped, backing up. The animal kept coming, towering half a head above him, a goofy grin fixed permanently on its face along with a large purple nose and huge purple feet that stepped on Jason's shoes. "You must be Jason Thibodeaux," the beast said in a friendly voice, offering his furry, oversized hand.

The woman laughed. "This is Stomper. He just got back from the upholsterer." Stomper reached up and removed his head. Inside was a head almost as large, belonging to Bo Hatcher, owner of the Santa Rosa Stompers. Hatcher was a tall, big-boned man about fifty-five, with a broad, intelligent face and mischievous blue-green eyes.

"I bet you don't have anything like that in the *Major* Leagues!" Hatcher bellowed. He put his arm around Jason's shoulders and pulled him into a small office containing a desk and a photograph of a group of young people huddled around Hatcher outside a modern office park. He pulled off the oversized feet and sat down heavily behind the desk, still wearing the hairy body suit.

"So you want to play for the Stompers," he said with friendly amusement.

Jason smiled weakly. 'Want' was a debatable term. During the intense courtship of his son by the paid suitors of organized baseball, he had begun making calls on his own behalf, starting with Bill Vucovich in Cincinnati. And beginning with Vuco's "We don't need a lefty" to Vince Lasky's regretful, "Sorry, JT, we filled the position," he'd heard a numbing litany of reasons why he wouldn't be pitching for a professional baseball team, major or minor league, that year or any other. Most of them brought up his age — thirty-eight. But reading between the lines, he realized that what they really held against him was running out on his teams. Marv Denton, VP for player personnel with the Pittsburgh Pirates, seemed to be reading from some sort of bio sheet as they talked. Quit his college team; asked to be traded from the Reds; quit the Rockies in mid-season. "We need somebody who's gonna stick with it," Denton said.

"C'mon, Marv, it's a business."

"Exactly," Denton said before hanging up.

The last guy he called was Bo Hatcher, a Silicon Valley software entrepreneur who cashed in at the top of the market and bought the minor league franchise in Santa Rosa, about fifty miles north of San Francisco. The Stompers were an 'independent' team in the Western Baseball League, unaffiliated with any major league franchise. It was, in the lowly world of minor league baseball, the dregs. Young players who missed the draft, Cuban exiles showing their wares, thirty-year-olds clinging to the fantasy of breaking into the big leagues — and hangers-on like Jason — made up the bulk of the rosters.

"To be honest with you I just want to get back to the Show, but I'll do whatever I can while I'm here," Jason said. As he spoke he watched a man wearing a Stompers uniform circling the field on a sit-down mower.

"That's Nick Isely, our manager," Hatcher said.

"The manager's cutting the grass?"

"Makes some extra money that way," Hatcher nodded enthusiastically. "He's excited about you being here. Says he might use you tomorrow in long-relief."

"You don't want to see me throw?"

"You told me on the phone you could throw! You weren't bullshitting me, were you?"

"No —"

"Frankly, I don't give a shit if you can reach home plate," Hatcher laughed. "People wanna see the guy who quit to raise his kid. Where is he, by the way?"

"He signed with the Dodgers. They've got him in Single A — "

"The Yakima Bears! Great franchise. I spent two summers checking out teams. This is real baseball, not that corporate crap they play up there," he motioned towards San Francisco. "This is where the game is played for love."

"Love means there's not much money."

"We pay sixty-five a game."

Hatcher slid a one page contract across the desk. Jason scanned the standard clauses. His heart sank when he reached the concluding line: 'For the payment of $65 per game for the remaining twelve games of the season, for a total of $780.'

"Didn't you forget some zeroes here?" He didn't need the money, but he could have used what it stood for. Just ten days before he had stood proudly beside his son at a press conference where Rafe signed with the Dodgers for a bonus of $1.8 million, a salary of $120,000 for the rest of this season and $450,000 the following year if he made their AA team.

"Everybody makes the same," Hatcher said. "I'm trying to get this operation to pay for itself." He picked up one of Stomper's giant furry hands and reached across the table. "Welcome back to the Great American Pastime." Hatcher flashed a big smile as Jason grabbed the hairy index finger and squeezed.

He returned to Stompers Stadium the following afternoon. The locker room was a prefabricated bungalow with two Porta-Potties standing like sentinels at either end. One player sat on a stool in front of a small metal locker, wearing nothing but headphones and bobbing his head to music. Another sat in a scratched plastic chair with his foot resting on a table, getting his ankle taped by the manager, Nick Isely.

"JT Thibodeaux," Isely said amiably.

"Hiya, Nick."

"Locker's over there," Isely pointed. "Suit up and take some BP." Neither one of them said anything, or asked anything, about how they ended up in a sad-ass outpost like Santa Rosa. Baseball was a game of archetypes and legends. It had a self-contained history, the longest and most eventful in American sports, full of stories and statistics that men young and old told over and over again if you gave them half a chance. Isely was the Utility Infielder, the classically scrappy guy who could play any position, turn a double play, hit .250 and lay down a bunt in a heartbeat. He had stopped playing a year before Jason did, after several seasons of injuries. Jason was the Lefty who came up throwing heat and got to the Big Dance — and then threw it away. Neither one wanted to talk about which baseball archetype they were fulfilling with the Stompers.

Jason glanced at the uniform hanging from his locker. "Fifty-seven?"

"Herb Score," Isely laughed. "Bo was a fan."

Jason dropped his duffel bag. "Herb Score's comeback never worked."

"You didn't go out on a stretcher with your eye socket crushed," Isely said, finishing the expert taping with a flourish.

"Yeah, I guess I should count my blessings."

At batting practice he raised some eyebrows with his solid stroke. In the era of the DH and spot relievers, good-hitting pitchers were rare — more a luxury than necessity. A few of the players floated by to check him out. "Not bad for a senior," one player cracked. "Rookies go last!" another called. The nickname stuck. He became "Rookie" — or "Rook." He wasn't crazy about the name but appreciated the sentiment. It took time to fit in with a new team, and a nickname always helped.

As Hatcher had hoped, the stands filled with locals eager to see a major leaguer make his comeback after a hiatus as uncommon as Jason's. The smell of hot dogs, kettle corn and cotton candy wafted over the field, and the reverent shouts of kids calling out to players set all other concerns aside. True, they were only making $65 per game — more if you mowed the lawn — but how many people in the world could claim they got paid for playing baseball? He was on the field, a professional baseball player, along with twenty-one teammates. They were special, they were selected. They were the beneficiaries, for the next three or four hours, of the divine right of swings.

JASON WAS stretching in front of the dugout when Ralph Kees, the Stompers' pitching coach, approached. Kees worked for the Sonoma County Highway Department by day, then on game days drove up Highway 101 from Cotati to Stompers Stadium. He was a well-built man with a deep tan and mirror shades that hid his eyes.

"Let's see you throw." Jason followed him down the third base line to the bullpen area. After watching him warm up, Kees reached over and turned on the radar gun.

"I wouldn't expect too much," Jason warned.

Kees waited, arms folded. Jason wound up and fired. There was the reassuring pop from the catcher's mitt, and even better, a reassuring neutrality from his shoulder. He took the return toss and wound up again and threw what felt like an OK fastball, socking into the catcher's mitt with an emphatic whack. Kees turned to look at the radar gun, then turned back, expressionless. "Coupla more." Jason threw six more pitches before he noticed Stompers stepping outside the dugout to watch. He fired another pitch. Kees looked at the gun.

"What the hell are you doing here?"

"What do you mean?"

"You're clocking ninety-eight. Nobody throws ninety-eight in this league."

Jason shrugged. "My arm's fresh. I haven't thrown in awhile."

"What were you throwing when you quit?"

"I don't think of it as quitting. More like family leave."

Kees looked at him, giving away nothing behind his shades. "You ready to go?"

"You mean start?"

Kees shook his head. "Fifth inning. I've got to look at some Cuban guy just washed ashore in the Bronx."

The Cuban was Alain Ochoa, an allegedly twenty-four-year-old cousin of Red Sox pitching sensation Enrique Ochoa. But if he was a day under thirty, Jason was a teenager. He had an OK curveball and sinker but no fastball to speak of, and by the middle of the fourth inning had already given up three runs and had runners on first and third. They had Jason warming up, and when Ochoa walked the next batter, Kees signaled him to come in.

Jason strode across the third baseline feeling strangely nonchalant. Maybe it was because he had done it so many times before, maybe because he was earning $65 and there were only seventeen hundred people in the stands. Whatever it was, he felt as relaxed as Jacques Pepin walking into a kitchen. The catcher, a broad-shouldered kid named Drew Potts, peered at him through his catcher's mask as Kees laid the ball in Jason's glove.

"Show 'em how it's done."

The first batter was a wiry black kid wearing number 1. As he crouched in the batter's box, all Jason could envision was Rafe. Rafe standing as awkwardly as an ostrich, swinging at wild pitches out of the strike zone, scowling at him and blaming him for not being able to hit. Rafe was the only person he had pitched to over the past four years, outside of batting practice at St. Frances de Sales. Most of those times, he was trying to let them hit. Now he was supposed to fool them.

Potts signaled for a slider and Jason shook it off. He wanted to throw heat and waited for the signal. He went into his stretch, checked the runner on third and wondered for one fleeting instant what the hell he was doing. This wasn't his game anymore. He was an aging interloper, intent on turning a clock back that didn't want to go that way.

He threw as hard as he could and the kid slapped it sharply to left for a single, sending two runners home and leaving runners at first and third. He looked in and again Potts signaled for a slider, and again Jason shook him off. Potts signaled slider again, and again Jason shook it off. Potts finally called for a fast ball and Jason nodded. He checked the runners, reared back and fired a pitch as fast as he could down the center of the plate — a pitch the batter delivered with just as much authority into the Big-4 Rents storage yard for a three run homer.

Kees walked slowly across the infield grass. "You watch much TV?"

"Mostly sports," Jason said.

"Good," Kees nodded, reaching for the ball. "Go watch the Giants game and see how those guys pitch. You're just throwin' the fuckin' ball."

Jason trudged towards the dugout, ignoring the two hundred people informing him that he was a washed up hack. He threw his mitt onto the bench and sat down, staring at the field. As a young man, he'd been able to let it roll over him, convinced of the enormity of his talent and the inevitability of its unveiling. But now he had no such reserves. He was angry at himself — for giving up his career, for giving up his son, for giving up the coaching job at USF, for giving up five runs in a Single A game in Santa Rosa. "God dammit," he muttered, pounding the bench. "That sucked!"

"That's OK, Rook," someone called from the end of the bench. "You'll get 'em next time."

HE CALLED Rafe later from the Motel 6 in Santa Rosa. "Hiya Buddy. How's things in Yakima?"

"Great. How's things in Santa Rosa?"

Jason started. He always forgot about the ubiquity of Caller I.D. He didn't want Rafe to know about his stint with the Stompers. "Just blowin through," he said. "How'd you do? Today was your first game, wasn't it?"

There was a pause, then a voice weighted with hopelessness. "Oh-for-four."

"That's *what* you did. *How* did you do?"

"Three strike outs," Rafe mumbled. "I didn't really see the ball ... "

Jason stared out the window at the empty drive-thru lane for a Jack-in-the-Box next door. The menu stand glared in the darkness like a buoy in a shipping lane. He imagined him and Rafe in the Pathfinder shooting through for a couple of burgers, the Giants game on the radio, looking forward to practice tomorrow at USF's Dante Benedetti Field. He was sorry now he had let Rafe go, though there wasn't anything he could have done to stop him. Rafe didn't need him anymore. Other coaches would solve his slumps, iron out his wrinkles, mine the ore of his talent and see if there was enough gold to establish a fortune — or buy him a ticket home.

"It's different under the lights," Jason explained. "Just stick with your mechanics, you'll get used to it. You're at a different level now. These are guys who got you out in high school, you gotta notch it up. In, out, up, down, outside, outside, outside — they won't show you anything and then they'll challenge you, inside, on your fists. Not all of them though. Every other guy you see *isn't* going to make it. They're just throwing the ball and hoping for the best. You've got to feast off those guys and learn from the others. Keep notes on everybody — you haven't been doing that, I bet."

"I forgot."

"You gotta do that. Find the hole they see in your swing and fill it. You sleeping all right?"

"Yeah."

"You got some friends?"

"There's a guy here from Menlo Park, Alex Noor. He played for Mitty."

"I remember him — first baseman, right? Get to know your coaches too. Ask for help — that's what they're there for, they like doing that. Your buddies may be gone in a week, but the coaches'll be around all season."

The line felt dead. He realized that everything he said to Rafe could be applied to himself. Listen to your coaches. Elevate your play. Approach the game like a science, break it down, take it seriously. Earn that $65.

"You want me to come up?"

"No!" Rafe said quickly. "I'm fine."

Jason watched as a pick-up truck pulled into the drive-thru lane. If Rafe had said yes he would have checked out right then and headed north. He wanted his son to need him. But most of all, he wanted to not have to prove that he could pitch again.

"You gonna coach at USF or what?" Rafe asked.

"I don't know," Jason replied. "I'm up here thinking about it." He paused, watching the truck glide towards the pick up window. "Actually, I worked out today with the Santa Rosa Stompers."

"Really? You gonna make a comeback?"

"Naw, just playin' a little ball, staying in shape."

His first road trip was to Yuma City, Arizona, a sixteen-hour bus ride through Nevada and along the western edge of Arizona in the middle of August. They left just before midnight and at first light the next morning Jason was staring at quicksilver frills on the surface of Walker Lake, stirred by some fleeing night breeze before the onslaught of the summer sun. They were seven hours out of Santa Rosa, on their way to an 8 PM game a couple of home runs from the Mexican border. Most of the guys were asleep in poses that would make a chiropractor weep. Jason had slept for an hour at most, from Dixon to the sprawling suburbs east of Sacramento. He had awakened at the sound of the bus's gears changing as they began their ascent into the Sierras, and watched the lights of towns clinging to the sides of mountains give way to silent stands of pines and spruces on the long ascent to Donner Summit. Several times they passed other buses on their way to gambling vacations in Nevada: "Reno Express"; "Lucky Lines"; "Lady Luck Express." Their worn seats stuffed with sleeping gamblers weren't much different from the dreamers on his bus. One or two of these guys at most had a future in baseball. Everyone else was running on love of the game, the adrenaline of competition, and the fantasy — or delusion — of how big it was going to pay off.

Their bus skirted Reno, where the other dreamers were whisked off to the gaming tables. It was pure desert then, a landscape as barren as Mars. Jason smiled as he thought of his son getting ready to play tonight somewhere else in America. He hadn't told Rafe what he was doing. He hadn't told him he was going to start tomorrow night against the Yuma City Bullfrogs. He'd dedicate the game to him and if he won, maybe he'd call and tell him. If he didn't win, maybe he'd just hang up his spikes and forget it.

He closed the curtain on his window and slept the innocent sleep of a rookie.

DESERT SUN STADIUM was just that — a bone-white circular arena set in the burning palimpsest of the Yuma Desert. For batting practice it was 105 degrees. By the time they hit the field for stretching and infield practice at 7 PM, it was down to 101. Jason strode into the sauna-like air towards the visitors' bullpen area, where a Bullfrog player waited with his hands shoved into his back pockets. Neither man had to say a word. Jason embraced Willie Herrera so hard that Willie's spikes lifted two feet off the ground.

"What the hell are you doing here?" Jason said. Willie shrugged, his eyes flashing. "Liliana with you? The kids?"

"You know Liliana — *Mexicaníssima*," Willie laughed. "They're in Mazatlan."

Small colloquies of players gathered around the field, friends catching up, men stretching together, the camaraderie of professional athletes filling out the contours of something resembling a personal life. Jason and Willie looked at each other again and laughed. "The Bullfrogs!" Jason roared. "The Stompers!" Willie shot back. Then a gleam came into Willie's eyes. "I read about Rafe, man. Congratulations."

"As soon as he figured I wasn't going anywhere, he blossomed."

"I told you man, you gotta believe in *la familia*."

The Stompers' backup catcher Dominic Valparaiso clomped out in his catcher's gear. "*Listo, joven?*" he said to Jason.

Willie groaned. "You pitching tonight?" Jason nodded. "We win two out of three, we go to the playoffs," Willie said.

"The Bullfrogs ain't gonna hop into history on my lily pad," Jason smiled.

The warm night air, the stands filled with raucous, brown-skinned fans, the presence of his old friend was wonderful inspiration. Jason pitched like he hadn't pitched since the year he went to the World Series. Potts's mitt looked as big as a satellite dish, his fast ball traveled in the desert air like a whisper. His own team was mesmerized, chattering him up when it was clear by the third inning he was throwing stuff the Bullfrogs were never going to hit. Unfortunately, the Stompers didn't hit anything either. By the eighth inning it was zero-zero. The Stompers had two outs when it was Jason's turn to bat. He was the first pitcher to hit in the league for years, because he was better than half the guys they had available for DH.

Jason looked into the Bullfrog's bullpen and caught Willie's eye. He'd intended it only as a friendly gesture, but to his amazement Willie touched the middle of his left ear, then scratched the right corner of his mouth. It was a signal they used when they picked up signs from the other team — fastball, inside corner. He set up a half step further from the plate, and when the pitch came he swung with the smoothness perfected over thirty years of playing this boy's game. The ball shot off his bat and into the sand beyond the right field wall. He didn't look at Willie when he rounded the bases, but reveled in the scene of twelve Stompers waiting to pummel him in appreciation.

After setting up the Bullfrogs all game long with fastballs, he struck out the side in the ninth with an array of off-speed pitches, finishing the game with a 1-0 shutout. To Willie's relief, the Bullfrogs came back and won the next two games, including a 12-3 laugher that saw Willie pitch three effective innings. After the last game the Stompers' bus was scheduled to leave at midnight. Jason showered quickly and hurried to the parking lot. Willie waited for him in his Jeep Cherokee, the door open, listening to the plaintive *Norteño* ballads of Vicente Fernandez.

"So what are you going to do, *hermano*? You going to be a Stomper?"

"Nah. Three in Long Beach, three more at home and I'm done."

"Why don't you come to Mexico?"

"There's nothing for me there," Jason said.

"The Mexican League starts in December. You earn more, and the cost of living is nothing." Jason gazed at the desert sky. He could do worse than the Mexican League — the one he was in, for example. "Give it a try," Willie said. "It'll be like old times."

The smells of Mexico blew across the border, roasting meat and ancient dust and the faint scent of desert blooms mingled with diesel. Maybe it was some kind of omen, finding Willie along *La Frontera*. Mexico had helped him find his soul before when he was wandering in the desert, the prodigal father searching for his son.

"Let me think about it," he said.

"*Si, claro.*"

"I want to make some more calls. If I can throw a couple more shutouts, they've got to take a look at me."

Willie clapped him on the shoulder. "You'll make it back, *amigo*. Either through the front door," he said, then motioning towards the border, into Mexico — "or the back."

Martha Evelia Uribe. MAR-ta Ay-VAY-lee-ah Oo-REE-bay. Jason sounded the syllables over and over as he walked down the street. He smiled at a gaggle of school girls who stared at him. "*Buenas tardes, señoritas,*" he called out. They giggled and poked each other as the impossibly tall gringo passed like a latter day conquistador.

He strode past the small café where he had met Martha Evelia Uribe three weeks before, the *Café Mar Lindo*. He had been half way through a home stand, with a 2-0 record and an ERA of 1.94 in his first three starts with Vera Cruz. *Vera Cruz* — The True Cross. The oldest city in the western hemisphere, the entry point for the conquistadors, the sore through which the virus of modernity oozed into the world of *los indios*. Tryout camp with the *Aguilas* looked more like an international peacekeeping force, with Japanese, Australian, Dominican, Cuban, Puerto Rican, Nicaraguan, American and even a Swedish baseball player, predictably nicknamed "Meatball," vying for the twenty-two slots. Jason was amazed — and inspired. The twelve games with Santa Rosa had whetted his appetite and reminded him he could pitch. In and out, up and down, fast, slow … and slower. He knew, looking around, that he was the best pitcher in camp. Within a week, everyone else knew it too.

HE TURNED right two blocks past the café. Around the corner was a small garden of flowering camellia and hibiscus bushes sheltering a grotto of the Virgin Mary. It was here, on the fourth night he had walked Martha Evelia home from her waitress job at the *Café Mar Lindo*, that she had tugged him off the sidewalk. The street was dark. The café was not a night spot, but they served dinner until 8:00 PM and it took another hour for staff to close up. They loved to tease Martha when the big gringo showed up for lunch on the *Aguilas'* homestand. On nights when the *Aguilas* didn't play, Jason walked her home from the restaurant. They took the long way through the *Zócalo*, past the marimba bands playing beneath the hotel balconies. He bought her ice cream at "Pops", a garish parlor of white linoleum and florescent lighting that clashed with the stylish Spanish colonial buildings around the ancient square.

He met her three children the second night he walked her home: Luis, twelve, Maria Evelia, ten, and Carla, seven. And her mother, Lourdes, who watched the children six days a week while Martha Evelia worked at the restaurant. It was a house of missing fathers. Martha Eveilia's had gone to *El Norte* and never returned. For awhile he sent money from Texas, Colorado, Kansas — then nothing. They knew he wasn't dead. They always heard about the ones who died. With Martha Evelia's husband, the news was more certain, but certainly no better. He died when a Pemex rig collapsed on him and three other men in the oilfields outside Villahermosa. The coincidence of her husband and Jason's father perishing on oil rigs bonded them — along with some basic chemistry.

Martha Evelia was 5 foot 3 with a long pretty face, shoulder-length black hair and smooth, copper-colored skin. Jason was unsure of courtship rituals in Mexico, though suspected they were lengthy, based on social rituals he had seen at Willie and Liliana's house — day-long birthday parties, week-long *quinciñeras*, *Semana Santa*, *Las Posadas*. He decided to err on the side of caution, gallantly parading publicly with her around the square after dark — the Widow and the Gringo. He was wary of their differences, after what had happened with Vicki. But after their second walk, he sent flowers to the café; another time, a signed poster of Isaac Sands for Luis, an avid baseball fan.

The night they stopped in the grotto, everything changed. He thought it was something religious when she pulled him towards the statue of the Virgin. But instead of praying, Martha Evelia wrapped her arms around him and turned her face up to his. He had never wanted to kiss a woman more, and was never more uncertain about doing so. He had never knowingly kissed a woman with three children before, *especially* one who was living with her mother. He certainly had never kissed a woman in front of Our Lady of Guadalupe.

"I thought you would never kiss me," she said, when his lips reluctantly parted from hers. He could taste the peppermint ice cream on her lips.

"I thought Mexican girls were shy."

"How could Mexico have ninety million people if we are so shy?"

HE TURNED off Calle de las Flores onto her street overlooking the
port of Vera Cruz. The climate usually felt like a warm wash cloth, but
tonight something was blowing in from *El Norte*, a fastball of cold air
straight across the Gulf. The steamy intimacy of the neighborhood
was swept away by the January wind, the palm fronds and stiff banana
leaves clacking like plastic trinkets. Martha Evelia's single-story stucco
house was in the middle of the block, with a small flower garden behind
a black metal railing set into a low cinderblock wall. He paused at the
gate. The house was uncharacteristically dark, with the glow of a single
lantern visible through the living room window. He wondered if he had
misunderstood her Spanish again and come on the wrong night. When
he knocked on the door, he discovered he hadn't.

She was dressed in tight black jeans, a thin silver looped belt, and
a white off-the-shoulder cotton blouse cut low across the top of her
breasts. Her long black hair was braided tightly and tied in a single
strand with a red velvet ribbon. Long silver earrings gleamed in the
lantern glow from the living room, where a vaseful of flowers, a bottle
of Don Pedro special reserve brandy and two glasses waited on the
coffee table.

"My god, you look beautiful," he said. She smiled and kissed him
shyly, then steered him towards the kitchen. "Where is everyone?" His
eyes searched the dim and unusually neat house.

"Mama took them to Serena's house," she said, speaking of her
younger sister, who lived three blocks away. He could smell roasting
pork and the deep metallic odor of *nopales* and *salsa verde*, his favorite
dish at the café. A basketful of warm tortillas sat on the candlelit table,
and a bottle of Spanish red wine. Jason stood transfixed, astonished by
the simplicity, the completeness, the promise of it. She hurried to the
stove and took a pot off the burner, then turned off the flame.

"You miss the children," she teased him. "It's only for them you
come and visit."

He crossed the room and drew her to him. He did miss her children.
The vitality of their home comforted him, as Willie and Liliana's home
always did. It had the warmth and richness his never had. He kissed her
on the neck, lured by the scent of her perfume.

"I figure if I'm nice to you, you'll let me play with them."

"Be careful," she said, pushing the *carnitas* to the back of the stove. "Or you'll get burned." She turned and he kissed her full on the lips. In the warmth of her own kitchen, her lips sought his as they had never done in the grotto of the Virgin Mary.

"Can I help with anything?"

"You can keep doing that." He kissed her again, deeper. She moved her hips against his in a slow, timeless gesture.

"You are hungry?" she asked.

"I am hungry."

She slid away from him and filled their plates with *carnitas* and *nopales* and mounds of rice as white as snow. "I do miss the kids," Jason laughed, pouring himself a Sprite. "But I'd miss this a lot more." She had forgotten he couldn't — wouldn't — drink. She put the cork in the bottle and set it aside. There wasn't any shortage of uncles and cousins who would make short work of a good bottle of Spanish *rojo*.

"How is Raphael?" she asked. "Have you called him?"

He had told her the whole story, or at least the highlights. Their children were their main topic of conversation on their strolls in the *Zócalo*. He always explained that his sadness was due to missing major league baseball, but she could see how much he missed his son. She asked him once if she thought that her father had ever missed her like that, and he assured her that he had without a doubt.

"Rafe's doing fine," Jason replied, but in fact he hadn't talked with him in three weeks. It was such a pain in the ass to find a phone that worked in Mexico. What he did know was that Rafe had finished his season with the Yakima Bears, hitting .268 in thirty-one games, and then done something so astonishingly mature that Vicki had hunted him down on a road trip to Campeche to tell him. In the off-season Rafe had enrolled at San Francisco State in musicology, with plans to earn a degree in case the "baseball thing" didn't work out. He also hired a financial adviser who invested his signing bonus and the bulk of his first year's salary in a way that ensured he would be able to pay for whatever level of education he wanted to pursue. In two more weeks he would finish spring training with the Dodgers in Vero Beach, Florida. What did he need his dad for?

"You should call him and tell him you pitched a ten hitter," Martha Evelia said.

"Two hitter. I pitched a two hitter."

"What is a two hitter?"

"When the other team only gets two hits."

She smiled, because he did. He would teach her about baseball someday, but not now. On this cold Mexican night, her house had a safe, hermetic feel, warmed by the oven and sealing them away from the world. Besides their children, they talked about the people in her restaurant. They talked about *El Norte* and the people who went there and never returned, like her father. They talked about sports. To Martha Evelia, being with a baseball player was like being with the President of the United States. Baseball was America. He certainly looked the part. She lost herself in his dancing eyes and the smooth, muscular rhythm of how he moved his hands, his head, his arms. She smiled as he settled deeper into his chair, comfortable in her home, watching her in the candlelight as she talked.

When they were done eating she cleared the plates and came to him. She stood before him and rubbed his soft sandy hair and pulled his face into her chest and held him tenderly. Jason wrapped his arms around her and breathed in her perfume. Turning his head, he could see down to the harbor where almost five hundred years before Hernan Cortes strode ashore to clasp the sweet vulnerable waist of this new world and crush it.

Martha Evelia began to hum softly, as if singing a lullaby. Jason kissed her tenderly on her lips. She closed her eyes, then opened them when he drew back and smiled broadly.

"You are happy," she said. It was a statement, not a question. They both knew there would be problems and misunderstandings, sadness and disappointments. But they were old enough to know what was important now. They had both lost enough to know the enormous value of what they had found.

"*Si*."

JASON CALLED from the Hotel Presidente Benito Juárez in Nuevo Laredo. He'd looked through three newspapers before finding news about the Texas League, and a box score of Rafe's team in San Antonio. Rafe was not in the line-up. He could hear the guy who answered the clubhouse phone bark loudly, "Thibodeaux — telephone!"

"Hi, Buddy," Jason said when he came on. "How's it going?"

"Fine." Rafe's voice was low and emotionless, just like the old days.

"You all right? I didn't see your name in the box score."

There was a long pause. He heard voices in the background, then someone's blow dryer start up. "They're sending me down."

"Down where?"

"Vero Beach." It wasn't difficult to hear the discouragement in his voice. At nineteen, the word 'down' didn't fit the script of anything.

"What's going on?"

"I'm not hitting."

"Like what — what are you hitting?"

"One-fifty ... one-forty-eight, actually."

Jason closed his eyes. He could feel Rafe's depression, and strangely, his own impatience. "You doing like we practiced? Swinging at strikes?"

"That's not what it is, Dad."

"Well what is it? Tell me —"

"I gotta go."

"What do you mean, you gotta go? You just got on the phone."

"We've got batting practice in five minutes."

Jason took a deep breath. He'd been watching a neatly dressed Mexican couple with two small children, a boy and a girl, walking through the hotel lobby, the little girl demurely holding her father's hand while the boy ran and swirled his hand through the fountain at the center of the room. He remembered Rafe at eight, so sweet, so trusting, so open with his needs. "I'm right down the road from you, on the other side of the border," Jason explained. "I thought I'd rent a car and see you play."

"I'm not playing. I'm flying out at nine-thirty."

"In the morning?"

"Tomorrow night."

"Look," Jason said. "It's always the same. Keep your head down, your hands back ..." he paused, waiting for Rafe to chime in. But he didn't, so he said it himself. "And swing at strikes."

RAFE ANSWERED the door wearing his Dodger-blue sport coat and pressed khaki pants. A large suitcase sat inside the door, and a duffel bag that contained, among other things, his bats. He looked at his father in bewilderment. "What are you doing here?"

"I rented a car at the border." Jason pointed at the duffel bag. "You ready to hit some?"

Rafe stepped aside and his father brushed past him. It was a garden apartment with a large dining room containing a round glass table and two chairs, a spacious living room furnished with nothing but a couch, television and stereo, and beyond that a bedroom with a king size bed and nothing else.

"I thought you weren't leaving until tonight," Jason said.

"I'm going to work out. It beats sitting around here."

Jason looked closely at his son. So tall, so strong ... so scared. In his blazer and khaki pants, he could have been a college kid waiting for the team bus to take him across town. But he was a pro. He already had a million and a half dollars in the bank and a head full of impossible expectations.

"You all right?"

"Yeah," Rafe replied — too quickly.

"Whatever it is, you can talk to me about it."

"Everything's fine. I just can't hit."

"Sure you can. You can hit me."

"I'm not even sure of that any more."

"I brought some balls," Jason said. "I think we should go hit some."

"Are you serious?"

"Have I ever not been serious?" Rafe looked at him as if for the first time. Here, in the dusty dregs of West Texas, a month into this nightmare season and his father appears. And he wasn't just his father any more — he was a ball player, someone who rode buses and chewed sunflower seeds and warmed the bench on April nights in games that meant nothing in the scheme of things except to the men playing out their dreams.

"You want some juice or somethin'? I was going to stop and have breakfast."

Jason smiled at the mention of breakfast — it was noon. "Let's get out of here," he said. "You can show me San Antonio."

They changed into sweat clothes and Rafe drove the rent-a-car to a local diner, then to a high school field behind Fort Sam Houston. They stretched, ran a couple of perimeters around the huge, spring-green field, then tossed the ball back and forth for ten minutes. Jason had pitched the night before but only lasted three innings. Throw, catch, turn ... throw, catch, turn ...

Then he gestured with the ball and Rafe set up in his stance, the bat high over his head like the Grim Reaper threatening final justice. Jason stared from the mound, flirting with the idea of suggesting an adjustment. "What!?" Rafe shouted, dropping his hands. It wasn't difficult to see what was running through his father's head. Another lecture series, Baseball 101, I've been there and you haven't blah blah blah blah.

"Just get ready," Jason called.

He threw a fastball about 86 miles per hour on the outside part of the plate, and Rafe let it go. It wasn't a bad pitch to take if you weren't prepared to drive it the opposite way, but it was clearly a strike. He threw the same pitch again but slightly faster, and Rafe swung and fouled it high off to the left. There was a loud metallic clap as the ball landed squarely on a car — maybe their own. Rafe peered at his dad, expecting the worst. Jason doubled over at the waist, laughing loudly.

Rafe began laughing, too. "I'll pay for it!" he shouted.

"Who cares — it's a rental car! Straighten it out now."

He threw a slow curve that Rafe missed badly. Then a slider low and away, and another on the inside part of the plate that he pulled down the right field line just inside the bag. Rafe's swing looked smooth, potent. He also looked as tight as a teenager on his first date. It was one thing to be intense; it was another to be in knots. Rafe was trying to make a career out of every pitch.

Jason grooved a series of batting practice fastballs that Rafe sent deep into a stand of cottonwood trees beyond center field. He followed with a series of breaking pitches off the edge of the plate that Rafe chased, missing badly. Jason took two steps in from the mound.

"I know, I know," Rafe said, setting up for another pitch. "Swing at strikes."

Jason set up again and uncorked his best fastball, just to see what would happen. It started at the height of Rafe's lower rib cage and began to climb. Rafe pounced on it like a viper, crushing it into left center, over a fence and into some kind of thick greenery.

"That was my best fastball," Jason called.

"That was my best swing," Rafe grinned.

The next pitch was a wicked, wide-bending curve that fell off the outer edge of the plate. Rafe flailed at it, chasing it into the dirt and sinking to one knee.

"Swing at strikes!" Rafe shouted to himself. "Swing at strikes!"

Jason reached for another ball. He had packed about forty of them, and there were only five left. Rafe fouled off two, hit one that would have been a single, and missed a change-up completely. The last pitch was a 92-mile-per-hour slider that Rafe just missed as it dove under his bat and crashed into the metal fence behind him. He picked up the ball and tossed it to his father.

"C'mon, strike four, like we used to."

"That's when you were a little shit. There's no free lunch up here."

"C'mon, just one." Rafe took a couple of half swings. "Two outs, bases loaded, last of the ninth, full count. What are you going to throw, *Obi-Wan Kenobi?*"

"You down one? Two? Three?"

"Three," Rafe said. "It's 5-2."

Jason nodded. A boy's dream of heroism never had him slapping a single or a sacrifice fly, or trotting down to first base with a base on balls. It was always an operatic finale — the crack of the bat like lightning tearing the sky, the roar of the crowd, the majestic trajectory of the ball sailing high over the heads of your foes. He knew he could throw a slider a foot off the plate and Rafe would flail at it. But why do that? He hadn't come all this way, made all these sacrifices, to deny his son the certainty that he could hit.

He set himself against the rubber and held the ball inside his glove. Rafe waited, his bat held high, his front leg twitching imperceptibly. Jason kicked and threw. The ball exploded from his hand and headed right where he wanted, belt high and rising towards Rafe's chest. And Rafe hit it exactly as he hoped he would, a towering drive high over the fence in right field.

Rafe dropped his bat and ran towards first. "Thibodeaux has done it!" he shouted. "Thibodeaux has done it! Thibodeaux has won the World Series!" He touched first base and continued into right field, stooping to pick up balls and flinging them in against the backstop. Jason trotted after him and when they reached the fence they scaled it together and dropped to the other side. It was only then they discovered that what they thought was a field was a lily pond. A soft breeze began to blow and cottonwood seeds filled the air like snowflakes, settling silently across the dark skin of water. Only one of the balls was visible, sitting on the bank. Rafe picked it up and tossed it back over the fence. He found two more that hadn't made it to the water and tossed them back too.

"Dad?"

"Yeah."

"Thanks for comin' up."

"My pleasure."

He hoped Rafe would say it, but he knew he wouldn't. He'd never told his own father that he loved him, that he missed him, that he thought about him a lot. He recalled that day in Galveston before his father left for good. He remembered how they'd played catch seemingly forever, with no banter, no complaints, no instructions. Jason realized he had spent nineteen years trying to be the father to his son that his father had never been to him. He was the one who wanted a man to come home with a ball glove and a gleam in his eye, and toss a baseball until the last light of day drained from the sky. He knew now what he should have known all along — he wasn't here for Rafe. He was here for himself.

THEY HURRIED down the concourse, Rafe in his blue blazer and khaki slacks, Jason in jeans and a red *Viva Vera Cruz!* t-shirt. Jason talked quickly as they swayed under the weight of their luggage. "You gotta stop worrying about the Dodgers getting their money's worth. Stop worrying about all the things you can't control, and control the things you can. The hits will come."

When they reached the gate there were only a handful of people left in the lounge. "You think you'll stay in Mexico?" Rafe asked.

"I hope not," Jason replied. "If I can come back for just part of a season, I'll be eligible for my major league pension."

Rafe stared at him. "You left without a pension?"

"I'm half a season short."

"Jesus, Dad. Is that why you're living in Mexico — because of the money?"

"Naw, I'm there for baseball." And Martha Evelia, he thought to himself.

The last person in line began to move down the gangway. They were minutes away from another parting — Rafe to Florida and his upward trajectory, Jason back to the center of the Aztec Empire, without a pension. He clapped Rafe on the shoulder. "Baseball is a game of the mind, more than any other sport. You've got to let yourself fail. Hank Aaron grounded into more double plays than any player in history — did you know that?"

"Yes, actually."

"Then don't forget it."

"Thank you, Mr. Rogers."

"Screw you. Mr. Rogers can't throw a fastball 98 miles an hour."

"Neither can you," Rafe laughed. "But you're still a damn good pitcher."

Jason grasped his son's hand firmly. He could feel their bones slide together like pieces of a puzzle fitting. "I'll always love you," he said. "So will your mother." Rafe draped his arm around his father's shoulder and gave a little tug, a gesture of extravagant intimacy for him. Jason watched as Rafe picked up his duffel bag and slung it over his shoulder, surrendered his boarding pass and slouched down the gangway to his future. Halfway to the plane he turned and Jason raised his hand to wave. Rafe smiled and tapped his temple above his right eye.

"Swing at strikes!" they called out together, and broke out laughing.

THE DEAL

Top o' the 10th …

Tobias Barlow USA TODAY

—

Down Mexico way comes word that former
Rockies ace Jason Thibodeaux has found an
unlikely home, pitching for the Vera Cruz
Aguilas — or 'Eagles' for you Spanishly
challenged. I mention this only as a contrast
to the fortunes of his son, Raphael. Last
year, young Thibodeaux was runner-up for
NL rookie of the year, with 27 homers, .299
average and 94 RBIs for the New York Mets,
and this year he's suffering from nothing
like a sophomore jinx. Early scuttle that
young Thibodeaux was a head case luckily
didn't go to his head. The kid's been a class
act, which doesn't come as any surprise to
anyone who knew his dad.

T HE TAXI DRIVER TURNED TO him in the back seat. "You pay how much you want. We go estadium now." But then he pulled over in the next block and picked up a woman nearly invisible behind two bulging shopping bags, and two blocks later a man with a machete and another woman coming from market. Rafe looked impatiently at his watch — fifteen minutes to game time. The old Toyota listed like an overloaded canoe as it hugged the shoulder of the road into town. Brass-heavy *corridos* blared from a portable radio taped to the dashboard. Rafe could see how his father had found a home here. It was loud and friendly and chaotic, a country running on humor, instinct and a kind of valiant dignity.

"*Ahí — el estadio,*" the driver pointed, half-an-hour and four fares later. The stadium loomed above a poor, fallen-down neighborhood like a space ship from another planet. The streets were filled with vendors — men tending smoking carts of tacos, women selling *licuados* from trays balanced on their heads, children hawking gum, combs and homemade pastries. The smell of charcoal roasting meat wafted everywhere.

Rafe handed the cabbie what he would have paid for a trip from JFK to Shea — $15. "I come back later," the driver beamed. Rafe bought a ticket for the equivalent of a dollar and hurried inside. It was like a fairy tale, where an ordinary door is opened to reveal a place of total magic. In the midst of the surrounding poverty was the classic configuration of a baseball field — the diamond circumscribed by emerald-green grass, the powder-white bases, chalk lines running to the wall, athletes stuffed into superhero suits. It could have been Vero Beach as easily as Vera Cruz. It was baseball.

He squeezed past two men passing a bottle of mescal and sat beside a quiet, gray-haired man. The first inning was over. The scoreboard showed no runs, no hits, no *errores* for either team. The Aguilas' last batter of the inning stood in the base path between first and second, waiting for someone to bring him his hat and glove. Then there he was, jogging from the dugout. He was forty but clearly in better shape than most of the guys on the field. All the stories about players who put in time lifting weights, running, doing whatever it takes to excel — his father was living proof it worked. True, he was pitching against the Tabasco Olmecas and not the Texas Rangers, but he was pitching.

Rafe slumped down in the hard wooden seat and adjusted the fishing hat he'd bought at the Vera Cruz airport. Watching his father take his warm up pitches for the second inning, it was clear to him why people loved this game so much; why his father had reinvented himself; why he would do anything to play again, even here. The currents of colors through the crowd; the towering banks of lights; the shimmering carpet of grass; the sweat of working people in the stands. Nations went to war, economies collapsed, marriages began and ended but the beauty of *el beisbol* went on. His father was right — it *was* a privilege to play this game. And the full weight of what he had given up for him settled onto Rafe's shoulders.

He took a deep breath, pushing the sudden urge to cry back where it came from. Then he saw his father slip a slider on the inside edge of the plate for a called strike and his body erupted in goosebumps. There he was, throwing as well as ever. There was an ease and economy to the way he played, as if he knew the exact amount of energy he had and how to conserve every ounce. Rafe thought of his own agent calling so excitedly a couple of weeks before. "You get me thirty homers, I'll get you sixty million dollars." I don't want sixty million dollars, he had told him. Not while my father's stuck in Mexico.

Jason sped through the Olmecas' lineup — one, two, three in the second, and again in the third and fourth. He gave them off-speed stuff that was tantalizing but never over the center of the plate, and all they hit were grounders and harmless flies to the outfield. Then he struck out five of the last six batters throwing heat, capping off a thoroughly efficient five-hit shutout. Even the most cynical scout would have to classify it as a masterfully pitched game by a wily veteran, mixing speeds, locations and finishing with fastballs somewhere in the nineties that exploded past the hitters.

His teammates seemed to take it in stride. A few patted him on the back; it must have been old hat. He'd gone 16-5 the year before, astonishing for a team that won only forty-one games all season. Seven of the wins were shutouts, which is why, Rafe's increasingly drunken seat mates explained by the end of the game, they called him "*Señor Zero*."

After the game Rafe blended with the crowd filing from the stadium, careful not to be seen. His cabbie was waiting by the entrance. "Hotel?" he smiled, nodding towards his cab, where a man was sitting in the passenger seat smoking a cigarette.

"*Aeropuerto*," Rafe replied, handing him a twenty in advance. "*Directo*." He knew what he had to do. The gift his father had given him was too awesome to go unrewarded. It wasn't going to be easy, but he knew that doing the right thing was sometimes not the easiest thing. His father had taught him that.

ROB MACLEAN'S New York penthouse comprised the top three floors of a high rise on Second Avenue at Fofty-first. A beautiful Latina led Rafe and his agent to a glass-walled living room with a dizzying view over the East River, all the way out to Shea.

"Rob's plane just landed at LaGuardia," she said. "Would you like something to drink while you're waiting?"

"Sparkling water," Donny Brashears replied. She looked at Rafe, who shook his head. "Check it out," Donny said, after she left. "Black Abbyssinian marble floors, Laotian hardwood panels, ferns from Borneo, toucans from the Guatemalan jungle." Brashears was one of the most effective sports agents in the business. He was also the shortest, one of 200-300 dwarfs born each year in the U.S. He had bright, close-cropped red hair, fierce blue eyes and large teeth chemically whitened to a gaudy gleam. He looked like a warrior from an ancient civilization, though dressed in a $3,000 hand-tailored suit from Hong Kong. "That table alone," he pointed, "is probably worth half what you're asking for."

Rafe watched a jet touch down like a feather on the runway at LaGuardia. Donny's job was to get Rafe money, but that's not what they were there for and it was driving Donny nuts. He could smell money a mile away, and here it was right under his nose. Maclean's father had founded Burger Hut, one of the world's largest fast food chains, and sold it to PepsiCo. He'd retired to his own island off the coast of Florida and left his money in his eldest son's hands to manage as he pleased. Besides owning the Mets, Maclean supported worldwide environmental causes, doling out more than $3 million a year to winners of the "Maclean Award" for activists working to preserve the part of the natural world that Burger Hut hadn't already devoured.

"This is divine intervention," Donny said, joining him at the window. "The gods are giving you time to reconsider."

"I think they've got more important things to do."

"Sixty million dollars!" Donny whispered. "They crave studs like you — guys who can yank the ball out of the yard." He gripped Rafe's forearm. "Real men."

A helicopter banked across the East River and hovered over the penthouse. "You can go if you want to," Rafe said over the sound of the helicopter landing on the roof. "I've got business to attend to."

"No way," Donny snapped. "I want to get out of here with cab fare at least."

In a few minutes Rob Maclean entered, escorted by a tall, creamy-complexioned woman carrying a leather briefcase. He was a delicately-built man about thirty-five, with wary, intelligent brown eyes and the casual aggressiveness of an heir.

"Sorry to keep you waiting," he said, walking straight up to Rafe and shaking his hand. "It's a pleasure to see you again."

"Me too, Mr. Maclean."

"Hello, Rob," Donny said, offering his hand. Maclean shook it as if it were contaminated. "Please, sit down," he said, turning to Rafe. "Jennifer?" The woman drew a sheaf of papers from the portfolio and handed them to Maclean. He smiled at Raphael. "This is probably the most unusual deal I've ever made — and I've made a number of them. You're sure this is what you want?"

Donny held up papers he had pulled from his briefcase. "I want to alert you that the section on incentives has changed. Should the team

260

make the playoffs —"

"I'm speaking with Mr. Thibodeaux, Donny." There was a long silence. Tropical birds stirred in the trees, the sound of trickling water came from somewhere.

"This is what I want, Mr. Maclean."

"Have you talked this over with your father?"

Rafe shook his head. "This is just between us."

"He's going to find out sometime. What happens if he refuses his end of the deal?"

Donny squirmed miserably on the couch, trapped in some nightmare in which the bottom line was somehow reversed and a moral code put in its place. He'd been against the whole thing from the beginning. But there was absolutely nothing he could do to change Rafe's mind.

"He'll play," Rafe said. "If he doesn't, I'll make up the money myself."

Maclean set the papers on the glass table in front of him. "Come on, Rob," Donny pleaded. "You know what this kid's worth."

"The offer I'm prepared to sign was proposed by *your* client," Maclean said with some irritation. "I don't want to pick up the newspaper tomorrow and read about stingy Rob Maclean." Used to high stakes bargaining, they had to have one final face-off before pen went to paper. Donny wanted Maclean to pay the most money possible; Maclean wanted to pay the least, in some instinctual tribute to his father's business acumen. But the details of the deal were entirely Rafe's: the Mets would finance a major league contract for his father to play for whatever team would have him, and Rafe would play the following season for one million dollars, no questions asked. There were some incentive clauses, of course — for average above .300, home runs above thirty, RBIs, playoff wins, the World Series — conditions that were as much to Maclean's advantage as Rafe's. Maclean was touched by the sentiment of it, though doubtful of finding another owner who'd play along. But he'd found a taker in Bill Sharpstein, owner of the Cleveland Indians. Sharpstein was a young buck like Maclean, who imagined himself the George Steinbrenner of the Midwest, wheeling and dealing and building a baseball empire. He'd never heard of a deal like this, so he sent a scout down to Mexico to make sure, as did Maclean, and accepted the deal on the strength of the scouting report on Jason Thibodeaux. What did he have to lose? Sharpstein got a pitcher who might be able to help, with Rob Maclean paying his salary.

"There won't be any stories, Mr. Maclean," Rafe said. "I really appreciate this. I know it's kind of strange ..." He glanced at Donny, who had fought him every step of the way. He'd have to get a new agent, that was one thing.

Maclean spread three copies of the contract across the table. "Every day I remind myself that I wouldn't be here, my children wouldn't be here — we wouldn't be here — if it weren't for *my* father," he said. "Every contract I sign is with the knowledge that it was his sweat, his vision, his determination that gave me this privilege."

Maclean handed a Mark Cross pen to Raphael and used another to sign the contract. "To our fathers," he said. Rafe stared at the line for his name, then re-read the terms of the deal. It was only money. His dad had given up the game. He signed and set the pen down. Maclean gathered the papers and gazed with a sober respect at the young ballplayer. "I'm curious what you would have done if we hadn't made this deal?"

Rafe replied without hesitation. "Play out the year and quit."

"Then I'm glad we did this. I want you around for a long time. I want you to help us beat the Yankees."

"And the Indians," Rafe smiled.

THE NEWS came over ESPN. Rafe was pulling on his uniform in the visitor's locker room at the Tigers' spring training facility in Lakeland, Florida when Lenny Diamond's distinctive voice oozed from the clubhouse TV.

"It's *adiós* for former national league hurler Jason Thibodeaux, who made a huge leap today from Vera Cruz, Mexico to Cleveland, Ohio. The Indians have reportedly signed Thibodeaux for half a million dollars to fill the role of left-handed set up man Bobby Clayton, out for the season with rotator cuff surgery. Thibodeaux pitched for the Reds, the Giants and Rockies in a major league career that included 127 victories, 108 losses and a very public custody battle for MVP candidate Raphael Thibodeaux. Daddy T was found pitching for the Vera Cruz Eagles under the nickname Señor Zero." They flashed a clip of Antonio Banderas as Zorro, slashing a "Z" into a tapestry, vaulting over a railing and galloping away on his horse. "Not bad for a forty-one-year old," Diamond cracked.

A magnum of O'Doul's was waiting in the Indians' clubhouse at

Winterhaven, Florida. Jason opened the note and smiled. "Throw Strikes." He called Rafe that night from the deck of a condo, the sounds of his showering roommate splashing through the screen door. Some twenty-two-year old kid — a year older than his son. His roommate.

"Congratulations," Rafe said. "I knew you'd make it."

"Yeah, well, you were the only one ... Hey, is this all right with you?"

"Is what all right with me?"

"Your old man coming back. I mean, I don't want to steal your thunder."

If he only knew the half of it, Rafe thought. "There's plenty of thunder for everybody. You deserve this. Everybody knows that."

"All of a sudden the place was crawling with scouts," Jason laughed. "The night they came I pitched a two-hitter." The happiness in his voice delighted Rafe. He thought of seeing his father pitch in Mexico. "That's why they call you Señor Zero."

"Don't *you* start that shit," he said. "Señor Zero left his ass in Mexico."

"They gonna use you as a starter?"

"I don't care how they use me — I'll mow the lawn if they want." He paused, then added quietly. "It was hard leaving Martha Evelia and the kids."

"Well I'm glad you're here," Rafe said. "We gotta get together."

"You bet. It'll be great to see you, man."

"You too, Dad."

—

Top o' the 10ᵗʰ ...
Tobias Barlow USA TODAY

There have been only three father-son combinations in big league history; none have lighted the firmament like the Thibodoze. Thibodeaux *pere*, pitching under the arm de plume *Señor Zero*, is entering the stretch run with the stats of a man half his age — 37 appearances, 6-1 record, 2.89 ERA. Add to that the intangible influence of his experience in the clubhouse and you've got a good idea of why the Indians(!) lurk just two games behind the Twins for bragging rights in the AL Central.

Thibodeaux *fils*, Raphael, is having what is known as a break-out year — which at his age could just as well refer to acne as slugging percentage. 21 years old, .312 average, 26 home runs, 87

RBIS. Thibodeaux, Jr. is a principal reason why the Mets (!) are eleven games up in the NL East with just nineteen to go.

These two are the toast of baseball, a testament to what natural selection and good Mexican food can do for a baseball career. Some thought the return of Thibodeaux the Elder would distract the Younger, runner-up to last year's NL Rookie of the Year winner Mark Elliot. "Just the opposite," Baby Thib told me the other day. "Seeing my dad back in the Majors really inspires me. I can watch him on ESPN now and talk with him whenever I want. Knowing he's there helps me focus on baseball more."

This is good for baseball, for families, for columnists who don't have a clue what to write about. It would be nice if it lasted forever, though we know it can't. But we'll always have Cleveland.

—

IT WAS September before they crossed paths, at Chicago's Comiskey Park. The Indians were finishing a series with the White Sox, the Mets coming in for three games with the Cubs. Rafe got to the stadium too late to see his father pitch, but went down to the locker room afterwards. It wasn't exactly an intimate moment. Reporters crowded them, asking the same questions they'd been asking all summer. Did you ever imagine you'd be playing in the Big Leagues together? How does it feel to see your son playing so well? What happens if the Indians and Mets make it to the World Series?

Jason and Rafe grabbed a few minutes alone in an empty lounge before the Indians left for the airport, sitting on opposite sides of a table littered with the detritus of an industry they helped fuel — empty beer and wine glasses, half-eaten plates of nachos and fries, peanut shells. They beamed at each other, happy — and incredulous — that much of this was about them.

"You know who I wish could be here?" Jason said.

"Martha Evelia."

Jason shook his head. "My father."

"He'd really be proud of you," Rafe said.

"Proud of *us.*"

Rafe nodded. What he'd pulled off was far beyond what he'd ever imagined. He thought his father would pitch a few innings and go back to Mexico with his pension. Instead, he had become an integral part of a playoff contender, in the full spotlight of the world. He had no doubt that he had done the right thing, though what he really wanted to say to his father was, 'we're even.' But he never would. How this had happened was a secret only four people in the world knew about. Or so Rafe thought.

THE PHONE rang and before "Shifty" Gehrs could answer it, the fans overlooking the bullpen started their chant: "Ze-ro, ze-ro, ze-ro." The Indians' starter, Andy Toms, had given up a lead-off single and was in a hole to the second batter, 3-0. Bernie Deckman, the set-up man, spit a spray of sunflower shells across the top of Jason's shoes. "You seen that Swarzennegger movie where that invisible thing's killing people?"

"*The Terminator?* He wasn't invisible."

"Naw, *Schwarzenegger's* not invisible. He's hunting this thing he can't see, it takes place in some kind of jungle ... *Predator!* That's it. You seen that?"

"Stan!" Shifty called out, signaling their big right handed reliever, Stan Bileschi, to get up and throw. "Zero! Loosen up."

"That's you, man," Deckman said. "*The Predator.*"

Jason slapped his glove across Deckman's back. "You can't hit what you can't see." He trotted to the mound on the far side of the bullpen where his fans posted their signs: "Zero is Everything." "Zero is my Hero." "o = $". Top of the seventh, second game of a doubleheader. The Indians had taken the first three games from the Twins and were leading this one, 4-1. They'd drawn 137,000 people in three days, and the stadium literally shook with excitement at the possibility of the Indians going up two games on the Twins with just six left.

As Jason threw his first pitch he heard the crowd moan — the batter had walked. "Ze-ro! Ze-ro! Ze-ro!" they chanted, louder this time. It didn't get any better than this. He threw four, five, six more warmup pitches and thought what the hell, if he could pitch this well into September, he could do it next year too. Martha Evelia would understand; she knew how much he loved the game. The money would be spectacular compared to what he could earn in Mexico, enough to build houses for the whole family and send the kids to the best schools.

The Twins' next batter was a lefty, and playing the percentages everyone in the stadium knew what that meant. The bullpen phone rang again. "Ze-ro! Ze-ro! Ze-ro!" Shifty answered just as Jason snapped off a curve and glanced towards the field. They'd use him for the third out, then bring in Deckman to pitch the eighth, and their closer, Brent Shicker, for the ninth. A batter here, a batter there, he didn't see why he couldn't pitch another two years, maybe three. He'd talk with Beuhler in the morning.

"Zero!" Gehrs called out. "Let's go — one up, one down."

MARTY BEUHLER was in his office studying matchups for that night's game against the Tigers. He was a tall, narrow-shouldered man just a couple of years older than Jason, which was more of a problem for Buehler than it was for his seasoned reliever. Managing a team owned by Bill Sharpstein wasn't easy either. Like most managers who had worked for Sharpstein, Beuhler felt everything was shoved down his throat — including the decision to sign Señor Zero. Jason had never been part of Buehler's original scheme for a winning season. And as often happens with men, practicality took a back seat to pride.

"Hey Marty, got a minute?" Jason asked, peering in.

Beuhler looked up from his stat sheets. "About that much. What's on your mind?" Maybe it wasn't the best timing. The night before Bileschi had given up a two run homer in the 8th, and the Twins had won it in the 10th with a pair of two out doubles. But Jason had done his job — a simple two-hopper to the second baseman, side retired. The Indians were tied for first, and he was a big part of their success. He figured he should strike while the iron was hot.

He closed the door behind him. Beuhler made no gesture for him to sit. "You know Mr. Sharpstein better than I do," Jason began. Beuhler set down his pencil and watched the pitcher with characteristic detachment. "I was wondering … in your experience … how he might react to considering a contract extension for next year."

Beuhler shrugged. "Jeez, I don't know, JT The guy you should really talk to is the owner of the Mets — he's the one paying your salary."

"Come on, Marty, a straight answer would be just fine."

"I always give straight answers. I wish someone would give me one around here," he said testily. "As far as I know, your kid made some kind of deal so you could come up and get your pension. His team is paying your salary and nobody's supposed to know anything about it."

RAFE GOT the call in Denver — from Mr. Maclean himself. The Mets had clinched their division the week before. They had one game left against the Rockies, then on to Atlanta for a four game tune-up before the playoffs.

"Your father found out about the deal," he said. "He's disappeared."

"Disappeared?"

"AWOL. Any idea where he might be?" Maclean asked.

Rafe was numb. "I need to find him and explain what's going on."

"Let me talk to Bagot," Maclean said. He called back in twenty minutes. "There'll be a private jet waiting for you at the Denver airport, at Butler Aviation. You've got two days, then get back here for the playoffs — whether you find him or not."

Rafe called his father's cell phone, standing at the window on the eighteenth floor of the Marriott and marveling at the irony. Six years before he was roaming the streets of Denver, riding shotgun in Lo-Jack's borrowed cars and messing up a whole bunch of lives. Now his father was probably doing the same thing in some sleazy bar in Cleveland. And he wasn't answering his cell phone either.

His mother met him at the San Francisco airport. He knew his father wouldn't be there, but he had to start where it made sense for him. He had to talk to somebody who understood how badly he'd screwed up before he could think about fixing it.

Rafe told her the whole story on the way in from the airport, his voice faint and self-accusing. "I've ruined everything," he said. "He'll never speak to me again."

Vicki got off at the first exit for San Francisco and pulled to the curb. She sat holding the wheel, tears streaming down her cheeks. "I'm so proud of you," she said. "It's such an incredible thing you did."

"Except I've totally fucked things up."

"No, Rafe. You couldn't have told him, he never would have done it. But he couldn't have done it without you."

"No, he would have made it," Rafe said. "He's that good, Mom." Though he knew it wasn't true. His father belonged in the Majors, but he never would have gotten there without The Deal. And he knew that his Dad knew that — which is why he took off.

Vicki had a new home, a spacious condominium on Russian Hill with a view of Alcatraz and the Golden Gate Bridge. Rafe was surprised to see pictures of himself all over the house, a retrospective of his life until he was fifteen, when he'd decided he didn't need his mother. She fixed a pot of tea and they sat at her kitchen table overlooking the Bay.

She stared at her son, smiling hopefully.

"Are you still playing music?"

"I'm a professional baseball player, Mom."

"I know, but I thought there might be some opportunity ..."

Rafe looked at her and held out his huge hands — his father's hands. "I know it's hard for you to understand," he said. "I think it's about competition. You come out and you see the other team — there's no feeling like it. It's rock and roll, gloves off, who's the best. You just don't get that when you're sitting behind a music stand. I mean, there's some mystery if you can pull off a piece, but you know you can do it if you practice enough. Imagine if Mozart had to play the harpsichord with 95-mile-an-hour fastballs coming at him. Or Prokofiev finishing symphonies with fifty thousand people screaming and the umpire ready to call him out if he makes a mistake."

She looked at him, smiling with a mother's pride. "I'm not sure what you're talking about, but I can see it makes you happy. And that makes me happy."

Rafe pointed to the newspaper on the table opened to the National League standings. "But now even you're reading the sports section."

She looked frankly into her son's eyes. "I'm seeing someone ... he's a judge."

"Sleeping with the enemy!"

"He's not in my line. He's a juvenile court judge," Vicki said. "I met him at a party."

"Anybody I know?"

"Of course not." Then more softly, "He's going through a divorce. He's got two children in high school — a son and a daughter. I think you'd like them."

Her hands circled her tea cup. She smiled uncertainly, then rose and set her cup in the sink. "What time do you want to get going in the morning?"

"I told the pilot 6:30. With the time change —"

"I'll be ready."

"I can take a cab."

"I'm going with you."

Rafe stared at his mother. She crossed the room and kissed him on top of his head. "Get some sleep. We'll take care of everything tomorrow."

But as tired as he should have been, Rafe couldn't sleep. He turned on the television in his room to the PBS Channel he watched as a kid. There was a black and white movie with actors he didn't know, playing scenes with no relation to his life. At one o'clock his cell phone rang. He glanced at caller ID and quickly answered.

"Who do you think you are, Florence Fucking Nightingale?"

"Dad, where are you? I want to explain."

"Go fuck yourself. Everybody knew why I'm back in The Show except me."

"Are you in Cleveland?" Rafe could hear voices in the background. He figured his father was calling from a bar — except it was 4:00 AM in Cleveland. He suddenly realized the voices were the same as on his TV. His father was at home, watching the same shitty movie.

"It's not what you think. Nobody was supposed to know, just Maclean and Sharpstein. Beuhler's an asshole — you told me yourself. He doesn't know the real deal."

"No — you're the asshole," he said, and hung up.

—

ZERO FROM ZERO IS ZERO
by Bob Jennings, *columnist*
CLEVELAND PLAIN DEALER

Let's talk today about a little known baseball statistic. Not RBI or OBP or ERA, but DNA — "Didn't Nobody Ask!?" A player's DNA is comprised of all those things that a team could have found out about a player when they signed him, but didn't ask. This can range from injuries to emotional breakdowns to assault and battery charges, things that players prefer to hide and teams too often oblige them by not looking.

The disappearance of Señor Zero involves a lot of DNA. First is, how did Tribe owner Bill Sharpstein push onto the team a player who was being paid out of another player's salary — and WHY??? Didn't Nobody Ask?

Secondly, Didn't Nobody Ask about the strange track record of this fellow? Jason Thibodeaux never met a commitment he didn't run from. A brief check of the *public* record finds a personal legacy of unprecedented woe. In chronological order, the Indians' beloved Señor Zero:

Married at nineteen and divorced at twenty-one, losing custody of his son in a divorce proceeding that featured court records attesting to "physical abuse and child neglect." Abandoned his wife and child to play professional ball. Demanded a trade from the Reds to the Giants to be back with his son, then traded again and for some reason didn't see his son for six years. Went through alcoholism and rehab, quit the Rockies to take care of the son (again), who by that point was in jail. And now he's run out on the Tribe while they're fighting for a playoff spot.

Studying Jason Thibodeaux's DNA would have let anyone predict — and hopefully avoid — this unfortunate sidelight. I say sidelight because I don't think his disappearance is damaging to the Tribe's chance of a pennant. Señor Zero means more to the team as a mascot than a pitcher. Do the math. In forty appearances, he's faced the grand total of sixty-one batters — that's less than three complete games worth of pitching in a schedule of 162 games. Zero's absence simply means each of the Tribe's able relief corps has to pitch to one more batter every few games, hardly an insurmountable task.

Let this be a lesson to Bill Sharpstein about hiring ballplayers and not paying for them. You get what you pay for — in this case, Zero.

—

THE ADDRESS was three blocks from Jacobs Field. Television trucks were parked in front of the tidy, two-story house, a knot of reporters conversing on the lawn. Rafe slowed the rent-a-car, then kept going. "Cleveland hasn't won the World Series since 1948," he explained to his mother. "It's the biggest story in years."

He turned into the alleyway and parked behind the house. There was a gleaming Weber grill in the overgrown yard. Rafe knocked on the porch door but no one answered; Vicki shouted through the screen. "Is anybody home? We're Jason's family."

An inner door opened just as they turned to leave. An old woman shuffled across the porch. She fumbled with the lock, then stood uncertainly behind the screen door.

"We're sorry to bother you," Rafe said. "Is Mr. Thibodeaux in?"

The woman looked worried. "You're not one of those newspaper people? He said not to tell them anything." Her eyes were focused somewhere beyond Rafe's shoulder. It was another moment before he realized that she was blind.

"No, no," he said. "I'm his son … and this is my mother. I see my dad's set up his barbecue in the yard there."

The woman's face lifted with a smile. "He smoked a whole chicken the other night. It was the most delicious meal I've ever had." Rafe turned and smiled at his mother. "Can you tell us where my father is?"

"He left to catch a cab on Carlin Avenue. He said he was going on a road trip."

VICKI SPOTTED him through the window of the Lake Shore Tavern. "Let me go in," she said. "You guys will start fighting and he'll leave." Rafe looked at her skeptically. "Trust me. There's nothing for us to fight about anymore."

Rafe hunched in the vestibule between two doors, watching his parents through a smudged, diamond-shaped window. His father sat in a booth with a drink in front of him, wearing his Indians' hat and reading a book.

Vicki walked straight in and sat down across from him. Jason looked up.

"Of all the gin joints in all the towns in all the world, you walk into this place."

She laughed. "I know this looks strange —"

"Strange? It's bizarre! This isn't any of your business."

"It is, Jason. He's our son." He closed his book and angrily shoved it aside. Vicki took a deep breath and closed her eyes. When she opened them, he was sliding his book into his suitcase.

"He did it for you, Jason. He loves you so much. You've got to stay and —"

"As usual, you don't have any idea what you're talking about. But *he* knows what he did." He gestured around the sad, dark bar. "Tell me what's lower than getting laughed out of Cleveland."

The bartender glanced over, then drifted discreetly to the other end of the bar. An elderly, bearded man half-turned on his stool and stared.

"He made a mistake," Vicki said heartfully. "God knows we've all made mistakes. And we always make them doing what we think is right." She stared at him, open, honest, demanding. He looked at her, exasperated by her reasonableness.

"Jesus, Vicki, that's not the issue. I know *why* he did it. But I can't go out there now and pitch to guys who know my son paid my way. Half of what goes on out there is illusion. Without that, I'm just another fucking guy wearing a glove."

"Can't you just finish the season?"

"It's already finished."

Rafe watched his father slide toward the end of the booth and he knew he had to do something. He knew enough about being a man that if he let his father break this off now, it would remain broken for a long, long time.

He turned and pushed open the outer door, then burst through the inner one as if he'd just arrived. "You found him!" he cried as Jason reached for his suitcase. "Wait — Dad. C'mon, you can't just walk out without discussing this."

Jason's face knotted with disbelief. "Did you discuss this ridiculous deal with me? All that time you were lying to me — to everybody."

"You're right, you're right," Rafe said. "But you know what? I'm twenty-one years old. You were twenty-one when you had *me!*"

Jason took a deep breath. "If you have to say something, hurry up and say it. I've got a plane to catch."

Rafe slid into the booth beside his mother. It was the last of the ninth, everything on the line. The wrong word, the wrong tone, and Rafe could lose his father for good.

"I'm only here because of you," he said, looking at his father. "Not here in Cleveland, but here — in the world. I mean you too, Mom, but I wouldn't be who I was, what I'm doing, if it weren't for you." Jason looked up with an expression Rafe knew so well — eyes narrow, his jaw set as if to say, "is that the best you got?" Rafe looked down. He suddenly realized he was in way over his head. "I'm sorry," he mumbled. "I just wanted to pay you back for what you did … to give you something in return."

"I don't *want* to be paid back!" Jason bellowed. "I didn't quit because of you. I quit because I wanted to." He stared hard at Rafe, who tried to stare back and take it like a man. "All I ever wanted was for you to be the best ball player, the best person, you could be. That's all. Not all this bullshit deal-making."

Rafe feared that his father would leave on the crest of his anger. He couldn't say goodbye again. He wasn't ready for that. He pulled out his wallet and extracted a frayed sheet of paper he'd been carrying since his sophomore year in high school. It was something he had written for Father Baldassare after a counseling session in which he had complained about his father the entire time.

"Do you love your father?" Baldassare had asked him. He couldn't answer it then, so Baldassare gave him an assignment. He could have blown it off — it wouldn't have been the first assignment he blew off. But Rafe wrote it that night and gave it to Baldassare, who returned it to him a couple of days later, saying, "I recommend you show this to your father." He never did.

The paper was soft with age and drooped as he held it with both hands. "I wrote this at Holy Innocents." He stared at his own handwriting, then began reading:

"*Why I Love My Father*, by Raphael Thibodeaux.
I love my father because he's a great ballplayer.
I love my father because he picks me up at school every day and
doesn't ask, 'how was school?'
I love my father because he cooks for me. Last night he made
barbecue chicken on the grill outside, even though it was raining.
I love my father because he watches *X-Files* with me.
I love my father because he bailed me out of jail and didn't lord it
over me.
I love my father because he helped get me into this great school.
I love my father because he wakes me up by putting on Tom Petty
and the Heartbreakers and sings really bad in the shower.
I love my father because he tries to teach me to do the right thing.
I love my father because he took care of me when I was a baby, and
he took care of me when I was a jerk.
I love my father because he helps me with my homework.
I love my father because he's different and doesn't care what
people think.
I love my father because I'm pretty sure he loves me."

He folded the paper and put it in his shirt pocket. Vicki looked from Rafe to Jason, tears streaming down her cheeks. The old man at the bar was crying. Rafe looked up at his dad, who stared back at him with a look of aching disbelief.

"I did what I did so that *you* could be the best ball player you could be," Rafe said. "That's all I wanted."

Top o' the 10ᵗʰ ...
Tobias Barlow USA TODAY

The new reality show, *Beanball Island,* took another surreal turn
this week with the three day suspension of Jason Thibodeaux for
going AWOL after discovering his own team wasn't paying his salary
(as opposed to those of us who have nobody paying our salaries).
But do you really want to be slapping your 41-year old relief
pitcher's wrist on the eve of the playoffs? I guess Marty Beuhler
had to do something, and he wasn't about to fine the less-than-
sharp Bill Sharpstein. If you're going to make a confidential deal,
it's supposed to be ... well, confidential. Maybe Sharpstein wanted
everyone to know he was the Sultan of Swap.

Now everyone's agog over this family thing — who paid whom
how much, etc. The talk lines are buzzing with more nonsense
than usual. 'What if David Ortiz held the Red Sox hostage until
they hired his son?' they ask. 'What if some superstar decides to
integrate the majors with his daughter?'

Hey, if David Ortiz's kid can rack up a sub-zero ERA and take
the *Cleveland Indians* to the playoffs, I say bring him on. If Derek
Jeter's daughter can jack out thirty dingers and hit .313, as Raphael
Thibodeaux has, I say bring her on. Baseball's an American game,
and America's about success. But success isn't only about the
numbers we put up on the scoreboard — or on our paychecks. It's
about what's in our hearts.

For me the question is, can they play? And that one's more
than settled. Thibodeaux Junior's Mets cakewalked into the
playoffs ten games ahead of the pack, while Señor Zero's Indians
tomahawked their way into a division series with the White Sox
with a dramatic 5-4 win at the Twinkie Dome. Zero never got in the
game physically, but his teammates wore their appreciation on their
sleeves. They all drew Zeroes on their uniforms ... with Sharpies!

"Zero's our leader," Indian hurler Johnny Eberhardt said after
the Twinkie implosion. "He knows how to take care of what's
important." No one gave the Indians a chance of reaching the
playoffs at the beginning of the season, yet here they are, led into
battle by a 41-year-old lefty who five months ago was dodging
mescal bottles in Vera Cruz. Marty Beuhler saved himself a lot of

trouble — and probably his life — by including Señor Zero on the post-season roster. Let the games begin!

—

RAFE STOOD in the batter's box and imagined his father on the mound. The eyes buried beneath the hat brim, the long stride, the ball on a trajectory as familiar as a stroll home from school. But it wasn't his dad, it was Miles Grant, the Phillies' number one starter, an inning away from knotting up the series at two games apiece.

The crowd was as loud as a hurricane. Carmelo Fox stepped off third, Julio Perez off first, waiting for the pitch. A 2-2 count, a 4-2 Phillies lead, top of the eighth, two outs. Rafe stepped out of the box and breathed deeply, adjusted his batting gloves, surveyed the outfield. "Just relax and play your game," Buck Bagot advised them before Game 1. Then when they dropped the opener 5-1, he chewed them out for being too nonchalant. Nonchalant, my ass. He hadn't slept in days. The season-long run he had been on — one of those zones players talk about, where the ball looks as slow as a mobile home on a mountain road — had come to a crashing halt. He was 2-for-12 at the end of the season, 1-for-15 in the playoffs. The whole thing had backfired on him. All anybody wanted to know about was Señor Zero. Señor Zero and his salary. Señor Zero and his son. Señor Zero and his date with destiny. He was the one who had given up the big contract, and Señor Zero somehow ended up the hero.

He stepped back in the box. One swing could end all that. He was sure Grant was going to give him something off-speed, and off the plate. Then at 3-2 he'd have to come in with a fastball and POW! — he'd take him long.

Grant checked the runners, then whirled. Rafe saw the ball bearing down on him not like a mobile home but in the tight reverse rotation of a fastball headed for the inside corner of the plate. His best hope was to foul it off — if he could catch up to it.

He didn't.

BY THE time Rafe got back to the hotel, the Indians had beaten the White Sox to even their series 2-2. His father had retired two batters in the seventh, extending his playoff ERA to 0.00. The reporters were all over him after the game.

"What happens if you make it to the Series and have to pitch to your son?" a TV reporter asked. "Will you pull punches because of what he did for you?" Rafe turned off the TV. He knew his father would say all the right things. 'I'll cross that bridge when we come to it … we're just focusing on the next game, etc. etc.' He was the word man, which wasn't Rafe's medium. When a reporter had asked him the same question before the game tonight, he had shaken his head and said, "I don't know."

He paced his room, pursuing the elusive damsel of sleep. A joint would work wonders right now. He knew at least five guys on the club who smoked, and half the cabbies in Philadelphia could score him some for a price. It would help him relax. It would help him forget the Señor Zero show. It would help him sleep.

He picked up the phone and punched in the familiar numbers.

"Hi Dad."

"Hey Buddy." They had spoken only twice since the barroom encounter in Cleveland — once after his father's public apology to his teammates and fans, once after the Indians clinched the division. Rafe had initiated the call both times. He could hear the sound of wind rushing by; he guessed his dad was in a cab heading for somewhere. He didn't know how to begin. Thankfully his father did.

"You all right?"

"Not really."

"What's going on?"

"Remember that conversation we had a long time ago — about being able to talk about anything?"

"Of course. You in trouble?"

"Sort of," Rafe replied. "I'm hitting .062." He heard his father say 'go right — right there,' and he felt a surge of loneliness. All season they had talked — on the phone at least. Then suddenly it had stopped, the consequence of his own stupidity. He heard a voice say, "twelve dollars." He imagined a neon sign, a crowded restaurant filled with friends. In fact, the cabbie had left Jason at the front stoop of Mrs. Harburton's house.

"I haven't seen any of your games," Jason said. "What's going on?"

"I don't know. The playoffs started and everything fell apart."

Jason looked around the quiet neighborhood, wanting nothing more than to go to bed. He had his own pressure-packed game tomorrow; but this was important, too. He sat down on the front steps.

"The playoffs are different. Teams use their one, two and three starters almost exclusively, and bring in their relievers faster than during the season. Most hitters are anxious and try to win games with one swing. Pitchers know that and give the big guys a little more off-speed stuff." He paused. "Just be patient. Stick to your fundamentals. Two or three hits and that .062 will be .200 and you're on your way."

"Are you still pissed at me?" Rafe asked.

"Why would I be pissed at you?"

"This whole mess about the deal. You never call any more."

Jason sighed. "Ah hell, Rafe, I'm over all that. But it's been kind of hard on me, yeah. I just want to play ball. The rest of this stuff is bullshit."

Rafe remembered the other part of their conversation on the reservoir, the part about his father being as scared as he was every day. For some reason he always forgot that. His father was so expert at putting a lid on it, that most times he forgot it himself.

"Can we do that?" Rafe asked. "Just play ball?"

"We can do whatever the hell we want."

—

Top o' the 10th ...
Tobias Barlow USA TODAY

We've had the Subway Series, the Earthquake Series, the all-Missouri "Show Me" Series ... now the first Father-Son Bestball Series. And thank God for us members of the press. Without this family saga, we'd have absolutely nothing to write about. The Indians, after all, simply don't have a chance.

But the Cleveland Indians, I wish to remind the skeptics, have been defying common wisdom all year — if not common sense. They won a division title that belonged to the Twins, a division series that was the White Sox's to lose (which they ungraciously did), and snatched a seven game thriller from a Yankee squad that was supposed to be one of history's best (the ALCS certainly was, Scott Spencer's bases loaded ninth inning strikeout a moment to cherish in all but the Spencer household). After the Mets ho-hummed their way to an NLCS win over the Dodgers, we now have America's most stirring family saga since the Clinton White House.

But let's keep our heads, shall we? One columnist has compared

this with Greek tragedy — *Oedipus in Cleveland*. Another cited
a psychiatric study comparing this upcoming confrontation to
Hamlet challenging his step-father Claudius — with the World
Series ring as the "Queen" both men crave. C'mon folks, this is
baseball. I've followed the Thibodoze for years and they're both fine
players. Neither man's a prince, nor has anyone murdered a king on
the road to Colonnus, let alone Cleveland.

Two Birds, One Stone Department: Beside filing my so-called
"normal" column, I'll also be providing daily coverage of World
Series games. Have no fear, I used to be a straight reporter, and
I promise I'll go straight again. Look for coverage of Game 1
tomorrow, I'm sure it will be a doozy.

—

HIS FATHER was already seated on a riser behind a table full of
microphones and tape recorders, separated from at least a hundred
members of the press by a yellow security tape stretched along the first
base line. It was a beautiful late October day, with bright sunshine and
a stiff breeze off Lake Erie. Red, white and blue bunting draped the
stands, sky boxes and press table. Rafe hadn't seen his father since that
afternoon in the Lakeshore Inn. He looked relaxed, his Indians' hat low
over his eyes, wisecracking with some reporters in front.

"We're just here to make sure the Series is played," he joked. "On
paper, we're like that team that used to play the Harlem Globetrotters
— what'd they lose, 450 games in a row? According to you guys, this
thing's over and done. Just put a fork in us."

When Rafe appeared, the cameras whirred and clicked like a
swarm of locusts. Jason rose and embraced him, a photo that would
land on news desks around the world in seconds. "Father-Son Meet on
Baseball's Mount Olympus." It would supplant the one Rafe saw on the
front page of the *Cleveland Plain Dealer* that morning, a photo of his
father pitching underhand to him at PacBell Park when he was eight
years old: "Can Zero Continue Mastery of Son?"

He tried to hug his dad back, but his arms wouldn't move. He
ducked into the seat beside his father. Jason wished they had talked
beforehand and discussed some of the questions. Rafe looked like the
proverbial deer caught in the headlights.

The first question came to Rafe. "How do you feel about your
decision to help bring your father up to the majors, now that you have

to face him in the World Series?" Rafe squirmed. He'd rehearsed with the team's PR guy, but he couldn't remember a thing. He'd never paid attention to this part of the World Series. Maybe after a game — or after the Series — when they asked players about the pitch they hit or what it felt like to rob somebody of a hit. But no one had played a minute of baseball yet!

"Good," he finally managed to say, without looking at anyone in particular.

Jason leaned forward, his heart aching for the pain and confusion Rafe seemed to be going through. He wanted to intervene, but this was Rafe's moment. He needed to stay in the background and let Rafe's star either shine or collapse in a black hole.

More questions poured from the herd. "Will you help him get a contract for next year? How often do you two talk? Will you split the World Series money if you win?" Rafe stared at the grass in front of the table. He tried to envision the questions like pitches, either inside or outside the zone. Anything outside the box, he wouldn't swing at.

Rafe looked up at the rows of squirming reporters. "As my father once said, I just want to play baseball. The rest of this stuff is bullshit." Jason smiled and draped his arm across Rafe's shoulders. The shouting, the flashbulbs began again.

"Are you surprised by what your father's done this year?"

"I'm never surprised by my father, he's an amazing man. He kept pitching, he believed in himself … just like he believed in me."

"Was it worth it, giving up what you did to get your father a contract?"

Rafe looked sideways at his father, then back at the reporters. "You know, I'd prefer to answer questions about baseball." Their collective groan was as loud as a herd of cattle. "This *is* about baseball!" someone yelled.

"Look," Jason smiled. "We're just a couple of guys struggling through the muck. Millions of families are out there working at it too, day in and day out, a lot of them single parents, raising kids and wondering if they're doing the right thing. As far as I can tell, the right thing in any of this is just being there and caring for each other."

"But you weren't there for a long time. Your son had trouble with the law —"

"Precisely," Jason replied. "When you're there, when you care, it works."

"Was it worth it to you, giving up $40 million to raise your son? And do you think your son made the right decision giving up what he did to bring you up?"

Jason laughed and shook his head. "Does it look like we gave up something? We're in the World Series, man! I did what I had to do to be the best father I could be. And the last I looked," he smiled, "I can honestly say I did a pretty damned good job. There isn't any amount of money you could pay me for the feeling I have right now."

A few hands came together in applause. Another voice spoke up from the back. "How do you plan to pitch to Raphael when you face him?"

"Carefully," Jason replied, igniting a spark of laugher.

"How about you, Raphael? Can you hit your Dad's stuff?"

Rafe shrugged. "You never know until you try," he said. "Before he was Señor Zero, he was my dad. And I used to hit him pretty good."

—

Top o' the 10ᵗʰ ...
Tobias Barlow USA TODAY

They're not called "odds" for nothing. Favored 7-5 by the gambling gurus, the Mets dropped the first two games 6-3 and 9-2 but are still favored to win. They're not pitching, not hitting, and their skipper, Buck Bagot, doesn't seem to grasp the most obvious strategies around the DH, leaving in his starters way too long. The theory is, the Mets have too much talent to blow it. And the *Titanic* leaves New York Thursday morning for its return to Southampton.

Highlights so far include Frank Wilmott's three run shot in Game 1, and Señor Zero's appearance in the seventh inning. It was a classic Zero moment — two men on, two outs — his own son on deck if he failed to get his man. It looked like he didn't want any part of that match up. Zero dispensed with Mateo Hernandez on three pitches — two of them 95 mph. How's that from a 41-year old arm!

The lowlight has to be the Mets' lackluster 9-2 loss in the second game. Second-to-low is Raphael Thibodeaux going 0-8 with four strikeouts. The New York tabloids started out calling him "Zero, Jr.," now it's "Señor Subzero." Ouch.

—

THEN IT all changed. Raphael finally found his groove in Game Three, roping a double down the right field line in the fifth inning, and a solo home run in Game Four that splashed into the koi pond Maury-the-grounds-keeper kept behind the center field wall. It couldn't have come at a better time. Rafe's teammates were resenting his family distractions, without any compensating production at the plate.

While Rafe struggled with an .087 average, Señor Zero faced five Mets in the first three games and got four out — three by strikeout. He never got into Game Four, the Mets banging out fourteen hits and winning 7-1. In Game Five he had his worst outing of the year, blowing a three run lead and leaving with the go-ahead run in scoring position. The Mets went on to win 7-5, moving up 3-2 in the Series. After Game Five, Jason appeared in the press room at Shea — alone this time, wearing a Vera Cruz *Aguilas* t-shirt and his Indians cap. A Japanese reporter called out the first question. "Did you have good stuff today?"

"I've had better stuff taking out the garbage," Jason said to much laughter. "I'm just sorry I let the guys down. I do my job, we go back to Cleveland in the driver's seat."

"Do you think it's over?"

"I wouldn't count the Mets out yet."

"Are you looking forward to facing your son?"

Jason shook his head. "Did you see that ball he hit last night? It landed in some body of water out there, Maury's Cove or somethin'. He does that in Cleveland, that's called Lake Erie. Look, us guys in the bullpen, we want to play. But the less we're in the game the better it is for everyone."

The Mets arrived in Cleveland at noon for their workout. There was an envelope waiting at Rafe's locker at Jacobs Field. "Dinner at my house seven o'clock," the note said. Inside was an address and the phone number for a livery service.

When the car reached its destination, a two-story condominium complex east of the city, three cars screeched behind them and a swarm of journalists jumped out. The flashes began popping before Rafe could even pay. He hurried towards a metal gate with the number of his dad's building. The gate popped open and an arm pulled him in.

"I can't believe what hyenas these people are."

Jason laughed. "They've spent the last two weeks trying to locate that bar where you found me." Rafe followed him up a flight of stairs to a plain white door marked 17. Jason clapped him on the back. "I'm glad you came."

"Me too." Inside Willie Herrera and his wife were salsa dancing in the kitchen. Martha Evelia, Luis and Maria Evelia transferred enchiladas from a platter in the oven. Mexican music blared from the living room. When Rafe appeared, a huge shout went up, "*Hola, Raphael!*"

It was a wonderful evening. Nobody talked about baseball. His dad had just lost his first World Series game, faced the international press, and flown back to Cleveland one game away from elimination, yet he looked as happy as Rafe had ever seen him. It was warm, it was welcoming ... it was home.

When dinner was finished, Rafe carried a pile of dishes into the kitchen and found his father and Martha Evelia deep in a discussion. She turned and when she saw Rafe, quickly left the room.

"Is this a good time to talk?" Rafe asked.

"It's the only time, I think. What's on your mind — Sex? Drugs?"

"Baseball," Rafe replied.

Jason groaned. "I'll help you anyway I can, *hijo* — after Sunday."

"What do you mean?"

"This is my swan song. Win, lose or draw, I'm going back to Mexico."

"I thought the Indians wanted you back."

Jason leaned against the counter. "So does Martha Evelia. She's afraid I'm going to disappear on her, like her father did. I'm sure you can sympathize."

Rafe shifted on his feet. The butterflies in his stomach felt more like a swarm of bats. "The series is too big for me," he finally said.

"Don't tell me this."

"I'm afraid all the time, I can't shake it."

"Please don't tell me this."

"I don't have anyone else."

Jason closed his eyes and took a deep breath. "OK."

"It's all that stuff we've talked about. Who the hell am I, what am I doing here ... what's the difference between me and fifty thousand people out there yelling my name?"

Jason opened his eyes and studied his son, then spoke in the fatherly, semi-impatient way he had when a lesson, in his mind, should be obvious. "If you hit .315 in the regular season, you belong here. If you hit 110 RBIS, you belong here. If you're in the World Series, you belong there!" he said, his voice rising. "Jesus Christ, you saw me pitch last night — do I belong here? Every day, Rafe, every time you go out there, it's like those first steps on the moon. You don't know whether your feet are going to burn off or monsters reach out and grab you, or whether you'll sink into some goo and disappear. Every day you just put on your space suit and jump out of the landing craft."

Rafe nodded. He knew that already, but it felt good to hear it from the horse's mouth. He looked at the clock — 10:10. He had an 11 PM curfew. He had to hurry.

"I'm sorry," he said. "About everything."

"Everything what?"

"Everything, growing up. I'm sorry I was such a jerk."

"Aw Jesus, Rafe. You don't have to do this. Not now."

"Yeah, I do. I'm embarrassed by what I did. I was angry when you weren't there and I was angry when you were. I was scared, mostly. I didn't want you to leave."

"I didn't want to leave either."

Rafe felt himself getting ready to cry and looked desperately around the kitchen for something to distract him. He grabbed a wooden spatula and tossed a grid of uneaten dinner rolls to his father, motioning him back towards the patio doors. Rafe snapped into his stance in front of the counter cluttered with dirty dishes and pots.

Jason went into his stretch, then fired a fastball past Rafe's flailing spatula. Two more rolls sailed past him. "You're out!" Jason grinned.

"C'mon, four strikes you're out, remember?"

Rafe watched the new dinner roll in his father's hand as intently as a cat watching a bird. It came towards him with an end-over-end rotation, towards the magic zone of his box. He swung the spatula and sent the roll crashing into the top corner of the patio door. It ricocheted to the counter, knocking over a wine glass and shattering it against the tiles.

"Whoops," Rafe winced. Jason crossed the room and engulfed his son in a massive hug. "You can do it," he said. "You're a player."

METS' CHAMPAGNE STILL ON ICE —
SEVENTH GAME TONIGHT
by **Tobias Barlow**

Every player's dream of appearing in the World Series looks the same: last of the ninth, two outs, all the marbles on the line. Cleveland Indians' rightfielder Daryn Burks got to live that dream last night and made it pay, powering a dramatic three-run homer off Mets closer Ernesto "Pancho" Villa and sending ten cases of French champagne back to the cooler for another night at least. Game Seven will be played tonight at Cleveland's Jacobs Field.

The game began ominously for Cleveland when the Mets jumped on Indians starter Ron Ricketts for three runs in the first inning. Leadoff hitter Nic Weise opened the game with a walk, then successive singles to Bruce Molinaro, Carmelo Fox and Julio Perez brought home two runs. Raphael Thibodeaux drove in a third run with a sacrifice fly. Thibodeaux also homered in the sixth, his second in the Series.

While Ricketts settled down to retire the next eleven Mets in order, Mets starter Hideki Oh was painting a masterpiece. He entered the fifth inning throwing a perfect game, but then the Indians broke through for a pair of runs. First baseman Marc Shulteis doubled to left, and following a walk to Armando Valentin and a sacrifice bunt, moving the runners to second and third, Rich Koskie doubled home two runs with a blooper just inside the rightfield line.

The score held at 4-2 until the ninth, when the Mets brought in Villa. The All-Star fireballer saved forty-one games during the regular season and had a perfect seven-for-seven save record in post-season play. Things looked bleak for the Indians when Villa struck out Valentin to start the inning. But then shortstop Jesus Almonte battled Villa in a tense fifteen-pitch at bat, fouling off nine pitches before drawing a walk.

The encounter seemed to rattle Villa. He gave up a first-pitch single to Rich Koskie, his third hit of the game, but struck out Indians centerfielder Ward Cameron on three wicked fastballs. With Mets fans holding their breath and waiting for their first world championship since 1986 — and Indians fans banging a hundred thousand Thunder Stix — number seven hitter Daryn Burks blasted a 2-2 curve ball into the seats just inside the left field foul pole.

"He started me with heat," Burks said. "But for some reason I knew he was going to try to sneak a curve ball and chill me." But the only thing chilled today are those ten cases of champagne. Who gets to drink them tonight is anybody's guess.

—

It was a cold, still autumn night in Cleveland, chasms of black sky opening and closing between cloudbanks drifting across Lake Erie. The voices of fifty thousand Indians' fans rose visibly on their breath, giddy with the taste of victory as their team took the field for the ninth inning, leading 8-4. But for Raphael Thibodeaux and his teammates, the taste was one of ashes. One out away from victory the day before, they faced imminent defeat today. The one consolation for Rafe was, he wouldn't have to face his father. Facing men you'd idolized was one thing — he'd hit against Martinez, Johnson, Smoltz, all experiences filed away under 'Baseball.' But facing the man who raised you, cooked for you, bailed you out of jail and quit baseball for you — they didn't make photo albums big enough for that. In the end, he would be happy for his father. Rafe had twenty years to chase the dream of a championship. Let his father have his.

But when he reached the dugout he found his teammates pounding each other on the shoulders, coaches clapping their hands and shouting, players whistling as if calling their dogs to a hunt. They'd seen the Indians put together a five-run inning — why couldn't they? The Indians had beaten their All-Star closer the night before, why couldn't they? They were the *New York Mets!*

Sure enough, Indians' closer Brent Shicker walked the first batter. Then Nickie Weise rapped a single to right and it was men on first and third with nobody out. Rafe joined his teammates on the dugout step. He could feel the momentum shifting their way — then just like that it was gone. Bruce Molinaro hit into a double play, sending home a run but bringing the Indians to within one out of their first world championship since 1948. Their closer was on the mound, it was 12:07 AM. It was time to call it a season.

Then Carmelo Fox shocked the crowd with a line drive that arrived so quickly in the right field bleachers that most people weren't sure it really happened. The Mets were sure though, greeting Carmelo like a rioting village in the dugout. It was 8-6 now, and when Julio Perez rapped a soft liner to center field for a single, doubt swept through the stadium like an avenging angel, ready to punish Indians fans for celebrating prematurely. The crowd mumbled, then rose to its feet, clapping, shouting, demanding the last out, appealing to the heavens for justice so long denied.

Rafe selected his bat and helmet and made his way on to the field. This was it, what every player lived for — a chance to bat in the ninth inning with the World Series on the line. He hadn't even reached the on-deck circle when he heard the crack and saw the ball pulled so sharply down the left field line for a double that everyone knew Shicker was done. A deadly silence fell over the stadium, then Rafe's heart stopped.

"Ze-ro! Ze-ro! Ze-ro!" the crowd yelled.

The Indians had three men warming up, but only one of them was a lefthander — and in baseball wisdom, they needed a lefthander to face Raphael. But somehow, Rafe thought they'd go against the wisdom. They'd bring in Johnny Eberhardt, he'd had three days rest, he'd won sixteen games during the season. Rafe watched Marty Beuhler stride to the mound. He watched him take the ball from Brent Shicker and pat him on the back. He watched him signal with his left arm and the bottom fell out of his stomach. The gate to the bullpen opened, and like a gladiator entering the Coliseum to the roars of an empire, his father emerged and strode across the outfield toward the mound.

"Ze-ro! Ze-ro! Ze-ro!"

Rafe turned away in the on-deck circle, rolling his shoulders, taking short practice swings as his father smoothed the area in front of the mound with his cleats. He had never felt more alone in his life — maybe once, in Juvenile Hall. 'It must have been like a dream,' people would say later. But it was more like a nightmare, and he couldn't get out of it. He always thought if he got this far, he could count on his father to help him. He'd never imagined that it would be his father who would stand in his way.

He watched him take his warm up tosses, as familiar a sight as the sunset. He was the only person who knew it was his father's last hurrah. He was the only one who knew he could throw with everything he had, because there was no tomorrow. Rafe took a few practice swings in synch with the pitches, imagining the ball sailing over the wall. His father looked strong and in control, though Rafe knew otherwise. He knew he was walking on the moon, uncertain of everything. He knew his father was just as scared as he was. Except he didn't look it.

When Jason finished his warm ups he walked off the mound and looked into the stands, remembering all the times he had gazed there so longingly in search of his son. And now, when he turned around, it would be his son in the batter's box, facing him for what would be the biggest moment of their lives. He couldn't believe he had come all this way, paid the price he had paid — and now he had to pay again. Baseball, or Rafe. Rafe, or baseball. He had always wanted to be the man who helped him, as a good father should. And now, if he did his job, he would humble him in front of the whole world.

Jason stepped back to the mound and stared in with his classic scowl. And there was Rafe. He wanted to tip his hat at least, acknowledge the blood and history between them, but he knew he couldn't. You couldn't show you were weak, even if you were. You couldn't acknowledge it was only a game, even if it was.

Rafe stepped into the box and tapped the plate with his bat several times, then rose into his distinctive stance. The crowd was delirious, the ground literally shaking. Rafe stepped out of the box, took another deep breath and more practice swings, then stepped back in and studied the pitcher's menacing scowl. He tried to conjure the feelings he had for his father when he was eleven, twelve, thirteen — the hatred and anger and betrayal he felt as his father made his mark in the major leagues, and he made his way to jail. He wanted to hate him just long enough to get a hit, to flare the ball somewhere and tie the game. That would be enough. He'd be happy if someone else on his team won it.

Then his father went into his stretch. What would he come with first? Something off-speed, or a fastball? Rafe's mind raced as the ball left his father's hand and headed for the outside of the plate. Fastball! He stepped toward it, then held up as it warped off the edge of the plate — Ball One!

Rafe backed from the box again. He'd survived the first pitch, and now it was all different. It wasn't about them. It wasn't about their history or their future or their pain — it was only about baseball, whether he could hit the ball or not, whether they would win or not. It was suddenly that simple. Maybe it always had been that simple.

He set himself and again watched the ball leave his father's hand. He knew he wouldn't get two fastballs in a row, but as soon as he saw the pitch he knew he was wrong. It was a fastball. It flashed by the letters on his uniform and he waited for the call. "Ball Two!" the umpire shouted.

At 2-0, he'd have to come in with a strike. Rafe settled into his stance, his hands even with the crown of his head. Jason stretched, then sent the 2-0 pitch homewards. It came in spinning, a slider over the plate — but too low. "Ball Three!" the umpire shouted.

Jason pounded his mitt against his leg and asked for a new ball. He'd been half again too smart, thinking Rafe would be overanxious and swing at something out of the strike zone. He tried to summon the anger he always pitched with, but all he could feel was frustration — and pride for his son. Then fear — of fifty thousand fans getting on his case, and an army of cynical pundits if he walked his son on four pitches. He couldn't walk Rafe; he couldn't put the winning run on base with two outs in the seventh game of the World Series. With two outs everybody would be running, and the hitter behind Rafe was Mateo Hernandez, who had 102 RBIs that season.

Rafe stared up the third base line for a signal. To his astonishment, Ireland flashed 'hit away.' Rafe rolled his shoulders and rose back into his stance. Maybe he gave something away, maybe someone stole the signal. Expecting a grooved fast ball, Rafe took an enormous swing and missed a changeup by a foot.

Jacobs Field trembled beneath the weight of the fans' desire. His dad still had to come in with another strike, or walk him and put the winning run on base. The next pitch came spinning out of the lights, a slider towards the inside corner. He should have taken it. It was a perfect pitch — for the pitcher, a strike down and in. The best he could do with it was hit a chopper somewhere in the infield. Instead, he topped it onto his foot. He hopped away, walking off the pain as the umpire called for time.

His father took a new ball and turned his back. The count was 3-2. The crowd wasn't just on its feet — it was on each other, pounding, hugging, holding, squeezing, jerking each other back and forth. Zero had him now. With two outs and first base open, the pitcher had a margin for error which the batter didn't. If Zero missed his pitch, Rafe takes first base, setting up a force at any base. If Rafe misses the pitch, the ball game, the Series, the season is over.

Jason looked in for the signal, never making eye contact with his son. Then suddenly the noise of the stadium faded away. Rafe saw his father on the deck of the reservoir, a duffel bag filled with baseballs at his feet. 'The strike zone is like a refrigerator box,' he explained.

'Visualize it front to back, side to side, top to bottom. Every pitch inside the box is yours. Anything outside, you let it go.'

Rafe saw it coming — a curve ball. He'd seen it a thousand times, sailing towards his shoulder like an overstuffed pigeon, then darting down and over the plate for a strike. He slashed at it and fouled it down the left field line — a soft liner into the stands above where his mother sat with Willie and his family, Martha Evelia and hers. Jason got a new ball and roughed it up, then turned towards the plate again. With each pitch the volume of the crowd increased, but somehow Rafe couldn't hear them. It was like the wind or the sea, some natural force that had nothing to do with him.

But now he had to be careful. His father was expert at lulling batters to sleep with off-speed stuff, then breaking their hearts with 95 mph heat. But no fast balls came. Rafe fouled off four straight sliders. But he knew his father would come in with it sometime. He had to challenge him, like he said they always did in the National League.

And then it came, as big as a planet, letter high and rising. He knew he shouldn't swing but he couldn't help it. He swung and the ball clicked off the top of the bat and headed high into the air above the leftfield line. The Indians' third baseman drifted over, tracking the ball like a man expecting to catch it. Rafe watched, not believing it would end like this. The whole stadium seemed to hold its breath as the ball, the fielder and the huge blue tarpaulin in place in case of rain all came together — and the ball fell into the front row of seats just out of Koskie's reach.

Rafe glanced at the mound. He was sure he could see the glimmer of a smile in his father's eyes. He had another chance — "Strike Four," just like they always played it. Only this time it was for real.

He watched his father shake off two signs. Rafe hoped he would get another fastball and crush it into history — but he knew he'd never get one. He knew his father would throw something outside of the box, get him to swing at some piece of shit off the plate. The perfect pitch, his father said, was when you offer water to a man who thinks he's dying in the desert — and deliver a mirage.

Jason nodded and went into his stretch. What happened then was the reverse of Rafe's life flashing before his eyes. At that moment, his entire life was wiped out. He had no history, no future, no fuckups, no triumphs. There was only him and his dad, right here, right now. He saw the front leg rise up, the body surge forward, the ball emerge and to

Rafe's surprise it left his father's hand in the tight clean spin of a heater, exploding down the chute like a freight train. They told him later it registered 99 on the radar gun, the fastest he had thrown since Denver.

Rafe's weight shifted forward, his shoulders and hips pulling him around, his hands hungering for the sweet vibration of ball-to-bat-to-bone ... but he checked his swing. The sickening thud of leather-on-leather sounded behind him, punctuating the screams of fifty thousand delirious fans waiting for the umpire's call.

CELLO CONCERTO IN D

THIS TIME WILLIE WAS WAITING in a black Buick Regal, twenty pounds lighter and "on the *carretón*." Carlito rode with him in the front seat, both men dressed in identical white suits, white ruffled shirts with black trim, and black bolero ties. Carlito wanted to know all about his favorite players — Vladimir Guerrero, Albert Pujols, Manny Ramirez, but Willie called him off. "Come on, *hijo*. He came all the way from New York."

They took him around the inner edge of the Vera Cruz harbor to a seaside park where caterers were setting up huge barbecue grills, three bars, and dozens of tables beneath a huge white canopy. "The reception's going to be here," Willie said excitedly. "We have ten cases of tequila, twenty cases of beer, champagne," he announced. "And plenty of Coca-Cola for me!"

They drove a half mile further to the Church of the Virgin of Guadalupe on Avenida de la Revolución. The old adobe church dated from 1728, featuring heavy, tree-sized pillars supporting a classic Spanish bell tower. Inside was a simple wooden altar, and two hundred people waiting in their Sunday best. Willie's second-oldest daughter, Maria Emma, waited nervously at the back of the church. Raphael beamed when he saw her. "*Buenos días*," he said shyly, kissing her lightly on her cheek. She wore a pretty cream-colored dress, her jet-black hair pulled up to reveal the copper-colored skin of her neck. She smiled, seeing the sullen teenager she had met seven years before grown into a tall, composed young man wearing an elegant tuxedo.

She kissed him on both cheeks. "How was your trip?" She spoke with the slightest accent, more a flavor than a flaw.

"Great," he replied. "I'm so glad to be here."

"It's not every day you go to your father's wedding."

She offered her arm and they walked together down the aisle. This was actually the second time he had been to his father's wedding. He was rather young the first time — still in the womb — but he'd been

293

there. There was, in fact, a strong feeling of familiarity to this whole thing, with Willie and his family, Martha Evelia and his soon-to-be-step-siblings, his father's obvious happiness. In the warm Mexican air, it all felt right.

He guided Maria Emma by her waist into the pew. Willie was already at the altar, transformed from chauffeur into best man. Raphael found the music stand and cello set up on a small riser to the side of the altar. Just as he sat down, the door on the other side opened and his father strode through. He wore a white tuxedo and scarlet red cummerbund, with a red bolero tie. Rafe quickly picked up the bow and ground out the opening chords of "Take Me Out to the Ball Game." The crowd laughed and applauded. Jason folded Raphael in a giant bear hug.

"Jesus, I'm glad you came!"

"I wouldn't miss it for the world. I was at your last one, remember?"

"Yeah," Jason whispered. "But this one's going to be a hell of a lot better."

They were ready to go but like everything in Mexico, 'ready' was a process rather than a destination. Flowers were suddenly rushed to the altar; two men began hooking up the sound system as if it had just occurred to them. Rafe looked up from his music and saw that the groom himself had disappeared. He struck off down a set of stone stairs into the bowels of the church, where Willie said there was a bathroom. With its brick walls and dark wood beams, the basement felt like Zorro's lair, and he laughed thinking of his father's nickname. "ZERO SAVES THE DAY," the headlines said the morning after. "Father-Son Encounter Marks Tribe's First Title Since '48." It was a moment few people would forget. The eleven-pitch confrontation between father and son, the first in baseball history, climaxing with a 99 mph fastball two inches off the outside corner — a pitch Rafe would have swung at if the man who threw it hadn't spent a lifetime teaching him not to.

His father had finally gotten the third out, though not without working for it. Mateo Hernandez had taken him to 3-2, then launched a fly ball to the warning track in left. Rafe watched from the base path as his father's teammates lifted him to the top of the world. Now he was going to watch him go up there again.

He found a toilet in a bathroom crammed with boxes of hymnals. When he was done he wandered down a hallway lined with centuries-old portraits of priests and public officials. Many paintings were deteriorating in the damp Gulf air, and he vowed to look into doing something to preserve them. Tradition was important to him, starting with baseball. Mexico offered him something special too. He had family here now.

He heard the cry of the pipe organ and hurried down the hall looking for the stairs. By the time he found his way back to the altar, the first flower girl was half way up the center aisle. He sat down behind the music stand, pulled the cello familiarly between his legs, and picked up mid-bar harmonizing with the organ. Little Carla dropped rose pedals along the white satin runner, then came Maria Evelia, Martha Evelia's oldest daughter, followed by a niece and the six maids of honor escorted by Carlito, Willie, and the entire infield of the Cleveland Indians.

It was a beautiful ceremony, complete with prayers offered to the deceased father of Martha Evelia's children, and gratitude to God for helping them find a father as wonderful as Jason Thibodeaux to live out the rest of their lives. When the Mass was finished, their hands entwined and their wedding rings gleaming, Jason and Martha Evelia turned towards the riser where Rafe sat poised with his cello. Rafe bowed his head and clutched the neck of his instrument. He could hear the piece in his head he had practiced over and over since the World Series, but he wasn't sure he could do it. When his father had first asked him if he would play at his wedding, he reminded him he hadn't picked up an instrument in five years.

"So?" Jason replied. "I hadn't pitched in five years either."

He drew the bow across the strings of the cello — too heavy, he thought. His arms felt rigid. He took a breath and relaxed and the bow slid more lightly now, like a breeze through a stand of pines. The languid chords of Luigi Boccherini's *Cello Concerto in D* rose from his instrument and filled the spaces of the ancient church, circulating like spirits. Rafe had chosen the piece. He had wanted to do more for his father and his bride than just show up. Music was the part of his life he had rarely shared with his father. Until now. The notes poured from his hands, from his heart. As long it came from there, he knew it couldn't be wrong. He played to the end without flaw, feeling in his hands the same pure vibration as a baseball struck solid and true.

SPECIAL THANKS to Dr. Lawrence Fisher; Jason Berry; Bill Dodd; William O'Malley, S.J.; James Motlow; Deborah Hayden; Hilary Gordon; Virginia Van Zandt and Jim Bruen; Scott Ostler; the San Francisco Public Library; The Beat Within; Ken Bowman; Blake Rhodes and the San Francisco Giants; Bob and Susan Fletcher, Dolf Hes, Tim Davidson and the Sonoma County Crushers; Ezra "Sly" Hunter; Dan "The Produce Man" Avakian; Paul Blum; Ted Farber; Peter Keville; Richard Marx. Special thanks to teacher, poet and baseball aficionado Rich Yurman for his insightful editing and unending faith; and to Katie Kleinsasser, whose inspiration, love and inexhaustible supply of sunshine were indispensable to the growth of this book. Not least, thanks to the hundreds of fathers, children, spouses and ex-spouses who helped inspire and inform this book.

JEFF GILLENKIRK is an author and journalist whose articles and book reviews have appeared in the New York Times, Washington Post, Miami Herald, Los Angeles Times, San Francisco Chronicle, Parenting magazine, The Nation, Mother Jones, America and other publications. His nonfiction book, *Bitter Melon: Inside America's Last Rural All-Chinese Town*, won the Commonwealth Club's Silver Medal award for best California history. In addition to his writing, Gillenkirk provides strategic communications support for community-based organizations in California and across the country. He lives in San Francisco with his son and extended family. *Home, Away* is his first novel.